LAST CHANCE

"Hold it, Chandler." It was Cole. He was standing ten feet away with his gun drawn.

Chandler froze. He had his hand on the hot barrel of the dead woman's .45. His leg burned where the bullet she fired had grazed him.

"Just don't move, Chandler."

The technician staggered out of the bathroom and stood over Chandler, breathing hard and weaving.

"Get out to the car," Cole said. "Call the reinforcement code number. Tell them what's gone down and get some help over here."

Chandler still had not moved. He was gathering his strength.

"Just stay exactly where you are, Chandler." His voice was tight with fear. "Is she dead?"

Chandler didn't answer. He was measuring his space, his chances. His movement would have to be quick if it was going to work, quick and startling. First he moaned weakly, to distract Cole, then he suddenly lunged back into the darkness, using the woman's body as a shield. Cole fired four times . . .

MORE THRILLING READING!

THE LUCIFER DIRECTIVE (1353, $3.50)
by Jon Land
Terrorists are outgunning agents, and events are outracing governments. It's all part of a sequence of destruction shrouded in mystery. And the only ones who hold key pieces of the bloody puzzle are a New England college student and an old Israeli freedom fighter. From opposite ends of the globe, they must somehow stop the final fatal command!

THE DOOMSDAY SPIRAL (1175, $2.95)
by Jon Land
Alabaster—master assassin and sometimes Mossad agent—races against time and operatives from every major service in order to control and kill a genetic nightmare let loose in America. Death awaits around each corner as the tension mounts and doomsday comes ever closer!

DEPTH FORCE (1355, $2.95)
by Irving A. Greenfield
Built in secrecy, launched in silence, and manned by a phantom crew, *The Shark* is America's unique high technology submarine whose mission is to stop the Soviets from dominating the seas. As far as the U.S. government is concerned, *The Shark* doesn't exist. Its orders are explicit: if in danger of capture, self-destruct! So the only way to stay alive is to dive deep and strike hard!

Available wherever paperbacks are sold, or order direct from the Publisher. Send cover price plus 50¢ per copy for mailing and handling to Zebra Books, 475 Park Avenue South, New York, N.Y. 10016. DO NOT SEND CASH.

THE LAST PATRIOT

By James N. Frey

ZEBRA BOOKS
KENSINGTON PUBLISHING CORP.

ZEBRA BOOKS

are published by

Kensington Publishing Corp.
475 Park Avenue South
New York, N.Y. 10016

First printing: July, 1984

Printed in the United States of America

A man who goes forth to take the life of another he does not know must believe one thing only — that by his act he will change the course of history.

— Itzhak Yizernitsky,
Terrorist

BOOK ONE

ONE

"You have tested the weapons?" Ferris asked.

"Yes."

"Were they satisfactory?"

"Most satisfactory."

"And what about the toxins to take care of the dogs?"

"We have tested them too."

"The cars we got for you, the Plymouth and the Ford. They've checked out all right?"

"Fine."

"Your cover identities, all the papers you need are there?"

"Everything has been checked and rechecked a dozen times. The only thing left to do is the job itself.

Ferris rubbed the palms of his fleshy hands together. "I know I do not have to lecture you on the subtleties of your trade, my friend, only this is so . . . so momentous." His gaze drifted downward and as they walked he kicked a clod of dirt with his foot. "Perhaps we should go over the itinerary again, to be certain of every detail."

"No, Ferris. Too much rehearsal can kill a performance."

They were walking up a steep hill and the path was

slippery. When they reached the top they paused to catch their breath. The sun was setting and the western horizon was orange and dark with thickening storm clouds.

After a moment, Ferris said: "If he were an ordinary target, I would tell you . . . what? Good luck? Good hunting? But this— It is so momentous, I can't find the words."

"Don't fret so, Ferris. The bullets won't bounce off. You worry that I may change my mind as the hour draws near?"

"Many men would."

"I didn't come to this decision quickly or easily. We both know it is something that must be done. I couldn't back away from it now even if I wanted."

They continued over the crest of the hill and down the other side to where the path divided and the shadows were long on the ground. "You have done your part, Ferris; and now you must wait while I do mine. Good-bye." They shook hands and Ferris watched him walk down the hill and disappear into the darkness of the woods beyond.

TWO

"They're going to kill you, Clement," Jules LaVale said.

"Nonsense."

"Sometimes I think you don't read the papers."

"I read them," Clement Jamison said. "Never like what's in them much, but I read them."

"This country seethes, I mean it. It's in a foul, foul mood."

"Moods change, Jules. The country's a menopausal old lady. She changes with the moon." Clement Jamison smiled confidently. He had a pleasant, strong face, warm blue eyes, and thick auburn hair streaked with gray. Carrying the burdens of the Presidency for three years and three months had etched dark lines deep around his eyes, but he still looked younger than his fifty-six years by perhaps half a decade.

"Come on, Jules," he said, "what the hell's really bothering you?"

"You're going to be killed, that's what's really bothering me. You've seen the Gallup, Mervin Field's, UPI. We're stuck like the proverbial pig and we're bleeding from Spokane to Sheboygan."

Jules LaVale had a pink, pudgy face and large brown eyes. His cheeks were flushed with mild anger.

"Hold your water, Jules. We'll handle it." The President poured them both more coffee from a stainless steel pitcher. It was Sunday, April 20th, 6:35 A.M. They were seated at a table in the small dining room of the President's private suite on the third floor, south wing, of the White House. They had just breakfasted on poached eggs and grilled lake trout with orange juice, cottage cheese with peach slices, wheat toast, and strong Brazilian espresso. A servant cleared the dishes and left them with a second pot of coffee.

"Used to think I understood you, Clement," LaVale said, "but lately you can't seem to make up your mind whether to fly north or swim south. This thing with the Russians and the Cubans down there in the Caribbean has got you crazy."

"More than you could know," the President said heavily, raising his eyebrows. "More than anyone could know."

LaVale paused and took a sip of coffee, studying the President carefully. "I've got to call it as I see it," he said. "If you think I'm out of line, say so."

"Say what you came to say."

"The campaign is in very bad straits. Financially we're okay for now, maybe half a million behind projections, but we're paying our bills. But the rest of it, it's sad city. In Philly and most of eastern Pennsylvania and upstate New York we couldn't get enough grass-roots support to hold a car wash. We need telephone dialers and door knockers, but they aren't signing up. The college kids even are staying home and drinking beer and smoking grass. The housewives would rather watch soap operas. There's just no excitement in this campaign, no spirit, no pizazz. We're playing the old tired tunes and nobody's dancing."

"Awful early in the morning for all this gloom and doom," the President said with a smile.

LaVale was not amused. "A President earns his bread on the home front, Clement. You don't think some unemployed black in Gary or Detroit gives a damn about banana land. We've got to give a damn about what that black gives a damn about. That black and the farmers and the truck drivers. For God's sake, you know where your support is, you know who put you here."

"What do you want me to do?"

"There are some plump primaries coming up. Nebraska, West Virginia, Maryland, Georgia, Indiana. It's time to get hustling. Shake a few thousand hands, kiss a million babies. Let them see you, Clement. Show them you care."

"Nobody's going to mount a challenge against me there. I own most of those states, Jules."

"I'm talking about momentum."

"I can't spare the time. Honest to God."

"Be warned, then. When the tougher states—Tennessee, Ohio, California, New Jersey—when they come up, we're going to be in a stall. C. Miller Petri isn't loafing. He's breathing fire and smoke and billowing volcanic ash. Domestic issues are his ammunition. You've got to hit hard on your economic recovery program and forget the goddamn Russians or you won't have enough delegates to overload a small elevator in the Chicago Hilton when convention time rolls around . . . You've got to level with me, Clement. You haven't been yourself. Something's been going on. It seems like you ha-

13

haven't been giving a damn. There's disaffection in the ranks. Rumors are flying like rice at a royal wedding."

"Without rumors, politicking would be as dull as a Jewish wake." The President's face clouded. "I'm not sure I like being hammered like this, Jules."

"I can't run your campaign unless I'm completely in your confidence. I have to be inside your head."

"No one has my confidence more than you do, my friend. I'll tell you this . . . the country nearly had a jellyfish for a President. All I can say at the moment is, trust me. I'll be getting out to kiss those million babies, don't you worry. I'll shake every damn hand in the country if I have to. We're going to steamroller over C. Miller Petri until he's flat."

LaVale was incredulous. "When?" he asked. "Next week you have three state dinners. You're supposed to meet with the NSC. And the Italian President will be here for talks."

"Who's more important? An Italian President or the American voter? We can fit in a couple of whistle stops in between the state dinners. Get some good material worked up, something we can whack Petri with on the behind. How's that?"

"I've got some TV spots that have been waiting for your approval a week or more. They whack Petri pretty good."

"I'm playing golf this morning. Afterward, I'll be at the club until maybe six or seven. How about I take a look at them at nine tonight?"

"Great."

"We'll see who gets killed, eh?"

THREE

After LaVale had gone, the President smoked a cigarette and sipped some more coffee. It was quiet. There was a newspaper put beside him, but he didn't look at it. When he finished his cigarette, he went downstairs to his study and looked at what had come in on the intelligence night wire. There were half a dozen yellow communiqués sealed in an envelope. He read and initialed them, put them in a drawer and locked it. They were progress reports on the war in Chad and the coup in Guatemala and were of little interest to him. He wrote a memo to his appointment secretary to coordinate campaign speeches with LaVale, and a memo to his personal secretary to expect LaVale at nine that evening. He then checked the staff work assignments for the day. Stewart Ott, the President's domestic affairs man, would be in charge of the White House. Jamison heartily approved. Of all the senior White House people, he trusted Ott the most. Ott was cool as a snake charmer and knew whom to call if he needed something done in a hurry. In Washington, people who could get things done were as rare as billfolds at a pickpockets' convention. The telephone rang. It was his pilot; the helicopter was ready anytime.

"Crank it up, I'll be right there."

The President walked back upstairs. He never used elevators if he could help it. He said it was better exercise to walk. The truth was, he was slightly claustrophobic. On his way upstairs he paused to ask himself whether he had forgotten anything. Small details were the bane of his existence. Men were elected President for their supposed leadership qualities, but their success or failure rested more with their handling of petty details. He made a mental note to write an executive order putting somebody in charge of little details. Maybe make it a cabinet post. Secretary of B.S. He smiled to himself. It was Sunday. Sunday it was okay to think ludicrous thoughts. It relieved the pressure.

He went down the hall to his wife's room. He had something to tell her and he didn't want to wait until dinner time. He knocked gently and went in.

"You awake?"

She opened her eyes. Omi Jamison was young and Eurasian, dark and delicately featured; her black almond-shaped eyes were exquisite.

"What time is it?" she asked.

"A little before seven."

"Is something the matter? I thought you were going to play golf this morning." She brushed her hair out of her eyes and sat up, fluffing her pillow.

"There's nothing the matter. I was about to go, I just thought I'd stop in to let you know."

She reached for a cigarette out of a gold case on the night stand and he lit it with his lighter.

"Jules was here," he said. "About the campaign. He wants me to kiss a million babies."

"Aren't you going to be late? What time did you say it

16

was?"

"It's a little before seven. The headwinds aren't bad this morning, I've plenty of time." He paused and looked at her in the soft light. "I was thinking about you last night," he said.

"Oh?"

He sat down on the edge of her bed. "This is a crap job. The Presidency, I mean."

"I know."

"Do you think maybe that things could have been a little different between us?"

"What do you mean?"

"Maybe our marriage had too much pressure on it. Maybe it cracked before we gave it a chance — before *I* gave it a chance. I've got a damn big ego, I maybe didn't handle everything like it should have been handled."

"I haven't really thought about it. I never waste time on what could have been."

"We never even had a chance to get to know each other. As private people, I mean. It was all a media thing. Even on our honeymoon we were watching out for photographers, remember? We were like fugitives."

"You're not becoming sentimental are you, Clement? Believe me, it is far too late for sentiment."

"I don't think it is."

"We have an arrangement and I'm sticking to it," she said firmly. "I play my part until the election. You don't fight me on the property settlement and I stay until you get your four more years."

He stood up and paced to the window; then he lit a cigarette. It was gray outside and there wasn't much traffic on the streets. The helicopter was warming up, its blades spinning, stopping, spinning again — finally

17

going. "You're a hard woman, Omi. I want to tell you something. I'm fond of you. Is it all right to say that?" He wasn't looking at her now. "I don't think I've ever been as fond of anyone. I want to have something between us. Friendship, perhaps. If not that, at least amicability. I don't want our marriage to go down in flames and smoke and malice."

"Once there was fire in me that was for you," she said. "I thought like an adolescent girl that it would burn for you, for all eternity. But the fire is cold. Dead. You crushed it out, my husband. You stamped it out with the heel of your ambitious boot."

"At least can I say I'm sorry?"

"Even for that, it is too late."

At two minutes after seven the Presidential Sikorsky helicopter lifted off its pad, rose over fifteen hundred feet, and circled northeast, gaining altitude. Clement Jamison watched the White House shrink into the distance below him. The Potomac and the Chesapeake Bay glistened blue and green and calm in the morning sun.

FOUR

It was cool and still in the Blue Ridge Mountains and on the course the fairways were soft and played slowly. At first the black clouds to the west were far up the valley, but then the wind came up and it grew cold and dark as the thunderheads moved down the Shenandoah Valley toward them. The President played badly but did not complain. He had his mind on other things — on the Soviets, on the economy, on the campaign, on Omi.

His companions that day were Art Armstrong, Jerry Chryslerhurst, and Dr. Hubert Samuelson, who was over seventy and golfed with the precision of a diamond cutter. Chryslerhurst was tall and rangy; Armstrong, shorter and stouter, wore heavy-framed glasses and walked with a limp. Armstrong and Chryslerhurst were both fifty four. It sprinkled for a few minutes while they were on the seventh fairway. They continued to play. Others left the course and play speeded up as a result.

The course at the Fire Creek Country Club was laid out along both sides of Fire Creek. It was hilly and narrow, dotted with oak and poplar trees, and well trapped. The old brick clubhouse had a slate roof and white-painted Colonial shutters and was surrounded by a stand of Virginia and short-leafed pines. It was built at the site of an old inn, said to have been visited by Benedict Arnold in 1778, while he was still fighting for the colonials. Someone had nailed a plaque commemorating the event to the little-used rear door of the clubhouse.

The President and his party finished the eighteenth hole a few minutes before noon. They left their powered carts at the pro shop and walked up the steps to the clubhouse. Six Secret Service men followed; four more were flanked out to the sides; another with binoculars watched from a second-floor window of the clubhouse. The President knew fourteen more were patrolling the grounds and more circled the perimeter. Fire Creek was as secure as any place in America outside the White House and Camp David, they had told him. The wind gusted strongly. Most golfers were inside already because the heavy rain would soon start.

The dining room was crowded. The Presidential party ate at a circular table in the corner of the bar. Afterward the President greeted some people he knew and shook some hands. He was feeling better. He genuinely liked people and they liked him. A couple asked him to sign an autograph book for their grandchild. He signed it a dozen times.

Harry Brill was in charge of the Secret Service crew. Brill was forty one, experienced, meticulous, a devout Mormon, as reliable as an atomic clock. He had soft features and friendly eyes and was wearing a checkered sport coat and slacks. He was solidly built, angular; his gray hair was close-cropped.

At ten after one the President followed Brill to the second floor. With them went Armstrong, Chryslerhurst,

Dr. Samuelson, and R. B. Reis, the club's assistant golf pro. There was the sound of distant thunder, soft, prolonged, rumbling. It started, some said later, at the time when the President went upstairs with his friends for their poker game. Brill had cleared a room toward the front of the clubhouse for the game, but the President objected. Brill defended his choice. It had a private bathroom and was closer to the fire exit, Brill explained. The President said he didn't give a damn; the fluorescent lighting was too harsh and the room was too large. He wanted something more intimate. He wanted the room they usually had, he insisted, and there was a sliver of anger in his voice.

Brill went downstairs and spoke with the manager, George Higgins. Of course, no problem, he said. Higgins was always anxious to please the President. He made a few phone calls and the kitchen and maintenance people were notified of the change. Harry Brill alerted his crew and made a quick inspection of the old room. There was a storage room adjoining; Brill checked it too. He found it the same as it had been in the past: crammed with holiday decorating supplies for the outdoor bar, used on the patio during the hot months. Against the far wall were some scoreboards. The dust looked as if it had not been disturbed for months. Satisfied, he closed the door and locked it. He made a note that the room had been checked in his notebook.

At nineteen minutes after one Harry Brill reported to the President that the old room was ready. Sam Blackburn, the Presidential Press Secretary, had joined them. Blackburn had bushy sideburns and a ready smile, gray curly hair, and a wine-colored birthmark on his right cheek. He was outgoing, affable, forty six.

21

The Presidential poker room was twenty-two by eighteen feet, windowless, lit by a single soft-color lamp which could be pulled down closer to the table. There were some chairs, a couch, a small bar, and a serving table where sandwiches would be placed at three-fifteen. There was a sink and towel rack, a cabinet well stocked with cigarettes, cigars, chewing gum, Kleenex, and aspirin and No-Doze tablets. On one wall there was a collection of old photographs of participants in the annual Pro-Am Leukemia Society fund-raising tournament held at the club; on another was a large, ornate clock with a brass pendulum swinging below it. It ticked noisily as the President and his party came into the room and took their places.

FIVE

The game began at one thirty-five.

The President sat with his back to the far wall in front of the storeroom; to his left was Chryslerhurst, then Armstrong, then R. B. Reis. Reis had his back to the door to the hall and was directly opposite the President. To Reis's left was Sam Blackburn and then Dr. Samuelson. Dr. Samuelson lit his pipe as soon as he was seated and let out a deep sigh, rubbing his hands together in anticipation. He had a passion for cards. "Who's the banker today?"

The job fell to Armstrong. He was an accountant and usually served as the banker. He grumbled as always, and went to work. The white chips were five dollars; the reds, ten; the blues, twenty-five. Soon they were ready. The ante was five dollars. They cut the cards to see who would deal first and the President won. It was dealer's choice. The President called five-card-stud low-ball and promptly dealt himself a pair of kings. He folded. Reis won the hand with a seven-five.

Brill was sitting on the couch by the door to the hall-way, sipping orange juice and going over his check lists, making certain each procedure was being followed exactly as the manual dictated and that nothing was overlooked. There was a second Secret Service man standing nearby, a former Marine captain named Wesley Que. He was black and muscular. Both the President and Brill had great confidence in him.

The President passed the deal to Chryslerhurst, who shuffled the cards with relish and dealt with a quick, snapping motion. The game was five-card draw. Three men had betting hands: Chryslerhurst, Blackburn, Reis. They raised each other again and again until the pot was over three hundred dollars. Reis finally called, Blackburn made a final bet, and the other two stayed. Chryslerhurst won with a small straight. Chortling, he scooped up the chips. The first big pot of the day. "Good karma," Chryslerhurst said.

Though Chryslerhurst was fifty-four, he hardly looked thirty-five. He had met the President at Ohio State when they were both sophomores, and they were as close as brothers.

It was Armstrong's turn with the deal. He called "California Poker"—which meant five-card draw, a pair of jacks or better to open. Armstrong dealt slowly, with precision. After he dealt he carefully cleaned his glasses before he fanned his cards in front of his face and studied them. Poker to him was a serious undertaking. He was often the winner on Sunday, and he liked winning. This time he dealt the President three kings and the President bet heavily on them. The others folded quickly, leaving him the pot. It was small, but the President was pleased.

The game had fallen into its rhythm. A waitress was called just after two and she brought Reis and Blackburn each a beer and Dr. Samuelson a gin and tonic.

24

The President had coffee and so did Chryslerhurst. By two-thirty, the President, having won three small pots, was eighty dollars ahead and had lit a cigar. He was feeling relaxed; his mind was clear. The deal had come around four times and Chryslerhurst was dealing again. They had been hearing more thunder. It was still distant, but distinct; it rolled through the valley like a volley of far-off cannon fire.

"Sounds ominous," Chryslerhurst said, turning to the President, who had just looked at his cards. "Openers?"

The President dropped two white chips into the center of the table. The clock ticked noisily.

Reis and Blackburn and Dr. Samuelson anted up; Armstrong and Chryslerhurst folded.

"Tickets?" Chryslerhurst said.

"Three," the President said. Reis and Blackburn took one card each and Dr. Samuelson, thoughtful for a long moment, took two.

The President fanned his cards out slowly. "Well, well . . . lookie, lookie . . . . Price of poker just went up." He dropped two blues onto the table. Fifty dollars.

Reis, the golf pro, stared at his cards, then at the President. He drummed his thin fingers on the table, then pushed four blues into the pot. "One hundred to you, Mr. Blackburn."

"Blackburn folded. "Too rich for a poor Georgia boy like me."

Dr. Samuelson stayed, but didn't raise.

There was thunder again. Diminished now. The President called, dropping two blue chips onto the pile of chips in the center of the table. "Let's see your power."

"Two little pair," Reis said. "Kings and queens."

"Close," The President said. "Close, but no brass

ring." He spread his cards on the table. "Three bullets," he said, looking at Dr. Samuelson.

The doctor flicked his cards onto the table one at a time: a diamond flush. "All pups of the same litter," he said, reaching for the pot. "Guess this isn't your day, Clement."

It was then that it happened:

Another roll of thunder ripped loose from the mountain and rolled over the clubhouse, shaking it and rattling the glass in the windows. Under cover of the sound, the door to the storeroom burst open and two figures appeared. It happened as quickly as if a bomb had exploded.

Wesley Que reacted with the swiftness of a striking snake; he dropped to his knees and a gun appeared in his hand, but the first intruder fired his silenced weapon for a short burst, sounding no louder than a child snapping his fingers; Que's face exploded red and his whole body seemed to jerk to the side, then twisted backward, flopping onto the carpet.

Harry Brill had not moved; he had tensed and his right hand had jerked an inch or two toward his shoulder holster—but no more. Slowly, his hands moved outward, upward in surrender.

One of the intruders looked exactly like Reis, slight, blond; the other like Blackburn, medium, dark, graying hair and sideburns, wine-colored birthmark. The intruder who looked like Blackburn, the larger of the two, stood next to the President, pointing a gun at his head. Everyone at the table was astonished that the likeness could be so close. Blackburn mumbled repeated curses and stared blankly at his twin and there was great fear on his face.

The President withdrew the cigar he had jammed in his teeth and looked up at the man. "Call it off," he said, his voice steady. "Call it off and I'll make you one wealthy son-of-a-bitch. I'll get you a jet that'll take you any goddamn place on the face of the earth with iron-clad immunity. You've got my word on it."

The intruder shook his head slowly. "I'm sorry, sir. . . ."

There was a long, empty silence. The clock ticked like a hammer on an anvil. No one moved. The smell of fear and cordite was strong in the air and the silence was heavy and long and the ticking of the clock pounded on them.

"Why don't they do something?" Chryslerhurst said.

The President answered: "They're waiting for the thunder again."

BOOK TWO

SIX

The tennis game had been a bore, Omi Jamison thought. She played her best when the competition was stiffer. The Henry Ormonds were pushovers; neither Henry nor his wife could handle Omi's deadly accurate crosscut backhand well, and her powerful service had scored seven aces on the day. Her speed, as usual, was moderately good, and her ground strokes had been unerring.

Omi's partner, George Draper, was past sixty, deeply tanned, played at being a stockbroker, and gave his life to tennis. He was competent as a player, dull in conversation, four times a grandfather, and considered socially "safe" as the first lady's tennis partner. He played close to the net, she played deep. She and George had won the first two sets — six-love, six-two — and were ahead 2-0 in the third. It was growing colder; a weather front was moving in. Omi was wondering whether they would have time to finish the set. She was serving in the third game when a Secret Service man ran onto the court. Having drawn her racket back, she was about to toss the ball up in the air when she saw him. Stepping back, she waited for him, annoyed at the interruption. Security people and their problems seemed always to be intruding on her life.

"What is it now?" she asked.

"There's been an incident, ma'am," the Secret Service man said breathlessly. "I'm sorry."

"An incident?" She had no idea what he meant.

"Yes, it's terrible — I'm terribly sorry." He couldn't find the right words. There were tears in his brown eyes and his lips trembled.

She still didn't understand. "An incident?"

"Yes, ma'am. They've shot Mr. Jamison. He's dead, ma'am."

She looked at George Draper who had joined her. He shook his head in disbelief. She handed him her racket. "I have to go," she said vaguely.

"Yes, of course."

"Will you be returning to the White House, ma'am?" the Secret Service man asked.

"Yes," she said.

The Secret Service man led the way off the court and down the shaded pathway to the waiting limousine. George Draper went with them, holding Omi by the arm. The only thing he could think of to say was how sorry he was, how very, very sorry. That, and what a great man and President Clement Jamison had been for the country. He opened the door of the limousine for her. She patted his hand and thanked him. "Thank you, George," she said. "I'll do my part fine," she said. He didn't know what she meant.

The limousine drove down the driveway, where a dozen police officers on motorcycles formed an escort. George Draper watched them go. He suddenly felt stupid and naked standing there in his tennis shorts. He turned quickly and went back up the path to where Henry and Grace Ormond were waiting. It had just started sprinkling. There would be no more tennis this day.

SEVEN

A few moments before, at three twenty-two P.M., John Matheson Haas, the Vice President of the United States, was having a late lunch with his eighty-two-year-old mother at the old and elegant Manhasset Hotel in Manhasset, New Hampshire. They had lunched on fresh shrimp and a small salad, with tea and English biscuits. The Vice President's mother was talkative and goodhearted, occasionally irascible, always witty. They both loved to gossip about family and friends, neighbors, and Washington bigwigs. They had each saved their best stories for the last and it was almost time to start exchanging them. Having finished his meal, John Haas pushed himself back from the table, took his napkin from his lap, refolded it and put it back on the table, and began listening to his mother start an anecdote.

John Haas was regarded as anomaly even by his closest friends. He was, it seemed, a master politician, yet liked playing second string. He was urbane and mannerly, an immaculate dresser, reserved. A Yale Law School graduate with an M.B.A. from Harvard, he had served as a supply officer in the Navy, had been a deputy D.A. in Boston, and later an assistant secretary of trans-

34

portation. Twice elected to the House of Representatives and once to the Senate, he had the credentials, experience, and bloodline for leadership.

John Haas's ancestors had settled in Massachusetts before the turn of the eighteenth century. There had been a Haas in state politics for a hundred and fifty years. This Haas cultivated friends easily and had few enemies. Much of his support was from the ranks of big labor and the nonworking poor, government workers, teachers, small businessmen. He was a bachelor, sober in his judgments, slow to form opinions. His style was conciliatory; his strength: his ability as a negotiator, a go-between. He despaired of political backbiting. When the liberal wing of his party called on him as a compromise candidate at its nominating convention, he demurred. Instead, he threw his support to the more conservative but exceptionally vigorous Clement Jamison, and his eventual reward was the Vice Presidency. He would apprentice for the top job, he told his friends, find out where to get his pencils sharpened; where they kept *the* button.

A Secret Service man interrupted his meal.

"Yes?"

"Stewart Ott phoned, sir. I'm afraid there's some bad news. Could I have a moment?"

"Excuse me," he said to his mother. "Business."

"Can't they get along without you even on Sunday?"

"Unless it's World War III, it'll only take a minute." He winked. She laughed mildly.

John Haas followed the Secret Service man into the lobby. Such interruptions were common. He had learned to bear them good-humoredly. It was policy to keep him just as informed as the President, even though he had no input whatever into the decision-making process. The Secret Service man marched stiffly in front of him through the dining room. Why were security people always so grim, he wondered. They all seemed to have a penchant for making simple foreign affairs briefings — or whatever — into *Oedipus Rex*.

The Secret Service man led him to a quiet corner of the lobby. Haas noticed the man's lips seemed tight, his eyes narrow.

"This doesn't have anything to do with our illustrious leader, I hope," Haas said.

"Afraid so, sir. There's been a shooting."

"Oh, my God!" He felt the room sway, as if the earth had moved beneath him.

"The President's dead, I'm afraid, sir."

Haas let some air out slowly pursed lips. His skin tingled as if it had been sprayed with gasoline and someone had just thrown a match.

"A judge is being located to swear you in, sir."

Haas nodded, even though he didn't hear what the man had said exactly. A judge? Swear to what?

"Stewart Ott is standing by for a call, sir. He says everything is under control. You needn't worry."

"No . . . I needn't worry . . . Who did this? This is quite impossible."

"Party or parties unknown. They ambushed him at the Fire Creek Country Club. Looks like radicals."

"It's not possible. Is this a drill? It's a test of some kind, isn't it? Mr. Jamison dreamed this up to test me, didn't he?"

The Secret Service man shook his head slowly. "No, sir. This is no test."

Haas looked toward the front of the hotel. Police cars

were arriving. Beefing up his protection. He looked toward the dining room. His mother was talking to someone she knew. The whole room was buzzing; they were all looking at him. They had all heard. It must be on the radio, the TV. Across the lobby more people were looking at him. He told the Secret Service man to wait a moment. He crossed the lobby and went into the men's room. It was small and unoccupied. He leaned over the sink and looked into the mirror. Small beads of sweat were forming on his forehead. *The President's dead . . . A judge is being located . . .*

He washed his hands and face and rinsed his mouth. His legs were weak. He breathed deeply. Suddenly he was lightheaded; he turned quickly and went into a stall and threw up his lunch.

"Is this Mr. Richard Knebel?" the caller asked. It wa
a woman, officious, curt.

"Yes, I'm Knebel."

"The White House calling, sir. Mr. Stewart Ot
Could you hold please?"

"Of course."

At forty-seven, Richard Knebel was, some said, th
greatest criminologist in the United States. He was ro
bust and bearded, with a thick neck, flaring bushy eye
brows, and powerful shoulders. He wore black-rimme
glasses and his eyes were narrow. A private man, fero
ciously independent, he was known as circumspec
often intractable, sometimes mulish. He was at home i
Rancho del Sol, Surfside, California, watching th
breaking story on television.

A man came on the phone: "Richard, is that you?"

"Stewart? Nice to hear from you. How's Omi Jamiso
taking it? Must be vicious for her."

"She's holding her own. True aristocrat, that one
Stoic. Haas is the one teetering."

"From what I know of him, he'll be a challenge fo
you, Stew."

"Don't I know it. I've tamed a few lions—this is my first outing with a lamb. Jamison, I'm afraid, will be sorely missed around here."

"You want me in?"

"Yes. As coordinator in the investigation. We'll get you a small staff. Be our eyes and ears. We've got to make damn sure our investigating agencies cooperate with each other. No glory grabbing—and no atrocities committed in the name of expediency. It hasn't hit the news yet, but some bunch calling itself the Manhattan Red Brigade has claimed credit. Slogans were left on the wall at the country club. They had the slogans right when they called in."

"Adolf White's group. I remember reading about him. Strange character. It's remarkable they effected an escape after hitting a President. Quite a feat . . . How do you think the Bureau is going to take it, my butting in like this? I'll be as welcome as the plague."

"By some—others, a little less. If you help wrap it up quickly, Mr. Haas will look good, I'll look good, we'll all look good. As time goes on, things will sour. If the case lasts any time at all, the good old boys will maneuver us both out. Sanchez-Flint, our illustrious FBI chief, will be among the ushers. . . . You'll be working with a guy named Hans Ober. Him you can trust with a capital *T*. But watch it, the medium to semi-big bananas over there will follow Sanchez-Flint's lead like lemmings to the sea."

"I'll get a flight out as soon as I can, Stew."

"There's a jet waiting at Edwards. A car will pick you up in thirty minutes."

Richard Knebel had advanced degrees in law and forensic sciences from Duke University, and another in police science from the University of Chicago. He had been a policeman, a prosecutor, a criminal consultant to the Texas Bureau of Prisons, a newspaper reporter, book editor; he once headed a special crime commission in Pennsylvania and helped reorganize the Federal Bureau of Investigation under Ronald Reagan. Lately he had been doing research for a West Coast think tank and taught graduate classes in the rights of the criminal, the duties of the investigator.

As a member of a formal organization he was indifferent to his superiors and a Simon Legree to his subordinates. He once said putting away a jilted boyfriend who had hacked up his lover held no fascination for him. It was like taking out the garbage. He left those jobs for the neophytes. He preferred complex, premeditated, high-stakes crimes. A Presidential murder was, he thought, perfect.

Knebel walked out onto the patio and found his wife, Laurie, sitting in the sunshine, painting at an easel and listening to the grim news on the radio. The circular stone patio overlooked the sea. She was facing the water and her hair was white-blond in the sun. She turned off the radio when she sensed him standing behind her. Laurie was in her early thirties, slight, graceful, delicate, serious about her art.

"They want you, don't they, Richard?" she said, without turning from her work.

"Stewart does." He lit his Meerschaum pipe, cupping the match in his hands. After a moment he said, "Something like this—a man can't say no."

She put down her brush. "I'd been hoping they wouldn't ask. I'll miss you, Richard. We've had it nice here."

"Yes, we have. I'll miss it."

"Swear you'll take care of yourself. I'll go crazy worrying."

"They want me to coordinate. It'll be mostly paperwork, make a few recommendations, snitch on inept bureaucrats — that kind of thing."

She stood up and kissed him. "You do it and make me proud, Richard. You make me damned proud, hear?"

He hugged her and ran his hand gently through her hair. "When they find out I'm after them they usually just turn themselves in to the nearest constable of the law. . . . Anyway, it'll be a matter of filling out a couple of forms . . . getting my picture on television.

He looked at her painting. There was an orange-black sun shining blackness down on a gray sea and a gray beach littered with dead sea birds. The sky was brown and streaked with red. It was hideous and powerful and grotesquely beautiful. There was great finality and sadness in it.

"I love it and I hate it," he said.

"As you should."

"I'd better pack, Laurie. They're sending a car."

"How long will your enlistment be?"

"Three to six months. That's just a guess."

"Patty Hearst was loose for years."

"I didn't make it to that show. They didn't pull out all the stops. This time they'll pull out all the stops, believe me."

"You get whoever did this, hear?" Jamison was a jackass, but he was *our* jackass, and they should be made to pay."

"They'll pay."

They went into the bedroom. She helped him pack

two suitcases with clothes and toilet articles. Then he went to his study and put some new thick, spiral notebooks and a few ball-point pens into a briefcase with a few pouches of strong Latakia tobacco and pipe cleaners. She was waiting in the living room with a glass of champagne for each of them when he was ready to leave.

She handed him his glass and they chimed their glasses together and each took a sip. There was a car turning into the drive.

"Good-bye," he said.

"Maybe while you're gone I'll have a torrid affair with our gardener."

"Katsu is seventy-four years old."

"I'll give him vitamins."

"You'll have to explain things to the university and the foundation. It's the President, they'll understand."

"You burn your bridges and I get to put out the fire, is that it?" she winked.

"I knew you'd understand."

NINE

It was dusk, deep dusk. The shadows of the trees were blending into gray and the sky was gray and burnt orange. The old Ford moved slowly around the bend and stopped beneath a gnarled old oak, flashing its headlights. Up the hill in the trees another light flickered twice, then again a moment later. The downpour had been steady for the last several hours and the potholes were filled with gray water as the Ford moved around them and up the hill. At the top of the hill the driver pulled off the road onto a flat place and got out and fixed an auto-club tow pennant on the Ford's antenna. He gathered the collar of his raincoat tightly to his neck, walked quickly into the trees, and found a trail. It was dark. He moved more cautiously down the trail a half mile to a clearing. There was a large camping trailer here and Ferris was waiting for him in the doorway.

"Greetings," Ferris said. "Come in, the coffee is hot."

He entered, took off his coat, and then sat at the table. "Where's Lucretia?" he said.

"A change in plans. She won't be coming, sorry to say. A regrettable chance happening. Her transfer vehicle was burglarized overnight — the battery stolen. Alternative plans were effected."

Ferris poured them both coffee and sat down at the table. He was a corpulent man, round-shouldered, slow and deliberate in his movements, and his eyes were large and strange.

Ferris said, "How do you feel now? Now that it's over. You were right, the bullets did not bounce off."

"The one Secret Service man was fast. The black. Like lightning, he was. That was the only hard moment."

"I have found it best not to look into their faces—and not to think of it afterward."

"For me, that is not possible. . . . Have the arrangements been made as we discussed?"

Ferris gestured with an undulating movement of his hand. "A few alterations—nothing of consequence. Did you have trouble with the road blocks?"

"It was simple. I went south, as we planned, and left my car and took the local bus north again. They had thousands of cars to search and no time to look for anything but an averted gaze, a nervous twitch, a choking voice. I offered none of these clues. What else could they have had to go on?"

"Have you had anything to eat?" Ferris asked. "I just opened a can of stew. Want some bread? It is not splendid, but it nourishes."

"I couldn't eat. Earlier I vomited. For me it is always like this. . . . You are certain that Lucretia is safe?"

"Yes."

"She has the blood of a shark, that one."

"She is very good, yes," Ferris said. He was eating stew with a spoon. "The Koran says that a woman has no soul—perhaps in her case the Prophet was right. No matter, for our purposes she is a godsend. What counts is that the assignment has been carried out. What needed doing is done. We will go on from here, go forward."

Ferris peeled open a bread wrapper and stuffed the end piece of bread into his mouth. He was smiling now. "You are a great man, my friend," he said. "You have courage in your convictions and the courage to impose your convictions on history."

"I heard on the radio that one of them didn't die."

"An unfortunate thing. For now, he is comatose and matters little. Still, it mars the beauty of the thing."

"When I heard he was alive I was glad. I want him to live. It was a terrible sight, Ferris. We waited until the thunder rolled to cover the sound of them hitting the floor. We went for head shots so it would be quick and they would not cry out. One second they were alive — the next, they were red pulp on the floor."

Ferris reached across the table and patted him on the shoulder. "It is over. Do not think of it. It is as much in the past as last year or the last war. It is a nightmare you had and now you are awake and you are free. I want you to change your clothes. Have a shower. Get all of your makeup off. In the cabinet under the sink in the bathroom you will find some grease to rub into your skin and get under your nails. Your papers say you are a working man from California and your name is Jim. Have a drink and relax, Jim. I'm afraid that in my anxiety to see you I left your papers and your travel money in the trunk of my car. I'll get it while you change. My car is over the hill a little ways."

"I should get rid of this old Ford."

"We have a pickup truck for you not far from here. A

very old battered Dodge. I'll drive you to it when you're ready. Fear nothing. Your path out of the country is open."

Ferris put on his heavy coat and went out. It was still raining and as he walked up the hill and through some trees, the path was slippery. Now it was quite dark. He found a clearing and stood for a moment shivering in the rain. He listened, hearing only the wind and the rain. He lit his lighter and after a moment a woman appeared from the trees. Two men were with her. They were swarthy men, coarse and hard, and they carried assault rifles with them.

"He is inside?" The woman asked.

"Yes. His mind is full of nonsense like a recruit full of regret after his first battle. His professional reputation is a falsehood. It will be an easy thing. He is trusting of us. I told him you had difficulties and could not make it."

"How is he armed?"

"With his usual, I think. The nine-millimeter automatic. . . . Wait until you hear the shower going. Strike then, Lucretia."

She motioned for the two men to follow her and moved off down the hill. The two men nodded and went with her. The rain was steady and they could see the light on in the trailer below them. There was good cover along a gully near the trailer and they moved along it, keeping spread apart. They moved close to the trailer and then one of the men, keeping low, circled around in back of it and hid himself in the pine trees. It was dark and the woods were still. The shower was going inside the trailer.

Lucretia moved to the door and opened it and crept inside; the second man went with her. The coffee cups and the plate of stew were on the table. They moved further inside, wrapped in silence. She pointed to the bathroom door. He nodded. Rainwater dripped from his chin and his cheeks were ruddy with the cold. He glanced down nervously at his weapon and took a deep breath. She stepped back and stood beside him. He raised the weapon quickly and fired. A wave of noise rose up and the trailer shook. The door to the bathroom splintered and disintegrated before the spray of fire and the lights flickered and went out when the bullets found wires in the wall. In the silence that followed Lucretia switched on her flashlight and they listened. The air was choked with dust. The water was running. The man reloaded with another long clip, slamming it into the magazine. There was rain on the roof and the wind brushed some tree limbs against the walls in the stillness. The man had backed away and was waiting for her to order him to fire again, but she did not. Cautiously, she moved down the short hallway and pushed the debris aside that a moment before had been the door to the bathroom. She half expected movement. She listened for the telltale sound of breathing. Besides the rain on the roof, she could hear only the trickle of the stream that ran past the trailer outside. Nothing more. She shone her flashlight in the bathroom and looked for blood and a body, but there was nothing—nothing but a busted sink and shower, and splintered sheets of paneling. The window was open; the shower curtain swayed in the wind. He was gone.

Lucretia and the two men with guns went down the hill and searched among the trees and the gullies for footprints, but found nothing on the pine-needle floors of the groves or the slate-rock sides of the stream beds.

47

Ferris joined them. He was out of breath from climbing down the path. "I want to see his body," Ferris said. "Where is it? I must know that he is dead."

No one said anything.

"You didn't miss him? You couldn't have missed him!"

They kept searching for a long time and then Lucretia came back to where Ferris was standing. "He isn't here," she said. "Somehow he knew and got past us."

"But how?"

"He is a spy. For a long time he is a spy. The ones that last know things. He just knew, there is no other way of explaining it. So do not blame yourself or anyone."

"You make him sound not quite human."

She turned off the flashlight and turned around and walked up the hill without saying anything more.

TEN

"I feel like a foolish understudy called in to play the lead in an absurd play and I don't know my lines," John Haas, the newly-sworn President of the United States, said.

"You'll do fine," Stewart Ott said. Ott was sixty, gaunt, gray; he wore a thin mustache and a bow tie. He looked deceptively like a used-car salesman, but was as tough as old shoe leather, they said, and as crafty as the bogeyman.

The two were alone in Haas's spacious ornate office at Blair House.

"I never wanted this," Haas said, "believe me. They wanted to balance the ticket. It was good for the party, they said. They flattered me and I listened to them."

"Give it awhile, Mr. President. The office always comes as a shock. Even if a man's elected, he's awed by it when the moment comes for him to take the oath. Carter was in a daze for a week or more, I heard."

"I hope you're right, Stewart. At the moment I feel as if everything is spinning around me and I'm powerless to stop it."

"The feeling will pass."

"Clement Jamison relied on you a great deal, Stewart. He told me the President's job was soft — all you had to do

49

was listen to Stewart Ott."

"He didn't always."

"He wasn't the kind of man to take too much advice . . . Is it true that you never went to college?"

"Hard knocks."

Haas toyed with a gold ring on his right hand. "That's good, I suppose." He smiled faintly. "You know, Stewart, they say the President is the most powerful man in the world. I don't feel powerful now — powerful or wise or any of those things I always thought of a President as being."

"Perhaps you haven't had time to get things into perspective, Mr. President."

"Are there many more out there waiting to see me?"

"Afraid so, Mr. President."

"God . . . Can you do something, Stewart? I don't want to see anyone right now."

"No problem, I'll handle them." He stood up. "Have you signed the executive order I left on your desk, sir?"

"Was there one? . . . Oh, yes. Knebel. I wanted to talk to you about that. You want him appointed some special coordinator?"

"I do, Mr. President."

"Why him? I don't understand."

"Knebel has no vested interest, career-wise. You can expect complete objectivity. The public trusts him one thousand percent. I do, too."

"Why not just let the regular FBI handle things? They assured me on the phone they were doing everything that could be done."

"Listen, Mr. President —"

Haas interrupted. "Call me 'John' please. You're making me feel like a stuffy institution."

"Sure thing — John. There are political considerations

50

here worth taking into account. We've yet to assess the effects of the assassination, but you'll probably be in a red-hot convention dogfight for your party's nomination in a few months. In between are the primaries. This investigation thing will still be dragging on. As far as the public is concerned, you're responsible for what the FBI does—if they goof it up, you're going to have sit in the fat and fry with them. Whatever they find will be criticized anyway. And you're going have to eat at that table. If you give oversight authority to Knebel—who's supposed to be some kind of superman—well . . ."

"It's always nice to have a Christian around to throw to the lions when the crowds get ugly, is that what you mean? You know, I hadn't given running for the office a single thought."

"You will, John. The Presidency grows on you, you'll see. Right now the country's rallied behind you. You've got to keep it rallied. Believe me, there are few men that doubt the integrity, honesty, and dedication of Richard Knebel. Naming him as a consultant on the investigation will do you credit. And it will go a long way toward dispelling any possible misgivings about our prioritizing this."

The new President sighed discontentedly. "We have these agencies set up to handle problems, then when a crisis comes along we call in outside consultants." He paused. "But if you insist—all right, I'll defer to your judgment." He signed the order and passed it back to Ott. "How soon can he begin his inquiries? I'll want to mention his appointment in my address this evening."

"He's already started, sir."

ELEVEN

It was still in the night air. The rain had ceased in the afternoon and the wind had died down early in the evening. Water, made sanguine by the red clay, ran in the ditches along the road which led to the clubhouse. In the distance they were blasting at the Fire Creek stone quarry; the sound echoed down the valley like summer thunder, rolling and sweet across the vacant fairways of the country club. Guards with shotguns stood by the gates and men with dogs patrolled the boundaries and farther up there were road blocks manned by the Sheriff's Department. During the day people had driven their cars in a slow steady stream along the ridge above the club and some got out with their small children and looked. They all drove away quietly when instructed to by the Secret Service and the deputies. Reporters and photographers and many TV people stood around on the crushed white gravel of the parking lot; they smoked, drank coffee, and talked amongst themselves. They had not been allowed in to see where the President had been slain and they were impatient. The bodies had been removed on stretchers in black plastic bags. At eleven-fifteen in the evening, when Knebel arrived by helicopter, all was still.

The reporters had questions. Were there any new facts, and were they any closer to catching the monster, Adolf White? There were many leads, Knebel said, many more by the hour. The public was helping enormously, and he hoped that they would not take any actions without the police. Innocent people could be hurt. He reiterated that. And yes, they had some hot leads, which Hans Ober of the Federal Bureau of Investigation was following up on and he had great hope for some speedy arrests. The reporters thanked him. They asked whether they might soon get in to see where it happened, and Knebel said he would check with Hans Ober and the lab people. He asked them to be patient.

Knebel was met on the steps of the clubhouse by a blond FBI special agent who introduced himself as Chad Priest. He was well over six feet, muscular, smooth featured, and smooth mannered.

"My instructions are to offer you every assistance, Mr. Knebel. Mr. Ober is waiting to see you."

Knebel followed him inside. Lab men were busy dusting for prints on virtually every surface. Others were vacuuming for fiber samples. Polygraph machines were set up in the foyer and dining room, where witnesses and employees were still being questioned.

They found Hans Ober in the cramped and crowded manager's office, talking on the phone. He finished his conversation abruptly and hung up, then shook Knebel's hand. Chad Priest excused himself and left them alone.

Hans Ober was a career cop, big, solidly built, black-eyed, tough. There were dark lines under his eyes and his tie was loose at the collar. His grip was strong.

"I've heard you're class all the way," Ober said, "straight arrow to the bottom of your boots. Okay, we need all the help we can get and we know it. One thing. I can't wet-nurse. This isn't the usual Federal feathered nest. You're here to do a job, to assist us, and we're here to do a job, too. If we aren't doing it right, you let me know. I'll tell you straight out, I think it's pure bullshit for you to be in, but I'm a game player, and if this is the game they want me to play, okay."

"Very inspirational speech, Mr. Ober. Now tell me, what's gone down and what have you turned?"

Hans Ober lit a cigarette, inhaled, and let the smoke out slowly, studying Knebel with his black eyes.

"Okay, the chief suspect is Adolf White — suppose you already know that. Called yesterday afternoon. We've got a ton of paper on him. He's been underground for two years. He's into drugs big, and sex. Supposedly he'll screw anything — man, woman, beast. He's supposedly humped half a dozen broads in one night and made them all purr. Three years ago he bombed a subway and killed two citizens. Mad-dog-type radical. Knows the rhetoric. Going to usher in the Marxist millenium by sacrificing innocents . . . Okay, you probably haven't seen the death scene yet. Pretty grim. Blood everywhere — and the slogans. Approximately two hundred rounds fired. The weapons experts are looking into the gun we recovered — they left one behind. We figure they had two of them. Sophisticated handmade deals. Quiet, reliable. Modified Uzis. They fire maybe eight hundred rounds per minute. Nine millimeter."

"Is it still here?"

"No. We've got good polaroids of it, if you'd like to take a look. We sent it to our gun shop in D.C."

54

"Have Art Lowenstein take a look at it. Remember him?"

"Lowenstein, Lowenstein . . . Is he that Philly detective who went up some years back on a corruption rap? A rotten apple in a rotten barrel, I remember."

"He's no altar boy, but he knows guns like Mother Hubbard knows baby bottoms."

Hans Ober made a note. "Okay, I'll get our franchise in Philly to dig him up."

"Tell me more about Adolf White. Who bankrolls him and what rock might he be hiding under?"

"Okay. The group has been linked for years to the Benson shipping fortune heir, Vincent Benson III. We've got people checking on him. Apparently he's disappeared. We've got photos of White and his people going out on every TV station in the country, okay? And so far the public has phoned in a third of a million leads, mostly junk.

"Okay, we're having every recent guest and all the employees at the Fire Creek Country Club screened, given thorough background checks, and interviewed with polygraphs. Some of them—if they had seen the killers—were also given hypnotic drugs. Composite drawings are being made. We've got no fix on the getaway car. A green Plymouth sedan, we think. Laboratory personnel are going over every square inch of the country club. We've got six hundred agents working the area. The organization needs fine-tuning—we've got people stumbling all over each other. Okay? What else? Progress? Damn little. Adolf White and his creeps have so far eluded us. They won't for long. You can put your paycheck on that. I'll have some of our staff brief you more fully whenever you're ready. I'll have them give you all the meat and potatoes. If you get any hunches, we're not proud." He took two quick puffs on his cigarette and crushed it out in a glass ashtray.

"I'll need a complete summary of events leading up to and subsequent to the shooting, but first I want a close look at the scene."

"Our people are just finishing up and the reporters have been kept the hell away. There's an archivist on the way over to give you a complete rundown on White and company. McHenry will give you the lowdown on what we've been up to."

McHenry was a monkish, balding man in a white lab coat. Knebel and Chad Priest found him in the dining room talking to George Higgins, the club manager. Higgins looked like a man who had spent a lifetime living the fiction that life's larger horrors would never reach him, and now that they had, he was reeling from the blow. "We won't be needing you," Knebel said to Higgins. Higgins excused himself and wandered off.

"I'm looking forward to working with you, Mr. Knebel," McHenry said. "I've read your books, of course."

"Where's the room, McHenry?" Knebel said.

"This way." Knebel and Chad Priest followed him down the hall and up the stairs to the poker room. The technicians had finished up and had left white lines painted on the carpet to show where the bodies had fallen. There were dull brown stains on the walls and ceiling where the rain of blood had splattered. On one wall there were blown-up photos taken before the bodies had been removed.

Chad Priest was ashen. He had not been in the room before. "Jesus," he muttered. "Jesus-oh-Jesus . . . could you ever imagine it?"

Knebel was standing by the wall behind the poker table where the blood had not splattered and this was the place where the killers had written the slogans on the wall in foot-high letters.

"Jesus-oh-Jesus," Chad Priest said again. "Could *anyone* imagine such a thing?"

McHenry stood close to Knebel. McHenry's features were smooth, stonelike; his dour expression, immutable. "They were standing about here when they fired," he said. "Wesley Que, the black, was over there by the door. Secret Service. We figure he must have gone down first. You see he had his weapon out. It's in the photograph over there, marked 1-A. The others went down pretty much simultaneously as far as we can figure. The President was hit square in the forehead from about a foot away, judging from the cordite residue imbedded in his skin. After he was down they pumped in twenty-eight more to be sure. It must have all happened like this" — he snapped his fingers — "because nobody cried out . . . at least that could be heard in the hall. There was some thunderstorm activity at the time and it may have masked some of it."

Knebel glanced at Chad Priest; there was sweat on his forehead and he was staring fixedly at the slogans painted with blood.

"Give me the sequence of events known," Knebel said to McHenry.

McHenry pulled a leather-bound notebook from his lab coat pocket. "This is incomplete at this time — we're still collating the data."

"Give me what you can."

"I'll start with last night. There was the annual Spring Dinner Dance at the club to kick off the Spring Tournament. It started at eight. Three hundred-four guests by invitation only. It was over at one o'clock. Some of the members stayed in the bar and drank until three or ten after. The bartender finished cleaning up and locked up and went home. He left at fifteen minutes to four and was the last one out of here. The club assistant pro, Reis, opened up at five-fifteen to get ready for the day's activity. He, of course, was a victim, so we don't know if anything was out of place when he got here or not. We figure the assassins made entry between three forty-five and five-fifteen."

"Has the bartender been fluttered?"

"*Everyone* has been given a polygraph test. I've gotten the preliminary reports and so far everyone has come clean with us."

"Continue, please." Knebel was still staring at the writing on the wall. The strokes were broad, hastily done, but legible: Jamison is Hitler; Murder is the cure of oppression; Death to the imperialist warmonger.

"They did the usual pre-Presidential check and found nothing," McHenry said.

"Were dogs used to cleanse the area?"

"No."

"Why not?"

"They kept the dogs at McFarland Kennel in Potter City, a mile from here. The dogs were sick. Something got into their diet."

Knebel was still looking at the writing on the wall. Chad Priest excused himself. "Sure," Knebel said, and then turned to McHenry. "The assassins must have poisoned the dogs, is that how you figure it?"

"Yes. We're nearly certain."

"What procedure was followed to make up for it?"

"Brill switched rooms, for one thing. Then the President switched them back. The President was a man of regular habits."

"It seems that the assassins had it pretty well figured."

"That, or they were lucky."

"What time did the President arrive?"

"Eight forty-five. He changed his clothes and they teed off at nine-ten, their regular starting time. They played eighteen holes. It was clouding up; everyone was getting off the course. They finished up before noon, had lunch, and retired to play poker at one-ten. There was a few minutes' delay while Brill straightened it out about the room. That's the last anyone of them was seen alive. Except Brill. At two forty-seven, two men came out. One was the image of Reis, the other of Blackburn. The Secret Service men suspected nothing amiss. The two suspects walked down the stairs and through the bar and as far as we can tell, vanished. It's possible one drove off in a green Plymouth. . . . Do you want to see the space they hollowed out of the wall in the supply room where they waited to kill the President?"

"Perhaps later. Thank you, I'll have more questions after a while. For now, I'd like to study the communication they left us."

Knebel pulled up a chair and stared at the writing some more. Then he got a tape measure out of his briefcase and made careful measurements. After that he sat in his chair again, staring for a long time and occasionally making notes in a notebook. McHenry left him there for over an hour. When he returned Knebel was still staring at the writing on the wall.

"Excuse me, sir," McHenry said.

"Yes?"

"They think they've boxed Adolf White on Long Island. Mr. Ober is leaving immediately and wants to know if you'd like to go along."

"Posses are not my style. Tell him thanks anyway."

"Mrs. Mancuso is here."

"Who?"

"She's to brief you on Adolf White."

"Love to talk to that lady."

TWELVE

Knebel met with Mrs. Mancuso in one of the small upstairs meeting rooms. It was two in the morning and she was visibly tired. She was past middle age, with short gray hair and gray eyes. Her long fingernails were polished rust red. They sat at a small card table and she opened a thick manila folder in front of her. She smoked a parade of French cigarettes held at the tips of her fingers and spoke in a monotone, with flat, machinelike precision.

"For now I'll give you the high spots, Mr. Knebel. You may want to glean the material in greater detail when time permits. . . . Right after it happened we received an anonymous phone call. The caller stated that the Manhattan Red Brigade was, quote, 'gloriously responsible' for the just end of the quote, 'tyrant' Jamison. Station A subsequently made a voiceprint comparison of that conversation with one known to be Adolf White—from an antiwar rally speech White made at Columbia Park, Manhattan, in nineteen and sixty-eight."

"Does the physical description of the assassins fit Adolf White or his people?"

61

"The larger of the suspects, yes. It could have been White himself. The other doesn't seem to fit any of them. We suspect he was a hired professional."

"What about the slogans? Supposedly they had them right."

"They did. The caller gave them verbatim. It's standard radical sociopath rhetoric, but they quoted them exactly. 'Jamison is Hitler' and 'Murder is the cure of oppression' were painted on the walls of the New York subway the Manhattan Red Brigade blew up two years ago. 'Death to the imperialist warmonger' is the group's motto."

Knebel wrote more notes in his notebook. "Tell me what you know about White personally."

"White's thirty-four, bisexual, a Dartmouth dropout. In the early seventies he was a Weatherman, spent some time in Huntsville for bank robbery. The prison psychiatrist listed him as schizophrenic paranoid. The complete psychiatric evaluation is in Records—if you'd like, I'll run it for you."

"Perhaps later. What is there about White that would bring him to this?"

"I'd have no way to know."

"Is it personal with him? Some real or imagined injustice?"

"Not that I know of. He's charismatic, does most of the thinking for his group. They say his Marxism is of the SLA type, though he's more literate. One thing, he's an intriguer, makes elaborate plans right down to the smallest detail. What is *most* interesting about White is his link to Vincent Benson III."

"Tell me about him."

"He's a left-wing groupie. Spoiled, fabulously

wealthy—with most of it tied up in trusts he can't touch. Before being radicalized he was heavily involved in yacht racing. He was raised mostly in prep schools—four of them—and then went on to Yale where he majored in hash, coke, and amphetamines. Our best analysts think he: one, feels guilt for his wealth and advantage and seeks repentance by supporting the proletariat in what he's sure is the coming class war; and two, that he's rebelling against his father, who has been dead since he was twelve. I guess the father was a pretty cold, distant sort. Rejection, and all that."

"So he had a deprived childhood, what a shame. . . . How about White's followers?"

"None of them has particularly distinguished himself or herself. Most are rootless, vaguely revolutionary, sociopathic. They are into drugs and sex. The single possible exception is the one they call 'Marya.' Ober has people looking into her past right now. In the file you won't find much. Apparently she keeps to herself, doesn't take drugs or even smoke pot. She seems completely committed to White, though—but doesn't sleep with him. At least that's what we've had reported by a close informant. She's the light of reason in the group. We don't know who she is or where she comes from." Mrs. Mancuso pushed the files across the desk. "I'll leave you these: surveillance reports, psychiatric evaluations, arrest records. It's everything we've got on all of them at this point." She inhaled on her cigarette and stood up to leave. "Give my section a call if we can be of any service. I've admired your career, Mr. Knebel. Nailing that L.A. mass murderer last year was a brilliant piece of work."

"We knew he liked blondes, Mulholland Drive, and Saturday nights. He was as easy to catch as a Greyhound bus."

THIRTEEN

It was nearly closing time. Arthur Lowenstein was sitting on the soft edge of sobriety, gently sinking into the calm sea below. Yet his senses detected the tall man coming into the Dolphin Room as not belonging, and he sensed too that the man was looking for *him*.

Except for a few dockworkers playing serious nineball on the pool table, most of the customers were at the bar watching a special about Clement Jamison. The tall man went over to the bar and looked at everyone and talked to the bartender. Lowenstein watched the bartender nod and point toward him.

The tall man was all business. He wore a gray suit. His expression was fixed, his gaze steady. He walked directly to Lowenstein's booth.

"Are you Arthur Lowenstein?" The tall man was used to being listened to and obeyed.

"Who wants to know? You a cop? Sure, you're a cop. A Federal cop. You can tell by the swagger."

"Peace, friend. I'm the bearer of good tidings."

Toward the front of the barroom a heated argument erupted over some small interpretation of the rules of nineball. The bartender quieted it with a threat to close the game. Didn't they have any respect? the bartender asked. The President had been killed, for Christsake, he said.

"How good are these tidings?" Lowenstein said. He downed the rest of his drink.

"You are Lowenstein?"

"Yeah, I'm Lowenstein. Arthur Zimmerman Lowenstein. Have a seat. Have a drink." He swished the ice cubes around in his glass and leaned his head back against the booth. "So what are you? FBI or what?"

"FBI." He showed his ID card. Lowenstein squinted at it. "Mann? George Mann. Kraut, maybe?"

"Dutch."

"When I was a kid, we always said 'dumb as a Dutchman.' " He looked vaguely upward. "You can't say things like that now."

Lowenstein wore an old plaid shirt and a worn overcoat. His white hair needed trimming and he hadn't shaved in two days.

"You are the Arthur Lowenstein who was a lieutenant here in Philly? Homicide, wasn't it?"

"Twenty-three years in Homicide. Twenty-three years, four months. I was thirty-four years a flatfoot altogether. Long time, catch? Robert Peterson Dawes wrote a book about me. Called it *Supercop*. It was novelized, but it was all true stuff. It's gone out of print. After I took my fall nobody wanted to read it. . . . What do you want with me, George Mann?"

"Knebel wants you."

"Knebel? *Richard* Knebel?"

"Maybe you haven't heard, but the President of the United States has been assassinated."

"So?"

"Knebel thinks you might be able to contribute some expertise."

Lowenstein laughed. "Don't that beat all," he said. "That son-of-a-bitch. He's the cracker who pulled my plug."

"We couldn't believe it either."

Lowenstein pulled a pint bottle from his coat and dumped a little bourbon into his glass, checking to make sure the bartender wasn't watching. He laughed again.

"Whenever you're ready, I'm to take you to Washington myself," Mann said.

"Let's get to the nitty-gritty. In what capacity do they want me?"

"As a consultant. To look at the weapon and give us an opinion. You'll be paid, of course. Two hundred-fifty per day plus expenses."

Lowenstein studied him and smiled. "Consultant? What's that, exactly? I've never been one of those. When you hire a man to do detective work you ought not to call him a consultant. The President's been shot, this shouldn't be a halfway thing." He took a few swallows of bourbon. His face hardened. "I want full police powers, catch?"

Mann shook his head. "All Knebel wants is for you to study the weapon the assassins left at the scene and give us what you can."

"You tell him I want to be a cop again. I'll help him. I'll look for these creeps under every rock in the country. But I got to be a cop, catch? Special investigator. Something like that. He's a big shot now, he can arrange it. They're looking for the killer of a President. They could suspend the rules."

"Not a chance."

"If they want me, they've got to give me a little something."

"My car's outside. You coming or not? It has to be our way."

"Tell Knebel to piss up a rope."

FOURTEEN

It was past four in the morning when Knebel came out of the poker room and began an inspection of the rest of the clubhouse. It was quiet. Most of the technicians had left and there was only a skeleton crew of guards and FBI men. The reporters had been moved inside the dining room. The club personnel had all gone home. All except George Higgins, who offered Knebel a cup of coffee when he came downstairs.

"Fine — and a sandwich or something."

"Tuna okay?"

"Anything."

Knebel looked around every room and said hello to the reporters. Chad Priest and George Higgins were waiting for him in the bar. Chad Priest was on the phone in one of the booths. When he saw Knebel coming to the table, he hung up and joined him.

"Anything interesting?" Knebel asked.

"We're getting close to White. And Brill didn't make it. He died about an hour ago."

"Did he say anything?"

"Yes. The assassin who looked like Blackburn called the President 'sir' before he fired."

"Anything else?"

"No, just that . . . By the way, I'm sorry about up there. I haven't been exposed much to this kind of thing. I don't get much field duty."

Knebel said, "You're human—a pardonable weakness. Where's McHenry?"

"He'll be right back."

"Brill was quite lucid, was he, when he made the statement about calling him 'sir'?"

"Yes."

Knebel stirred a tablespoon of sugar in the coffee Higgins had brought him.

McHenry came back and sat down. He was wearing a sport coat, muted herringbone. His dour expression was the same, his eyes steady and tired. "Reports," he said, indicating a pile of papers on the table. "Everything everyone had said so far—the people who were here. Mostly Secret Service stuff," he added, "all preliminary and sketchy." Knebel scanned some of it while he waited for the sandwich and then leafed through the rest while he ate. Afterward he made a few notes and asked McHenry some questions about the positioning of the Secret Service men; then he went back to the poker room for a while longer. When he came out he asked Higgins to please get him some fresh coffee. He sat down with McHenry and Chad Priest and loaded his pipe. His mood had changed. He seemed more at ease and confident. It was by then almost five-thirty in the morning.

"All right, Chad, I've got a question for you. Why here, and why now?"

"I don't think I understand, Mr. Knebel."

"Why did the killers choose this place and this time?"

"Opportunity, I assume."

70

Knebel shook his head. "I don't think so. These were sophisticated killers with damn good intelligence and plenty of resources. They knew the President came by helicopter — why not just shoot him down with a heat-seeking rocket?"

"I don't know. Maybe the expense?"

"Maybe the President wasn't the target — or wasn't the only target."

"Never thought of that."

"I want to know about the other victims — who loved them, who hated them. Find out their relationship to the President, any big business deals brewing, political connections . . . I want to know who are their debtors, creditors, and what skeletons they had rattling around in dark closets."

"Yes sir, will do."

"Now, here's what we have. The murders occurred at approximately two-thirty. The exact time of death is not critical. We assume that after the shooting they took a few minutes to write the slogans and then left. Ballistics tests have shown that two weapons were used, yet only one was left behind. No latent prints, of course. There were two killers; one medium height and weight, disguised as Blackburn; the other, shorter, thinner, disguised as Reis. They come out of the room, go down the front stairs and through the bar; They turn to the right — in all likelihood — and exit at the side entrance by the kitchen."

McHenry nodded and Knebel checked his notes and continued. "One Secret Service man noted that Reis walked 'peculiar' but couldn't articulate what he meant. He did not note it in the log, but did in his report. Did you see that?" McHenry nodded again and Knebel resumed: "A guest, a Mr. Ralph Blunt — who had seen Blackburn many times at the club—reported that he saw him in the parking lot getting into a car. This would be the suspect disguised as Blackburn. He was alone. The car might have been green. It was a late model and fullsized, definitely not a compact. At two-fifty, the gate duty officer for the Secret Service noted a green Plymouth leaving with a man driving. He thought it was Blackburn, but checked the license number and found the car belonged to a club member by the name of Allison."

"Allison, right," McHenry said.

"His car had been left in the parking lot overnight Saturday. It was noted as being in the lot when the Secret Service arrived early Sunday morning."

"Allison was probably at the dinner dance and may have had too much to drink," McHenry said. "It's common for club members to leave their cars here when they've had too much to drink. There were four cars parked here when Brill arrived. He didn't think anything of it apparently, except for just mentioning it in his notes."

"So the suspect disguised as Blackburn left in that car at that time. That's clear, is it not?"

"We've had an all-points out for the car, yes. And we're looking for Allison."

"What about the second suspect, Reis?"

"He's a mystery. We haven't got a clue."

"On the contrary, there are plenty of clues."

McHenry reddened. "I can't imagine what they would be. We've had dozens of top people sifting every detail."

Knebel puffed on his pipe. "What I am about to tell you may seem fantastic at first, but I'm confident it will be borne out by further investigation. There are so many pieces that it is not possible to fit them all together today, but I have an outline and I know a great deal about what has happened here and who **perpetrated** it. Bear with me even if you think it is fantasy. . . . Suspect Blackburn is first. Here we have an interesting enigma. He is the one who called the President 'sir.' He is five-feet-nine or ten, probably in his mid-forties. I doubt he's a radical at all. Perhaps he is a hired gun. He is a professional. You will notice that one of the brushes dipped in blood is lying on the floor all the way across the room. It was not dropped there, it was flung. One stroke was made by that brush. You see, he has no stomach for it. He tries to do it, but can't. He is a man who is respectful even to the President he is about to kill, and he cannot do the ghoulish thing they set out to do. The rest of the writing is done by the other, suspect Reis."

McHenry had reddened more, and his eyes were alive with skepticism and doubt. Chad Priest was obviously doubting too. George Higgins brought the coffee and Knebel poured in the sugar and cream, put down his pipe, and went on.

"Suspect Reis is more interesting. Figuring out Suspect Reis was a bitch, and even when I figured it out I didn't quite believe it for a while. But one's handwriting is a window to the personality, a clean window. Suspect Reis is a woman, gentlemen."

McHenry and Chad Priest looked at each other and then at Knebel and their eyes said they didn't believe it.

"She's a malevolent woman. She's about thirty-five, but I may be a little off on that. She could be as young as thirty or as old as forty-four or -five. She was educated in Europe or North Africa under the French, but since the liberation. She probably has had guerilla training. She may be one of White's people, the one called Marya. I think her general description would fit. She is slender enough—or could

73

have lost weight — and she's the right height. Nothing much is known about Marya. We ought to consider making her our prime suspect for now." He looked at them both; their expressions were blank.

"Do either of you remember that the Secret Service man on duty in the hallway reported that one of the suspects walked 'peculiar'?"

They both nodded.

"The hips of a woman are different from a man's. If you told him it was a woman, he would find that there was not the least thing peculiar about the way she was walking. She came out that door with suspect Blackburn and went down the stairs over there and through the bar. They turned and went down the short corridor on the other side where suspect Blackburn exited into the parking lot. Suspect Reis ducked into the small restroom reserved for women — the waitresses use it — changed into a waitress uniform, perhaps, and walked out across the patio. In all likelihood, she took the path that leads to the bus stop. You see, Mr. McHenry, you had it all wrong. They came as a couple in here last night in Allison's car. They mingled with the guests, might even have danced. After a while, they slipped into the poker room, dug out their space — the dance band would cover the noise — and then all they had to do was wait. They waited as quiet as mice in their little mouse hole, and then in the afternoon the mice came out and killed the President and all the President's men."

FIFTEEN

"We were told not to expect you, Mr. Lowenstein," the young woman behind the security desk said.

"Yeah? Well, I'm here. Must be a mix-up someplace in communications, catch?"

"I think Mr. Reed is still in, I'll tell him you're here."

Lowenstein paced around the lobby under the eye of a second, stone-faced security guard. The clock over the elevator said it was six-twenty-five. He took off his raincoat and shook the water off it, then straightened his tie. He paced to the end of the lobby and looked out some windows into the street. Outside it was dawn and raining steadily. He paced back toward the other end of the lobby. Many flattened cigarette butts littered the marble floor. At twenty minutes to seven the woman reappeared and asked for some identification. Lowenstein produced his Pennsylvania driver's license. She looked at it carefully. "Follow me," she said. They took the elevator to the sixth floor. Here a gray woman in a green dress had him sign some papers including a loyalty oath. His check would be mailed, she said. He scratched his signature on the papers without reading them.

"It's all politics," the woman said. "We have very competent people here."

"Meaning what?" Lowenstein asked.

She looked at him coldly. "It's all politics, that's all I'm saying." The woman stuffed his papers into a file folder.

Back in the elevator the woman who had brought him up from the lobby said, "I'll apologize for her. Federal snobbery, pure and simple. Really you can't blame her though. Richard Knebel coming in was a slap in the face, sort of. And now him sending for you does kind of make the statement that we need help. We don't. We've got White cornered out on Long Island. You must have heard that. There's been little else on the news for hours."

"I'm here for the weapon," Lowenstein said. "I don't give a damn about the rest of it."

At the end of a long hall on the twelfth floor there was a windowless door with a bell. She rang the bell and a moment later a young man in a white jacket opened the door. The woman left. The young man said that Lowenstein should follow him. They went down another hallway with large windows along one wall; on the other side of the windows there was a large room where serious-looking men and women were working with scientific equipment. There were many computer terminals and panels with digital read-outs and switches and dials. At the end of the hall there was another door. The young man knocked softly and a voice from the other side said to come in. It was an office. A middle-aged man with thick eyebrows said his name was Reed. He asked Lowenstein to sit down.

"I'd rather just see the gun. I won't be staying."

The young man was excused. Reed said, "We have to set the ground rules. We are responsible for the evidence, after all."

"I am here as a consultant."

"We know all about you, Mr. Lowenstein. I had your records pulled. Knebel, when he was assistant D.A. for Philadelphia, headed up a special police corruption unit. You took a fall for six years. Maybe Mr. Knebel feels sorry that he did that and he's trying to make it up to you."

"Where is the item I've come to see, Mr. Reed?"

"Be patient. I want the ground rules set. It is nearby. It has been disassembled and we're doing every kind of test on it known to science. We will soon know more about who made it than the persons that made it. What were your specific instructions?"

Lowenstein shrugged. "I am a consultant, that's all they said. You can make of that what you want, catch?"

"I don't approve, I want you to know that. I will have my people cooperate, but I don't approve. We are doing every conceivable test that can be done. What do you expect to find out what we won't?"

"Maybe nothing."

Reed studied him with his thick eyebrows raised, then he nodded and stood up abruptly. "All right. You may see the article. You may touch it, but any testing must be cleared through this department. Clear?"

"Yeah."

"You may use our equipment only if one of our people is standing by."

"Anything you say, Reed. Let's get on with it."

"All right, fine. Just so long as we're straight."

Lowenstein went with Reed down a hallway and then through a doorway and down another hall and they stopped in front of a door with a red plastic sign in white letters: SPECIAL PROJECTS CLASSIFICATIONS ROOM. Reed had a key and opened the door with it. It was a room with tiled white walls and white linoleum floors and fluorescent lights. Voices sounded hollow and the light was intense. On a long, green, felt-topped table the disassembled parts of the gun were displayed, each piece placed on a clear plastic dish with a typed index card.

If a piece was missing there was a blue check-out card signed with the name of the person who had accepted responsibility. There were two technicians in the room, a woman and a man. They were taking small filing samples from each part and indexing the filings and putting them in small ampules, each carefully labeled.

"Our work here is exacting and time consuming," Reed said. "That is the only way to learn everything."

Lowenstein bent over the table and surveyed the pieces without touching them. He asked for a magnifying glass and bent low over the table and looked at the pieces. "May I see the can—the silencer?"

Reed nodded. "Properly, it's a sound suppressor."

Lowenstein picked it up and sighted down it, and then he looked at the short barrel.

"Nine millimeter?"

Reed nodded again. "Basically it's an Uzi S.M.G. Modified, of course. Standard clip on it would be thirty-two rounds. Using these circular cannisters, they had ninety. Ingenious really."

"Yeah," Lowenstein said.

"The whole thing was tailored," Reed said. "No mass produced parts. No sir, this is specialty shop stuff."

"You'd suspect for close work they'd want something larger, more knockdown power at the same muzzle velocity. How come so small?"

"Perhaps to make the chambers in the centrifugal clip accommodate another row. We don't know."

"They must be sub-sonic."

"Of course," Reed said. "The sonic boom would otherwise nullify the silencer. That's really obvious."

"You fired it?" Lowenstein asked the technician.

"Yes," the technician said. "We measured heat and sound. Both remarkably low. High-speed firing mechanisms. Ten and two-tenths rounds per second. There are mass-produced weapons that'll outperform it, but we suspect the reliability is much higher here and the lightweight design was a decided plus for the purpose the weapon was intended. It's an extremely well-made piece — the tolerances are within three ten-thousandths of an inch."

Lowenstein nodded and went back to the weapon and sat down. He studied it for a long time, holding the parts, turning them in his hand, sighting down the short barrel, checking the precision fittings. Reed excused himself and returned to his office. Lowenstein continued studying the parts for a long time. Someone had borrowed the trigger mechanism and he asked to see it; a technician brought it to him. It was in pieces and he wasn't interested in the pieces. He asked to see the cartridges and he was given one. It was a rim-fire type and the bullet was tipped with a hard plastic which the technician said would split and tumble through the flesh "like a backhoe through soft mud."

"Cyanide in them?"

"No."

"Strange. You'd think they'd go the whole forty miles. Unless they were worried about being nicked by a ricochet."

"Nose point's too soft to ricochet. Soft and fibrous," the technician said. "We figure it's some kind of polyester. The tests are not completed."

"So why no cyanide?"

79

"Maybe they weren't ghoulish enough."

Lowenstein nodded and studied the weapon again for a long time; then he asked where he might go for a cigarette. He was taken to a lounge area where he smoked a cigarette and drank lukewarm coffee from a machine. Two technicians sat with him and one asked him whether he had any idea about where the guns were made and he said so far he was baffled. After his coffee and a second cigarette he went to Reed's office.

Reed was studying sheets of computer print-outs. He continued reading while Lowenstein stood over his desk for a few moments and then looked up. "Well, what do you have for us?"

"Nothing yet."

"We're learning more by the minute. The tests are coming in in a flood. A veritable torrent. The aluminum for the carriage-return housing was made by Halyard in Detroit. We even have a fix on the lot number of the stock. The springs for the trigger return were made in Italy and were wholesaled through a New York distributor. This is coming together like a marvelous jigsaw puzzle. I meant it when I said we were going to know more about that gun than the people who made it."

"I want to fire the weapon. I've got to know the feel."

"That's nonsense. It will serve no purpose, reveal nothing. How do you describe it? What indexing can be done about a 'feel?' I'm sorry. Definitely no."

"Reed, you can know nothing about a voluptuous woman until you test her in bed, catch? It is the same here. You must test the performance."

"You asked—I said I was sorry—but no."

"Get your director on the phone. Him and Knebel."

Reed brushed his hands through his hair, then sighed

deeply. "It will take a while to get it assembled. We could spare you no more than a few rounds."

"Twenty-five would be enough."

The firing range was in the basement. The weapon was light in his hand when he pointed it at the man-size silhouette target, and when he fired, it spoke with a voice no louder than a hiss. All the shots were high of center, but concentrated, and Lowenstein and the technicians agreed that the accuracy was good.

Lowenstein went back to the coffee room and Reed returned to his office. Fifteen minutes later Lowenstein was in Reed's office with a list of names.

"You recognize these men?" Lowenstein asked.

"They're gun freaks. Most work on the other side."

"You have dossiers on these men?"

Reed sighed heavily. "I'm sure we do."

"Get them."

Lowenstein read the dog-eared files in the coffee room. A technician sat with him, a fat, lugubrious man with dark circles under his eyes. The files were full of surveillance reports and arrest records, probation reports, lists of known associates. Lowenstein leafed through them, shaking his head and mumbling and smoking cigarettes and drinking more coffee. It was nearly eleven A.M. when he finished. He got up and stretched and said he was done. He had seen enough.

"What do you think?" the fat technician asked.

"I think I should have stayed in Philadelphia."

Reed wanted to see him before he left. Reed was tired, but beamed when Lowenstein told him he had drawn a blank.

"So you have no theories, no answers, nothing whatever to report?"

"Nothing at all."

Reed tried to suppress a smile and couldn't; it spread slowly across his pale face. "We are finding out more by the minute. Stick around, perhaps you'd like to see how we match and cross-verify every piece of evidence. Facts must be extracted painfully, carefully. We are like master chefs creating a great soufflé one mistake and it goes poof. We are not about to allow that one mistake."

"I'll leave you to your cooking, then," Lowenstein took Reed to be a buffoon and he had no patience with such men.

"Mention in your report — about our cooperation, eh — We're team players here and we like them reminded of it every chance we can." He was smiling broadly now. "Couldn't come up with anything, eh?" He put out his hand and Lowenstein shook it.

Outside it was drizzling and the streets were empty. Lowenstein walked a few blocks north toward the Capitol dome, then turned west and found an open liquor store where he got a half pint of Jack Daniels and two dollars worth of change. From a payphone across the street he called the airport and made a tourist-class reservation for a two-thirty flight to Chicago.

SIXTEEN

It was a large, brown-brick building on K Street, built in the 1890s for the Interior Department. It had once been a school for Naval Intelligence during World War I. Later it was a warehouse for office furniture, renovated in the sixties to house a War on Poverty program task force temporarily, then given over to the Federal Bureau of Investigation. A sign in front proclaimed it to be the "Center for Independent Counter Civil Disorder Research and Coordination Facility." FBI staffers referred to it as "the Annex."

Knebel arrived by car from the airport at ten thirty in the morning, Monday. He didn't like the office they had given him. It was large enough and had an anteroom for a secretary, but it was in the basement and had no windows. The air conditioner was too noisy and it had a musty smell. He grumbled, but decided against mounting a protest. His secretary was in her late twenties, mousy, thin, efficient as her IBM Selectric. Her name was Ms. Pressman.

Already there were reports and memos stacking up on his desk. He spent half an hour going through them, then called in Ms. Pressman.

"Take a memo," he said.

"Sir." She readied her pad.

"Tell Hans Ober I have no desire or need to get photo-copies of every goddamn report coming through here on the way to oblivion. I want summaries of investigation findings — clear, concise, and readable, with notations indicating where I can find out more if I want more. All right?"

"Yes, sir."

"I'd also like a coffee maker and some good Colombian coffee. And a cot and some blankets, a small refrigerator, and a couple of more telephone lines — and some room deodorant."

"Yes sir."

"Who's running the computer section?"

"Mr. Thaddeus Gore."

"How do I find him?"

"He's on extension one thirty four. His office is on the third floor."

"Thanks."

Knebel took the stairs. He didn't like elevators. The halls were crowded and there was a buzz of voices. Knebel glanced into the offices and departments. Telex machines and typewriters clacked away. Clerks were at computer terminals. Telephone men seemed to be everywhere laying cables and installing equipment. More computer equipment and office machines were coming in, and desks and filing cabinets. The third floor was jammed with computer hardware, software, and technicians. Knebel found Thaddeus Gore in his small, cluttered office. He had a pile of computer print-outs on his lap and was marking them up with a felt-tipped pen.

"You're Richard Knebel," Gore said. He was young

and blond, brittle and intense. His complexion was sallow for a young man, Knebel thought, and the worry lines were deep around his eyes. Gore extended his hand and Knebel shook it.

"Have a seat," Gore said, indicating the only chair not piled high with papers. Knebel sat down. "What can I do for you?" Gore asked.

"How's it going so far?"

"We're keeping up. Until yesterday we were a sleepy little department with twelve dozen programs and God knows how many operators. We've got so many clerks all of a sudden we're falling over them."

"Good, I've got something to keep them busy. I want you to do a correlation of all incidental information on any and all suspects, victims, witnesses, investigators, public officials — from place of birth to rank in the Army, religious preference, national origin, brand of toothpaste. Absolutely anything, no matter how trivial."

"I don't get you."

"Simple enough. If Jamison, say, went to kindergarten with some suspect's sister-in-law's neighbor, I want to know about it. If a suspect chews tutti-fruiti chewing gum and so does the head of the Post Office, I want to know that too. The Bureau's been squirreling away reams of information on citizens for years. Time to use some of it."

"Jesus Christ, Knebel. Do you know what you're asking? Our machines are only human."

"Can you do it?"

"Sure, but can't you imagine the mountain of meaningless crap it'll generate?"

"I'm hoping for a little gold among the meaningless crap."

The phone rang. "Gore . . . Yeah, he's here . . . Okay, I'll tell him." He hung up. "Hans Ober has White's gang surrounded out on Long Island. They've got hostages and will negotiate only with you, personally."

"The price of fame," Knebel said with a wry smile.

"We'll have a ton of coincidences for you to frolic in when you get back," Gore said. "It'll be a lot of fuddle, believe me. These machines can't tell what's significant from doggy-do."

"Neither can a lot of people."

SEVENTEEN

The helicopter put down in the mud of the baseball diamond behind Our Lady of Mercy Elementary School at one o'clock in the afternoon. It was misting and cold. The wind gusted strong off the North Atlantic. A deputy sheriff waited in a black-and-white sheriff's car. Knebel and Chad Priest, crouching low, dashed for the car and got into the back seat. Knebel carried a briefcase under his arm.

"Anything break?" Knebel asked the deputy.

"Nothing, sir. We've got them treed. There's been one exchange of gunfire. Couple of shots is all."

"Casualties?"

"None on our side. One suspect—maybe."

"Any communication?"

"They want to parley with you; that's all they're saying."

"Has it been confirmed about the hostages?"

"The household staff—best we can determine. There's at least a butler, three maids, a Jap houseboy."

"Let's go," Knebel said.

They moved out with siren and red lights. The neighborhood of Belle Island was an expensive one; the houses were large and the lawns expansive, the shrubbery sculptured. The trip took three minutes at sixty to seventy miles an hour. Suddenly they were there: crowd and police cars, fire trucks, ambulances, confusion. There were dozens of TV mobile crews and men with cameras. The crowd parted as they approached and the police waved them through and directed them to park next to a row of police cars.

They were more than a block from the house. Now it was quiet and the houses around them were empty. The wind was blowing stronger and the misting was heavier. They got out of the car and turned up their collars against the wind. Two uniformed police officers met them and asked for identification and then let them pass. A little further there was a line of police cars forming a security perimeter and hundreds of policemen were standing around.

The house they had surrounded was a large one, built on three levels with columns on either side of the front door. The shades were drawn. Knebel inquired where they might find Hans Ober and was directed to a large gray truck parked down another street. They started walking in that direction. On the lawn across the street newly arriving cops were reporting in and being given assigned positions around the security perimeter. Knebel stopped to watch for a moment.

"Look at them," Knebel said. "Like jackals."

"You can't blame them," Chad Priest said. "It was the President, after all."

"I didn't say I blamed them."

The truck was a SWAT team command post. Inside, they found Hans Ober, a State Police SWAT commander named Fixx in a fatigue uniform, and the

88

county sheriff, named Pete Sparks. Sparks was young and chewed gum. There were other police officers there too, Federal men and State Troopers, and the sheriff's chief assistants. In the front of the van there was a communication center with two radio men in fatigue uniforms. Someone passed Knebel a cup of coffee poured from a steel thermos. He took a sip, puckered, and pushed it aside. He then told Hans Ober he had a message from the President and Ober quieted the men down.

When they were quiet, Knebel said: "The President wants no unnecessary killing. Not the hostages. Not us. Not the suspects. Everyone is to understand that. I'm sure everyone has been told to follow standard SWAT siege and standoff procedures. We will stall, we will talk, we will cajole." Many nodded; they understood. "Unless, of course, a command decision is made to take them by force."

"What if they open fire on us?" someone asked.

"The standing order is to maintain the security perimeter. If they fire from positions inside the house we will not return fire. I repeat that. For the time being we will *not* return fire as long as they maintain their position. If they attempt to break out—even if the hostages are endangered—they are to be stopped by all necessary force. Does everyone understand?"

No one had a question.

Hans Ober said, "Fine. Pass that along to every man. Have each man sign something that says he understands what the standing orders are. There are to be no mistakes." They all left to pass the word.

When they had gone Hans Ober said, "You've identified the second killer as a woman, is that right?"

"Yes. Possibly Marya."

"Based on what evidence?"

"Her handwriting — the slogans."

"Graphoanalysis?"

"Yes."

"Pretty damn slim, I'd say."

"You'll have to take my word on it."

"If you're right, a whole lot of other people are goin[g] to look a little stupid."

"I don't give a damn if they do."

"Okay, you were right about the Allison's car bein[g] the getaway car. I guess McHenry had that figured ou[t] too. The Allisons are dead, both of them. Found th[e] bodies in a wood about half an hour ago, okay?"

"That makes ten."

"I guess it does. Would you like to see what we've go[t] going down here?"

"Sure."

It was warm in the van. Voices rattled on the trans[-] mission equipment. Knebel and Chad Priest took of[f] their raincoats.

"They think from watching the TV that you somehow speak for the President," Ober said. "They've stated cat[-] egorically they'll only deal with you. If you don't want t[o] play, I'll tell the goddamn media people I decide[d] against it for jurisdictional reasons."

"I prefer to play."

"Okay, hoped you would."

Ober unfolded a penciled sketch of the area, don[e] with considerable detail, and spread it out on a table[.] "As you've probably noticed," he said, "the house is th[e] second one from the corner. We were put onto this b[y] one of the ten jillion citizen leads we've gotten since yes[-] terday. A neighbor lady noticed a suspicious-looking van with young people in it around noon. Our people didn't show up till about six. They didn't think this a particularly hot lead. Before knocking on the front door, a man was sent around back to check things out. Somebody—maybe White—was out back. Whoever it was just opened fire on our man without so much as a whistle. We returned fire and possibly scored a hit. We called up the reinforcements and set up the security perimeter. Nobody got out. Okay, we evacuated the citizens from the area. We've sent for some parabolic microphone equipment so we can listen in on them— maybe figure out what room they're keeping the hostages in."

"What weapons were they using?"

"Rapid fire stuff, probably an M-16. Somebody reported seeing a shotgun too."

"Tell me about the house."

"Okay. It's on three levels excluding the basement. Normally there are five servants. We've verified they're in the house. We're making assumptions, but it looks like there're nine in White's bunch—four men, four women—and Vincent Benson III. The backyard is fenced. Inside there's a garden and an empty pool, a patio. There's some cover here along the walkway. The State Troopers have eighteen men stationed here with automatic weapons and tear gas. It's forty-eight feet to the houses on either side. There are thirty men stationed in these two houses and another fifty at least behind these vehicles in front. Probably more like a hundred and fifty the way reinforcements have been showing up. Okay? They're sealed like in a sardine can. We cut their phone off, except to us."

91

Knebel's pipe had gone out and he relit it. Then he said, "Let's get them on the phone and see what the stakes are in this game."

Chad Priest punched the numbers into the phone, listened for the ring, then passed the phone to Knebel.

A woman answered: "We will speak to Knebel, no one else."

"I am Richard Knebel."

"We have civilians in here, do you know that?"

"Yes. To whom am I speaking?"

"I am a member of the Revolutionary Council of the Manhattan Red Brigade."

"Are you Marya?"

"I am."

"One of your people has been wounded. We'd like to suggest he be taken to a hospital."

"That is out of the question."

"Was it Adolph White who was wounded?"

"Mr. Knebel, listen. We are not going to surrender anyone or do anything until we have our message heard. We demand that you restore our phone service and do it now. Lives are at stake, Mr. Knebel, and we're not fooling around."

"Wait a moment," Knebel said. He pushed the hold button on the phone and looked at Ober.

"A very tough little bitch," Ober said. He had been listening in on a monitor.

"Tough enough to gun down the President?" Knebel asked.

"Maybe."

Chad Priest said, "What are we going to do?"

"We're not giving them phone service," Ober said. "I'll guarantee you that."

92

"I've got a suspicion they aren't about to be stalled very much," Knebel said.

"If they want to wrestle, we're ready," Ober said. "We've got enough fire power to blow that house down."

Knebel said, "Once the firing starts, all we're going to get out of this is a lot of dead bodies."

Knebel punched the button and got Marya back on the line. "Let's talk this out face to face. I want to see the folks you're holding in there are all right."

"Just a minute, Knebel."

There was muffled talking at the other end of the line and some shouting; then it was quiet for a few moments. Finally:

"Come alone, unarmed, no hidden transmitters. Your safety and freedom are guaranteed by the Revolutionary Council. Come now."

The line went dead.

Knebel sat for a while smoking his pipe. Ober asked the men at the communications desk to play back a tape of what had just been said. They all listened. When it was over, Ober said, "No way in hell you should go in there, Knebel. Their guarantee isn't worth crap. Let me get you a volunteer instead. There's a couple of hundred red-hots out there who would be giddy at the chance to be a hero."

"They wouldn't know what they were looking for." Knebel turned to Chad Priest. "Get her on the phone again. Maybe I can negotiate a little insurance."

Chad Priest dialed the number, then handed the receiver to Knebel. Marya answered.

"This is Richard Knebel. When I come in, you send one of your people out."

Again there was a muffled discussion on the other

end, this time a short one.

"The Revolutionary Council agrees."

"When you start your person, I will start up the walk Tell whoever you're sending out to walk slowly — and t carry no weapons."

"We will be ready in two minutes."

Knebel hung up. He puffed some more on his pipe then put it down. "They're negotiating. We've showed them at least we won't let them dictate."

"This is a big chance you're taking," Ober said. He sa down. "I wouldn't go in there for a bucket of Kruger rands."

Knebel double-checked his pockets to make sure the were empty. He looked at Ober. "While I'm in ther maybe you could send out for some fresh coffee. Th stuff in the thermos tastes like paint thinner."

"Thanks."

"Thanks?"

Ober smiled. "We've been looking for the damn thir ner all day."

EIGHTEEN

Outside it was cold and still misting. Knebel and Chad Priest walked up the block. Hans Ober stayed in the van.

"It's nasty for April, isn't it?" Knebel said.

"Yes, it is," Chad Priest said. "It's been a nasty winter and a dismal spring so far."

"In many ways," Knebel said. "If they sacrifice the stooge they exchange for me, you're not to let them deal for me. I don't want to be a martyr, but I don't want any deals made either."

"It will be up to Hans and he won't deal. I know him."

They were at the end of the block across the street from the security perimeter. Knebel stopped and looked around, taking several deep breaths. Then he said, "Some climatologists say the temperate zones are in decline."

"I remember reading something about it."

"This place will be under three hundred feet of ice. It'll last fifty thousand years."

"It'll play hell with property values," Chad Priest said. They both smiled.

Knebel rubbed his hands together to warm them. "I'll

see you in a little while if the fates are favorable." He crossed the street. Young Sheriff Sparks was waiting for him. Hans Ober had communicated what was about to happen, he said. Sparks shook Knebel's hand and wished him luck. The men standing nearby wished Knebel well too. There were many men there, most of them in uniform and wearing flak jackets, chest protectors, and gas masks. The scene had the look and feel of war: the tension, the fear, the nervous waiting. Knebel could see in the men's eyes and their bearing that they wanted it to happen soon. They wanted it badly. He thanked them for their good wishes. They stepped aside and let him pass. Knebel stood at the edge of the perimeter, his hands in his pockets. A few moments later the front doors of the house opened and a young man in a white jacket stepped out on the front porch and waved. He yelled something, but no one could hear over the wind. Knebel started forward and the young man, longhaired, cocky, started down the walk with his hands held high over his head, an amusement-park grin on his face. They passed on the walk but did not look at each other.

As Knebel walked up the front steps the door opened. He walked directly in. The door closed behind him and he found himself standing in a large foyer under a chandelier. A large china cabinet had been blocking the door; behind it a couple of dressers were stacked to reinforce the barricade. A barefoot woman in jeans and a sweatshirt was standing in front of him. She had long auburn hair and a pleasant face and very blue eyes and there was a small automatic stuck in her belt.

"How do you do, Mr. Knebel?" she said.

"Marya?"

"Yes."

Two men appeared from around the corner. Both had guns. One was tall and dark and thin. The other was younger and blond, with severe acne on his cheeks. Both looked fatigued by the strain. They were wearing camouflage fatigues, berets, and bandoleers full of ammunition. The one with the acne searched Knebel. He was thorough. The taller one lit a cigarette with one hand and held the gun steady on Knebel with the other. When the one with acne was finished searching Knebel, he stepped back and said, "The fucker's clean, nothing on him at all."

The taller one said to Marya, "You going to tell him now?"

"Be patient, comrade." She turned to Knebel. "Come this way."

He followed her into the living room. The room was large and covered with a thick white carpet. There was a fireplace at the far end. The furniture had been pushed up against the windows and patio doors. Knebel wondered whether they knew a couch and a chair would not stop a high-powered rifle bullet. Even the wall of a house wouldn't. He looked at Marya. She was young and her blue eyes flashed with the excitement of the moment. He noticed too that the automatic in her belt was a .22 Beretta and its safety was off.

"May I see the hostages first?" Knebel said.

"An ugly word," she said. "*Hostages* is such an ugly, ugly word. *Detainees,* let us say, shall we?"

"Detainees, then."

"This way, please."

He followed her up the stairs and the two young men went with them. They nudged him in the back with their rifle barrels. In the hallway above there were many gasoline cans and the odor of gasoline was strong. In the master bedroom she showed Knebel five frightened people, three women and two men, tied and huddled in a corner. A gaunt, bearded man in his thirties sat on the bed. He wore camouflage fatigues and had a Soviet-made AK-47 assault rifle in his lap. He looked over at Knebel and his face was impassive, but in his eyes there was the look of one who loved death. The man was calm, but under the calm and deep behind the eyes was a great hatred for mankind and Knebel could see it too.

"Are you people all right?" Knebel said to the five people huddled in the corner.

They nodded their heads. There was fear, heavy and terrible, on them, but they nodded and some of them looked relieved, their eyes flickering with hope.

Knebel said nothing to them. He turned and walked out of the room and Marya went with him. She led him back downstairs. Knebel glanced toward the dining room where two young women stood by the window; they smiled and saluted him. One was large and naked to the waist except for the crossing bandoleers; her breasts sagged heavily to her belt. She had a rigid face and large, confident eyes charged with determination. The other young woman was hardly into her teens and her face showed fire and great excitement. In her hand was an M-16.

"You do see we are ready," Marya said. "An attack on us would be very costly."

"Isn't Vincent Benson with you?"

"He's in the kitchen—would you like to see him?"

"Yes."

He followed her through the dining room to the back of the house.

Vincent Benson was lying on the floor, groaning. He had been severely beaten and there was blood on his face and shirt and his face was swollen and black.

"He decided he'd rather be elsewhere, but we persuaded him to stay," Marya said. "If we don't have our demands met he will be the first to die. Tell them that out there."

"I will," Knebel said.

Vincent Benson looked up at Knebel and mumbled something. The young acne-faced man was standing near him and kicked him twice. "Shut up, motherfuck," he said. Vincent Benson III rolled over and groaned and then was still.

"There is no mercy for those who betray the people," Marya said.

Knebel went back into the living room. His hands were sweating and his mouth was dry. Marya stood with her arms folded, was looking at him severely with her cold blue eyes. The tall young man sat on the couch, automatic in hand, and the one with acne leaned against the doorjamb, his face hard and cruel.

"May I have a cigarette?" Knebel asked.

"None of us smoke," she said. "We don't poison our bodies so tobacco companies can make profits."

Knebel nodded and said, "I have to tell you all something. It's a matter of formality. May I speak?"

"Say whatever you wish," Marya said.

"You are all under arrest. You are hereby ordered to lay down all your weapons and come with me."

The taller one laughed, but the other flushed with sudden anger. "Will you listen to this? Who's he think he's talking to? God how I'd love to blow up the son-of-a-bitch. Let's make him eat shit." He raised his weapon and cocked it, but Marya glared at him and he pointed it away. "It's because of fuckers like him," he said with disgust, "that there has to be a revolution."

"Forgive our exuberance," Marya said. "You see, we are committed to the freedom of all peoples now under the domination of the American capitalist classes. We have, through the justifiable and meritorious liquidation of Clement Jamison, an enemy of the people, made a great leap forward toward permanent liberation for a quarter of a billion people. This will serve as a warning to other tyrants. Our oath is to make no compromise with injustice, never to cower before the might of the oppressors, and to show no mercy for warmongering imperialists." Knebel said nothing and she continued. "It is necessary for a revolution to succeed first to raise the consciousness of the masses. Tomorrow at noon we plan to hold a teach-in right here. All three networks must be present."

"Then you'll release the hostages and surrender?"

The acne-faced young man stamped his foot. "Can you believe the arrogance of the motherfuck? Hey, we're in the driver's seat here, man. People are going to die-die-die if we don't get what we want and we don't mean the fucking TV cameras."

"Just what is it you do want?" Knebel said.

The tall one said, "We want thirty million Swiss francs and a fueled seven-twenty-seven. We don't get them and there's going to be a lot of dead bodies all over this place. You got to ten tomorrow to bring the money. Ten-oh-one and we start blasting."

"I see," Knebel said.

"We would also like the telephone reconnected so we can talk to the world and not just the police out there,"

Marya said.

"I will relate your demands. You do understand, I'm just an intermediary."

"The world will hear us tomorrow. Nothing can contain us and the truth. One way or the other, our message will get out."

"May I go now?" Knebel said.

The tall one said, "It's up to Adolf."

"I say he can go now," Marya said sternly.

The two young men looked at each other. The tall one said, "Adolf wanted to talk to him."

Marya sighed heavily. "He isn't feeling well. He doesn't have to see him."

The two young men talked among themselves for a moment; then the tall one said, "I'll check with him, Marya. It's got to be his choice."

"Never mind!" Marya snapped. "I'll do it. This way, Knebel."

They went back up the stairs and down the hall. At the end of the hall she paused and knocked softly on the door, and when there was no answer she pushed it open. "Dolf? You awake?"

She took the automatic out of her belt and motioned for Knebel to come inside. "You two wait out here," she told the two young men. "I'll keep watch on Mr. Knebel."

Heavy paper covered the windows; it was dim in the room. A chair faced the window and someone was propped up in it. In front of him was a water-cooled thirty-caliber machine gun on a tripod, its ammunition belt in place.

As Knebel got close he could see whoever was in the chair was slouched over, his head askew, his eyes staring blankly into space.

"He's dead," Knebel said, "isn't he?"

"If you tell Jerry and Stephen, I'll shoot you."

"I won't tell them."

"They believed in Adolf White. They would have fol
lowed him anywhere. Adolf White was as great as
Lenin, Mao, or any of them. He was a giant."

"Was he?"

"Yes! He was a great, great man, miles out in front of
ordinary men!"

"All right, Marya. He was a prince. Was he the one
who got Jamison? Who went with him, you?"

"What?" She didn't seem to comprehend the question.

"We know the one dressed as Reis was a woman. Benson financed it. White must have planned it—with your
help. Pulling it off was some trick. I figured you must
have gotten into one of the waitresses' uniforms, then
hiked up the path to the bus stop. White took the
Plymouth that belonged to Allison."

"Members of the movement disposed of Clement
Jamison, that's all you have to know. We aren't seeking
individual glories. Everyone takes part."

Knebel studied her. "It wasn't you, was it Marya?
And it wasn't Dolf either."

"You have answers enough, Mr. Knebel."

"Wait, Marya. You do know your situation here is
desperate, don't you?"

"You mean we're not getting thirty million Swiss
francs? I know that, Mr. Knebel. That was Stephen and
Jerry's idea and Dolf went along because he was like an
overindulgent father. I strongly suspect you aren't letting TV people in here either. You see, Mr. Knebel, I'm
not self-deluded. I have a very firm grasp of reality."

102

Mencius, the Chinese sage, four centuries before Christ said that when tyranny and oppression rule, a minister of heaven will rise up from among the masses and rescue the people. Dolf was such a minister. . . . Have you ever heard of Galeazzo? He was a tyrant in Italy, maybe around fifteen hundred. Olgiati was the man who killed him. Before his execution, Olgiati said his death was untimely, but his fame was eternal. His deed, because it was just, Mr. Knebel, will endure forever. So will ours."

"One of the girls downstairs is very young. Perhaps you might consider sending her along with me."

"Dahlia is fourteen, Mr. Knebel. Our sisters in the Viet Cong were enlisted at twelve."

"How about the detainees? Why involve innocent people?"

"The masses must sacrifice."

"Five very frightened nobodies are not the masses!"

"I'm sorry," she said. "No."

She ushered him out of the room and down the stairs. "We're letting you go so they will know that we keep our word." In the hallway downstairs her two young companions were waiting. "It's cleared," she said. "Dolf says to let him pass."

"So be it," the taller one said.

Knebel walked to the door and Marya went with him. The two young gunmen stayed behind.

"You probably think I'm a fool," she said.

Knebel said, "I don't pretend to understand, I'll admit."

"Maybe to you Jamison wasn't a tyrant — that makes the difference. I know we're all going to die soon," she said. "But everybody dies. Isn't it better to die *for* something?"

"I think it's better to live for something."

"And what do you live for, Mr. Knebel?"

"Maybe a little more justice in the world."

"Then we're both on the same side," she said.

"No, we're not," he said.

She opened the door. The young man they had exchanged for Knebel started up the walk.

"Please reconsider," Knebel said. "You can make your statement without spilling innocent blood."

"We're going to do it our way," she said.

Knebel walked toward the police lines. He didn't look back at her.

NINETEEN

"Did you see their guns?" This from Hans Ober.

"Yes. Plenty of small automatics, an M-16, one AK-47. They have an old water-cooled thirty caliber too."

"Christ. How many hostages?"

"Five, as you said. They seem to be okay for the moment. They have them in the master bedroom at the top of the stairs."

"See any explosives?"

"No. But there was gasoline in the upstairs hallway. Twenty to thirty one-gallon cans."

They were in the SWAT van. It was warm and steamy with damp clothing.

"I doubt these are the people who killed the President," Knebel said. "These are amateurs. They are bluff and rhetoric, they lack the skills. Marya doesn't even know enough to keep her safety on."

Ober said, "They've taken hostages and they've claimed credit. It's enough for me. They must have been involved somehow. Did you talk to White?"

"Adolf White is dead. Marya is keeping that unhappy news from the rest of them."

"She is in charge now, would you say?" Ober asked.

"Precariously."

"We've got some additional information on her from the Secret Service, okay? They have a file on her. She's a kindergarten teacher, believe it or not. Real name's Mary Ellen Sanders, from Oshkosh, Wisconsin. She's twenty-six years old and until two years ago was as straight-arrow as a Presbyterian. Okay. Then she takes a vacation to New York City and meets Adolf White on a bus. Would you believe it? He turns her completely around. Next thing you know she's an urban guerrilla. Jesus."

"They've beaten Vincent Benson savagely. He wanted out, they said."

"He's still a hostile as far as I'm concerned," Ober said. "So how many hostiles we know about?"

"Seven besides Benson. Four men, three women — counting the man who came out when I went in. That's all I saw."

"What do they want?" Chad Priest asked.

Knebel told them about the money, the plane, the time with the press.

"Did you make a demand for their surrender?"

"Yes. They scoffed at it."

Ober said, "They must be fourteen-carat crazies. We aren't letting them out. They've got to know that."

The young sheriff said, "We can't mess around on this one."

"At least they're negotiating," Fixx, the SWAT commander put in. "They've got the idea. It's a good start when they're dealing. We've showed them we keep our word. They let Mr. Knebel go — I'd say we might be able to keep this one cool."

"We can't mess around," the young sheriff said again.

Hans Ober asked, "Okay, what are you saying?" This was said to the young sheriff.

"We pop them."

"When? *Now?*"

"Just before dawn would be good."

"They've got heavy stuff for Christsake."

"We can't mess around. The whole goddamn world is watching us, we've got to take them and take them fast."

The SWAT commander said, "If they weren't dealing they wouldn't have let Mr. Knebel go."

"I say we pop them hard just before dawn," the young sheriff repeated.

"No sir," the SWAT commander said. "We've got to think of the hostages. Finesse them out if we can."

"If they don't get their cake and cookies by ten in the morning, they're going to ice Vincent Benson." Knebel stated.

"Okay, so what do we do?" Ober asked.

"As Mr. Fixx said, we've got to finesse them if we can."

"And if we can't?" the young sheriff asked.

"We'll have to wait and see," Knebel said. "They aren't going anywhere, that's for sure."

TWENTY

At nine-thirty in the morning Knebel called Stewart Ott at his office in the White House.

"Good morning, Richard, my friend. I see here on the TV you've got a real Super Bowl going on up there. What do you think? Is it going to be one of those long siege deals? The President liked the way you went in there last night, told me so. He admires guts. Everybody admires guts. You've won the nation."

"Whatever goes down, the President might draw flak on this, Stewart. Maybe he ought to be in on the decision-making process."

"Nooooo, boy, why do you think we hired you? You're the whipping boy. My friend, if you can't stand the heat . . ."

"You're a hard man, Stewart."

"I know."

When Richard Knebel stepped from the van, it had just started raining. It was a few minutes before ten. It had been clearing since before dawn, but now the sky was dark again and it was raining hard. He walked down the block to where the men were waiting. He looked at them and asked Ober whether the men were ready. Ober said they were ready. The SWAT commander said his men were ready; the young sheriff, wearing a bullet protector like a catcher's breastplate, said his men were ready. There were many men now, over five hundred. The assault squads had bullet protectors and gas masks. They all wore fatigues and looked like Marines and carried M-16's or pump shotguns.

They had been listening in with parabolic microphones, Chad Priest told Knebel. Some of it was garbled, some couldn't be picked up at all, but as far as they could tell the hostages hadn't been moved. He added that an assault team in the first wave would make an attempt to save them, but its chances of success were not promising.

"Did she tell the others Adolf White was dead?" Knebel asked.

"Yes."

The anticipation now was great. The men held their weapons tightly and kept their eyes on the house and the rain came down steadily. Knebel walked down the street and could see the barrier beyond, where a large crowd was waiting. The police were moving them back even further. Ober joined him. He had his hands in his pockets and a cigarette in his mouth. He hadn't slept and there were dark circles under his dark eyes.

"We came here to dance — I think the band is ready," Knebel said. "We'd better call them soon. I want them to know we won't open up first under any circumstances."

Ober jerked the cigarette out of his mouth and threw it down on the wet pavement. "We shouldn't give them too much time to think."

They walked down to the security perimeter. Chad Priest reported all units in position and ready. Knebel told him to get the hostiles on the phone. A momen[t] later Chad Priest handed the phone to Knebel. "Marya," he said.

"This is Richard Knebel. Can you hear me?"

"Yes."

"Kindergarten's out. If you lay down your arms and give yourselves up, I promise you no one will be hurt. I promise no one will be degraded. I promise you wil[l] have your time with reporters."

There was a long, empty silence. Knebel looked t[o] Chad Priest, who was in contact with the surveillance units, but they also heard nothing.

Marya's voice came back on the line: "It's no good."

"We've got to keep talking, Marya. There's no reaso[n] for violence! You *can* stop it. How about a two-hou[r] cooling-off period?"

"We have a message for the world. You're forcing us to take a life, Knebel!"

"We have tape equipment. We'll let you record you[r] message and we'll give it to the networks before you[r] surrender."

There was no reply.

"Marya?"

The line was dead.

Chad Priest said, "Surveillance units report they're picking up a debate—wait a minute." He listene[d] through another receiver for a moment, then said[:] "They're going to shoot someone. He's begging, but it'[s] not doing him any good."

"The poor bastard," Knebel said.

There was the sound of a single shot coming from inside the house. It was raining hard, but they all heard it[.] Suddenly the front door of the house opened and a body was hurled out.

Along the security perimeter, guns were aimed. Men stiffened. All were silent, waiting.

"What do you say?" Ober said to Knebel and the SWAT commander. Ober's hair was matted flat in the rain.

"They drew blood," the SWAT commander said gravely. "They got a taste; now they'll want more."

"Knebel?"

"Kindergarten is over, like I said."

Ober signed a written authorization for an assault without restraint, smearing his signature in the rain.

Chad Priest picked up a radio microphone and said: "There is a green light. Green for GO!"

For a long moment nothing happened; everyone seemed frozen. Then with a poof-poof sound the first tear-gas cannisters smashed through the front windows and the small arms fire erupted from inside the house and then automatic rifle fire opened up inside the house and from the men crouched behind the cars along the street. Shotguns boomed above the crackle of the automatic weapons firing and the windows disintegrated and white clouds of tear gas billowed from the house and across the lawn. A figure appeared in a downstairs front window waving its arms, but vanished in a burst of firing. After a few moments Ober gave another order and gray SWAT teams, with their faces hidden, monsterish, swept across the lawn like the black death, firing as they went. Suddenly the muzzle of the thirty-caliber machine gun appeared in an upstairs window and clacked away at the swarm of men crossing the lawn and many of them dropped; then the men firing from the houses across the street and from behind the vehicles in the street trained their guns on the window and a rain of bullets silenced the weapon. A second and third assault group smashed in through the front door and through the patio, and the firing on the inside was intense.

Knebel followed the swarm across the lawn and in the front door. The air was thick with tear gas and his gas mask leaked so he couldn't stay inside. It was over quickly; the firing diminished and then it was quiet. He had seen some men go down inside, but didn't know who they were. Rushing outside, he washed his face and eyes with a garden hose. Others gathered around with the same problem. They were all coughing, yet excited about how well it had gone. The rain was still coming down and none of them seemed to mind. He helped with some of the wounded on the front lawn. Two FBI men were dead and another was seriously wounded. They were trying to save the hostages, someone said.

Knebel saw them carry out the body of the big girl, who was still naked to the waist. She had taken a shot-gun blast in the head and her face was unrecognizable. Knebel saw the acne-faced kid too; he was dead and bloodied. After a few minutes Knebel went up the stairs and into the living room. It was torn apart by gunfire; there were holes everywhere and the tear gas lingered and the floor was covered with broken glass and plaster and spots of blood. Gagging on the tear gas, he went out the back door to the patio and found Hans Ober under the shelter of a plastic cabana, comforting an FBI man who had been shot in the neck. Knebel asked Ober about the hostages.

"They got it first."

"All of them?"

"Yeah, all of them."

"What about the hostiles?"

"Two still alive. The fourteen-year-old, Dahlia, for one. Somebody knocked her on the head and stuffed her into a broom closet. She's already on the way to the hospital."

"Who's the other?"

"Don't know."

Knebel watched them carry out the last of the dead and wounded. The rain was heavy. A deputy had been killed and the young sheriff was kneeling by the body, white with grief, shaking his head in disbelief.

A moment later Chad Priest came down the back stairs, taking off his gas mask. There were less fumes now. More ambulances were arriving, sirens going.

"They're bringing Marya out the front door," Chad Priest said to Knebel. "She's pretty bad."

They went around the house together and found her lying on the sidewalk. There was a crowd around her; a cop was holding an umbrella over her. Knebel bent over her. She wheezed horribly. Blood ran from her mouth. She said something, but Knebel did not make it out. He knelt beside her and listened closely.

Her words trickled out: "Am I going to make it?" she asked.

"An ambulance will be here in a minute."

"Never imagined it would burn like this." She coughed. "How about my comrades?"

"All dead, except Dahlia. You saved her, didn't you?"

She didn't answer him or acknowledge the question. She winced with pain for a moment and then caught her breath. "We died well. I saw Jerry and Stephen go down on the stairs. They died well— Oh Jesus it hurts! My guts are on fire!" She caught her breath. "A revolutionary must die well, it is our *raison d'être*."

The cop holding the umbrella wiped away the blood from her mouth.

"The two who shot the President," Knebel said, "it wasn't White. It wasn't any of you."

"Yes, yes, yes," she said, her breaths more labored. Sweat formed on her forehead. "Yes. We did it. Dahlia was brave. She'll fight again. She'll be there at the final victory. Are the reporters here?"

"Who pulled the trigger on Jamison? Tell me!"

She shook her head. Ambulance attendants put her on a stretcher and into an ambulance, but before they closed the door an attendant shook his head and said she was already dead.

Knebel and Chad Priest stood in the rain and watched the ambulance drive off. The SWAT trucks were pulling out too.

"You really think they didn't do it?" Chad Priest said. "I mean to Jamison and his party?"

"I think we killed a kindergarten teacher from Oshkosh who took the wrong bus one day." Knebel lit his pipe with a butane lighter. "This bunch had about as much to do with icing Jamison as my fairy godmother."

"How is it when they called in they had the slogans right?"

"Somebody tossed them a crumb so they could grab the glory. Terrorists stay up late nights trying to figure out how to get their names on the front page and their faces on TV."

"Why would somebody else give them the publicity?"

"So the hounds would be chasing the wrong rabbit, maybe. Look at what's coming."

Swarms of reporters had been let through the barricades and were running down the block toward them, followed by dozens of vans carrying on-scene camera equipment.

"What shall we tell the ladies and gentlemen of the press?" Chad Priest asked.

"Luckily they prefer pleasing fictions to complex enigmas. Let's tell them what they want to hear."

"It'll be nice to see the Bureau being made the hero of the six o'clock news."

"Won't it, though?"

BOOK THREE

TWENTY-ONE

It was mild and windy in the old Hyde Park section near the University of Chicago. Greenwood Avenue, near Fifty-fifth. Three lanky black youths played basketball in the street, shooting for a hoop nailed obliquely to a telephone pole, yelling, swearing, enjoying; playing with speed and grace, cutting, dribbling, shooting, blocking out each other. They went at it with championship intensity.

Lowenstein watched them for moment, admiring them for their skill, envying their agility. He was on the porch of the house across the street. It was an old clapboard house with a wheelchair ramp running out to the sidewalk. One of the windows on the porch was broken and patched with cardboard and masking tape. Lowenstein turned from the boys and knocked on the door. The doorbell was out of order.

"Yeah, who's there?" The voice was an old man's voice, hoarse and gruff, tinged with anger.

"That you, Tower?"

"I'm Tower, yeah. Who are you?"

"Art Lowenstein."

The door came open. Tower was in a wheelchair. He

was thin, needed a shave, looked old. He said, *"Gee*zus H. Christ! Will you look at this? Detective Lieutenant Lowenstein. Thought they locked you up and threw away the key. Come in, man."

"I heard you'd taken disability, Tower. How'd it happen?"

"Nigger got me. Twenty-six years a cop and a twenty-year-old nigger got me in a two-eleven. Somehow I let the bastard get behind me. I'd chased him down this alley and he circled back on me. . . . Come on, sit in the living room. *Gee*zus, man, it's good to see you."

The living room was cluttered and smelled of solvent. The television was on. Tower turned it off with a remote control.

"You hear they got those assholes shot Jamison? Cut 'em to pieces. Knebel's a pious jerk. The press boys and girls are licking his ass. I'll hand it to him, though, he sure nailed the lid on this shit in a hurry. They don't fuck around when it's the President."

Lowenstein sat on an old green couch. "Had a bad time finding you, Tower," he said. "Your precinct station wouldn't give me the time of day. I remembered your old watering hole, the Blue Panther. They still remembered you. You ever going to get out of that chair?"

"When they plant me in the ground."

"How about the suspect? They get the bastard?"

"DA let him go. Lack of sufficient evidence for a conviction. I swore I saw him clear, but they let him go. Rodney Johnson his name was. A tall, ugly fucker . . . Good to see you, Lowenstein. Art's your first name, eh? How come you're just about the only Jew I ever met I liked? I mean, as a friend. Most Jews are—I don't know—closed up, I guess."

"I was a cop."

"A Jew cop. They've got fag cops now in Frisco so why not Jew cops? Hey, why not crippled cops?"

"Why not crooked cops?"

Tower laughed, then he was suddenly serious. "You must have fallen hard. Shit, every dick on earth takes a little grease. It comes with the territory. Knebel got a couple of good men here, too, when he was Assistant Attorney General. . . . Want a drink? What is it with that guy? He thinks he's God's right-hand man. . . . What'ya drinking?"

Lowenstein took his bourbon straight, two shots, then two more to sip. Tower drank brandy and water. There were hundreds of photos and yellowed news clippings and a few plaques on the wall. Tower pointed at them.

"That's all there is to my career. Wasn't fuckin' worth it, believe me. We worked together on a gun case once, didn't we? Stolen guns. How many years ago? A hundred and fifty? My brain's all fucked up, can't remember shit. What the hell was it? Did we get convictions? Did we bag 'em?"

"Frankie Giacone's mob. Eight arrests, no convictions."

"Oh, yeah — guinea fuckers. Bad people . . . *Geez*us, good to see you."

"I'm not here socially, Tower, catch? I need help."

Tower poured Lowenstein some more bourbon. "It's about the President being killed, ain't it?"

"Yeah."

"Sweet fucking Christ. They ain't fucking around. You were good about hardware, I remember. What's the pitch? They got the bastards this morning on Long Island someplace. That's all that's been on television, for Christsake."

Lowenstein shook his head. "Those punks didn't ice Jamison. I've seen the gun that hosed Jamison and it wasn't a punk weapon. It was artwork. It was precision. Maybe somebody wants to lay it on the punks for some good reason. I don't give a damn about that. I think I know who it was, catch? The gunsmith, I mean."

Tower rolled his brandy around in his glass. "You gotta get there before Knebel, that right?"

"Yeah."

"I get it. They don't like it when you make 'em look stupid." Deep worry lines appeared on his forehead.

"If you don't want in," Lowenstein said, "go back to whatever the hell it is a crippled old cop does."

Tower stared at him angrily. His mouth got tight and he stared for a long moment. "I get drunk and feel sorry for myself. What's the big fuckin' deal? What could they do to me?"

"Not a goddamn thing."

"How can I help? As you can see, I ain't worth a solid fart anymore."

"You remember Max Sunday?"

"Vaguely."

"He made the gun that got the President."

"You sure?"

"Sure enough."

"He'll be a mile underground."

"You make a few phone calls. Find his friends. You must still have connections in the gun trade."

"He made those weapons he'll be shitting greener than green."

"That's why he'll want to talk to me. I'll let him know

122

I'm a friendly."

"You always did make them come to you. Smart. Jew cunning." Tower wheeled himself to the phone. "Make yourself another drink, Art. Knebel sure gave you a bad rap. How'd you make out in the slammer?"

"I'd rather be in that chair with a plaque on the wall."

Tower's expression clouded and the lines on his forehead deepened. "No, you wouldn't."

TWENTY-TWO

The woman said she didn't know any Max Sunday. She never heard of him, she said. She was a slender woman, a redhead with round brown eyes and creamy skin. Her mouth was small and hostile.

"Where did you get my name?"

"I heard you knew him, that's all."

"I've never heard of him."

"It's important, catch? You are Elizabeth Bunting?"

"I never heard of him."

"If he's hiding, I may be able to help."

"I told you I don't know the man. I'm calling the police!"

"You give Max my name, Miss Bunting. Lowenstein. Arthur Lowenstein. From Philly. Tell him I know about the guns, catch? *All* about them. Tell him I got connections in Miami. Good people, people he can trust. They can get him in with friendlies in Brazil. People who appreciate what he can do. The cops are right behind me, tell him that too."

She stared at him through the crack in the door.

"This is on the level," Lowenstein said. "Tell him I want ten grand and he's out of it." He passed her a slip of paper which she let fall to the floor. "That's my motel. I'm going there now. I'll wait for him."

"I don't know the man. I never heard of the man. I don't know anything about any guns."

She shut the door.

Lowenstein went back to his motel. It was windy and clear. He had some supper in his room, a hamburger and coffee. And then he waited. Tower had been sure that the Bunting woman was Max Sunday's girl friend. If Tower was sure, Lowenstein was sure, because Tower had never steered him wrong.

Lowenstein watched television and drank cheap muscatel. Knebel was being interviewed on television. Lowenstein could sense that Knebel knew more than he was saying, and Lowenstein worried that time was getting short. He hated Knebel with a cold hatred that thickened with time and never thawed. After the interview there was a discussion and commentary by two well-known "news analysts." Lowenstein turned off the set. These men were silk-tongued but ignorant fools, he thought. He had no interest whatever in what they had to say.

He waited by the window and watched the cars move in and out of the parking lot. He drank more wine, but it did not relax him. His stomach was sour and his head hurt. He was tired and weary. He say down in the stuffed chair by the door. His cheeks felt warm and after a while he drifted off to sleep. At a little after ten he woke suddenly. There was a noise outside, somebody skulking around. A moment later there was a loud knock on the door. When he opened the door he found two men standing in the hallway. Big men in overcoats. One of them stepped inside and looked around the room. "You

Lowenstein? That your name?"

"It is."

"Assume the position."

Lowenstein put his hands out against the wall and submitted to a body search. They were fast and thorough. One of them went through his overcoat, then handed it to him. "Let's go."

Outside it was still windy and colder. Lowenstein followed them to a black sedan and got into the back seat. They headed north. Tape was put over his eyes. No one spoke. After a while there wasn't much traffic. They made many turns. The radio was on loud, turned to a country-and-western music station.

When they stopped Lowenstein was taken out and walked up some stairs and into a house. The tape was taken off. He found himself in a barren room, its windows covered with newspapers. There was one chair. Lowenstein was told to sit. The two men stood by the door with their arms folded, idly watching him. After a few minutes the door opened and a man came in. He was of medium weight and height, had thinning hair and penetrating green eyes. He wore thick, wire-rimmed glasses. It was Max Sunday. Lowenstein recognized him from his mug shot.

"You're a stupid, stupid man, Lowenstein," he said pacing.

"Yeah, maybe. A lot of people tell me that."

"Who knows besides you?"

"A friend. A confidant. In case I don't come back. He can be trusted."

"That's it?"

"Yes."

"I could deny it, you know."

"With the technology they have today? Not for long."
Sunday rubbed his face with his hands. "I suppose you're right."

"Do you know who I am?" Lowenstein asked.

"Yes. I knew the Giacones. You tried to put them away. Then you took a fall on a corruption conspiracy rap. I had you checked out. Why are you helping me? Not for a lousy ten grand." His eyes were darting.

"I saw one of the guns last night," Lowenstein said. "I fired it. Sweet. Nobody can make them as sweet as you."

"You said ten thousand would get me to Brazil. That's what you told Elizabeth."

"Tell me about the guns. Who bought them?"

"I'm not saying nothing to *no*body."

"I didn't think you dealt with meatballs like this White."

"Guns change hands. They're bought and sold every day like tickets to the Super Bowl."

"I tell you what, Max. I give you the name of the people in Miami—free. No ten thousand. You check them out, the connections are there. All you've got to do is tell me who, what, where, and when."

"What's with you, Lowenstein? You don't look like the good Samaritan type."

"I have my reasons."

"Knebel sent you up. You want him to have egg on his face." Max Sunday smiled. "I'm starting to get the picture." His face seemed to relax. "I don't want to go to prison. I've got to sort this out. I'm seeing my lawyer in half an hour—he says he's got some ideas. One thing, I don't want to do time for this; I had nothing to do with it. I'm a businessman. If they put me in a cell, I go rootie-tootie."

"I know the feeling. Brazil isn't so bad."

"I heard you're a square shooter, Lowenstein. Give me the name of your connection. I'll check him out. I can't trust nobody. When I saw on television it was my work I crapped."

"My connection is the Barguzzi family. The old man left Philly. He's now in Miami. He's agreed. I let their son take a hike one time from a minor infraction and they still feel obligated, catch?"

"The Barguzzis are known even here. I've done business with their relatives in Detroit."

"Well?"

"Tomorrow morning. You'll have to wait. I've got to think this through, check out all my options. If we deal, I give it all to you tomorrow."

"It wasn't White's gang, was it?"

"No. When I tell you, you'll know why even Brazil may not be big enough to hide me."

It was three-thirty in the morning when Lowenstein got to Tower's place. Tower was still awake but quite drunk. Lowenstein had given Max Sunday Tower's phone number. Tower poured Lowenstein a straight bourbon and made him a cold-cut sandwich. The bread wrapper had been left open and the bread was stale.

Tower's head wobbled on his thin neck as he listened to Lowenstein tell what had happened. Then he said: "It may come up a dry hole, Arthur, my Jew-cop friend."

"He's got to deal. He's in the rat trap and there isn't any way out. The poor son-of-a-bitch has got no place to turn. That's how you bag a bad guy, Tower. You present yourself as the only solution to his troubles. Bad guys are human, and the human fish—when he's afraid—always swims in the direction of greatest safety, catch?"

"Do me a favor, Art. Please. Just mention my name, will you? If this turns out to be something, say I helped you a little, eh? It's important."

"A Jew cop never forgives an enemy — or forgets a friend."

Tower smiled. He smiled and poured himself another bourbon and one for Lowenstein too.

"What's now? You going to shove this up Knebel's ass? He got some good cops here too — friends of mine."

"I'm going to shove it all the way up to his neck."

Tower laughed. His leathery, ruddy face wrinkled deeply as he laughed and the veins on his cheeks glowed red.

"I haven't felt like this since I sent Danny Morse to the chair back in the fifties," Lowenstein said. "It's almost like being there again. Almost that good. Like carrying a shield."

"Nothing's that good," Tower said. He wheeled over to a locked wooden cabinet beneath the window. He opened the cabinet and produced a bottle of Wild Turkey, one hundred proof. He had hoarded it, he said, for two and a half years, for a special occasion. This occasion was indeed special. The two of them drank it and told cop stories and ate cheese and crackers until the dawn came. Then Tower fell asleep in his wheelchair. Lowenstein stretched out on the couch, happily singing and mumbling to himself, wrapping his arms around the near empty bottle, keeping it tight to his chest. He drifted off just before seven and woke to a banging on the door three hours later. Tower was still asleep in his wheelchair, a grin on his red face, his head cocked to the side, snoring loudly. Lowenstein got up, half sick and still-legged, and went to the door. He peered out through the curtain. There was a man and a woman on the ramp. Lowenstein asked what they wanted through the door.

"Federal Bureau of Investigation," the woman said.

Lowenstein opened the door and found it windy on the porch and cold. He blinked his eyes against the light of morning.

"I'm Special Agent Louise Foster," the woman said, "and this is Special Agent Dunn."

"So what's the deal?" Lowenstein asked. "You want to come in?"

"Are you Arthur Zimmerman Lowenstein of Philadelphia, Pennsylvania?" Special Agent Foster said. She was thirtyish, attractive, blond, businesslike.

"Yeah, sure, I'm Arthur Lowenstein. So?"

She took a small glossy black-and-white photo from her jacket pocket and held it in front of Lowenstein. It was Max Sunday; he looked younger, his hair fuller on top, cut shorter on the sides. But it was definitely Max Sunday. "Do you know this man?" she asked.

"Maybe I do know him. So what?"

"You met with him last night, we believe," she said, her eyes fixed on Lowenstein, her mouth tight. "Did you or did you not?"

A gust of wind caught the door and Lowenstein struggled with it for a moment until the wind died down. "Maybe I did and maybe I didn't. I'm saying nothing until I know what this is all about."

Special Agent Dunn moved closer to him. "We're afraid you might be in some difficulty, Mr. Lowenstein," he said. Dunn was a big man, with the shoulders and neck of a weightlifter, but his features were soft. He had another photo, which he handed to Lowenstein. "Do you know this man?"

Lowenstein looked at the two agents and they were both grimly serious; then he looked at the photo. It was a larger black-and-white, showing a man in a suit coat and tie. He was about thirty-five, well groomed, square shouldered, athletic; he was staring, bored, blankly into the camera.

"Nope," Lowenstein said. "Perfect stranger." He handed the photo back to Dunn. The wind gusted again, strong and cold, and Lowenstein backed into the kitchen. The two agents followed.

"The guy in the picture," Lowenstein said, "he's the guy who bought the guns that nailed Jamison, isn't he?"

Special Agent Dunn nodded and he looked to Special Agent Foster, who said, "Max Sunday showed up at WNBX here in Chicago this morning about six A.M. and detailed his involvement — and your involvement too, Mr. Lowenstein. Tracking him down was a considerable achievement. We applaud your skill."

"You're arresting me, aren't you?" Lowenstein said.

They nodded. "Obstruction of Justice," Special Agent Foster said. "Shall we read you your rights?"

"I know my rights. I was a cop when you were in pigtails, catch? The man in the photo, who is he? Sunday said when I knew, I'd know why maybe Brazil wasn't big enough for him to hide in. Is he Cosa Nostra? Maybe with these big Latino syndicates?"

"No," Agent Foster said. "He is not a criminal. He's not with any syndicates. He's an intelligence officer. He goes by the name of Chandler Smith."

"Intelligence. You mean like the KGB?"

"No, afraid not."

Lowenstein smiled. "You wouldn't kid an old blue-foot, would you? If he's not one of theirs, then he must be . . . what? A friendly?"

"He's with the CIA, it's been confirmed," she said.

Lowenstein laughed until tears formed in his eyes. "God damn! This is going to shake them all up," he said. "It's going to shake the whole damn country."

Agent Foster nodded. "Right up to the tippy-top."

TWENTY-THREE

"Thank you for coming, gentlemen," the President said. "This is the newest member of my staff, Mr. Wilson Wright, who is for the moment acting as sort of an advisor at large. Please be seated, won't you, gentlemen?"

Wilson Wright was of medium height and weight, unassuming, professorial, warm. He shook Knebel's hand first, then Ober's. He already knew Stewart Ott. They were in Haas's study at Blair House. The bookshelves were empty, the books packed in boxes to be shipped to the White House.

The President sat behind his large, ornate desk; Knebel, Ober, and Stewart Ott sat opposite. Wilson Wright sat to the President's right, his legs crossed, his hands on his lap. Ober seemed ill at ease, holding onto the arms of the chair as if to anchor himself. Ott was alert, waiting to react to whatever ball might be tossed into his court. Knebel, impatient, toyed with his pipe.

"Well now, Mr. Knebel," the President began, his hands folded comfortably on the desk, "although the business with Adolf White went extremely well, I want you to know I am not happy in the least with the latest developments. It was apparently shabbily handled and showed a lack of discipline in your organization. You man, Lowenstein, I am told, offered Max Sunday unofficial immunity — in fact, conspired to get him illegally out of the country — in exchange for information. Is that essentially a factual account?"

"It is," Knebel said, "as far as I know."

"The Bureau has brought Lowenstein in for questioning, sir," Ott said.

"He's cooperating fully," Ober added.

"We ought to give him a goddamn medal," Knebel said. "He's worth a thousand pencil-pushing pigheads. Maybe ten thousand."

The President's eyes flickered with amusement. "I might agree with you. He has nevertheless been an embarrassment."

"Admittedly," Knebel said.

"Using Lowenstein — I mean a man of his record," Stewart Ott said, " — shows the country we've taken off the brakes."

"I suppose . . ." the President said. He looked at Ober. "This nation is rife with speculation about conspiracy. Now one of our own CIA people has been implicated. This is a very upsetting business. Where do we go from here? Do you think he may have been one of the assassins? Is it possible other agency people are involved?"

"We have a full-scale investigation getting underway, sir."

"Good. And what is being done to find this renegade Smith."

"His photo is on TV nationwide every fifteen minutes. The public is turning in thousands of leads.

134

every hour."

"What about his accomplices?"

"We've got differing opinions," Ober said. "We hope to have something solid for you soon. Mr. Knebel thinks the suspect disguised as Reis was a woman. I'm skeptical, but we're gathering information from all sources world-wide on any woman capable of committing such an act."

"What I don't understand is, what did Adolf White have to do with all this?"

"That's what we'd like to know too," Knebel said. "His involvement with them was likely peripheral. It's possible Adolf White and his Manhattan Red Brigade may have been cashing in on the publicity and had no actual complicity in the crime."

"That would be a sorry turn of events at this point," the President said sourly. "The public has been so elated over their quick demise. No matter, we must pursue all lines of investigation vigorously. I want no Warren Commission–type cover-up, no clouds over this Administration. I believe it's imperative that we find out whether the CIA itself actually had anything to do with the killing of President Jamison and his party. I was on the Senate Intelligence Oversight Committee and can tell you with certainty they are not cooperative with their watchdogs. They've overstepped their charter more than once."

"Amen to that," Ott said.

"They've got nineteen thousand, three hundred people over there. If just half a dozen were working together—"

"We'll be looking into the CIA long and hard this summer, John," Ott said, "when the platform committee starts its hearings before the convention."

The President turned to Ober after a reflective moment. "I'm giving you full power to investigate the CIA," he said. "They are to show you whatever you want to see. I'll make that perfectly clear to the Director. Get digging as soon as possible. Put as many men on it as you need. I want to know who over there is involved and I want them out of there as soon as possible. I've already instructed them they are not to involve themselves in this Chandler Smith business in any way. They are to turn over any leads or information to the Bureau. Do what you have to do, Mr. Ober."

"Yes, sir."

The President tugged at the French cuffs of his shirt to square them with the sleeves of his jacket. "If we don't get cooperation, you tell them that Stewart is growing weary from holding me back from smashing them into nineteen thousand, three hundred pieces."

"Yes, sir."

"Mr. Knebel, I trust there will be no further embarrassments."

"Fast ships often make big waves, Mr. President, but I'll do what I can to see decorum is preserved."

"It will be much appreciated. Please keep us informed — and keep up your very good work."

"Thank you, Mr. President, I will."

"Nice meeting all of you," Wilson Wright said.

"You think we covered everything, Wilson?" the President asked.

"Quite nicely, yes."

TWENTY-FOUR

As they left the study, Knebel was stopped in the narrow hallway by one of the President's junior aides, who handed him a small envelope. "Special courier brought it, sir," he said.

Knebel opened it; it was from the Deputy Director of the CIA, Lucius Cole.

Hans Ober stopped next to Knebel. "Important new development?"

"Lucius Cole wants to see me."

"Oh? Is he a friend of yours?"

"Never met the man."

"Watch him closely, Knebel. Lucius Cole can be a vicious bastard."

Forty minutes later, Knebel was in Cole's office at CIA headquarters, Langley, Virginia.

The office was spacious, neat, sterile. A painting of a lonesome knight on horseback, riding into a blazing sunset, dominated one wall. Cole himself was short and broad, with flashing gray eyes and short black hair. His voice sounded brittle and flat. They sat down on opposite sides of a large, clean desk.

"Okay, Mr. Cole," Knebel said. Why am I here?"

"I'll get right to the point. Hans Ober and his legions of morons will never get Chandler Smith, I'll tell you that for a certainty. They corner that son-of-a-bitch Smith and he'll litter the landscape with bodies. He knows how to kill a man six hundred ways. They better hope they don't catch him, let me tell you."

Knebel was sitting with his arms folded. "I'm sure you didn't ask me here to boast of Mr. Smith's prowess, Mr. Cole."

"It's not a boast — it's a cold fact. Let me tell you who I am, Mr. Knebel. I'm a bureaucrat now. A paper-pusher. I love two things: a fourteen-year-old coon dog named Starbright and the Company. That's it. That's the whole world to me. I am a man of little subtlety and no guile. Wind and fire, they call me. I blow hard and hot. I won't pretend with you, Knebel. I'll tell you straight out that having Hans Ober come here and dig into our files and question our people is tragedy. The Agency is the goddamn backbone of the defense of the nation. We are many things. Many things our critics accuse us of being we are. One thing we are *not* is Presidential assassins. Having Hans Ober here trying to prove we are is high tragedy. High Greek tragedy. Max Sunday may have made up the whole damn story. I've known Chandler Smith for twenty years. He isn't the kind of man to really sour. He knew the enemy from the guts out . . . . Know what it is? It's the goddamn press in this country. Drunk on conspiracies. Why would the Company want to see the President dead? Clement Jamison was the first President since Kennedy to understand our historic mission. Maybe except Ronald Reagan. Even if Smith did buy the weapons, does that really mean we have an open window on conspiracy?"

138

Knebel shrugged. "Hans Ober is here to set the record straight. We know one bad apple doesn't mean a rotten barrel. Maybe the others are ripe as spring virgins."

Lucius Cole's cheeks reddened. "Listen to me, Knebel. Smith went mad, right? That's the concensus. That has to be it. Either that or hostiles sent in a manikin — a look-alike. I could believe that. I've known Smith — he's top-shelf. He wouldn't have flipped out, believe you me."

"I'm sure he's a prince . . . What do you want from me, Cole?"

"I think you're a man I can reason with. They say you give a damn." He was clasping and unclasping his hands. "You've got to understand what the hell is going on in the world if this is going to make any sense to you. The Russians are taking an active part with their little Cuban brothers in Latin America. They're going military. We've intercepted communiqués, we've documented it, we can prove it. We turned four top spooks in the GRU — their military intelligence — last year who have spelled it all out for us. This planet is taking a bath in Bolshevik Red. The mask is off. They're blitzkrieging in Latin America." He paused.

Sweat was glistening on his forehead: he was short of breath for a moment. He wiped his sleeve, then continued.

"This Chandler Smith stuff is high tragedy. It doesn't even matter if he bought the guns or not. None of it matters. Our credibility is all that matters. The Company is more than a network. It's a bulwark. It's an idea. It's an idea that we have to believe in if our way of life is going to survive: the idea that Communism can be countered, halted, turned back. That idea must persist. If this one agent somehow was turned, that's tragic. But you can't shred the Company because of one man."

"We don't know it was one man. In fact, there were at least two."

Cole rubbed his face with his hands. He was very red-faced now. "You haven't understood any of this, have you? You're a cop and you're looking for a killer. I'm talking about the future of Western civilization and you're interested in your pound of flesh for a few lousy killings."

"Clement Jamison was the *President,* Cole."

"He was a man! Men come and go. It's ideas that are immortal. I don't give a damn that Haas wants us out of it. You could convince him to let us in. We've got assets you and the Bureau don't have. Even in this country, believe me. We want Chandler caught. We'll prioritize looking for him. Hear me, Knebel! The *Times* and the *Post* both had editorials talking about dismantling the Company! That is a tragedy that makes the other tragedy microscopic. If we dismantle this bulwark we are naked and defenseless. They will crawl over our underbelly and gnaw at our guts." He was breathing heavily as he paused and the color ran from his cheeks. He stared at Knebel. "Look, we'll find him for you." His voice softened. "Get the President to let us do that. Then we can put this thing behind us."

"When we know it all, we'll put it behind us. The Bureau will find Chandler Smith. That's the game the President called, that's the game we play."

Lucius Cole sighed heavily, gesturing surrender. "We will cooperate. But please remember, you peel the skin off the fruit, it dies. I tried to tell Ober on the telephone. I don't think he heard. That's the one point that's got to sink in: you can't peel off the skin."

"They are not peeling off the skin, Cole, they're boring deep into the core. That's where you find the rot."

Knebel arrived back at the Annex at two thirty.

"Stewart Ott wants to talk to you as soon as possible," Ms. Pressman said as soon as he came through the door. Knebel asked her to get him on the phone.

In his office Knebel turned up the thermostat. There were dozens of memos on his desk and summaries of reports and briefs from analysts who were sifting the data. Ms. Pressman buzzed the intercom; she had Stewart Ott on the line.

"Richard, thanks for returning my call. Understand you spoke to Lucius Cole. What's he up to?"

"He lectured me on historical imperatives. Wanted me to intervene with the President and let the CIA hunt Smith. I told him nix."

"You think he might suspect some more of his boys are in on it? How worried is he?"

"He's plenty worried, but I don't think he knows any more than we do."

"All right, Richard. I trust your instincts. But there is something worrisome about a man who's always waving such a large flag so wildly."

"I'll let you know if he waves it in my face again."

"Thanks, Richard."

Knebel lit his pipe and went to work. He would have preferred to be at the CIA helping Ober and his staff dig through the records, but he had too much paperwork to catch up on. The President was expecting some recommendations and the Senate was getting up a committee to investigate the investigators, trying to head off another Warren Commission fiasco.

Already Knebel had found massive chain-of-command problems and procedural problems. There were bottlenecks between the field operators and the clerical sections who processed their reports. Some sections were short of personnel; others were overloaded. The computer people didn't have the program straightened out and personnel assignments had to be made by hand, which sometimes meant there were misassignments, and idle time. Interdepartmental rivalries and jealousies abounded. The Secret Service was screaming that the FBI was stepping on its toes. Both agencies were often following the same lines of investigation, each unwilling to surrender any responsibility to the other, each hoarding its findings to get a jump on the other. He found special investigation budget analysts were already bickering with the FBI regulars, the Secret Service, and local and state agencies over who owed what bill for which involvement. The SWAT action against Adolf White alone ran over half a million dollars and all the figures still weren't in. It was an accountant's nightmare.

At seven in the evening he sent his secretary home. He had started making a report to Hans Ober when he got a call from Thaddeus Gore, the computer section chief, who told him their computer was still down and the one at the Main Campus wasn't able to produce a woman candidate to fit the profile he had supplied of the second assassin. There wasn't one even close among all the hundreds of living agents in the world known to the United States intelligence network.

Knebel said, "How about the other networks? Keep digging. Vary the parameters. Get me some names."

"Will do, Mr. Knebel. We've got your first load of coincidental material. Couple of big boxes. Some of the coincidences are really staggering. Did you know both Chandler Smith and Clement Jamison wore a nine and one-half D shoe?"

A few minutes later Chad Priest called to tell him they had been working hard at the CIA headquarters and still had come up with nothing. Talking to spies, he said, was like talking to trained parrots. "They all say things like 'I have no direct knowledge of any such person or persons involved in any such activity or activities.' You'd think we were the goddamn KGB. This stonewalling has Ober madder than hell. Says it's like trying to cut a diamond with your index finger."

"Keep at it, Chad."

Knebel went through a pile of reports and then read Chandler Smith's personnel records with care. As he was finishing up, more reports arrived. A two-foot stack. He scanned them, leaning back in his chair smoking his pipe. After a while he stopped and turned to the wall. Something was terribly wrong, he thought. Thousands of trained and dedicated people were pedaling like mad, but the bicycle just wasn't going anywhere.

TWENTY-FIVE

Arthur Lowenstein had had a bad day. The flight from Chicago to Washington had been bumpy and he had had too much Wild Turkey the night before and not enough to drink on the plane. He was unable to sleep all day. They had interrogated him for endless hours about everything he had done and thought from the moment he'd arrived in Washington the first time and had looked at the specimen weapon until he was arrested in Chicago. They offered him the services of an attorney, a man named Simms, a young recent graduate of Yale Law School. Simms seemed nervous and unsure; he advised Lowenstein to say nothing. But Lowenstein didn't take the advice. He answered all questions asked. He didn't give a damn, he said. Let them do what they were going to do. They finally locked him in a cell around midnight and said his bail would be set at the arraignment in the morning. Simms promised to be there.

In the cell block the prisoner in the next cell groaned continually, complaining of illness, but the guards ignored him. About two-fifteen the man threw up and Lowenstein could smell the vomit. It made him nauseous. Lowenstein paced in his cell. When he lay down he felt dizzy. At two-thirty he had smoked his last cigarette and now it was nearly four. He wanted a smoke desperately. His time in Atlanta came back to him — the thousands of trips he had made from the bars to the back wall and back to the bars again. He told himself they wouldn't be holding him long this time — hadn't he found the goddamn gunsmith Max Sunday when the rest of them were sitting around looking in their microscopes? He was a media hero. A household word. But then he knew Knebel. Did Knebel give a damn? Knebel was a fanatic when it came to playing by the rules. You cross him, you get blasted with both barrels.

He rinsed his face in the sink and went back to pacing. After months and months he knew a numbness would set in and the numbness would make it possible to endure. But he promised himself he would outlast the pain. At four-thirty in the morning two black jailers came and opened the door to his cell. They had a clean shirt, a shaving kit, and a pack of cigarettes.

"What the hell is this?" Lowenstein asked.

"Get cleaned up. We're taking you upstairs."

"Why?"

"Just do it, man," a jailer said.

After he had washed, shaved, and put on the clean shirt, they took him upstairs and handed him his personal effects. He signed for them. They led him down a hall and into a small interrogation room and left him there. It was as quiet as the Pharaoh's tomb. Now what the hell was this all about, he thought. Hadn't they asked enough damn questions? A few moments later the door opened and Knebel came in.

"I guess you figure I've been bullshitting the small fry, eh?" Lowenstein said. "Is that it?"

"Not exactly." Knebel leaned against the table and folded his arms. "You've been treated humanely, I trust?"

"They asked me a lot of questions and I haven't had any sleep."

"You have heard of suppression of evidence and obstruction of justice, have you not?"

"Sure."

"We could criminally prosecute; you know that."

"That's what I've been hearing."

"You tried to make me look like an ass. Instead, Max Sunday made you look like an ass."

Lowenstein shrugged. "It almost worked. I've been out of things for a long time, Knebel. Maybe I lost a little of the edge, catch?"

"By enticing Max Sunday to consort with known criminals, you left us vulnerable to suit. It may even be entrapment."

"Why tell me all this? What do I give a damn? When your life is as putrid as mine, you're damn past caring what the hell happened. I wanted to get the man who bought the guns, that's all I could think about."

"You're supposed to be Supercop."

Lowenstein's red eyes flashed with anger. "I almost had the whole thing, catch? I was going to push your face in it."

"Your hatred for me has made you stupid!"

"Yeah, maybe it did. But it felt good for a little while, me knowing and you and your ten thousand clowns not knowing. I am Supercop compared to you and your legions of college kids." He shook his head and shrugged heavily. "But what the hell; Max Sunday blew the ball game for me." He rubbed his hands and looked at Kne-

146

bel, his features softening, his eyes narrowing. "What is this, Knebel? You didn't have me brought here just to chew my ass out."

"Do you know how many men there are working on this case?"

"No."

"Full-time Federal investigators alone number nine thousand. Thousands more are tracking down leads on a part-time basis. We've got lab men and research people, scores of them. Then there are local cops and state cops involved as well. We have a full-time computer just to keep track of them. It's the biggest manhunt in history. We've questioned everyone that lived within twenty miles of the place. All that effort results in a mountain of reports and nothing else. With one notable exception. You."

"It isn't luck, Knebel. I got the instincts and a whole lot of experience. The hard kind."

Knebel nodded and looked at him blankly for a long moment, collecting his thoughts. Then he said, "There's something wrong with what we've been doing. We're shotgunning and it isn't working."

"Yeah? That's what happens when you canvass the world, you end up in truckloads of worn shoe leather and enough paper to wipe every ass on earth."

"Most of it's on my desk. It's going to smother us."

"Yeah, and these guys you're after aren't sitting in the tulips. They feel the heat, you can bet on it."

"Suppose this were your case, what would you do?"

Lowenstein grinned and rubbed his chin and his eyes came alive. "I'd start, I guess, by remembering what it is we're dealing with here. This is murder. That's the first thing I told myself when I was going after the gun business. You can't let yourself be dazzled by the importance of the case — "it's still murder."

"Meaning?"

"Meaning, you ask who would like to see this man dead? And there was more than one guy dropped. Maybe the President was killed to cover up the murder of one of the others."

"Very doubtful."

Lowenstein spread his hands out. "You're still dealing with a simple homicide. You've got to sweep in all the corners and get all the dirt, catch? You've got to ask yourself the right questions .. . . Why did they leave that piece behind to lead us to Max Sunday? That had to be on purpose . . . . This had to be on purpose . . . . This White character was just a punk, yet the real killers were willing to let him take the heat and get all the headlines for a while . . . . You must have some kind of theory."

"Right now is looks like the CIA — or elements within the CIA — tried to pin it on the radicals."

"Then why leave the weapon behind?" Lowenstein said.

"Heat of the moment, it was overlooked."

"Two pros? Not a chance." He smiled, tucking his hands in his belt. "Why are you here, Knebel?"

"Maybe I just need somebody to bounce a few ideas off of."

"You're the man who got the L.A. slasher. You're big time, Knebel. Special Crime Commission Task Force in Pennsylvania. Why don't you just bounce your ideas off the wall?"

"It's late, Lowenstein, and I'm damned tired. A President has been murdered. Anybody else, and you'd be back in Atlanta picking your nose for the next five to seven years. I mean it. People who work for me stay in bounds or the sky falls on them."

Lowenstein frowned. "You think I give a damn about a President? He's just another stiff to me. The guy who hit him is just another slob with a gun, catch?"

Knebel lit his pipe and Lowenstein lit a cigarette; the small room began to fill with smoke.

"I'll tell you how I've always worked in the past," Knebel said. "I always begin by asking myself what brought the murderer and the victim together. Chandler Smith is our number one suspect. Let's assume for the sake of argument that he is the murderer. The President is the primary victim. Granted, we're just assuming that too. But what brought these two men together? There is always a bond between the killer and the victim, even if it only exists in the killer's imagination. Once you find that bond, you have the foundation for working out your case."

Lowenstein shook his head. What a bunch of crap. You've got a corpse, Knebel. You start with the corpse. Who loved him, who hated him? Work over the suspect: who loved him, who hated him? Then work both ends toward the middle. You surround a murder, Knebel, you wrap it all up and you find all the loose ends, and then you pull it tight."

"I want you in on this, Lowenstein. I want you in and I want you to play it straight."

"Give me full police powers."

"Impossible."

"You've got to give a man respect!"

"No police powers. There'll be an FBI man with you every step. He'll have all the police powers you'll need.

You're to cooperate with him and follow the procedures."

Lowenstein shook his head. "I'll haul in the fish for you, Knebel, but I'm not taking any chaperon. I'll do it without papers, but you've got to give me some room to move, catch?"

"You're going to play this our way or not at all. Your cell downstairs is waiting. . . . What'll it be, the rock or the hard place?"

Lowenstein glared at him with tired red eyes. "You're a son-of-a-bitch, Knebel."

Lowenstein got up and drifted around the room. He crushed his cigarette out on the tile floor. "All right," he said. "Your way. Let's get the hell out of here."

TWENTY-SIX

"Tell me about Smith," Lowenstein said.

Knebel had his notebook open in front of him on his desk and they were eating sweet pastry and drinking coffee. It was six-thirty in the morning. Knebel had called for an FBI man to serve as Lowenstein's partner and the agent was on his way from his home in Baltimore.

"You want to take some notes?" Knebel asked.

"I keep it all in here," Lowenstein said, pointing to his head. "That way it don't get lost, stolen, or mutilated."

"I'll give you the high points and then you can take the file with you."

"Fine."

Knebel took a sip of coffee and began:

"Smith was born in Breslau, Hungary, during the war and came west as a teenager in nineteen fifty-six. He's forty-five now, five-feet-nine, one hundred sixty-five pounds. He went to public grammar schools in New York City, played football, studied jujitsu, organized a dance combo, won a roller-skating contest. He had two years at City College of New York studying Biology, and enlisted in the Green Berets in nineteen sixty-one. He was quite a patriotic young man. On his original application to join the CIA he had written that he wanted to — quote — commit his time, his energy, and his sacred honor to 'fighting for liberty.' The FBI investigating agent noted that a cursory check of his classmates revealed that, indeed, he hated the Reds with an uncommon vehemence. If anyone even breathed a laudatory sentiment about the Soviet Union or Karl Marx, Chandler Smith was ready to bash in his head. This propensity was considered a decided plus in considering his application favorably."

"What was Smith's name before he came to this country?"

"It's not in the records. Seems they feared a mole might discover it and put his family in jeopardy. He was given the name Smith when he entered the CIA and all his previous school records were changed to conform. His mother changed her name as well."

"I imagine Smith was a star."

"He received six service awards, including the CIA Meritorious Service Award. He was the eighth most decorated agent in the Agency's history. He attended, all in all, eleven prolonged training courses and innumerable seminars. All of his instructors without exception lauded his diligence and he mastered all phases of his work. His supervisors in the field had some problems with his severe commitment and lack of patience with any slackers, but they all recommended him for promotion and raises. Copies of the reports are all here and you may read them if you like."

Lowenstein shook his head. "Spare me, please."

"The only curious thing is that three years ago he had ten months of — quote — 'administrative leave.' That may have meant that he was on some secret assignment, or he was taking a rest, we're not sure."

"That may be worth looking into."

"You know about the woman?"

"No. Just what was in the newspaper — some love affair that went sour."

"Her name was Mme. Rousseau. A very lovely woman, according to reports. They met at a Spanish embassy function. Her husband was the French Culture Minister. Affairs of the heart are a common thing in France and, if people are discreet, they are tolerated. Smith, however, is a member of the CIA. His boss, Gerald Hix, the Paris station chief, thought this might be a splendid entry into the inner workings of the French Cabinet. The fact that France is a friendly power means nothing in the game of international espionage, it seems. Smith, despite his loyalty and fierce commitment, refused. They threatened to expose the affair in the French press if he did not cooperate. They are ruthless men who run these networks. Smith still refused. He would break off the affair, but he would not use his lover for this seedy business."

"They blew the whistle on him, huh?"

"They may have. Someone did. The CIA files do not show that they did. It doesn't matter. Smith blamed the Agency. The irate Cultural Minister confronted his wife and she confessed. He shot himself in her presence. That was November fourth last year. It was not the idea of the affair. He could have stood having an unfaithful wife in good grace — it was the idea that she had done it with a foreign spy that was intolerable. Whether she had divulged any State secrets or not didn't matter. He couldn't face the scandal. But he botched his suicide somehow. It took him twelve hours to die, twelve hours of agony. All the time he cursed her and refused to accept her supplications for forgiveness."

"A hard man." Lowenstein finished his coffee and dumped the paper cup in a waste basket. "A very hard man."

"The French press made much of it, and though we denied Chandler Smith was an agent, it created a strain in our relations. Smith became despondent and his work went to pieces. They didn't recall him immediately because they thought it would look like an admission of culpability. He grew lethargic and drank heavily. Finally, they did recall him — supposedly for health reasons. The Agency has a sanitarium in Alcon, New Jersey, for burned-out agents. They figured to debrief him at Langley and then see to it that he had a good rest. Once you fall out of faith, it's hard to get it back. They probably would have retired him. They sent a man to meet him at the airport. Smith was spotted getting off the plane, but they lost him in the crowd. He failed to report to Langley. There were some routine notices sent around to keep a lookout for him, but no search was instituted. He was considered a burned-out agent. Happens all the time, they tell me."

"So the next thing you know he's buying guns to knock off the President of the United States. . . . You mentioned a mother. Tell me about the mother."

Knebel searched his notes and found what he wanted quickly. "She's in a nursing home in Massachusetts. The Bureau had a couple of men go up there. They didn't get much — nothing in fact. Apparently she's little more than a vegetable."

"Did Smith see her often?"

"Yes. They were close."

"I'll start with her."

"Your new partner should be here any minute. I'll get you some expense money."

"You should know something, Knebel. You should know I was a good cop. Sure, I was on the grease. Everyone was on the grease. But no bad guy ever took a walk on account of me. I want you to know that. They tried to buy me plenty of times, but no *real* bad guy ever walked on account of me. . . . I'd never have made detective if I didn't go along with what was going on. It was institutionalized, as much a part of the system as the pension plan."

"We offered to let you turn State's evidence. If your superiors were involved, we wanted them a hell of a lot more than we wanted you."

"Better to drink lye than be a snitch."

"You could have stayed clean. You didn't have to put your hand out."

"Didn't you ever have to make a choice when either way wasn't worth a damn?"

"You were bent, Lowenstein, I put you away! That's all there is to it."

"Listen, friend. I'm going to get to the bottom of this Jamison killing. You can put that in the bank. Then you and I are going to have a long talk about reality, catch? We're going to have a long, long talk."

"You get me the assassins and you'll have my undivided attention."

TWENTY-SEVEN

The Chevy Citation pulled into a parking space in front of the large, white-painted Victorian. It was late morning, sunny but cool; clear skies. There were poplar trees along the street and the house was surrounded by a black wrought-iron fence trimmed with gold at the tips of the bars. Lowenstein was in the passenger seat. He had been reading the file Knebel had given him; he closed it and slid it under the seat. He got out of the car. The driver, a black man, got out too. He was twenty-eight and tall, Harvard educated, careful.

"You said your name was what now?" Lowenstein said.

"Walter Byron."

"In there, I do the talking, catch?"

"My orders are to observe and report."

"Maybe I'll teach you something."

"Anything's possible, I guess."

They went up the walk. There was a small sign by the door which proclaimed the place to be the Goodfellow Rest Home. The sign was small and neatly lettered with gothic script. The lawn smelled strongly of fertilizer.

"We've already had qualified agents here,"

Walter Bryon said.

"I know," Lowenstein said.

"Did you bother to check what they said in their report?"

"No."

"The woman is senile. Completely unresponsive."

"Is that right?"

"You think this is a waste of time, eh?"

"I do."

"Maybe you'll learn more than a little something." Lowenstein rang the bell.

Walter Byron looked around. "My grandmother went out in a place like this."

A flat-faced, uniformed security guard opened the door.

"FBI," Walter Byron said. "We phoned." He showed the man a plastic identification card.

"Him too?" the guard said, meaning Lowenstein.

"He's with me," Walter Byron said. "Mrs. Fitch is expecting us."

"He isn't a reporter is he? They told me reporters are not to come near the place. They hang around like vultures."

"He's not a reporter."

"Let me see that ID again."

Walter Byron showed it to him. The guard examined it carefully, then let them in. He asked them to wait in the foyer. There was a large open room toward the back of the house. Patients in bathrobes and a few nurses and aides were watching television. On the screen Clement Jamison's funeral procession was moving slowly up Pennsylvania Avenue. The hearse was horse-drawn and flag-draped. Lowenstein and Walter Byron watched for a few minutes. The procession moved slowly. A band was playing a dirge.

After a while a little man with a gray mustache appeared. "Follow me, gentlemen," he said with formality. He took them down a narrow hallway to the back of the building. Mrs. Fitch was a stout woman in her early fifties with a heavy German accent. She asked them into her office. Lowenstein sat down; Walter Byron stood by the door.

"You vant to see Mrs. Smith, Mr., ah, Lovenstein? Vy, might I ask?" She regarded him severely. "They have qvestioned the poor vooman before und she has said—vat?—nothing. She loves her son deeply, Mr., ah, Lovenstein, und she vill not betray him."

"I wouldn't ask her to do that. It's not my way to do things like that."

"They told us no vun else vould bother the lady."

"If you want to throw me out, I'll go quietly . . . I'm looking for her son, I wouldn't kid you about that. But I'm also looking for the truth. I've read Chandler Smith's file. He isn't the kind of man to do something like this."

She regarded him with curiosity. "You are Yewish?"

"Yes."

"My mother vas Yewish." She eased back in her chair, smiling pleasantly. The office was small and well ordered, and the air was heavy with room freshener and masked cigarette smoke.

Lowenstein said, "Okay if I have a cigarette?" He took out a pack of Camels.

"Vee aren't supposed to smoke in the building."

"I won't tell if you won't." He winked.

Now she smiled broadly and produced a pack of mentholated Vantage and an ashtray from a drawer in her desk. She opened a window and they lit their cigarettes. Lowenstein offered one to Byron, who declined.

"It makes me feel like a naughty girl," Mrs. Fitch said. "I am an addict of the vorst kind." She said it as sort of an apology aimed at Byron.

"Life's pleasures—big and small—must be taken as they can," Lowenstein said.

"That is true," she said nodding. Then her expression hardened. "This whole thing has been terrible for Mrs. Smith. Her whole vorld come down on her. The poor, poor vooman. Now the owners here talk like she has some contagious disease. They are vorried our patients vill move out. Ver vould they go? The county home? I vould rather die in a toilet. It vas terrible about President Yamison. He vas kind, I think. He cared for people und that is the most important thing. He cared about the whole vorld und not yoost America. That is vat made him great. . . . But Mrs. Smith did not kill him."

"Tell me, Mrs. Fitch, did Chandler Smith come here often?"

"Ya, venever he vas in the country. He traveled a lot of the. . . . They took the guest book, the men from the government. I can't tell you, but ven he vas in the country he came ven he could. He loved his mother much. He spoke German vell, but in the throat like the Sviss. He had great concern for his mama und vee all liked him. I don't believe he had anything to do vith it. He vas—vat do you call it?"

"Framed?"

"Ya. Like he vas put into the wrong picture."

"If he was framed, I'll find out, Mrs. Fitch."

"His mother thinks they vill shoot him."

"Can I see her? With her consent, of course."

Mrs. Fitch nodded. "Something made him get involved, if he is involved. I know him, he is not the kind."

"I rely on your judgment."

She took a few more drags on her cigarette and cruched it out and Lowenstein crushed his out too. Then she sprayed the room with air freshener.

"Every time I do this ritual I hate myself," she said to Byron. Byron nodded that he understood perfectly.

"Everyone plays some games, Mrs. Fitch," Lowenstein said.

"Vat is yours?" She put away the air freshener.

"I drink."

"I know you do. Your liver is fading, your skin shows it."

"My liver has been fading for forty years."

"Vun day it vill qvit on you. Und then you can come stay vith us." She smiled, amused.

"A sobering thought."

Lowenstein and Byron followed Mrs. Fitch to the south wing. The place was impeccably clean, filled with spotless nurses and helpers. It smelled of cleansers and medicines and death. Mrs. Fitch had them both sign on a line in the guest book, with date and time.

On the way upstairs she said, "Vee exceed every single State und Federal standard here, both for nutritional reqvirements, cleanness, und patient-staff ratio. You vould like it here, Mr. Lovenstein."

"I'm sure," Lowenstein said.

They went down a long corridor. A janitor was repairing a light fixture and a nurse loaded lunch trays onto a stainless-steel cart.

"I doubt Mrs. Smith vill talk to you, Mr. Loven-

160

stein — she is qvite sickened by all of this. Vee ourselves vould not have told her anything, but ven the police came there vas nothing vee could do about it. Please, if she doesn't speak, try not to upset her. She has strong constitution, but she is very, very sick."

Mrs. Fitch checked first to be certain the woman was presentable and that she was awake; then she invited Lowenstein and Byron into the room. The room reeked with sickness.

"This is a Mr. Lovenstein, Mrs. Smith. He is from Vashington und he is here about your son." She turned to Lowenstein. "I told her you ver a decent man und that she should talk to you."

"Thank you." Lowenstein approached the bed slowly. He smiled tentatively.

The woman was thin, very white, and had large eyes which seemed to have the power to penetrate the thin surface of falseness. Her eyes fell on Lowenstein. He pulled up a chair and sat beside her and said nothing. Her eyes never left him. The silence was long.

"You will not find my son," she said finally. Her voice was surprisingly strong.

"Perhaps not."

"If he does not want to be found, he will not be found, sir."

"Please, my name is Arthur."

"You are not FBI?"

"No."

She glanced at Byron standing at the foot of the bed. "This colored man with you. He is one. He has the look. Like the CIA — the arrogance. Everywhere in the world the look is the same. I have hate for them all. Hate and contempt."

161

Walter Byron remained impassive.

She averted her gaze and her expression soured. "Spies and storm troopers are the same. They are not men at all—and I know—my son was one of them. They made him one. I encouraged him, and for that sin I am guilty. God will punish me. . . . Who are you, sir?"

"My name is Arthur Lowenstein."

"Chandler is clever. You'll not get him."

"Perhaps not."

"The Company may—you will not. . . . I'm not saying anything. They tortured me about my friends in Budapest and I told them nothing and I will tell you nothing."

"Chandler is one of the most decorated agents in the history of the CIA, did you know that, Mrs. Smith?"

She nodded gently. "He is clever and has will."

"Tell me, did he have any hobbies growing up?"

"Why should you ask that? No."

"Not even as a boy?"

"No. No, he played music and did the fighting. What do you mean? Why would you care?"

"What was he doing about three years ago when he took a ten-month leave of absence?"

She looked at him hard. "I will tell nothing about that. Nothing absolutely. What he did was for the country, that is all I will say."

Lowenstein nodded as if he understood. Then he said, "You don't believe he had anything to do with the death of Clement Jamison, do you?"

Tears formed in her eyes.

Lowenstein touched her hand. "I'll go. I don't know what I expected here anyway. I'm sorry to have disturbed you."

"No—I want to tell you something. Please. I want you to know. You should know he has not been made an animal. They will not make him an animal." Her hands were fists. "Events make men bestial when they are not bestial as God made them. Tell me, sir, what kind of a world is this? I do not understand the world. Is it true that they have bombs that will kill us all? Rockets to shoot them anywhere in the world? I can't understand such a thing. The whole world burnt, is that what we have been striving for all the centuries? Killing with the tanks I have seen. And guns. First the Germans, then the Russians. And our own people. Guns and tanks and bombs. One cries equality and the other, freedom. One kills you to save you from the other. Half of my life I have spent praying that I can forget. The Lord has cursed me with a long life to suffer. This life is all suffering, sir. My son, can he get away? Is it possible with so many looking? I am ashamed that I do not wish him dead for this terrible thing he has done. I do not. It is a terrible world. He hinted to me that he was about to do terrible things and I should have to be strong. God would forgive him, he said. God would know that he was doing the right thing, he said."

He held her hand and said nothing, waiting. Walter Byron looked at her and waited too. After a moment she said:

"He loved this country, sir. He loved her much. When you live under the boot of the Russian and then you come here, you love her much. He loved her more than a hundred others who say they love her. He gave up his very spirit for her."

She was crying now; her frail body trembled.

After a moment, Lowenstein kissed her on the hand

163

and said good-bye. He was sorry to have disturbed her, he said.

Outside in the car Walter Byron said, "Well, that netted us exactly *nada*. Now what?"

Lowenstein looked at him curiously. "In school you learned to read books. You hunt men, you learn to read people in here." He touched his chest. "We now know the most important thing, catch?"

"Which is?"

"The motive."

"The motive?"

"He did it for love — love of country."

"You're not buying that!"

"Every last syllable."

Walter Byron shook his head. "Even if it were true, what good does it do you to know it?"

"*What* a man loves tells you nearly everything. *Who* he loves is the rest."

"You mean this French woman, Mme. Rousseau?"

"You're learning."

TWENTY-EIGHT

"Thank you for coming today, Mr. LaVale," Knebel said, shaking LaVale's slippery hand.

LaVale's pink face flushed as he sat down. "This has been a gruesome week, Mr. Knebel, absolutely gruesome. But I understand the authorities must double-check everything and I wish to assist in any way I can. Whatever questions you have, please ask them."

They were in Knebel's office. It was late in the afternoon. Jamison's funeral had been earlier in the day and LaVale was still wearing a black suit and black tie. Knebel opened a notebook in front of him. He was fatigued; his eyes were burning. He had been working on paperwork all day and had not slept the night before.

"Let me explain something, Mr. LaVale. What I'm trying to do is get a better 'feel' of things before the assassination. Get an idea of the mood and so on. How things were that morning with the President. I've already spoken with the pilot of the helicopter, who said things seemed pretty much 'situation normal.' The President's valet was off that day. I don't know exactly what I'm looking for, so my questions may be vague. . . . Would you like a cup of coffee before we begin?"

LaVale declined with a wave of his hand. "My stomach won't hold anything today, thank you." He sighed heavily. "I can't believe it yet, Mr. Knebel. It seems so like something from an old newsreel. It isn't all quite real. Like Kennedy—I was just a kid then, but it had that same unreal quality about it. How's it been going with the investigation? What is this business with the CIA? The country is horrified. They had a demonstration at Langley this morning. It got ugly, I hear. People are angry. Do we really have to have all this spy business? We're training armies of these insane people. Libya isn't the only country unleashing these beasts on the world." LaVale eased back in his seat and smiled dimly, picking some lint off his sleeve. "How is it I can be of help to you, Mr. Knebel? I gave a full report to the FBI. They had me on the hot seat twice, the second time for almost nine hours. I tell you it has been a gruesome week."

"I read the reports, naturally," Knebel said. "There were some remarks in them that frankly puzzled me. As an example, you said that Clement Jamison had lost confidence in you."

"Did I say that? At the time they interviewed me I was naturally quite upset. They first interviewed me that Sunday afternoon and I was in a state of shock. I still am. Understand, Mr. Knebel, my background is public relations. This whole thing has been mind-blowing."

"For all of us. Did you know that I knew Jamison?"

"Yes."

"You say a lot of flattering things about him in your statement."

"They were true."

"All of them?"

"Yes. He was the greatest President of this century. Maybe the greatest ever—besides Abraham Lincoln, maybe."

"Why had he lost confidence in you?"

"I said *seemed to*. Didn't I?"

"Possibly. Had you given him reason to lose confidence in you?"

"Of course not."

Knebel combed his beard with his fingers and stared at LaVale. "I don't get it," he said. "Am I to understand that Jamison was acting irrationally?" Knebel was fishing and had little confidence that anything would come of it. He cleaned his glasses with a Kleenex. "Well, Mr. LaVale?"

LaVale shifted his weight in his chair. "It's difficult to state what I mean exactly."

"These questions are important, Mr. LaVale. Forgive me if I seem uncivil—but you do appear to be equivocating."

LaVale's cheeks reddened. "I'm not equivocating."

"Then he was acting perfectly reasonably when he lost confidence in you. So what was the reason? Give me his reason."

"I didn't say he was acting perfectly reasonably."

"Was he just being foolish?"

"I told you, he was a great man," LaVale flushed intensely. The redness spread to his forehead and down his neck.

"Ah, yes, a great man," Knebel said. "So you told me. What did you talk about with him that last morning?"

"The campaign. I recounted the conversation for the FBI nearly verbatim. Must I do it again? I said it was a painful time, you have it all already."

"Yes, the campaign," Knebel said. He was studying LaVale closely; LaVale folded his arms across his chest and then unfolded them.

"There was something wrong with Jamison, wasn't there?"

"No."

Knebel leaned forward on his elbows. Perhaps he had hit a good vein. He sensed he had. "I have some news clippings, Mr. LaVale. In the last four months Jamison took — what — six vacations?"

"Short vacations."

"He never had taken any before then, had he?"

"They were *working* vacations."

"He was exhausted, wasn't he? He'd been President for three years. He was just plain tired out."

"All Presidents get tired. It's a demanding job."

"So he was tired?"

"It was to be expected. What's wrong with that?"

"I didn't say anything was wrong with it. Was something wrong with it?"

"No."

"So he was suffering somewhat from exhaustion."

"Yes."

"Severe exhaustion?"

"I didn't say that."

"Come on, LaVale, Clement Jamison was falling apart, wasn't he?"

"I didn't say that either!"

"He was murdered, damn it — this is no time to hold back!"

"It has nothing to do with the murder!"

"You can't know that! Come on, LaVale, give it to me! Give it all to me, I'll decide if it had nothing to do with the murder.!"

LaVale was nearly purple. He wrung his hands, then stopped suddenly and took a deep breath. There was a film of sweat on his forehead. "You've got to know he was a great man, Mr. Knebel." His voice was calm now. He wiped his forehead with a handkerchief. "The last thing I want to do is besmirch the name of Clement Jamison. He was a great, great man. You've got to know that. Everyone should know that." He licked his lips, his eyes darting.

"The truth has got to be known, LaVale. Give it to me straight before somebody else comes on it and makes it into something grotesque."

"All right." LaVale's voice softened to a whisper. "It started about a year ago. Maybe a little longer. I can't tell you when exactly. Clement was very tired. It's a terrible strain being President when you're trying as hard as he tried."

"Stick to what happened, Mr. LaVale."

"All right." LaVale leaned forward in his chair, rubbing his forehead. "At first he was just a little sick to his stomach. That's the way it started. A little listlessness set in. He didn't seem to give a damn anymore. This was last summer sometime. He started doing strange things."

"Like what?"

"Please, you've got to promise me this won't get out."

"What strange things did Clement Jamison do?"

"For one thing, he agreed to divorce Omi. Just like that. He stopped fighting her and agreed. They made some kind of private settlement. Clement Jamison was a decisive man. When he made up his mind it was like it was set in concrete. That's what made him presidential.

169

But with this, he changed his mind back again. Vacillated like crazy. She wouldn't let him reneg on the deal and he became ugly. I mean he was moody about it, not really ugly. He was human, after all. I never said he wasn't human."

"You said he became a different person? What did you mean by that?"

LaVale let out a deep breath. He was at confession now and would let it all out. "Clement's energy level was low. I knew the man well. On the campaigns we sometimes shared the same room and we'd talk strategy on into the night. He was a genius when it came to strategy. When he started to run down I thought it was the problem with Omi. Jesus, he was crazy about her. Then he started drinking soft drinks in the afternoon. I mean a lot of them. Six, maybe eight at a time. I guess the sugar gave him a boost. That didn't last too long. One day he stopped altogether. Then for a long time he seemed to have changed. Personality-wise, I mean. I was terribly worried about him, but of course I didn't say anything. A lot of rumors were going around about his health. His physical health. To me it seemed worse than that. It seemed he lost his soul. He called me in one day and was in a rage about the Russians. I had never seen him so angry. He talked about rejoining the Hemisphere Brigade thing and tearing Cuba apart. He said they had attacked him in the vilest way, but he had saved himself in time. He was circling the room like a cat in a cage. I'd never seen him like that. Then all of a sudden he stopped and said that maybe it wasn't the Russians, that he had enemies in his own house to worry about. It could have come from anywhere. He was going to clean house, he said. The only housecleaning he did was to get rid of Harrison Cheney. They had been as thick as thieves. They quarreled; then poof, he was gone."

"When he resigned they said it was his health, as I recall."

"They always say it's personal or health, or some damn thing." LaVale straightened out the crease in his pants. "That's Washington, that's the game. It was right after Cheney departed Clement told me he wanted the campaign to get cranked up and he was giving me a free hand with the budget and the television people and so on. That was it. We spoke on the telephone a few times subsequently, but we didn't get together until last Sunday morning. Of course he had made a couple of weekenders where we spoke between rounds of politicking, but no serious strategy sessions until Sunday. We'd won four out of five starts, but we were starting to sink in the polls. By then I'd say he was preoccupied most of the time and he didn't seem to have the stamina he used to have."

Knebel stood up and circled the room, smoking his pipe. He stopped.

"Did you ever talk to anyone else about these changes?"

"No sir."

"Did anyone else mention them to you?"

"Not that I recall."

"Can you remember anything else that seemed strange to you?"

"There was something, yes. This will be difficult for you to understand, perhaps. You must understand my position. I was responsible for getting him reelected. That's all that mattered in my life. I felt he wasn't being open with me for a long time. God, this is hard for me —

I hated what I had to do. It made me feel cheap, but there were certain things I had to know. I asked questions around. I was always there, at the White House I mean, and so I nosed around a lot. There were some people I made friends with. Some that cared for Clement as I did. We talked a little. I found out about his visitors."

"What visitors?"

"I don't know who they were. No official records were kept. I asked the servants and the staff and even his appointment secretary didn't know anything about them. They came through the security tunnel at night using a special ID card. I couldn't get descriptions. That's all I could find out. Somebody called them the Old Guard — something like that. One came in the morning, too. Almost every day, I think. I don't know who he was."

"What did he look like?"

"He was medium tall, Caucasian, middle-aged. From all accounts, not a handsome man."

"Do you still have contacts at the White House?"

"I don't even know if I have a job. Apparently not — Mr. Haas hasn't sent for me. I'm pretty sure I'm on the outbound track."

"But you still must have friends over there."

"Sure I do. Among the Lilliputians — the little people — clerks and secretaries."

"All right. Find out what you can. Get busy. I want to know who the strange visitors were. Get me some names."

"I'll do what I can. Do you think this strange behavior had anything to do with Clement's murder?"

"What do *you* think, Mr. LaVale?"

LaVale appeared thoughtful. "I guess it's possible."

"Damn right it's possible," Knebel said.

After LaVale had left, Ms. Pressman knocked softly and came in. "Mr. Knebel? Sorry to interrupt, but you said this was important. That profile you made up of the second assassin? They've found a woman who more or less fits, but she's been dead for three years."

She handed him the memorandum from the computer section. "Her name is Raba Hakim. She's French-Arab, born in Algeria. They're getting her complete file from Interpol."

"I want to see it as soon as it arrives," he said. "In the meantime, I want to talk to Omi Jamison."

"Might I remind you, sir, that the funeral was just today." Her lips formed a small accusing frown.

"Can't be helped," Knebel said.

TWENTY-NINE

Omi Jamison was staying at the Georgetown House. Knebel arrived at six-thirty in the evening. He parked his Ford pool car by the entrance to the stately mansion hotel. The doorman said he was expected and showed him to an elevator. A maid in a black-and-white uniform showed Knebel into a library. Ancient books lined the walls; the floors gleamed. He was asked to wait. He paced. A moment later Omi Jamison came in and offered him a seat. She was in black. Her ebony hair caressed her shoulders. He gave his personal condolences, which she accepted graciously.

"My husband was unkind to you, wasn't he, Mr. Knebel? He never mentioned it to me, but others have said so."

"Unkind? Not really. Personally, our relationship was always amicable."

She smiled pleasantly. "There were rumors that he had promised you a place on his cabinet and then had gone back on his word."

"Definitely not true."

"I'm very glad to hear that." She was sitting with her hands together on her lap.

Knebel said, "I'm sorry to have come here today. The funeral, I hope it wasn't too . . . difficult."

"These things one goes through with the spirit dull, Mr. Knebel. I was there, but it passed like a dream, a very awful dream. Perhaps later I will receive its impact."

"I wouldn't have come if it wasn't important."

"Anything I can help you with, please. I was interviewed by a very nervous agent — I think he was FBI — just after it happened. I can't even remember what we talked about. I do recall he kept looking away from me and was very nervous."

"You will have to forgive me if these questions seem blunt, but I've had reports that you and your husband were having marital problems — that some agreement had already been reached."

"Those rumors did get back to us. Clement and I discussed them and decided it best to ignore them."

"There was no truth to them?"

"None whatever."

"I see. Tell me, Mrs. Jamison, did your husband ever meet with people privately — meetings that weren't recorded by his appointment secretary?"

"There was no way for me to know. In political matters, my husband pretty much just did what he did. On Sunday he met with Jules LaVale very early in the morning. I don't know if it was a scheduled meeting or not, you would have to ask Mary Farrington; she kept his appointments. He and Jules did quarrel about something. Clement never discussed these things with me. I think he wanted me to be free of such burdens and to concentrate on being First Lady. Forgive me, Mr. Knebel, but how is this pertinent?"

"I'm not quite sure yet, I'm still trying to piece it together. Sometime around last Christmas—it's been alleged—your husband underwent some kind of personality changes. He began acting somewhat . . . strangely."

"I don't think I understand."

"Did you notice any changes in him, any changes at all?"

"No."

"Are you certain?"

"No changes whatever."

"Did he not have a sudden craving for soft drinks?"

"He drank them from time to time. After he became President he cut down on alcohol, to be perfectly honest. He thought it unseemly for a President to imbibe. I wouldn't call it a change in him exactly."

"Did the two of you ever discuss a divorce?"

"Never."

"Did your husband keep a diary?"

"Not that I knew of."

"Notes for his memoirs?"

"No. He detested politicians who tooted their own horns after they left office. He cared nothing for history, only what he could do for the people."

"Did you ever have legal representation apart from your husband?"

"No."

"Was your husband a diabetic?"

"No—why would you ask that?"

"Diabetics get thirsty for soft drinks."

"I'm afraid I'm not being much help. My husband prided himself on being in perfect health."

Knebel stood up. "Thank you, Mrs. Jamison. I'm

truly sorry to have disturbed you. I'm surprised in a way to find you moved out of the White House."

"John Haas wanted me out as soon as possible."

"Really?"

"John Haas is an ambitious, small-minded man, Mr. Knebel. Clement distrusted him. He had a pet name for him, which wasn't at all complementary."

"Can you recall it?"

"Is this confidential?"

"Absolutely."

She smiled. "Horseface. Horseface Haas."

They both laughed.

THIRTY

Harry's was a Mediterranean-style restaurant near the Capitol where the food was average and the service fair; the booths were private and the customers minded their own business. This night the place was nearly empty because the President had been buried that day and it was not considered an appropriate evening for dining out. The city was quiet. Stewart Ott ordered Manhattan clam chowder and a shrimp quiche. Richard Knebel had the Hearty Irish Stew, which he ate with slices of French bread spread thickly with butter. At first they talked only about organization problems and the problems with the computer which had them temporarily paralyzed.

"I never said it'd be a cinch," Ott said. "Just make your reports skillfully, your recommendations broad enough to be listened to. And a little honey never hurts." Ott tightened the knot of his bow tie. "You're in the limelight, Richard, and the people upstairs will want to catch a little of the reflected brilliance."

"It's not going all that well. There are a lot of conflicting stories and unanswered questions."

"I gathered as much. Haas seems satisfied and the

press thinks you're God Almighty. When you've got that going for you, you should count your blessings and be happy. . . . Word has it you called on Omi Jamison today."

"Yes."

"Bad timing, I think. The funeral being just today, I mean. You forget you're the director of a media event, you've got to orchestrate it like a pro."

"I've got to get to the bottom of things."

"Some things don't have a bottom."

"What was going on with Jamison?"

"What do you mean?"

"He supposedly had clandestine meetings with mysterious persons not booked through his appointment secretary. He called them his Old Guard."

"If he did, this is the first I've heard of it. Honest Injun. Domestic affairs is my bailiwick. When you have a nest, feather it, that's my philosophy. And stay the hell out of the other fella's. There was some cackling, but I ignored it. The White House gossip mill is ever busy."

"Gossip about what?"

"Nothing in particular. You can tell when things are happening. The generals stop smiling; they look grim and square-jawed. There was a real shocker coming, a lot of us could feel it. But it never came. The cloud passed."

"Who would know about it?"

"Jules, probably."

"He doesn't."

"I'm surprised to hear that."

"Would State know?"

"Old Mack? He wasn't in on it. He asked me about it. He was grumbling that Jamison didn't tell him beans.

Nope, whatever was in the hopper, Jamison didn't tell any of the regulars. He mistrusted them. Me, too, I guess. He was scheming on his own."

"About what?"

"I don't know, honest."

"You think Harrison Cheney might have been privy to it?"

"More than likely. Cheney had clammed onto the President like a barnacle. Remember the Hemisphere Brigade business? Cheney was its chief advocate. . . . You know Cheney?"

"By reputation."

"He's a Casper Milquetoast on the outside and a Kaiser Wilhelm on the inside."

"What caused the rift between him and Jamison?"

"Don't know. Jamison thought he was Jesus Christ for a while, but he lost faith in him all of a sudden. Jamison was close mouthed about a lot of things, Richard."

"Okay, did you know Jamison was getting a divorce?"

"You're not serious?"

"You didn't know?"

"I don't believe it."

"I'm pretty sure."

"Did you ask Omi?"

"Yes."

"What did she say?"

"She denied it."

"I dined with them maybe a twice a week. If they were on the outs, it never showed. A more loving couple I never knew. He was absolutely wild about her."

"Did Jamison go through a change around Christmas time last year?"

"I was in the hospital with a wild and wooly gall bladder around then."

"Before that, did he seem peculiar in any way?"

"He was under a hell of a strain. Who wouldn't buckle a little?"

"You thought he was buckling?"

He paused and poked at his quiche with his knife. "Maybe. He wasn't Superman. He was inflamed about the Soviets. If you listened to Clement Jamison, he'd have you believing the Soviets were the authors of all the world's sorrows, miseries, and political vicissitudes. Clement came out of that, though. The last couple of months he was A-okay. He was the Clement Jamison we all knew, loved, respected, admired, and slaved for."

"Was he drinking a lot of soft drinks for a time?"

"Once in a while. He was off the booze. . . . What the hell are you after, Richard?"

"He was killed for a reason, Stewart. I want to know what that reason was."

"A nut doesn't have to have a reason."

"These were pros. And somebody paid them or somebody ordered them. And that somebody had to have a motive."

Stewart Ott shrugged and went back to eating. They finished their meal without talking except about the food, the service, and the good quality wine.

After the dinner Knebel paid the bill. They went outside. It was cool and quiet; they walked together across the street to the parking lot.

"How's it going with the lamb?" Knebel said.

"Haas? We thought he was a lamb because of the wool all over him. He's peeling it off a little at a time."

"What's underneath?"

"The usual. Wolf."

THIRTY-ONE

It was ten A.M. Knebel was on time for his appointment. He rang the bell; an Indonesian houseboy opened the door.

"Richard Knebel. I phoned earlier."

The boy bowed and invited him in with a sweep of his arm. A massive, muscular black man wearing a white shirt and tie stepped out of the kitchen. He was eating a piece of toast and wearing two matching shoulder holsters packed with large walnut-gripped revolvers.

"Mr. Knebel is expected, Benny," the houseboy said to him.

Benny smiled politely. One of his incisors was missing. "Are you armed, Mr. Knebel?"

"No."

"Welcome."

Knebel followed the houseboy down a hallway to the living room. Coming in out of the morning sun, his eyes had to adjust to the dimmer interior. The townhouse was in the Wilmington suburbs. It was crammed with early American antiques; the walls were covered with artwork, old paintings, and tintypes in gilded frames.

Harrison Cheney rose to greet him. Cheney was a

small man with a round, cherubic face and pale blue eyes. Knebel guessed he was nearly seventy. He seemed nervous; his eyes darted.

"A great pleasure and an honor, sir," Cheney said, shaking Knebel's hand. His hand was as small as a child's, but strong as a lumberjack's.

"Coffee, tea? What can we get for you, Mr. Knebel?"

"Nothing, thanks."

Cheney dismissed the houseboy with a gesture.

"Well, then, Mr. Knebel. You said you had some questions. How can I help you? You know, I hadn't seen President Jamison in, well, half a year."

"You resigned your office last December the fourteenth."

"Then I stand corrected. It has been somewhat less than half a year. Let's be accurate."

"You stated publicly the reason for your leaving was your health."

"Correct."

"Was there a private reason as well?"

"No, I needed the rest. Jamison drove his staff hard at times. As Foreign Affairs Advisor, I spent many sleepless nights, believe me. When he wanted a detailed analysis of a crisis, he wanted it right *now*."

"Isn't it true you and Clement Jamison had a policy disagreement?"

"We had many policy disagreements. I was not a yes man, and Clement Jamison had some very strong notions of his own. He was a man who could tolerate dissent. In fact he invited it."

"You resigned over the Hemisphere Brigade, isn't that right?"

He shook his head. "I don't know where you're getting

183

your information—it's patently not true, not true. My resignation came because, frankly, I was, well, getting run down. Yes. At my age, you're much too old for the demands and responsibilities of a job as demanding as that one. I don't know how Ronald Reagan ever managed the Presidency."

"Did you know Jamison was seeing visitors secretly at night?"

"No—was he?"

"Have you ever heard of a group called the Old Guard? Or something like it?"

"No. 'Old Guard,' did you say? No."

"Did Clement Jamison seem to be going through a personality change sometime last summer?"

He thought for a moment, then shook his head. "He was moody sometimes."

"Did you know he was having marital problems?"

"Was he? He never mentioned them to me. Personally, we weren't all that close."

"Would you say Mr. Jamison had 'low' energy at about the time you resigned?"

"Not at all."

"Would you describe him as having changed a great deal? Someone described it as having 'lost his soul.'"

"No. Absolutely not."

"Why did he hate the Russians so?"

"Because of their spreading their disgusting revolution, I suppose."

Knebel stood up. "Thank you for the time, Mr. Cheney."

"Could you tell me, Mr. Knebel, just what it is you're trying to get at? Your questions are most curious."

"It's beginning to look like I'm barking up the wrong tree."

Cheney smiled. "If you have any more questions, you come on out any time. I don't get many visitors."

"Thank you, sir."

The houseboy opened the front door; the sunlight flooded in.

"It certainly would be nice if they catch this Smith person soon," Cheney said with a heavy sigh.

"Indeed."

When Knebel got to his office he called Chad Priest on the phone.

"Yes, Mr. Knebel."

"I want Harrison Cheney put under surveillance — phone tap, eavesdrop, the whole forty miles.

"The Director might not go along without a powerful reason, Mr. Knebel."

"Then don't tell the Director. I'm working directly for the President and I want it done. That's all the authority you need. See to it, Chad."

"Yes, sir."

THIRTY-TWO

The barber stood in the doorway of his shop and watched the two policemen get out of the car. It was a clear day, breezy, the temperature in the mid-fifties. The two officers were young, both six-footers, both broad shouldered. One had a mustache and wore sergeant's stripes. He said his name was Yerkies and his partner was Patrolman Harry Green. Green smiled and touched the brim of his hat.

"What kept you?" the barber said. "I phoned maybe an hour ago." The barber was bald and sixty, small and slight. He backed into his shop and the two officers followed him.

"What's the problem?" Yerkies said.

The barber looked around as if worried about being overheard. Then he said, "That guy—Smith—that guy on TV, the one who bought the guns that got the President. I seen him. Honest to Christ, I seen him not three hours ago."

Yerkies glanced at Green, skeptical.

"Could I have your full name, sir?" Yerkies said.

"Charlie Henderpoole. Charles R. It's an English name, but I'm three-quarters Dutch. H-E-N-D-E-R-

P-O-O-L-E. Most people don't put the 'E' on the end.
. . . When you were late coming I figured you'd figure I
was nuts. I almost didn't call you."

"We'll check it out, Mr. Henderpoole. Where was
this?"

"On the beach."

Green was leafing through a magazine while Yerkies
asked the questions. The barber continued: "It was
about eight-thirty—maybe nine—this morning. I jog.
Me and the dog. I was out there on the jetty. They got a
few summer homes out there. You know, the dunes.
Most of them are boarded up this time of year. It was
windy this morning and misting a little. I sometimes
run between the dunes. All of a sudden there he was
right in front of me. I stopped dead in my tracks. All the
time I run out there and there ain't nobody except in the
summer. Then this morning, there he was. I had no idea
who he was or what the hell he was doing there."

"What time did you say this was?"

"Eight-thirty, a little after."

"Then what happened?"

"Nothing *happened*. He was just standing there. He
saw me and turned away—I guess so I couldn't see his
face."

"But you did see his face."

"Sure I saw his face. How the hell could I identify him
if I didn't see his face? I thought maybe it was him, but
then as I drove back here I wasn't so sure. I called the
wife and she thought maybe because I'd seen his picture
so many times in the paper, maybe it was my imagination. Hey, I didn't want to bother you guys for nothing.
So then, maybe an hour and a half ago, I have this cus-
tomer in here, Willy Fremont. Either of you know

Willy? He's been just sour since it happened. The killing of Jamison, I mean. Anyway, Willy was here and we have the set on. I don't watch it myself, I think those rays it sends out make you go, you know, limp. Maybe not, but why take the chance? So anyway, they have this guy Smith's picture on and I look real close. Then I'm sure. I'm sure it was him, and it wasn't no imagination. So I call you guys. I get home, I'm telling Elsie — that's the wife — she should maybe keep her mouth shut when she don't know what she's talking about."

"Did you see anyone else?"

"No."

"A car, anything like that?"

"No."

"Which of those two houses was he staying in — any idea?"

"No."

"Okay — we'll check it out."

Green said, "You want to see a bunny that *is* a bunny?" He held the magazine lengthwise.

Yerkies glanced at it and said, "Let's get going."

"Mind if I borrow this?" Green said to the barber.

"I have those for the customers."

"I'll bring it right back."

"Come get your hair cut — five-fifty — and you can read the magazines free."

Green scowled and dropped the magazine on a chair.

In the car, Yerkies and Green headed southwest toward the beach.

"This is nuts," Green said. "How many phony reports we get so far?"

"Why count them? You've got to check them all anyway, so why count them?"

"Let's get some coffee."

"After we check out the dunes."

"This is a lot of crap. Probably some old bum. They get a lot of bums out there looking for a place to sack out. Let's run a rubber."

"A barber ought to know faces — heads, anyway. That's what I'm thinking."

"Okay, Yerkies, you're the honcho. I still say it's a waste of gas."

They pulled out onto the road that went along the beach and passed the dunes. The road was in poor repair. The wind was stiff, the sky was gray; and the sea churned with whitecaps and the heavy surf roared in. The beach houses were closed up and dismal and at the end of the road was the old Coverman mansion, and it, too, was closed and boarded up. They looked for car tracks and footprints but found nothing except along the beach where two men had been fishing earlier. They stopped the car at the end of the road, where the Hamptontown Inlet began. There was a crumbling cement sea wall and the piles of a pier that had vanished in a long-ago hurricane.

"If you wanted to hide, this would be a damn good place." Yerkies said. "Any one of the cottages would be good. Nobody ever comes out here."

"What's with you, man? Monday the watch had sixty bogus calls about this Adolf White character. We've had how many already about this Smith? Twenty? The Federal boys have had a million — Christ."

"I'm going to have a look around. You stay in the car."

Green waited twenty-six minutes. It seemed more like three hours. He got out of the car and called for Yerkies, but his voice was lost in the wind. He walked a little down the road toward the main cluster of four cottages and called again, listened, and heard nothing. He went back to the car. There was the usual chatter on the police band. After a few minutes he unlocked the shotgun which was mounted to the dash, put it across his lap, and opened the breech. It was loaded. He got out of the car and started down the road with the shotgun at the ready.

He moved slowly at first and followed his partner's footprints in the sand on the road. The wind was not as strong now, but the surf was high and his voice didn't carry. Yerkies footprints circled a dune and then a cottage. There was a loose board on one of the windows, but the window had not been opened and it was nothing. The footprints continued and Green followed them. It was quiet, except for the surf.

There was a long stretch where the wind had funneled through the cottages and he lost the trail of footprints, but picked them up again further down the road. They circled a second cottage. There was a second set of footprints here too, off to one side. Green pressed the safety into "off" position. He stopped close to the house and listened. There was nothing. A sea bird was squawking someplace. He moved forward, turning the corner of the house. He hugged the side of the building and inched his way to the back, where he leaned around the corner to get a look. There was Yerkies. He was standing on a wooden patio near a brick barbecue pit; there was a young man with him. Green paused for a moment to relax and breathe easily. The young man had a pack on his back and long hair. Yerkies checked his identification and handed it back to him. The young man jogged off.

Green said, "Who was that?"

"Some kid from Maine off to see the world. He's been camping out here."

"He's not the one the barber saw."

"No chance . . . You were going to wait in the car, remember?" Yerkies started walking back toward the road and Green went with him.

"I thought you might be getting lonely," Green said. "Is that why you brought Betsy along?" He was referring to the shotgun.

"You never know," Green said.

"The kid did say he saw somebody here this morning. Didn't get a good look at him. Said he was pulling some weeds behind him, maybe to block out his tracks."

They walked between two cottages and down the road, where Yerkies stopped and looked around. "Maybe we ought to check this whole place out if we get the time."

"That'll take a hell of a lot of time, Yerkies."

"The watch commander has keys to all these places. We're supposed to check them out from time to time anyway. We'll get the keys and make a run through them—what the hell."

"Christ, Yerkies, what is it with you? Life's too short for spinning your wheels. So some tramp's been hanging around for Chrissake, so what?"

"I'm just thinking tramps don't try to cover up their tracks. What the hell for? We bust them, they get a nice thirty days at the county's expense."

They radioed in to the station. There were two hot domestic dispute calls waiting. They locked the shotgun back into the rack and drove quickly back down the jetty with their red light flashing.

From the second story of one of the small houses in the middle of the long row, Chandler Smith watched them go.

THIRTY-THREE

He had been watching with field glasses through a crack in the shutters. When they left he took his hand off his automatic and went back downstairs. It was dark in the house and cold. He lay down on the couch and put covers over himself to keep warm. He could not risk a fire until dark.

He wondered whether they would be back and figured it did no good to wonder. They either would be or wouldn't be. If they did come back, he would deal with them. He had a tiny pocket radio and an ear receiver. He listened to the news. They were talking about the massive manhunt for him and the dozens of theories and leads. Most commentators called him a psychotic killer, a rogue CIA agent, a turncoat. Speculations about conspiracies abounded. He turned it off. He closed his eyes and dozed off until four-thirty. He awoke with a start when he heard the police car coming back.

He went back upstairs and looked out. It was still gray and overcast, and the sea was calm. The wind had died down. The sun was hidden. The patrol car moved past him down to the end of the jetty and stopped at the mansion. He watched as one of them went up the stairs to the front door. He had a large key ring in his hand and it took him a couple of minutes to find the right key. He let himself in. The second officer stayed outside holding a shotgun and leaning against the car. It was obvious they intended to make a house-to-house search.

If they would go slowly it would be dark before they got to the end of the jetty and then he could slip away unseen in a small rowboat he had hidden in the rushes behind the house. If only they would take their time there would be no killing. He watched them closely. The mansion would probably take them the longest. He timed them. It took twelve minutes and then they moved on to the house next to the mansion: moved one house closer. There were eight small cottages now between them. If they took ten minutes each it would perhaps be dark enough to slip away.

He went downstairs and packed his things. He had a few shirts and a poncho, wigs and makeup kit for disguises, a razor, and some underwear and socks. That was it. He would wear his coat.

Opening a can of stew with his knife, he ate hurriedly, then went back upstairs and looked again through the opening in the window. They had moved two houses closer. The sun, now visible, was half submerged in the sea. The gray sky in the east was turning black, but the overhead grayness would last for forty minutes or more and that would make it close. He would have to get them before they could call for help, he thought. That was the important thing. He watched them closely now and timed them. They were moving more quickly through the houses. They were two houses away. One had a mustache and was a sergeant. He carried the shotgun and stood by the car. He was serious about the business. The other went through the houses in a great hurry. He shouted that things were clear as he went from room to room. The one outside held the microphone to the radio in his hand and kept talking into it. After a few moments they moved to the small house next door. There were probably only three or four rooms to check and it would not take them long.

Chandler Smith moved to the back of the house and looked out. It was almost completely dark. Perhaps it was dark enough. He thought about leaving for a moment, but decided against it. The risk would be unacceptable. He heard the car start, which meant they were moving again. He would have to work quietly now, quietly and quickly to get the thing done.

He went back into the living room. It was pitch-dark inside, and quiet. The car was in front of the house. They had switched off the engine, but he could hear the crackling of the radio. He took out his small jackknife and cut two curtain cords and tied them together, then twisted them and made a loop for a garrote. Picking up his bag, he headed up the stairs, keeping to the sides of the steps so as not to make them creak. At the top of the stairs he stepped into the bedroom and waited.

It was quiet for a moment except for the sea birds cawing. Quiet and still. The police radio crackled, then a moment later he could hear the two policemen talking, laughing, and in another moment there were footsteps on the porch. Another sound: keys jangling on the ring. Then the door squeaked open. Suddenly light flashed on the stairway; footsteps came inside.

"Living room clear!"

Chandler Smith listened. There was movement in the kitchen; closet doors opened and closed, cabinets opened and closed.

"Downstairs clear."

Chandler Smith barely heard the reply. It sounded as if the one outside was telling his partner to hustle.

The patrolman started up the stairs mumbling to himself, the light from his flashlight bouncing in front of him. Chandler Smith held his breath. He stood perfectly still, his garrote held in front of him, the ends wrapped tightly around his clenched fists. A garrote, to work, required surprise and speed. It would choke off the blood supply and cause unconsciousness in less than a second, before all but the quickest could react. If it was not done properly, if the victim dropped his chin or got his hand between the cord and his neck, he could stay conscious long enough to struggle, perhaps to strike back, to call out.

At the top of the stairs, the patrolman paused and got his breath. He shined his light around. He stepped forward and turned to check the first bedroom, complaining and cursing under his breath. The rope slipped over his head like a wisp of air and Chandler Smith jerked the ends, snapping the officer's head to one side, breaking a bone in his neck. The flashlight flew into the air, his body stiffened but for a moment, then sagged forward and sprawled onto the floor. Chandler Smith knew he was dead. He checked his pulse to be sure and there was none. He pulled the revolver out of the patrolman's holster. It was a well-oiled Smith and Wesson .38. He would use it rather than his automatic on the other one. He picked up the flashlight too and went downstairs. The front door was open. He waved the flashlight around so the one by the car would think his partner was still looking around.

The sergeant called for his partner to report.

Chandler Smith looked out the window through a crack in the closed shutter. It was very dark outside and the sea birds were cawing noisily. The wind was beginning to rustle through the tall grass that grew beside the house. Chandler Smith watched him by the car, his silhouette outlined against the last trickle of orange of the sun. He was talking on the radio. Chandler Smith didn't want to fire while he was talking. Finally he put down the microphone and took up the shotgun. Chandler Smith took a bead on him, but it wasn't a good one. The angle was bad and the man was pacing around, calling for his partner, getting impatient. Perhaps in a moment he would become suspicious. Chandler Smith moved toward the front door, carrying the flashlight. He stood in the doorway and flashed the light in the direction of the police car and then held it on the sergeant.

"Knock it off, Green," he said, covering his eyes with his arm.

It was then that Chandler Smith shot him twice in the chest, and as the bullets spun him around, he shot him twice more, driving him back against the car. He sank slowly to the ground like a half-empty sack of grain.

Chandler Smith waited in the doorway, waited and listened, and when he heard nothing and saw nothing he went outside and checked. He was dead. The police band crackled with voices, but no one was giving an alarm. Across the inlet he could see the lights of Hamptontown. He went back into the house and took the coat and hat of the young officer. Then he gathered up his things and put them in the police car and got into the driver's seat. He put on the young officer's coat and hat. He looked once again toward the town and could hear no sirens. No cars moved toward him on the jetty road. He looked to the black sea and the rising moon in the southeast. He knew there would be no more killing at least for the present, and he was glad. He started the engine and drove back down the jetty and turned onto the country road that would take him back to Hampton-town. There he noticed a young woman getting into her Volkswagen. She had been walking a small dog and was fighting with the animal, trying to get it to stay in the back seat. Chandler Smith stopped the police car behind hers. He got out and walked up to her car. She turned and looked at him. "Yes?"

"Just get in the car," he said. "I'll drive."

THIRTY-FOUR

At nine-thirty the following morning Hans Ober phoned Richard Knebel.

"We've got a confirmed location on Smith," Ober said excitedly. "New York. He killed a couple of police officers last night and took a hostage, Mary Ellen Sawyer of Hamptontown, Connecticut. He let her go not twenty minutes ago in Manhattan. We've got a chopper going to short-hop us up there, Richard. Want to come along?"

"No thanks."

"We'll get him, okay? If not today, tomorrow. We'll get him soon, believe me." He hung up.

Knebel looked across his desk to Dr. Franklin Cullen Crist. "Very sorry for the interruption," Knebel said.

The doctor gestured it was nothing with a wave of his hand. "I just hope they capture that mad dog soon." He smoothed out his hair with the palms of his hands. Dr. Franklin Cullen Crist was a high-born Virginian. He had jet-black eyes and smooth manners; he sat stiff and erect in his chair. "Let's see, I believe you were asking about the needle marks on the President's body? Yes, there were fifty or more, I think I said. So many it was difficult to count them."

"And what was their significance?" Knebel said.

"None that I know of."

Knebel stroked his beard and looked dully at the doctor for a moment, then asked: "To your knowledge, was the President a diabetic?"

"I've never heard that he was."

"Could he have been a diabetic?"

Dr. Crist tilted his head to the right and ran his finger around his right ear. "I don't mean to seem contrary," he said, "but I'm a medical examiner, not the President's physician of record. I performed an autopsy to determine the cause of death. The President was killed as an effect of severe trauma resulting from being struck by numerous bullets fired from very close range. There was no reason for me to care particularly about some ancient needle marks."

"Still, do you know if he was diabetic?"

"I have no direct knowledge one way or the other. Most diabetics inject themselves. It is not likely a man would inject himself in the buttock. He would have to be nimble indeed."

"Could you speculate then on what these marks might have been?"

"Perhaps he had a series of innoculations, perhaps for allergies or weight loss. Millions of people receive such injections for a myriad of complaints."

"You weren't curious?"

"No." He fixed a filtered cigarette into a short black holder and lit it with a gold lighter.

"You said there was no sign of pathology."

"I said there was no sign of *drug* pathology."

"But there were signs of some other pathology?"

"Mr. Knebel, as you know, I was assisted throughout by Doctor Amil Risson, who's reported to be the best forensic pathologist on the East Coast. He didn't think anything of those marks or the variant histology of the liver tissues. The President could have been recovering from the flu or a fever; it will sometimes leave lingering discoloration of the liver. It could be residual hepatitis effects. Or even malaria. Most of our cases have some anomalies and we don't do anything about them. The man died from multiple gunshot wounds—his brains were literally expelled from his cranium. The bullets and only the bullets were the direct—and indirect—cause of death."

"Did you, by chance, consult with his physician and check his medical records?"

"No, sir. Nor did we do so for the other victims. It is not procedure. Anyway, the President's doctor of record was Lamont Belzar as far as I know. Dr. Belzar committed suicide last November, I think it was. He jumped from the top of the McLearn Building in downtown Washington. I suggest you subpoena his records if you're curious. My job was to find the cause of death and he died from the bullets, believe me."

After Dr. Crist left, Knebel made a phone call to the number listed in the directory for Dr. Lamont Belzar. A woman answered.

"Dr. Hagarty's office."

"Has Dr. Hagarty taken over the practice of Dr. Lamont Belzar?"

"Were you one of Dr. Belzar's patients?"

"No, but I'd like to check the records of Clement Jamison, who was Dr. Belzar's patient."

There was a pause. "Perhaps I should have you talk to

Dr. Hagarty."

A moment later a man's voice came on the line. "This is Dr. Hagarty. May I help you?"

"I'm Richard Knebel, Doctor. I'm looking into the Presidential assassination and for our files I would like to have the President's medical records. Would I require a warrant? I'm sure I can procure one."

"I'd be happy to show you Dr. Belzar's records, Mr. Knebel, but President Jamison's file is not among them. I've looked for it everywhere — even at Belzar's house."

"Where are the records now?"

"Here at the office."

"I'll be right there."

Twenty minutes later Knebel was in his office. It was plush and spacious, thickly carpeted. Knebel spoke to Dr. Hagarty in his private office. There were white cabinets in the room and an EKG machine. The doctor was middle-aged and intellectual, gaunt, and gray-haired.

"Isn't it odd," Knebel asked him, "that there would be no record?"

"Yes it is. If you'd care to look through the files yourself, please feel free. I've got twelve hundred forty files of Belzar's, but not the President's. I even asked a former nurse of his. She said she never saw them. There are billing records for the President, though. Those records are most complete.

"Did Dr. Belzar see the President often?"

"Yes, according to the bills, very often."

"Tell me about the suicide. Did you know Dr. Belzar well?"

"Yes. No one who knew him was surprised. The war got him. Vietnam. It did something to his mind. He was never the same after Vietnam. His practice wasn't much because he didn't apply himself. He was a competent professional, but things were eating at him. No one ever knew what, exactly. He was a very private person. It was obvious his health was failing. He lost weight and would cry sometimes, just like that, out of the blue. I know the VA tried to help him, but what can you do? The President was his friend, and even that didn't help much. Lamont could have had so many patients. Everyone wants to be treated by the man who treats the President. But Lamont just threw away the opportunity. And then he threw away his life."

"Did he leave a suicide note?"

"No, no he didn't. It happened at night. About eight-fifteen in the evening. Around Thanksgiving. He was here, alone, apparently. Depressed. Possibly he was on drugs. Doctors aren't immune, you know. He went to the top of the building here and that was it. No note, no good-byes, no nothing. The police investigated. The coroner's inquest concluded there was no evidence of foul play."

"Did he have a family? Someone he was living with?"

"No, he lived alone."

"What was his financial position?"

"Apparently okay. He had a great deal of money just sitting in the bank."

"Who got his estate?"

"The District of Columbia. No will. No living relatives."

"Could I see the records?"

"Certainly."

Knebel went through the records quickly in the waiting room while the doctor saw his patients. By one o'clock Knebel was finished. Dr. Hagarty came out of an examining room, put on a sport coat, and was ready for lunch.

"Find anything?" the doctor asked.

"Yes. There is a woman here, M. Quesenbury. Note the height and weight. I think Mrs. Quesenbury is a pseudonym for the President. I think Belzar changed the name to protect the President."

"I remember trying to contact this woman. She didn't have a phone. We sent her a letter and it was returned marked 'addressee unknown.' I never linked her file to Jamison. I never even thought about it."

"You'll notice that her supposed visits compare exactly to the President's billing."

He glanced at the records. He blushed with embarrassment.

"I see that, yes. What was he treating her for?"

"Diabetes."

The doctor was still looking at the file. "Blood pressure wasn't all that great either."

Knebel called Omi Jamison, who was reluctant, but said she'd see him. He told her it was important.

On his way to Georgetown he stopped at a small restaurant and had a crabmeat sandwich and a glass of German beer. He bought some toffee peanuts to eat in the car.

At the Georgetown house he found he was a few minutes early. He sat in the lobby and waited, then went to the desk and asked for Mrs. Jamison. The clerk made a call upstairs. A few minutes later a matronly woman appeared wearing a tweed sport coat. She said her name was Miss Marsden, Mrs. Jamison's secretary. If Knebel would tell her his business, she said, she would do her best to help him.

204

"When I phoned, I said I wanted to see Mrs. Jamison."

"Mrs. Jamison is very tired. Please try to understand."

"I'll try to be as brief as I can."

Miss Marsden took him up in the elevator and he was shown to the small den where he had been two days before. Omi Jamison came in a moment later. She was dressed in an elegant yellow housecoat with a dragon embroidered on it and didn't appear tired in the least.

"I hope you don't think I'm being rude or ungrateful, Mr. Knebel." She offered him her hand, then invited him to sit down. "I am very busy. My mind has been a blank. How can I help you? Please—let me answer all of your questions now because I'm leaving tomorrow on a kind of a retreat."

"I'm here about the diabetes again."

"Oh?"

"You lied to me the other day."

"I did?"

"You knew perfectly well your husband was a diabetic."

She stared blankly for a moment and then she sighed. Her eyes smiled at him. "It was a little fib. What possible difference could it make?"

"Don't know. Unless I have the whole picture, I don't know what any part of the picture means."

"It didn't have anything to do with his being assassinated, believe me. My husband didn't want anyone to know about it. Could not his intentions be honored in his death? It was all completely legal and aboveboard. He had sugar diabetes. He found out about it perhaps a year ago."

"Why the secrecy?"

She brushed aside a lock of hair from her eyes. "My husband was very vain. Exceedingly so. He thought it unmanly for him to require a medicine. Also—and perhaps because of his vanity—he hated to give himself shots. Dr. Belzar came every morning through the tunnel and gave him an injection. Every morning for months. Until his suicide."

"And then?"

She lit a cigarette and inhaled the smoke deeply. "My husband was the President," she said, "but in some things he was foolish. He felt sorry for Belzar. He had known him in Saigon. Personally, I found Belzar to be a horrible, weird little man. It is a great irony, but after Belzar's suicide my husband sought other medical attention from a doctor he knew at his club, Dr. Samuelson—who, as I'm sure you know, was killed along with my husband. Dr. Samuelson treated Clement with diet and pills and he didn't have to take shots any longer. If you contact Dr. Samuelson's nurse, I'm sure you'll find her very cooperative."

"What about the divorce, Mrs. Jamison?"

"Our personal relationship is not for public scrutiny, Mr. Knebel. There was no truth in the rumors."

"I don't believe that, Mrs. Jamison."

"You may believe what you wish."

"Did Clement Jamison undergo some kind of personality change—a change of any kind? Even attitude?"

She thought for a moment. She looked at him and her mouth puckered slightly. "Perhaps he did. . . ."

In what way?"

"He was—I don't know . . . How could this be important?"

"There is no way of telling. It may be very important."

"My husband was always a very determined man, Mr. Knebel. Very self-assured and self-possessed. But there was a short time when he seemed most unsure and withdrawn. Then he pulled out of it. I think Mr. Cheney helped him get back on track."

"When was this, Mrs. Jamison?"

"Perhaps six months ago."

"He and Cheney had a falling out. Do you know what it was about?"

"No idea."

"How did Cheney help him get back on track?"

"By just being a good friend, I suppose."

"That's all?"

"Listen, Mr. Knebel. The Presidency is a terrible burden. Clement didn't have the simple-mindedness of a Reagan or the simple Christian morality of a Carter to get him through. He fought his way to the top and he fought with himself to stay there. It was damned tough on him. . . . I've told you all I can. The skeletons are out of the closet—at least those I'm willing to let out." She stood up suddenly. "Will that be all, Mr. Knebel?"

"For now," he said.

Knebel phoned Chad Priest from his car phone as he drove back to Washington.

"Chad, I need a couple of good men."

"Sure."

"Jamison's doctor, Lamont Belzar, committed suicide last November. I want to know the why's and wherefore's. Tell them to dig deep."

"No problem."

"I'd also like to see Dr. Samuelson's records on Jamison."

207

"No problem there either."

"How's Ober doing in New York?"

"Haven't spoken to him, but the New York police say Chandler Smith will be in custody by nightfall. They've sealed lower Manhattan tight as a time capsule."

"Wish them luck. Smith's playing games with them, I think. . . . Has Lowenstein checked in?"

"Special Agent Byron cabled from Paris. The French police grilled Mme. Rousseau for two days and they think she told all she knew, which was nothing. Some of our embassy people were there. They're satisfied."

"What's Lowenstein think?"

"He still wants to talk to her."

"See to it it's arranged."

"Okay, Mr. Knebel."

THIRTY-FIVE

There was a strong warm breeze from the south and the smell of spring and flowers was in the air. The Paris streets were clogged with cars and the sidewalks were crowded. Fine women in short skirts were everywhere. Lowenstein was surprised to see skyscrapers in the La Défense section. He wanted to see one of the pissers he had heard so much about, but didn't care about the rest of it. Walter Byron had spent time in Paris and knew the landmarks. He pointed out the Hôtel des Invalides to Lowenstein. "Napoleon is entombed there," he said.

"Good place as any," Lowenstein said, without interest.

The embassy man who drove the Ford Escorte was a clerkish, bald little man, curt and formal, who muttered to himself incessantly. The streets were narrow, crooked, bumpy; and the drivers seemed mad to Lowenstein. There was much fist-shaking and shouting and horns were blowing constantly. They made their way to the Belleville section, north of the Seine. Here there were more hills and the homes were larger and surrounded by walls and wrought-iron fences and hedges. Ville Rousseau was a large stucco-and-brick mansion surrounded by a wall. The driver stopped in front and let them out.

Walter Byron and Lowenstein knocked on the door. The embassy man stayed in the car with a book to read. There were birds eating out of a bird feeder near the door. A stiff, cold-eyed butler let them in. He led them through a massive living room filled with ornate furniture to a patio and down some steps to a garden. The flowers were blooming. Mme. Rousseau was waiting for them. She was a stately woman, wearing a tweed pantsuit, and her hair was short and blond. She was slender with high cheekbones and a thin, elegant nose. She extended her hand to both of them, first to Lowenstein and then to Byron.

"I know this must be painful for you," Lowenstein said. "We are grateful."

"Indeed," Byron said with a polite bow.

She turned and started walking down a paved path and they went with her. "There were others before you," she said. Her English was impeccable, her accent barely noticeable. "I told them everything that I knew about Chandler. I know nothing more."

"Perhaps they asked the wrong questions," Lowenstein said.

"Perhaps."

"May I ask you something personal?"

"As long as I may choose not to answer it."

"Why did you agree to see us? I know our embassy people pressured you, but you still could have refused."

"I thought about it for a long time after your embassy people called. You know, my country demanded that I tell all to a whole group of inquisitors. I resisted them and they pressured me. I grew weary and eventually I

210

told them. I don't think it meant anything. I don't know anything about the assassination. What could I tell them? This has been the worst week of my life. More terrible even than my husband's death . . . They were all men with tiny eyes and they squinted. Pale men with voices like . . . like iron heels on cement. But your embassy assured me that you worked for this Richard Knebel directly. He has great fame in France because of the Girard killing. You are his man? True or not?"

"True."

"I wanted to speak with you. I have the newspapers and the television which say nothing. I was hoping you could tell me more."

"What, for instance?"

"Did you know him? Chandler, I mean. You were never CIA?"

Lowenstein shook his head. "I am a former detective. Once, perhaps, a very good one. They called me as a consultant. So far, I have not consulted very much."

"Chandler, did he really kill the American President?"

"I would be lying to you if I told you no. I think so, but I don't know for certain."

"I think he did," she said. "In my heart, I know he did." They had come to an iron bench. She sat down on it. Lowenstein and Byron remained standing.

"There is speculation he may already be dead," she said. "What do you think? Be candid."

"I am sure he isn't," Lowenstein said.

"He was seen yesterday," Byron said. "Positively identified."

"I heard. In New York. He may have killed two policemen."

"Yes," Byron said.

211

"It is too terrible. Tell me . . . is it possible he can survive? Do not deceive me."

"He is a trained agent," Lowenstein said. "You have every reason to hope."

"When they catch him he will fight. I know that. . . . I told him I hated him and I never wanted to see him again. But it is not true. I love him and every waking moment I long for him. . . . Will you — will they — kill him deliberately if you find him?" She was resigned to the fact and it showed on her drawn face.

"I don't know," Lowenstein said.

"It is better that he die than go to prison," she said. "They will never give him rest until they have killed him. Let me tell you, he would not have killed the President unless his superiors told him to. I have read the American papers. It is not possible he would do anything his superiors did not approve, believe me."

"He did refuse to make use of your friendship," Lowenstein said.

"It was the line he drew. Still, it was hard for him. He was very dedicated."

"Tell me, madam," Lowenstein said, "when did you first find out he was with the CIA and was not just the embassy employee he pretended to be?"

"The whole story needs telling. . . . My husband was an aloof man, aristocratic, domineering. He loved three things: power, position, wealth. When we married I was very young. He seemed perfect to me. My imagination was active and I thought the man I was marrying had something behind the shell he always seemed to be wearing. A prince, that is what I thought. A prince who would sweep me away from all the troubles of everyday life to a grand castle — the childish dreaming of a young and foolish girl. The reality was darker." She got up and resumed strolling. "He treated me well, but coldly. I honored him and obeyed him, and I never did anything to disgrace him. For seventeen years, I did my duty. Then a terrible thing happened. I say terrible, because at first it *was* terrible. Terrible and wonderful. It was at a dinner party given by the Belgian Ambassador. I met Chandler Smith. Right from the first he stirred something in me — a warm place I thought had long ago gone cold. . . . He had just come back from Algeria, and was brown and full of life. We walked in the garden — a garden such as this — and we talked of silly little things: the restaurants of Lyons, the flowers in the garden of Petrice. Amidst flowers and at the seashore were our favorite places to be. He told me that he lunched every day while he was in Paris at a little restaurant on the Rue de la Carmogne and I agreed to meet him there. My heart was talking, not my — you say, I think — common sense.

"I did not go to the restaurant for a very long time. At home I fretted like a schoolgirl with a crush. He had intriguing eyes that fell upon me like — I don't know — a warm sun. Part of me scolded the other part: it was wrong for the wife of the cultural minister to have such feelings. I stayed away from the restaurant. I turned my back on myself for a long time. Finally, I could not help it. I had to know. I pretended I had forgotten he had told me to meet him there, but I think he knew I was fibbing.

"He was a wonderful man, Chandler was. Courteous and respectful. We met — I don't know how often — dozens of times? Hundreds? They all swirl around in my head. The wine became sweeter. Days, brighter. I was like a giddy young girl. It pained him to love me . . . and believe it or not, he never once even suggested that we meet alone somewhere where we might be intimate. No, that was for me to suggest. In Paris, love is everywhere in the spring. It was early spring then.

"I had some money that I had put away years before and let grow at interest, never knowing what I might do with it. Occasionally I drew some of it out for a surprise for my husband, a tiepin once, a gold watch five years ago. He never asked where I got the money, nor do I think he cared. I called it my happiness money. . . . This all seems a century ago.

"I rented a flat with my happiness money, overlooking the West Bank shops. Picturesque. A lot of Arabs live there and not much is talked about. No wagging tongues. I furnished it nicely and invited Chandler over. At first he was a reluctant lover, more like a boy than a man. But when two people love each other they find pleasure in each other as if by magic. I was ecstatic. As ecstatic as I ever dreamed it was possible to be."

"Did he ever talk about his work?" Lowenstein asked.

"Yes. He talked about everything and I talked about everything. We were exploring each other to the depths. Nothing sacred, nothing secret. One often has an insatiable curiosity about the person one loves. He told me of his many adventures—his extreme passionate hatred he had for the Communists. It frightened me a little. It was a part of him love could not touch." She stopped and turned to him. "What kind of man are you, Mr. Lowenstein?"

"I am a detective, madam. An old, broken-down, flatfoot who drinks too much."

"Flat foot?"

"Mouchard," Byron said.

"Ah. What a colorful idiom. Flatfoot." She was thoughtful for a moment. "I have a great fear for Chandler. Not just from the police."

"Ma'am?" Lowenstein asked.

"They tried to kill him. The people he was working with."

"You've heard from him?"

She nodded.

"Surely he hasn't phoned. The phone must be monitored. The mail is no doubt being checked."

"I'm sure it is. You have forgotten, Mr. Lowenstein, Chandler is a spy of the highest order. A letter came to the woman who owned the house where we used to meet. A Mrs. Sharmandar. She was fond of us. She suffered with us when my husband . . . passed away."

"May we see the letter?"

"It has been destroyed."

"What about these people, the ones he worked with?"

"They tried to 'get him,' the letter said. He called them 'Old Guard.' "

"Are they Americans?"

"Yes. I'm sure. I'm telling you this hoping you may be able to stop them from killing Chandler. That he may live is all I have to hope for."

"What else did he say?"

"Only that I should forgive him. Forgive him for being what he is. He regrets only the pain he has caused me, he said."

There were tears now in her eyes. She brushed them away with the tips of her fingers. They were at the end of the path, having circled the garden. They stepped onto the patio.

"One more thing," Lowenstein said. "Where was he the ten months he was away from Paris?"

Her eyes went wide. "It doesn't show in his records?"

"No."

She stared blankly for a moment. "Why, I don't know where he was—exactly. I sent my letters to American Express in Montreal, Canada."

"Was he in Montreal?"

She nodded. "He gave me his cover name—in case of emergency—and the hotel he was staying in. . . . Do you think his time there may be related to the killing?"

"I don't know."

"I do not remember the hotel, but he was called 'Robert Roberts.' I remember laughing when he told me. Robert *Roberts*. It is comical, isn't it? That was a bad time for him, you know."

"In what way?" Lowenstein asked.

"He came back in a very low mood. He was in great despair over what happened there. For the first time he was saying things against the profession. He was saying that you do not slay the dragon by becoming a dragon yourself."

"What did he mean by it?" Byron asked.

She turned to him. "In Montreal the CIA was doing nightmarish things, Mr. Byron. And Chandler was involved in them."

"Then his loyalties did waver," Byron said.

"His loyalties? No, not his loyalties." She thought for a moment. "Not his loyalties, nor his willingness to sacrifice. All that wavered was a tiny bit of idealism. He said he was maturing, as all espionage agents mature. He claimed he was becoming as cold-blooded as the best of them."

THIRTY-SIX

Knebel was working on a report to the President when Lowenstein phoned just after midnight.

"Madame Rousseau is a hell of a woman," Lowenstein said. "She thinks Chandler Smith is a super patriot and I believe her. He's not a turncoat spy, catch? He's red, white, and blue to the core."

"Hard to believe . . . How do you explain the slogans? What's the connection to Adolf White?"

"Damned if I know. I'm just telling you, Smith's no meatball terrorist. Listen, his pals tried to kill him afterward. She says Smith got a letter through to her. Called his pals the Old Guard. What the hell's that?"

"Don't know, but I've heard the name. Who are they?"

"She says they're American. Must be patriots."

"You're sure about this?"

"Hell yes! I'm giving you something here you can run with. This Old Guard, they must be old-timers. People Smith would trust. I'm on my way to Montreal — where Smith spent those missing ten months. He's becoming real to me, Knebel. We push the right button, he'll fall into our lap." He broke off the connection.

Knebel called the computer section and asked for Thaddeus Gore. The line clicked, then Gore answered: "Gore."

"Glad you're here, Thaddeus."

"Haven't got a home anymore. . . . We've got problems, Knebel. Backlogs and bottlenecks like you wouldn't believe. Coding is a mess. The program's fucked. There are people running around here who don't know a computer from a trash can. . . . How can I help you?"

"Ever hear of a group called the Old Guard?"

"Relating to espionage?"

"Yes."

"Sure, haven't you?"

"Just whispers. Smith may have been involved with them."

"Somebody's pulling your leg, Knebel."

"How?"

"The Old Guard is an old joke around here."

"I still want all you've got on them, joke or no joke."

"Okay, Knebel. I'll send you our resident expert in folklore. She'll fill you in."

Fifteen minutes later Mrs. Mancuso knocked on Knebel's door. She looked haggard and tired. Knebel offered her coffee and she settled into a chair, lighting a perfumed cigarette.

"You want something on the Old Guard, is that right?" Her voice was hoarse. She had brought a thick file with her, which she opened on her lap. "The Old Guard was a dumb idea that never came to be. Goes way back to the Nixon era. The days of panache and paranoia."

"Tell me about it."

218

"The Old Guard idea kicked around the CIA for a while and in the Bureau too. In late seventy-three there was a lot of fear apparently — both in the Intelligence Community and in the Administration — that when Nixon collapsed, if he did collapse, the Intelligence Community would collapse as well. America would be naked, her counterintelligence effort would be made useless by laws designed to control her. There was a lot of paranoid talk about KGB infiltration of Senate committees and so on. Legal search and seizure and disclosure laws that these men could see on the horizon terrified them."

"What exactly was the Old Guard idea?"

"Proponents wanted to entrust some loyal senior intelligence officers with the unofficial defense of the Constitution. They were to handle counterterrorism and antisubversion clandestine operations within the boundaries of the United States. Self-regulation — report to nobody. Private enterprise espionage."

"How were they to be funded?"

"Through CIA front organizations like Air America, Air Asia, Willoughby Electronics, and so on, whose books are closed to Congressional investigations."

"I see."

"The man most associated with the Old Guard is Bernard Ferris, a rather sensational figure in the Vietnam war years. Worked on Colby's safe hamlet program. Ruthless, fanatical. He was supposed to be a super spy, inordinately dedicated, highly skilled in tradecraft — the art of spying."

"Just like Chandler Smith."

"Guess so."

"Tell me about this Bernard Ferris."

"For a while he was the liaison between the Nixon White House and the Intelligence Community. Later he became a special projects director, then left the Agency in eighty. He died three years ago in Belgium. Stachel bomb disintegrated his car. Righteous witnesses, supposedly."

She lit another cigarette with a butane lighter and leafed through the file on her lap. "Most of this is Ferris's service record. He was an active player. Angola, El Salvador, Haiti."

"Gore said it had become an old joke."

"After the idea was trashed, you started hearing of the Old Guard from time to time. If an adversary agent showed up dead and there was no known official sanction, it was credited to Old Guard activity. A sort of mythology grew up. At the training centers there were whispers about the Old Guard being the brains behind the intelligence community, linking them to the Mafia and Nazis and all kinds of nonsense. The Old Guard is the poltergeist, the leprechaun, the gremlin of the intelligence community, Mr. Knebel."

Knebel lit his pipe. "This is all very fascinating, Mrs. Mancuso, but I don't believe in gremlins, leprechauns, and poltergeists."

"Mr. Knebel, there isn't any Old Guard. Never was. I'll leave you my file on it, such as it is."

"Were there ever committee hearings on this idea, anything along those lines?"

"Might have been."

"I want to know who argued for it, who was against it."

"All right."

"Prioritize it."

"Will do."

He read through the file quickly. Most of it was personnel matters, reports of training supervisors, copies of field reports Ferris had filed. He wrote with a fluid hand, tersely, without evasion. A direct and deliberate man, Knebel thought. Central European extraction, well read, highly educated in science, math, chemistry.

When he finished the file it was two in the morning. Knebel cleaned his pipe with a small jackknife, loaded it with fresh tobacco, thought for a moment, then called a familiar number. It belonged to Janet, his ex-wife. She was an editor on the Washington *Daily Chronicle*. It took her nine rings to answer the phone.

"This better be important," she said sleepily.

"How are you, Janet? Sorry to wake you."

"Richard! That's okay." She was fully awake now. "What is it? How are you? How's the investigation?"

"I'm fine. The investigation is a whirling dervish—lots of motion, little forward progress."

"How's Laurie?"

"This isn't a social call, Janet. I need your help."

"I figured you did, otherwise I wouldn't hear from you until Armageddon."

"I've stumbled on something," he said. "Have you ever heard of a group called the Old Guard?"

"No—doesn't ring a bell."

"Would you get me whatever you can as soon as you can?" He gave her his number at the Annex.

"How wild is this goose chase, Richard?"

"I wouldn't want to prejudice your investigation—let us just say there is some controversy about the nature of the organization, whether they're fact or Disneyland."

"I see. You are on the fact side."

221

"Yes. Arthur Lowenstein believes they're connected somehow to Chandler Smith."

"Give me a hint . . . animal, vegetable, or political?"

"Spies of some sort. Possibly counterintelligence."

"Foreign or domestic?"

"Ours, probably."

"If some goodies come out of this, the *Chronicle* wants the usual."

"Can't make any promises."

"Give us a bone if you can?"

"No commitment, Janet."

"Then I'll rely on your sense of fairness. I'll get the machine cranked up and get back to you."

THIRTY-SEVEN

The hotel was one of Montreal's oldest, catering to English speakers. It was ornate, smelled vaguely of mildew and decayed opulence, and was peopled with geriatric residents of modest means. Many of them were sitting quietly in the lobby in the vague stupor of age when Lowenstein and Byron came in. Two of them turned in their direction with dim curiosity. The desk clerk was young and swarthy. Lowenstein showed him Chandler Smith's picture.

Looking at it intently, the clerk said: "He's the guy who shot the American President, maybe?"

"That's right. He used the name Robert Roberts. He was once a resident here, years back." Lowenstein had made the same claim in eighteen other hotels and was able to make it still with conviction.

"Impossible, man."

"We're certain that he was," Byron said with equal certainty.

"The Queen Mother is a class hotel, man. No criminal element."

"How long have you been employed here?" Lowenstein asked.

"One month."

"Let us talk to the manager."

The clerk bowed and smiled and bowed again, then disappeared through a small door. A moment later he returned with an older man whom he introduced as a Mr. Ogilby. Ogilby was a nineteenth-century man: short, white-haired, wearing a vest, gold watch, and a striped suit with a wide lapel. He denied having any knowledge of Chandler Smith, absolutely.

"Perhaps he was using another name at the time," Byron said, "besides Robert Roberts."

"Aren't you even going to check your records?" Lowenstein asked.

"I was on the desk then," Ogilby said. "I know he did not reside here."

"We'd like to see your records," Lowenstein said.

"You have writs, do you? Canada is a nation of laws, gentlemen. We're not obliged to assist you without a writ."

"We can go to the local authorities for an assist," Byron said. "No problem."

"We can even go to the local papers," Lowenstein said.

Ogilby squinted. "That's always the bottom-line threat for you chaps, isn't it? Blackmail."

"We came a long ways, catch? Get the records."

Byron said, "Please."

"It won't be necessary to get the records." He glanced around to ensure his clerk was not listening. "You've got to keep the Queen Mother's name out of this. Some of our tenants would be very upset and management is nervous. Our profit margin is not that handsome. Our reputation is important to us."

"Yeah, sure," Lowenstein said. "So he was here, eh?"

"We had something of a scandal here having to do with our bookkeeper. She used to spend the night with Robert

Roberts sometimes and was dismissed over it."

"We want to talk to that lady," Byron said.

The bookkeeper's house was tiny, white clapboard with a brick front; the yard was enclosed by a white picket fence, the lawn was fresh-cut. It was near La Fontaine Park off Rue Sherbrooke E. It was late afternoon and the wind was gusting when Lowenstein and Walter Byron arrived.

Betty Franklin was in her mid-thirties; she wore a starched white blouse and a red full-length skirt. She had kind, intelligent blue eyes and a friendly smile. She asked them in and offered them a seat in her living room. The wallpaper, the couch, two chairs, were in floral patterns and there were potted plants everywhere. Ogilby had phoned, she said, and told her they were coming.

"You're not the regular American police, then?" she asked.

"No," Lowenstein said. "Mr. Byron is, I am not."

"Do I have reason to call my solicitor?"

"I have no authority here, ma'am," Byron said.

"I feel a little guilt. Perhaps I should have come forward as soon as this terrible business started. . . . Can I get you anything? An iced drink perhaps?" Neither wanted anything, they said. "I wanted it not to be he. He wasn't known to me as Chandler Smith, you know. He was Robert B. Roberts. I called him Rob. I knew he had other names. I knew he wasn't Robert B. Roberts even though he never said anything about it. I just felt it." She blushed. "Women, I think, sense things. I'm not claiming psychic powers or anything. I just think we sense things."

"What was he doing here in Montreal?" Lowenstein asked.

"I don't know, really."

"He was working, though."

"Oh yes, every day. Sometimes late into the night."

"What exactly was your relationship to Robert Roberts? We understand you lost your job over it."

"I wasn't discharged. They didn't tell you I was discharged?"

"What did happen?"

"It's really a rather dull story. He was in love with someone else. I never knew who. He was a very closed book, about his life, his work, his background. . . . Where should I start?"

"Anywhere you like," Lowenstein said, and he settled back into his chair. "Any place that's comfortable for you."

"None of this is a betrayal, gentlemen—I wouldn't betray him. I don't know what he was doing, so I can't betray him. . . . You know I was working at the Queen Mother. He was a boarder. That's what we called the guests then because we served meals as well. We had a younger clientele, at least partly. Salesmen and the like, mostly. A lot of Americans. Rob was a loner—quiet, some said gloomy. We—the staff, I mean—used to make jokes about him being a hermit, or an old man, and that kind of thing. I am spinsterish—is there such a word?—you probably can tell. I'm shy, or worse: reclusive. I felt a sort of kinship with him. He was almost morose, like he went around in a fog all the time. He wasn't ever rude or anything like that. Just completely private."

"You're giving us quite a different picture of the man," Lowenstein said.

"I knew he hadn't always been like that. I could tell. He wasn't a terminal case. In those days I used to collect the weekly rents if they weren't paid promptly on Monday.

Occasionally Rob would forget and I'd go to his room. He was always there in the evenings after seven with his head stuck in a book. There was something in him that made me like him. He was, I don't know — suffering. He was suffering intensely on the inside. Not physically. In his mind. I was sympathetic. Gradually we got to know each other and like each other. Honest to God, I don't know what he saw in me. He had been places and done things. I have been *no*where and done *no*thing. He knew all the restaurants of Paris, London, the pleasure palaces of the Orient. He knew all about what wines to drink and what champagnes were best. I knew none of those things. We used to go out every Friday. Saturdays and Sundays he would drive someplace to visit his mother. Boston, I think. *That* was true, wasn't it?"

"Yes," Lowenstein said. "What kind of books did he read?"

"Science books. Chemistry mostly. Books about how the organs of the body work. What do they call that?"

"I don't know," Lowenstein said.

"Physiology," Byron said.

"That's right," she said.

"Go on, please," Lowenstein said.

"Like I say, I don't know what he saw in me. He had known many glamorous women and he had a way with them. He seemed vulnerable. Women like that in a man. Strong and vulnerable both . . . In the evenings we would go for walks in Regency Park. He didn't like the out-of-doors, but he would go because of his health. Constant work was crippling him. He was always lost in thought and his stomach bothered him. Rarely did he complain or say anything. I know he envied people who were just regular people. We'd see them down by the river

227

playing with their children and their dogs and he would sometimes stare at them and smile at the children. He never said so, but I think he liked children a great deal. . . . I met Rob right after my mother died. I had taken care of her for years. I had done my duty. She was a loathsome person, vile-tempered, selfish, contemptible. She had dominated my life. She had made me into a frightened, groveling woman, unsure of life, myself, people. Meeting Rob was good for both of us. I had to free myself and he had to free himself from the domination of another kind of mother. His work, whatever it was. Gradually, as we began to know each other and to open up a little, I began, I thought, to love him. But I didn't love him, I loved the *idea* of loving him. I was fond of him and he of me, but there was no abiding love there. He knew it and I knew it. We used to talk all night sometimes. He'd do most of the talking — about life, what it meant. How precious it was. He knew a great deal about Communism and he hated it greatly and he hated whatever it was he was working on."

"He must have given some clues about what it was."

"No, never. But it bothered him. He thought it terribly wrong. You see, he was a very good man. You should know that. I don't think he did any evil. What else can I tell you about him? Nothing really that would help you. He cared terribly for his mother, but you probably know that. Dogs and cats could annoy him sometimes. Every morning he did some special calisthenics like fighting. His body was a mess of scars. I'm sure some were bullet wounds. His legs were very scarred. He told me it was done by a mine. Meat was his favorite food and he preferred red wines to white and he liked them dry and cold. Burgundies and sometimes Chardonnays . . . We never slept to-

228

gether." She blushed momentarily.

"What happened finally?" Lowenstein said.

She pinched her lower lip with her fingers, then said: Whatever it was that was bothering him, it began to bother him more intensely. He paced around a lot and hardly ever slept. He would ask me questions I could never hope to answer, like 'if evils were in the name of right, were they still evils,' and things like that. Was it wrong to sacrifice innocence in the pursuit of great goals? Questions no one could answer. And then about a week before he left that all stopped. Somehow he had found himself. He slept better. He was working on something, he said. And then one morning he said he was leaving. He said he was never coming back. Just like that and he was gone. We parted as the very warmest of friends."

"What was it he was working on?" Lowenstein asked.

"I don't know. At the time I thought it might have something to do with the fire. We watched it from the window of his hotel room."

"What fire was it?"

She gave the approximate location and date. Byron wrote it down.

"One more thing I'd like to say," she said.

"What's that?" Lowenstein answered.

"If he killed poor Mr. Jamison, he must have had a damn good reason."

"I think so too," Lowenstein said.

THIRTY-EIGHT

The East River, flat and gray beneath the Manhattan skyline, lay calm and streaked with orange in the dawn. It was cold, clouding to the west. Four New York City Police boats surrounded the docks and piers. They were supporting the fifty-five divers in the water, their powerful lights glowing under the murky surface. The divers worked their way south and west along the bank with the outgoing tide. Further down along the finger piers below the Brooklyn Bridge more boats and more divers were working their way back against the current. Two other boats dragged nets in the deeper part of the channel. As yet none of them had found anything.

On the shore a dozen TV camera crews waited with scores of police and curious onlookers. The police had set up barricades, but the crowds were not large enough yet to need them. The command post was a New York P.D. SWAT van.

Knebel got the story from a police detective named Kant, a fleshy, broad-shouldered man with a mustache and a heavy voice who had picked Knebel up at the airport.

There were three police officers, Kant had said,

working a search pattern with a team from the eighty-seventh precinct. Somehow they had made a wrong turn or had started in the wrong place. Anyway, it was a simple screwup. They were covering a street that had already been covered and were working their way from building to building east instead of north. They searched a building and had had good cooperation from the tenants. Nothing seemed amiss. And then one of them, a Lieutenant Holland, decided something wasn't right. He went back to check on someone's identity again. The two others stayed at the bottom of the stairs while Holland went up to the man's room. That's when the shooting started. Holland was shot in the face. When the two other officers started up the stairs they were shot as well. Police units quickly moved in and the suspect was chased down toward the wharf area, trading shots with police all the way. He was hit at least twice, witnesses said, maybe three times, before he went into the water. The man's quarters were searched and nothing was found to verify that it was Smith, but the police were certain it was.

Knebel found Hans Ober pacing nervously by the side of the wharf. With the dawn a breeze had come up. It rippled the water and smelled of raw sewage, and there was refuse in the water.

"About time we got lucky," Hans Ober said. "So far Smith's had all the good, we've had all the bad. . . . There's coffee and doughnuts, want some?"

"Sounds good."

They sat in the back of a police car. Ober stuffed his mouth doughnuts and washed them down with coffee.

"You've seen my memos on the Old Guard?" Knebel asked.

"Yeah."

"What do you think?"

Ober shrugged. "Been in the business too long to dun another man's hunches, okay? But there never was any Old Guard, except in Wonderland. . . . Ever hear of the Illuminati? Supposed to be behind every conspiracy ever walked the earth. Fascist, Communist, Trilateralist, everything. I don't buy it."

"What if there really was an Old Guard?"

"There really isn't, though."

"What if the mythology was used to cover up the reality?"

Ober's expression soured. "That's too Byzantine for me. The Old Guard is just bull. . . . You want my honest opinion of what this assassination is all about?"

"Sure."

"I think this Chandler Smith is a twenty-two carat crazy. He popped the President *simply* because he is a crazy. And I think White and his crazies helped him and they did it on Vincent Benson's money."

"Mme. Rousseau seemed to Lowenstein to be a pretty reliable witness. I'll put my money on the Old Guard."

"Chandler Smith may have been trying to throw us off through her. How can you believe anything that comes from him—he killed the President for Christ's sake!"

"All right, Hans. The Old Guard thing may turn out to be crap, but it fits with what the man is and has always been—a patriot, red-white-and-blue to his gills."

Ober helped himself to another doughnut. He chewed for a few moments, then said, "Pretty flimsy stuff, but I'm interested, okay?"

"Interpol found a woman who fits my profile. Name: Raba Hakim. French-Palestinian. They believe she was homicidally psychotic. Russian-trained. She worked out with the Italian Red Guard and maybe pulled a few bank jobs with the Bader-Meinhoff gang. Her file is on the way."

"Hasn't she been *D-E-A-D* for some time now?"

"Allegedly."

"She was reported killed when?"

"In Japan, three years ago. Found dead in a fire. Could have been staged. Think I've got my lady assassin."

"I don't see where she meshes into the other gears of this thing. Any contact with White and his bunch?"

"None known."

"Okay, have Chad put some men on it."

"Already have."

Ober rubbed his eyes. "This is the goddamnedest case. . . .Where's Lowenstein now?"

"Montreal."

"What the hell is he doing there?"

"Digging deep into Smith's background."

"I remember Lowenstein from Philly in the old days. He's a cagey old bastard. If there's anything to get, he'll get it."

There was some excitement just then; a diver had found the body and they were pulling it onto a boat. Knebel and Ober went down to the dock. There was a detective on the boat and he radioed in that it wasn't Smith. He knew who it was. It was a dope dealer named D'Angelo. They found narcotics on the body.

"Christ!" Ober said, kicking the pavement.

233

Knebel lit his pipe. "Smith's got us chasing wind-mills."

Ober took a deep breath and turned toward the TV camera crews heading toward them. "I admit he's making us look awful stupid, okay? Worst part of the job is alibiing to those one-eyed monsters."

"Give them something to chew on, they stop breathing fire."

Ober scowled. "Only thing they'll want to chew after being out here all night is a big juicy piece of my rump."

THIRTY-NINE

Ober crossed the street to talk to reporters. Knebel headed for the airport. Two hours later he was at Dulles International outside Washington. He slept on the plane. When he checked in with his office he was told that his ex-wife had called and wanted to see him as soon as possible. He phoned her at home.

"I've got someone who can tell you all you ever wanted to know about the Old Guard and then some. His name is Biskey. Harold Biskey. He's a bit skittish. Could you meet him over here? He semi-trusts me, but absolutely refuses to come to my office. Where are you now, Richard?"

"Dulles."

"I could have him here in an hour."

"I'll be there."

She had moved since the divorce. Her new apartment was in an elegant old building in McLean, Virginia. The doorman said he was expected and directed him to the fourth floor, apartment 4C. The halls were thickly carpeted; the elevator moved noiselessly.

Knebel knocked on the door; she opened it almost immediately.

"Come in, come in." She was beaming. "Welcome, welcome. I think this Mr. Biskey sounds good. Very good. He's on his way."

She showed him into the living room. It was austere, uncluttered. There was a writing desk covered with books and papers in the corner and a small bookcase packed with reference books and a typewriting table. That was the part of the apartment that looked used. On the wall was an oversize original oil portrait of Franklin Roosevelt looking severe. She directed Knebel to sit on the couch and she sat in the chair.

"So tell me about Biskey," he said.

"He's antiestablishment with a capital 'anti.' For years he's been harping about this Old Guard—nobody'd listen. He's gotten a little space in the small presses, that's about it. The Old Guard is the cutting edge of the apocalypse, according to Biskey."

"How reliable is he?"

"I don't really know. We'll find out, I guess. . . . So how have you been?"

He had taken out his pipe, but put it back in his pocket, remembering she hated it.

"Smoke if you wish, Richard. Really. I know how fond you are of that chimney of yours."

"Maybe later."

"Have you been up all night? I saw you on television this morning. Hans Ober must have been shell-shocked when the man in the river wasn't Chandler Smith. God, this whole thing has been just so shocking. . . . Would you like some coffee? I have some good Colombian."

"No, thank you." He loosened his tie. The portrait of Roosevelt seemed to be staring at him. He turned away from it.

She said, "How's California?"

"Sunny and warm. Just like the travel folders say."

"And the social climate?"

"Sunny and warm."

She smiled. She had a pleasant smile. She was forty-seven and had a round, pleasant face and intelligent, probing eyes. Her mouth was unusually small; she was self-possessed and had a quiet, professional demeanor.

"You never did like small talk, I remember," she said.

"Guess not."

"I'm assistant feature editor now. The first woman to hold that position on the *Chronicle*."

"I'm glad for you . . . if that's what you want."

There was a long silence. Knebel tried to get comfortable. "Think I will have some coffee," he said.

She disappeared through a door. She returned in a moment with the coffee and served it. She sat down across from him again, smoothing out the wrinkles in her skirt with the flats of her hands.

"Neither of us were ever really any good at small talk," she said.

"Guess not."

"It's supposed to be an art. A civilized art."

"Is it?"

"Remember I used to call you 'Joe Friday'?"

"I remember."

She smiled with her small mouth. "When you were on a killer's trail, you were like a tiger with the smell of blood high in his nostrils."

"Haven't even got a whiff so far. . . . You're sure this man is coming?"

"Yes . . . How's Laurie?" Her voice softened when she said the name.

"She's fine."

"I read she had a showing of her water colors in L.A. The critics raved. Even Templeton liked her a little, and Templeton likes no one who is still breathing."

"She knows Templeton. They argue a lot on the phone."

"Laurie is a great talent."

Knebel looked at his watch.

"He'll be here any second," Janet said.

After a moment he said, "Thanks for helping me on this thing."

"Patriotic duty."

He shifted around in his seat and changed his pipe from one pocket to the other again.

"Relax, Richard, I'm not going to bite."

"I know you're not."

"Are you happy?"

He shrugged.

"I want you to be happy."

"I'm making every effort."

"You really are happy, aren't you?" Her eyes narrowed; it seemed to mean a great deal to her.

He smiled uneasily. "I'll be a whole lot happier once Harold Biskey graces us with his presence."

"I meant—with your situation. I meant—with Laurie."

"I knew what you meant." He gave her a hard look.

She took a sip of her coffee, then put the cup down. "This probably looks like prying," she said. "Maybe I am prying just a little. Maybe I'm a little jealous things worked out for her and they didn't work out for me. Is it okay to admit maybe I'm a little jealous?"

"Sorry I got hot. I'm just not very good at talking

about — things. Let's not be so damnably polite and apologetic, shall we? We survived a twelve-year drought. Let's just be happy we both came out of it without too many scars."

She was quiet for a moment, then said, "There was an occasional oasis — at least for me there was."

"Please, Janet. No auld lang syne."

She nodded and smiled tentatively. "More coffee, Richard?"

"No thanks."

There was a knock at the door.

"That'll be our man." She rose.

FORTY

Harold Biskey was thin, sickly pale, and needed a shave. He wore faded blue jeans and a T-shirt beneath a shabby yellow jacket; his fingernails were down to nothing from biting them. They sat in the kitchen at the table; Biskey talked quickly and his eyes rolled wildly when he became excited.

"You use this, I want a by-line," he told Janet Knebel. "I've been trying to get an article on the Old Guard in your sorry paper for seven years."

She nodded agreement. He wanted something in writing; she said she couldn't give it to him. She'd have to know what the information was before she could give him a written guarantee.

He shot up from the table. "Forget the whole thing," he said. "Goddamn cheapskate bastards! You're as stingy with glory as a miser with his gold!" He started out the door.

"Hold it," Knebel said. "You walk out on me, you've got the FBI coming right behind."

"I don't scare."

"A fact, not a threat. If there is a conspiracy and you hold back, you could be held accountable as a

240

coconspirator."

He sneered. His teeth were yellow and large. "The irony of that!" he said sourly. "I've bean after these fucking creeps for ten years. Me, a coconspirator with *them!*"

"You have my personal assurance," Janet said. "Everything you say, if the *Chronicle* uses it, will carry your byline."

He thought about it, then sat down. He nibbled for a moment on the stub of a fingernail. "Man, I haven't slept ten minutes since Jamison got it. They might be coming for me. I know about them. These people are capable of anything. *An-nee-thing.*"

"Tell us about them," Knebel said.

"I've been tracking them almost ten years — writing about them. Getting absolutely nowhere. Like a madman screaming in the desert. Now the Guard is moving out of the woodwork. Jamison was the opening salvo in the underground war. These people are capable of annee-thing. Look at Smith. A monster. He's got to be one of them. I know he is. He worked for them on the Montreal Project, I think. I'm sure of it. Bernard Ferris and his merry men. Ferris isn't the head of it, you know. He's the titular head. The real head of it is higher. Nixon maybe. Or Jack McFarland, our illustrious Secretary of State . . . . No, Nixon, I think. You don't think it stopped at Watergate? Illegal crap, I mean. It didn't. I'll bet you think Ferris is dead. They told you he was dead, didn't they? That's what they'd like you to think. They call it 'possum' when they do that. They blow up some poor schnook and then they make you think it's one of them and then they are free to go on about their business. I know about Belgium. I've looked into this thing deep. Forty fathoms. I've seen the bottom of it. Ferris is not dead. No way. I seen him six months ago with my own eyes. I've been collecting stuff on the Old Guard for years. Remember the Cubans found dead in Manhattan when Castro came to the UN? They were gunned down by the Old Guard. The CIA took the rap, but it was Old Guard stuff all the way. I know, believe me."

"What do you know about the Montreal Project?"

Biskey glanced at both of them and licked his lips, then took a deep breath. "You've both got to swear you'll never ever tell where you got this." They both swore. "When you aren't a player you don't know what the spy game is. It isn't the secret codes and clandestine bank accounts. That's Mata Hari stuff. That's World War I stuff. This is the new age in intelligence. This is science. This is spaceships and spy satellites. We are on the threshold of conquest by espionage. Armies and all that crap are as old-fashioned as mustard gas. The Montreal thing was an Old Guard project. They were going to make zombies out of people. I don't know how it worked, but it was horrendous. Think of it. A drug that would make you their slave. I tell you, they are capable of *an-nee-thing*."

Knebel glanced at Janet. They were both skeptical.

"Can you give us any details of these experiments?" Janet Knebel asked.

"We need names, date, facts, witnesses. How did you find out about this?" Knebel asked.

"I had everything. I had a ton of stuff. But they were following me and they managed to get it from me. The Lexington Avenue subway. I was changing apartments and I had all the stuff in a suitcase. It had to be the Old Guard. Who else would want an old suitcase? They were on to me. That's why I have to be careful." He was speaking very excitedly and his eyes were flashing. "John Haas is not what you think. He's not the mild-mannered, Clark-Kentish type everyone thinks. He's like the intelligence higher echelon — they're all Ivy League. I know. They're Ivy League and they are ruthless as rattlesnakes. Inside that simpering shell, Haas is a Stalin. I've been chasing the Old Guard for a decade. I know of what I speak. The Old Guard had a program for Latin America. The same old stuff: torture, suppression, heavy-duty military action. Kissinger was Old Guard, what do you want to bet? Anyway, Jamison would only go down the road so far with them and then he had second thoughts and so they *un*elected him. They got this ace spy Smith to do the job and so — pop goes the weasel."

He folded his arms and turned sideways in his chair, satisfied that telling it was tantamount to proving it.

Knebel said, "Where did you see Ferris exactly?"

"Some of this stuff is secret," he said. "I can tell you but a smidgen of it. I'm sworn to secrecy. I protect sources. It's my religion. Private journalistic security. Friends would never tell me some of this if they thought it would get out. The Old Guard are dangerous men. In certain circles I'm quite well known. Intelligence people contact me every day. Anyway, I had this tip — I'll never tell you where I got it because when I say I'm going to protect a source I do — I had this house under surveillance. It was an Old Guard safe house in New Jersey. This is risky stuff, believe me. The Old Guard would kill you without so much as blinking an eye. I watched that house for three days and nights over the last Labor Day weekend from this van I've got. That's when I seen him. He's a fat man, that's how I was tipped off. I followed him all over

243

the place . . . to the Ambassador Hotel in Manhattan. I started snooping around, but was caught by the Secret Service. They shooed me away. Now I realize he was stalking the President. They were fixing to kill him even then. After the assassination, I figured it out. Now I think that the whole thing is a plot to put Nixon back on the throne. To get the country all messed up so people will demand a strong man. Like in Germany. Look at the violence in this country. Somebody's behind it. Somebody is making hay out of it someplace."

"Okay, Biskey, you've made a lot of charges, let's fertilize them with a few facts," Knebel said.

"I just gave you the facts."

"Let's have the address of this New Jersey safe house."

"Can't give it to you. Privileged information."

"You've linked Haas to them. How?"

"He's in the White House, they put him there. He *must* be one of them."

"You said McFarland was Old Guard."

"Must have been."

"But you don't know for sure."

"They're all Old Guard. At least he would be sympathetic. A fellow traveler."

Knebel leaned back in his chair. "I see."

Biskey tore at a nub of a fingernail with his teeth. Knebel took a hundred dollars out of his wallet and handed it to him.

"You don't believe any of this, do you?" Biskey said. He took the money.

"Like I said, I need facts. Proof. Witnesses."

"These are clever, clever people. They don't leave untidy loose ends lying around."

"I can't do much without proof."

"You're patronizing me now."

"I'm a cop and I need proof!"

"Jamison's doctor killed himself!"

"Does that mean something?"

"You bet."

"What?"

Biskey's eyes seemed to float in their sea of white. "I can't say."

"Listen, you've got to give me something I can grab hold of."

"I've given you it all, man. Fuck! You can't see shit when you're into it up to your ears."

"Give me some names. Show me some Old Guard people. Show me that safe house you mentioned."

"Can't."

"Just point one out to me, let me do the rest."

"I can't deal with this," Biskey said suddenly, coming to his feet. "They stay too well hidden. There will never be proof, not like you want it." He left, slamming the door behind him.

After a silent moment, Janet said, "What an odd little man."

"Isn't he."

"Let me scramble you a couple of eggs."

"I've got to get back to Washington."

"I'm sorry. I didn't realize he was quite so spaced out."

"Not your fault."

"I'll keep looking. I have four very good people on this."

At the door she kissed him on the cheek. "Thanks for inviting me back into your life," she said.

FORTY-ONE

When Knebel got back to the office the file on Raba Hakim had arrived from Paris Interpol, most of it in French, which he could read, but slowly. He noted the highlights of her life and the more he read the more excited he became. She had grown up in Morocco, was tied to the PLO, did time for gun running in Italy. He sent an urgent request to Paris Interpol to see whether they could get samples of her handwriting.

At five-thirty Hans Ober came down. He was tired and there were black rings under his eyes. He sat down heavily in a chair in Knebel's office.

"You haven't got a crystal ball someplace, have you, Knebel?"

"No."

Ober lit a cigarette. He wasn't wearing a suit coat and the sleeves of his white shirt were rolled up past his elbows. "Dahlia Nichols, the lone survivor of White's gang, has been talking. Her parents and her attorney finally got through to her, okay? Deprogrammers have been working with her, maybe. Who the hell knows? Fourteen, you don't know your ass from your lower lip . . . Christ." He puffed on his cigarette. "I'm shot. I've forgotten what a bed feels like. Okay, about Dahlia. She's started talking. She doesn't know it all, but it seems like White never did have anything actually to do with the Jamison killing. Some woman talked to him. Dahlia never saw her, okay, but she heard them talking a couple of times on the phone. White wanted the publicity. Christ, what the hell kind of people we got running around these days? Wanted the glory of shooting all those unarmed people. Okay. What else? We've got some pretty good stuff coming in now. Some good stuff about Smith before the assassination. We think we've got a fix on at least some of his movements. We're getting up some composite drawings of suspected accomplices. The men we put on Belzar's suicide phoned in a report — you should be getting a written copy. Looks like a righteous suicide so far. Depressed, had been undergoing psychotherapy, okay? The medical records on Jamison? No dice. Supposedly Samuelson had a private file someplace — as yet we haven't located it. . . . You wanted Mrs. Mancuso to find out who supported the Old Guard, who opposed it. Admiral Leher, who headed the CIA then, was for it. Bernard Ferris was for it. Harris Cheney was for it. A lot of Nixon people were for it. She's got a list coming over to you. You still hot on this Old Guard business?"

"Let's say I've got them stewing in the pot."

Ober crushed out his cigarette. "Keep your crystal ball polished, Knebel, you're doing okay."

Knebel went out for dinner at six-thirty, had a sandwich, and was back at his desk by seven-fifteen. At eight o'clock Jules LaVale called.

"I'm two blocks away, Mr. Knebel. I want to see you right away."

"What is it, Mr. LaVale?"

"I thought you'd like to hear what I found out. . . . I know who killed Clement Jamison and why."

FORTY-TWO

"What do you plan to do with this information?" LaVale wanted to know. His pink face was darker and he was agitated, gliding up and down the carpet, folding and unfolding his arms.

Knebel watched him. He sat in his chair, smoking his pipe and sipping coffee.

"What have you got, LaVale?" Knebel said.

LaVale stopped pacing. "I don't want President Jamison's memory ruined. I've seen this kind of thing before. Gossip and innuendo can make you or break you in the history books. Jamison's second term was going to be historically innovative. He was going to reach for the stars, I mean it."

"The truth has a way of wiggling its way out of its wormhole, LaVale."

"I found out who was coming through the tunnel every morning to see Clement."

"You mean Dr. Belzar?"

"You found out already."

"Yes."

"You know he committed suicide?"

"Yes."

"You don't think it's strange?"

"Is it, Mr. LaVale?"

"I don't know. . . ." He resumed pacing.

"When you called you said you knew something about the assassination, LaVale—who and why."

"Yes, yes I did. I have—First you should know about the international thing. It was big, *very* big." LaVale took a deep breath. "You remember when Clement pulled out of the Hemisphere Brigade thing?"

"I do."

"They were planning to invade Cuba. Honest to God. Clement at one point had tentatively okayed it." LaVale licked his lips and rubbed his hands together. "The media is going to blow this all out of shape if they get hold of it."

"You're certain about this?"

"Yes. Absolutely. When Clement pulled out of the Hemisphere Brigade and left those Latin American dictators high and dry he angered a lot of right-wingers in the Party. Clement felt the Russians had gone too far, that they were about to cut off the Panama Canal and that is absolutely critical to our national interest."

"What happened to change his mind?"

"He didn't want to risk World War III, I assume."

"You figure that's why he was killed?"

Jules LaVale sat down; he was wringing his hands and his face was growing red. "I thought this through very carefully. The first thing the detective is supposed to ask is 'who profits'? Isn't that right?"

"It's one of the first things."

"So I ask myself, who profits? And the answer is obvious. The Latin dictators, the CIA, and guess who?"

"John Haas."

"Correct."

"Go on, Mr. LaVale." Knebel shifted his weight in his chair.

LaVale was back on his feet. "I've got something else maybe you didn't know. Clement was going to dump Haas at the convention like Ford dumped Rocky. Clink, boom, bam, down the sewer of history."

"Every four years you hear the Vice President will be dumped."

"I can get you the draft of the speech he was going to deliver when he nominated Senator Southerland."

"Maybe Jamison thought Haas was going to quit the ticket."

"No, sir. He was more than half planning to dump Haas. He was vacillating, sure, but he was thinking about it and Haas knew it." LaVale sat down again. "It isn't *impossible* that Haas had something to do with it."

"This conversation is strictly between us, LaVale, understood?" LaVale nodded. Knebel said, "You know John Haas and I know John Haas. I ask myself, did he have the capacity? Ask yourself. Do *you* think he had the capacity?"

"I don't think I know what you mean."

"Capacity is many things. It's wherewithal, determination, singleness of purpose. You boil it down and in most cases it adds up to one thing: guts. I put it to you. Does John Haas have the kind of guts it would take to risk all to gain the presidency? To risk being a murderer, a traitor, a villain in history? Not the John Haas I know. Not even on a reckless impulse. Not unless he's a Jekyll and Hyde."

"He hated Clement. Hated his guts. Haas is a petty man, petty as they come. Petty but shrewd."

251

"That doesn't make him a murderer. . . . I'll need to speak to your source about this Cuban business, LaVale."

"I swore I wouldn't betray her. National security violations would be involved."

"If push comes to shove, I may have to produce this person. We'll get her immunity."

"Then you do think I've got something here?"

"Tell me this. How is it Haas doesn't seem to be supportive of Central Intelligence?"

"I know how he talks — he's supposed to be so damn liberal. But you check his record; you see how he's voted."

"How has he voted?"

"He's CIA right down to his Argyle socks."

"That doesn't make him a conspirator."

"I have more evidence. His people caught me asking his people questions — guess what he did? He called me into the Oval Office. He wants me to run his campaign — starting right now in Iowa. That sort of clinches it, don't it? He's getting me out of the way."

"Maybe he thinks you're a crackerjack campaign man. What did you tell him?"

"Of course I told him 'yes.' "

"What? You suspect him of complicity in the murder of Jamison and yet you'd help him get elected President?"

"If I don't some other ad man will. Working for him will give me a chance to observe him up close. I want to know the people he knows — nail him, if I can."

"Good luck then, LaVale."

LaVale shook Knebel's hand. "You think I'm way off base with this, don't you?"

"Yes. Really off base."

"In a way I hope you're right. . . . I'll be in touch if I uncover anything." He started for the door. "Say, awful about Stewart Ott, isn't it?"

"What about Ott?"

"You didn't hear? President Haas has replaced him with Wilson Wright."

FORTY-THREE

Knebel found Stewart Ott at his favorite bar, the Golden Horn. It was a quiet, subdued place, with a piano player and a discreet clientele. Ott was sitting by himself drinking martinis in one of the booths when Knebel arrived at nine-fifteen.

"Hello, Stewart."

"Richard Knebel, my old friend, have a seat."

Knebel ordered a scotch and soda and squeezed into the booth.

"I guess you heard about Haas's surprise for me today. The bastard didn't even do it himself. He sent one of his junior flunkies over this afternoon with a stupid note. My services were no longer required. You could have knocked me over with a whiff of smoke when I got that note. And I thought I had the bastard in my pocket."

He loosened his bow tie and unbuttoned his collar, finished off his drink, and signaled the waiter to bring him another.

"You know what it is? He can't respect me because I haven't got a diploma hanging on my ear. You know I've got more savvy in this finger than all the Harvard eggheads put together."

"I'm sure you do, Stewart."

"Lucky for me I salted away a few bucks . . . Does it make a hell of a lot of sense to you to can me when you publicly commit yourself to pushing through the last of Clement's five-point public security benefits packages — to fire the man who's been doing the pushing for almost three years?"

"Not a whole hell of a lot."

"See the Gallup this morning? Haas's popularity is rising like a rocket powered hard on. It's like LBJ after Kennedy, only more so. But this Haas, he's no LBJ. LBJ had big brass ones swinging from his loins. Big as watermelons. This guy — I don't know. He can't seem to make up his mind to doo-doo or get off the pot."

"What'll you do now, Stewart?"

"Don't know. Pound the pavement, I guess. Maybe it's time to cash in a few overdue debts. I'll bet you're wondering how your boat's floating right about now."

"Should I be packing my bags?"

"Two days ago Haas was saying he was pleased with your reports. He's looking forward to your reorganization plan. That means what? Zero. Every five minutes he changes his mind, slithering like a snake."

"First a sheep, then a wolf, now a snake. I wonder what kind of an animal he really is?"

Stewart Ott said he didn't care anymore. He was getting out of Washington. He had had it up to his ears. The waiter brought another double vodka martini and he ran the olive around the edge of the glass. "Senator Southerland is going to make a run for the Presidency," he said after a few moments. "Southerland could probably use a good domestic affairs man, somebody who

255

knew the ropes, had good connections, and a ton of experience. . . ."

"Something tells me I shouldn't worry too much about you, Stewart."

"Hell no. The cream still floats to the top, don't it?"

The waiter brought Knebel his drink. Ott ordered two more martinis and another scotch for Knebel.

"What the hell, I own myself a good drunk," Ott said.

"LaVale was just over to see me," Knebel said.

"What did the twerp want?"

"He thinks Haas is a petty man."

"Yet he'll run his campaign." Ott frowned and shook his head. "PR people haven't the decency of a two-bit whore."

"He's doing it for private reasons."

"I'll bet."

"Did Jamison really get along with Omi?" Knebel asked.

"You still beating that old drum?"

"They were on the outs, weren't they?"

Ott nodded. "After the election they were going to say bye-bye. Maybe I should have told you before, but the man's dead. The country thought they were Mr. and Mrs. Marital Bliss. What the hell difference does it make now?"

"I just want to know what was going on in the man . . . the Hemisphere Brigade thing. They were going to invade Cuba, true or not?"

"Friend Richard, allow me to graciously duck the question. Foreign affairs is a sticky game. War is a scary word to the voters. Just because a President okays a plan of action doesn't mean he intends to go through with it. With the Soviets you shadowbox." He shook his finger at

256

Knebel. "You go quoting me about any of this, I'll swear you're crackers. Maybe I'm out of the Administration, but I'm still vice chairman of the party. We're the party of peace, remember. Peace and the pursuit of happiness." He took a sip of martini. "John Haas isn't the earth and stars. He's as temporary as a hangover. So let us keep our discourse tuned to pleasantries." He downed the rest of his martini in a single gulp.

"Jamison did consider it, didn't he?"

Ott stared at him for a long moment, then nodded. "If you must know, yes. Haas is reconsidering the option now. I was totally against it and told them both so. Maybe Wilson Wright wouldn't be sitting at my desk this moment had I been a little circumspect. I swear to you I'm not saying any of this, Richard . . . what else would you like to know?"

"About the Old Guard. Jamison did meet with them secretly. They came through the tunnel."

"He met with military and intelligence people, yes. He didn't trust the CIA or the Joint Chiefs. . . . Listen, the Old Guard is just a word. You're beating a dead horse there, I'm sure. Somebody's always singing spooky songs about conspirators who go bump in the night. Show me one, I'm from Missouri."

"Is it even remotely possible Haas had anything to do with the assassination?"

Ott laughed. "You've got to be kidding."

"It's not possible?"

"*Absolutely* not possible. He'd pee his pants trying to hold onto a secret like that. Nobody'd trust him with it. Haas is a rich kid who's spent his political life saying yes to powerful people and buying poor folks' votes with government money. Christ, Richard, the man is a neb-

257

bish, not a conspirator."

"Good night, Stewart."

"Stick around. When I wallow in self-pity I don't care to wallow alone."

"Lowenstein and Byron are due in from Montreal. I want to get their report in person."

FORTY-FOUR

Arthur Lowenstein had been drinking a lot. He breathed heavily and his eyes were glazed and half closed as he sank into the chair in front of Knebel's desk. Byron, tired yet excited, paced the floor behind him. Knebel poured three cups of strong, black coffee, then sat down and lit his pipe.

"Strike out up there, did you?" Knebel asked.

Lowenstein shrugged. "We found some dirty laundry, smelly and old, but it don't mean crap far as I can tell."

"Let's hear it."

Lowenstein gestured to Byron, who took some notes out of his pocket.

"Some of this isn't substantiated completely," he said. "It would take months to get this ready for indictments, but here goes . . . Chandler Smith worked for the *Centre de Recherche Psychologique du Siècle Nouveau* in Montreal. His title was Business Manager, but his exact duties remain a mystery. We checked the records of the Bureau of Business Licenses and found that he signed as an officer of the professional corporation using his cover, Robert B. Roberts. Mr. Lowenstein cut into this thing so fast it astounded me. I give him most of the credit for this. The Center was into what they call 'stress management.' Their patients were mostly executives and professional people. They obtained their referrals from legitimate doctors and other health professionals. We talked to some of their patients. Lowenstein figured if they were up to funny business — as he called it — there would be lawsuits on file. And there were. Dozens of them. Most involved the Center's head doctor, Dr. B.V. Sabel, apparently a European. As yet I have not been able to find any evidence he was a doctor or ever attended any medical or graduate school."

"B.V. Sabel, you said?"

"Yes."

"You have a description?"

"Caucasian, early fifties, heavyset, medium height, spoke Belgian French and accented American English. Quiet, somber, all business."

"Any photos?"

"No."

Knebel opened his drawer and removed a file, opened it, then handed Byron a photograph of Bernard Ferris. "This him?"

"Could be."

"Go on, tell me about the lawsuits."

"They all involved charges of addiction and liver failure. The pattern is almost the same in all cases. A patient would be referred from a local doctor. Typically, he would be in his forties, successful, a mild drinker. Complaints would range from hypertension, elevated cholesterol in the blood, acid stomach, sleeplessness, and so on. The patient would be examined by a doctor and given routine blood tests and coronary capacity tests and so on. Pretty much as you might expect. Then the treatment would begin. Daily doses of a drug by injection. We have talked to fourteen patients; the routine and course of treatment were identical. Let's see . . . At first the patients would find little change. Daily stresses would gradually become less harrowing perhaps, but the changes were not spectacular. Some patients discontinued treatment during this stage, but were pressured to go on. Those who did so began to enjoy a mild euphoria and daily life became much more tolerable. Then they slowly underwent mood and personality changes. These complaints varied. Some became hostile, others had memory problems, others became talkative, still others, lethargic. I assume they were experimenting with dosages and various drugs or combinations of drugs."

"What results were they looking for?" Knebel asked.

"That's the damnedest thing. We have no idea. The only lasting effect seemed to involve the decision-making process. The executives would back away from problems, they'd vacillate, hedge. They'd commit themselves to course A one day and then switch to course B the next and C the next. Outwardly, mind you, they seemed perhaps more confident and in control than ever. And certainly more amicable. They just lost that certains toughness. Some became severely depressed and withdrawn. Two committed suicide. Traces of anabase trioxins were found in their livers, probably residual drug effects."

"What was the drug?"

"Allegedly it was a legal drug called Rodunperson, a mild tranquilizer. The manufacturer and suppliers categorically deny having ever sold any to the Center. It was not recommended for extended use in any case. I'm fairly convinced it wasn't Rodunperson — the side effects are completely different."

"What was their goal?"

"Don't know. They might have wanted to branch out into industrial espionage, but we were unable to determine what possible secrets these particular men had access to. Then again, it may have been part of a larger program, we're not sure. How exactly this relates to espionage, we're not sure of that either. The only thing we're fairly sure of is that Chandler Smith probably engineered the fire that destroyed the Center. Maybe he was covering his tracks. Everyone associated with the project has since disappeared. The Canadian authorities, unaccountably, have never instituted an investigation."

"See what our good old government has been up to, eh?" Lowenstein said. "What do you think, Knebel? You're a moral man. Give us a sermon here. Tell me how this is all justified according to the commandments of God and the Constitution of the United States. Or whatever. National security — isn't that the bull they usually give you?"

"According to an investigative reporter named Biskey, this is an Old Guard project. The government has clean hands this time."

Lowenstein laughed. "That's how they do it. Front groups. This was all financed by Uncle Sammy, let's not kid ourselves. What's going down here is just a tiny sliver of what's been going down all over the world. This is American foreign policy. These are high crimes done in the name of the goddamn national interest. Makes you want to puke to think about it. Experiments on people. Hitler in his camps did things like that. Is that what we've become, Knebel? Are we the Nazis now?"

"Maybe that's what we're trying to find out," Byron said. "The spy game damns all players. Once you accept the first premise that the end justifies the means, you no longer have a soul. You're a Machiavelli and you're damned."

Knebel stirred some sugar into his coffee. He was thinking and there were deep furrows in his brow. He sipped some coffee and looked at Walter Byron and then at Lowenstein, who had laid his head back and had his eyes closed.

"Tell me the symptoms again," Knebel said.

Byron checked his notes. "You mean prior to receiving the drug?"

Knebel shook his head. "After."

"Lessening of reactions to daily stresses . . . If treatment continued, they had memory problems, or they became hostile or lethargic. Sometimes they would become more complacent and changeable. They seemed less able to keep their resolves, I guess you might say. It depended on the strength of the drug and the dosage. They were apparently experimenting, trying different variables."

Knebel nodded. "Jamison had some of those symptoms," he said. "Jamison had a lot of those symptoms."

Byron stopped pacing. Lowenstein's eyes came fully open. He sat bolt upright.

"Bingo, bongo, bango!"

Byron sat down, rubbing his temples. "How the hell do you figure it?"

"Don't know," Knebel said, relighting his pipe.

Lowenstein took a half-pint whiskey bottle from his pocket and poured a third of it into his coffee and drank

263

it down. He looked at Knebel. "Pretty damn obvious what needs doing," he said.

"Let's hope it's just as obvious to the big guys."

FORTY-FIVE

"So you figure the only way to know for sure is to do another autopsy on Jamison," Hans Ober said.

"We do," Knebel said. "If anabase trioxin is present, we've got a whole new ball game."

"We've got to have Sanchez-Flint on this," Ober said, reaching for the phone. "This is going to have to be hush-hush. If the media gets hold of this, they'll make a circus out of it."

An hour and fifteen minutes later Sanchez-Flint, the FBI Director, and Wilson Wright, the President's Domestic Affairs Advisor, were in Ober's office. Both were red-eyed and irritated. They listened to what Knebel, Byron, and Lowenstein had to say without looking at them. When they were finished, Wilson Wright stood up and paced to the window, looking out into the darkness. After a moment he turned to them. "I'm against disinterment of the body. President Haas will be too, and I'll tell you why, Mr. Knebel. If Jamison was taking this drug and was debilitated from it, we would lose confidence in the eyes of the public. Our allies would lose confidence in us as well. You haven't enough facts to warrant such a move. Get some hard collaborative evidence."

"Could be handled secretly," Sanchez-Flint said.

"It would leak," Wilson Wright said. "The bureaucracy is like a giant sieve."

"When Kennedy was killed, we never got the answer," Knebel said. "We got the snow job from the Warren Commission and the country has suffered with that ever since. We got the snow job about Vietnam and Watergate and Laos and along the way we lost what the hell this country is about. We lost our sense of building something and having a destiny. You can't build your country on lies."

"You know what I think it is with you, Knebel?" Wilson Wright said. "I don't think you give a damn about the country. I think you want to solve a case, and that's all you give a damn about."

"If we don't do the autopsy I can guarantee this will get leaked anyway," Lowenstein said matter-of-factly. "Catch?"

Wilson Wright stiffened and he glared at Knebel hotly for a long moment. Then his eyes softened. "I'll overlook your man saying that, Knebel. I don't like being shoved."

"We're going to have to have the autopsy done sooner or later, Mr. Wright. It might just as well be sooner."

"I'll talk it over with the President and get back to you." He glanced sharply at Lowenstein, then left.

Knebel, Byron, and Lowenstein walked the four blocks from the Annex to the Holiday Inn. It was dark and quiet; the streets were nearly deserted.

"It's really inconceivable," Byron said, "a President could be the target of such a scheme."

"Kings and princes have been poisoned since time immemorial," Lowenstein said.

"Murdered, yes. But this, it's not murder. It's worse than murder. . . . I hope we're wrong."

"We're not wrong," Knebel said.

Knebel was asleep when Hans Ober phoned at nine-thirty in the morning.

"The President is on your side, Richard."

"Surprised to hear it."

"We'll get Mrs. Jamison to go along with it and Justice Fordham will sign the order. We've decided to issue a statement to the press up front. We'll say simply that the original autopsy might have had errors which we hope to correct. Sometimes it's better to be vague than evasive."

"Let me put it to Mrs. Jamison," Knebel said. "Personally."

"She's up in the Catskills, visiting friends. You'll be expected."

The lodge was a large one, made of pine logs and overgrown with vines. Omi Jamison was wearing a plaid hunting shirt and jeans. She met with him privately in a small game room at the back of the lodge. When he told her what he wanted and why, she signed the consent agreement without hesitation and handed it back to him.

"You thought I would give you a hard time, didn't you?"

"Yes, I did."

"He wasn't himself, Mr. Knebel. You were right about that. If this is the reason, I want to know it."

She walked with him down the path to the parking area where he had left his car. Her Secret Service protection followed behind at a discreet distance.

"I suppose you know by now Clement and I were planning a divorce."

"I know."

"Will it be kept out of the media?"

"Probably not."

She kicked a twig off the path. "It will be difficult for me, now that he's been martyred. The public will see me as a betrayer, or worse. Perhaps I was to blame a little, but not completely. Clement was a complex man. Very difficult to know, extremely difficult to love. If he could have been king of the universe, he'd have tried for it. I was just something he kept around to show off on state occasions. He wanted me to be there when he wanted me, and not to be there when he didn't. I felt like a pet parrot, shown off to impress guests and then put back in a cage. But you want to know something funny? I sort of miss him."

"Somehow I don't believe you do, Mrs. Jamison. Not very much at any rate."

"How very rude of you to say that, Mr. Knebel!" she said angrily.

"I'm sorry if I've offended you."

They were silent for a few moments. They had arrived at the parking area. Knebel opened his car door. "Good day, Mrs. Jamison."

"You were right, Mr. Knebel."

"About what?"

"I don't miss him very much."

FORTY-SIX

The rain was steady and hard. It was a dark night and the noise from the highway below Arlington was muted by the sound of the rain. Knebel was there and he watched the backhoe dig a slit into the earth and pull out the dirt from above the leaden box. The small crane stood by in the rain, to lift the box out of the earth and put it on a conveyance.

Byron waited silently. Hans Ober walked down the path and watched the men working for a moment and then he came up a small hill and spoke to Knebel.

"Mrs. Jamison give you much trouble?"

"Nope."

Ober put his hands in his pockets. The workers were putting the lifting gear onto the casket. They were solemn, working quickly.

"I give you a lot of credit, Knebel. You seem way ahead of us ordinary mortals on most of it. But I'm worried, okay? This could prove a disaster either way, heads or tails."

"I know."

"Did you get my memo about Raba Hakim?"

"No. I haven't been back to the office."

"You were right again, Knebel. The report of her death was quite premature. She got off a plane this morning in Costa Rica. Some of our people were there and I don't know how, but they recognized her."

"Have we taken her into custody?"

"She resisted being taken, there were shots fired, okay? She's dead. A man was with her. A heavyset man with a beard, probably our friend Ferris — another walking corpse. He wished to cooperate with arresting authorities, but she killed him with a karate blow."

"You mean she was not armed and they couldn't take her alive?"

"She killed six Costa Rican policemen before they got her. Couldn't be helped."

They had the sarcophagus in the air and it was being lifted onto the flat trailer behind the small tractor. Then they moved it down the hill to the chapel and the honor guard moved with it. Knebel, Ober, and Byron followed it at a distance and the rain was coming down in torrents now.

In the chapel the coffin was removed from the sarcophagus and put on a gurney and rolled out into the driveway where a van from the medical examiner's office was waiting.

They met Dr. Amil Risson at the morgue. He was a curly-haired man with thick lips and a droll expression. Byron gave him what he needed from the Canadian autopsies so he would know what he was looking for.

"Will it take very long, Doctor?" Knebel asked.

"An hour — perhaps a little less."

Knebel waited in the hall, walking up and down, and Hans Ober and Byron waited with him. They did not talk. Forty minutes later Dr. Risson returned. He saw

Knebel and shook his head.

"The liver was definitely spotted a bit, but otherwise there was really nothing. As far as the anabase trioxin is concerned, I could find no evidence."

"Thank you, Doctor," Knebel said. He walked down the hall and then back to Walter Byron. "Get Lowenstein and go back to Montreal. Keep digging."

"I'm sorry," Byron said.

Knebel then turned to Ober. "There are some reporters upstairs I ought to talk to."

"What are you going to tell them?"

"I won't have to say much. They'll see all this egg on my face."

BOOK FOUR

FORTY-SEVEN

A woman answered the phone on the fourth ring: "Yeah?"

"Auntie M?"

"Yeah."

"You know me. You know me well. I was your number one tenderfoot once. Do you know my voice?"

"Maybe I do — yeah."

"I need help. Say no if you want and I'll understand."

There was a moment's hesitation. "Where are you?"

"Remember the surveillance field orientation? The first one, I mean."

"I remember."

"Across the street there is a gas station and there is a phone booth by the street. Not the one by the station, the one by the street. In one hour's time."

She said she would be there.

He was in the phone booth outside a Seven-Eleven store, wearing a sailor's uniform. He had treated his skin to remove the appearance of age and his hair was tinted black. He walked up the street. It was a mild day; there was moderate traffic. He walked along the road where they were building an apartment house and a small professional center. A quarter mile further there was a vacant lot on a hillside covered with heavy brush. He waited for a car to pass, then ducked into the brush and followed a trail made by neighborhood children who played on the hillside. He retrieved his duffel bag from where he had concealed it near a large rock. In it he found his binoculars. He sat on the rock and, using the binoculars, surveyed the scene below him. Grant Boulevard ran east and west, a wide, busy thorough-fare. On the corner of Fern Road there was a large shop-ping center filled with cars and shoppers. To his left, at the corner of Grant and Harrison, was a Shell gas sta-tion. This is where she was to come. He watched the corner and waited. There was no unusual activity. Nothing suspicious.

She arrived fifteen minutes early. She drove up in a green Volkswagen bus, an older one, with a rusted scrape along the side and shabby curtains in the win-dows. She parked and got out. She was almost sixty, but was still lean and muscular; her hair was short and gray. She wore a bulky sweater, jeans, sneakers.

He scanned the area again for suspicious activity. There was none. She stood patiently by the phone, lean-ing on a pole with her arms folded. It was dangerous for him to trust anyone, he knew. Dangerous, but neces-sary. He waited until it was past the time he was to meet her. Still she did not move. Finally he walked back up the hill to the road to the Seven-Eleven store and dialed the number at the phone booth where she was waiting.

"Were you followed?"

"Hell no."

"Did they tap your home phone? If they tapped your phone they might have followed you."

"They could have before, but I had the line cleared. I figured maybe I'd hear from you. Give me credit for a few fucking smarts, Chan."

"Drive around the block," he said.

He hung up the phone and ran back up the street to the vacant lot and watched her through the binoculars. She circled the block, stopped again at the gas station and again stood by the phone. He waited, telling himself to be patient, to be sure. His mouth was dry. His heart pounded. He told himself that this was a necessary risk. He couldn't rely on disguises; sooner or later he had to come in out of the cold. And there was part of him that needed company, needed rest, needed some comfort. That part of him, that soft, human part, he mistrusted. He went back up the trail, moving slowly, weighing the possibilities. When he got to the road, he decided finally, and then he hurried down the hill and called the number quickly.

"This is a big risk, Auntie M. Are you sure you want to take it?"

"Where the fuck are you, Chandler? All these fucking games can get you burned if you're not careful. You and me go back a long way, Chan. I'm not going to fuck you over."

"All right," he said. "Drive south two blocks, turn right, then right again on Esterhassy. Drive slow."

"Got it."

He waited for her at a bus stop. He stood with his duffel bag and watched her slowly come up the hill. There were other cars that passed her, but no one was following her. He couldn't see any aircraft. His hand closed around the grip of the automatic in his belt. When she was close he waved to her. She pulled to the curb and he took a quick look inside. It was a camper and as far as he could see she was alone. He climbed in. She said she was very happy to see him. She smiled. Her teeth were large and gray. "You got your firepower in there just in case I ain't righteous, Chan? Going to pump a few into me, are you, if this goes sour?"

"Never trust a human animal, you taught us," he said.

He checked the back of the van, in the closets and cupboards for men or transmitting equipment.

"I'm playing it straight with you, Chan. You know how I feel about you."

He sat in the passenger's seat. "Sorry," he said. He pulled his automatic out of his jacket and reached his hand toward her. She opened her sweater and pointed to a .45 in a shoulder holster.

"That's all I'm carrying," she said.

He took it from her.

"Where to?" she said.

"I haven't eaten since yesterday morning."

She drove to a fried chicken place, parked on the street, went in and bought a bucket. He had set up the table in the back of the van when she came out and they ate the chicken, then some potatoes and gravy from plastic cups with plastic spoons.

He kept his hands off his gun now and relaxed.

"You were one of the best sons-a-bitches ever came down the trough," she said. "This sailor gag is great, really fucking great. I always said a uniform was a good gag."

"I want to thank you, Auntie M," he said. "Being with me could be bad for you if they caught you. You might even be tagged as an accessory."

"It isn't the big fucking deal you make it sound. What

the hell good are you if you can't bail out an old friend once in a while? Besides, they put me in the shallow end of the pool and maybe it's time I got myself back into the deeper waters."

"You don't owe me anything."

"I don't owe *them* anything either. We parted company with all accounts even-Steven."

"What happened? You were an institution."

"They've got a suite of rooms for the nursery now over at the Washington Hilton. They run the babies through like they were college seminars. It's all theory, no fucking practical stuff. It isn't going to work. You've got to train field people one way. The hard way. You've got to make them go out and do it, and that's all there is to it. Like you. I made you be able to get invisible. A real bonafide spook."

He was tearing at the chicken and slopping up the mashed potatoes and gravy with a roll. She had bought milk for him to drink but he didn't drink it.

She leaned back against the wall of the van and tucked her feet up. Her body was supple. "Yeah," she said. "Ever since Ferguson took over the Technical Services Division the whole training routine soured. Remember how we used to follow the Soviet attachés to the U.N. and listen in with good parabolic equipment at night? We'd hear them humping and farting and everything. That's all blown now. FBI has jurisdiction, they say, and should have had from the start. Besides, they say it's bad PR. Can you imagine the Company giving a damn about PR? The whole fuckin' sport has changed." She turned to him. "How about you, Chan, have you changed?"

He stopped eating. "Meaning what?"

"You cross the street, did you?"

"No."

"If you've crossed the street, there ain't nothing I can do for you."

"I haven't crossed the street."

She regarded him severely, her piercing eyes staring at him. "Better men than you have gone over, Chan," she said. "I used to sleep with Charlie Zinn and he went over. He was tough too, a spook's spook, and they bought him, I hear, for fifteen thousand bucks when he needed to fix it up with some bigamy rap. Just tell me to my face and I'll believe you, Chan."

"No one has bought me!"

She seemed relieved. "I knew it. Right from the start I knew it. . . . Listen, Chan, I still got high-up friends. Lucius Cole knows me. Why don't you give yourself up to him? He'll help you, Chan, whatever the hell is going down. He's a square shooter, believe me."

"You can't trust anybody. You always told me that. What am I to people like him? Like Lucius Cole. A President is dead, that's all they'll see. The Company is getting heat."

"Maybe you're right," she said. "You've put a lot of trust in me, Chan. Maybe more than you ought."

"I guess maybe I have to take some chances." He handed her back her .45. "If you were going to get squirrely on me, you'd already have done it. I'd be ducking bullets right about now."

"How can I help you, Chan?"

"Did you ever hear of a spook called Ferris?"

"Wasn't he the one who got himself blown to shit in Belgium a few years back? Fucking torture freak. He was redhot, though. I'll give him that."

"I've been working with him."

"Couldn't be the Ferris I'm thinking of. That fucker's double dead." She started the van.

"I think it is, Auntie M . . . Where are we going?"

"I've got a safe house you can use, Chan. Long as you want. Believe me, this is a *safe*, safe house. You couldn't be out of the cold better if you climbed back into the fucking womb."

They caught the Baltimore-Washington Parkway and headed northeast into Maryland. It was a pleasant afternoon. There was moderate traffic. Auntie M could not stop talking. She talked about the changes in the CIA and the trouble she had resisting them, the horrors of reorganization, the old-timers who had returned and what had become of them. Some of them were drunks, some were dead, some had just gone away someplace and no one knew much what had happened to them. Chandler Smith rode in the passenger's seat and kept a wary eye out. Every few minutes he went into the back and watched out the back window. Once into Baltimore, he had her twice circle blocks and double back before he was satisfied. Auntie M said she understood, but that she wasn't being followed. Nobody could follow her, she said, if she didn't want them to, because she had the instincts. In the last analysis they were all a good spy needed, she said.

"This guy Ferris," Auntie M said. "You've got to be mistaken about him. I know for a fact he's dead. McPherson was with him the night it happened. Cuban spooks, supposedly. Both of them got it—completely disintegrated. No great fucking loss. The man was a pig from what I hear. Fucking torture freak. McPherson wasn't much better. I trained that creep. Boy did he ever get off on hurting people."

"It was faked, perhaps. Before General Order Ninety-four it was done often. The Old Guard could have done it easily. Have you ever heard of the Old Guard?"

"The Old Guard. Sure. They used to talk about it to the recruits, tell them hair-raising stories of fantastic fucking exploits of the Old Guard when there never was such a thing."

"The myth was deliberately constructed to mask activities."

"No, no, Chandler. I was around then. I knew all about the Old Guard. I remember now. Austerhouse was supposed to assist in the setup and he was my boss then. I knew every fucking thought in his head before he thought it. I swear to you, it never got off the ground. There never was any Old Guard."

Chandler Smith leaned his head back against the headrest. "I spent ten months in Montreal working on an Old Guard project, Auntie M. And Ferris headed the project."

She shrugged and slowed down to change lanes. "So what will you want me to be helping you with, Chan?"

"For now I need some rest. I'm desperate for a little rest."

"No fucking problem at all."

FORTY-EIGHT

They were in a mixed industrial and old residential area now and the streets were dark. There were abandoned cars parked on the street; abandoned wine bottles were everywhere. The old factories and warehouses were dark and the windows were smashed out. A giant car crusher was working nonstop in an auto-wrecking yard.

She pulled into the driveway of a small house between two large warehouses. The grass was high in the front yard and there was a for sale sign in front. Inside it was dank and cold. Auntie M lit the gas stove in the kitchen and opened the door onto the back yard. Behind was a scrap yard and a deserted factory. Chandler Smith looked around, his hand resting on the butt of his automatic. The place was cluttered and dusty and hadn't been lived in for a long time. The furniture was worn and shabby and the wallpaper was faded and peeling. Some plaster had fallen away from the ceiling.

"You can have the bedroom," she said. "Better if someone comes to the door. I doubt anyone will."

"Thanks."

"A relative of mine fucking croaked and left this to me. The tax man said this dump was worth sixty-two thousand fucking dollars."

"Must be the land," Chandler Smith said.

They sat at a small kitchen table that wobbled with age. There was warm beer and a bag of pretzels she had brought from the van. He liked beer. This beer was dark, imported, expensive, and he liked it even though it was warm.

"If they capture me alive," he said, "and I am determined that won't happen — they will not get your name from me no matter what they do to me."

"Thank you, Chan. The same here."

He smiled. "Think I'll give that bed in there a tryout."

He slept for a while and when he got up it was past midnight. Auntie M had been cleaning up the place but it still smelled dusty. She had taped newspapers to the windows and the edges of the doors so that from the outside it would appear dark and deserted. She had carried the for sale sign inside and it was now against the wall in the kitchen. The space heater in the corner crackled with its fuel-oil fire, and the smell of the fuel oil was strong in the little house. She had bought some food, too; the refrigerator was working, she said, and the beer was cold. She fixed him a salami sandwich, with heavy brown mustard, on French bread, and he ate at the kitchen table and drank cold beer with it.

The radio was on. There was a special about the search for him and they were interviewing four authorities. One was an FBI man and two others were Secret Service. The fourth was Candice Penn, an in vestigative reporter, who was critical of the way things were being done. She was certain Chandler Smith was in South America and he was working for Fascist elements in the United States. They had killed Jamison because he favored controlling the profits of the oil companies, she said. He shut the radio off.

"Reporters," Chandler Smith said, "are liars and fools. None of them know me or the Company and yet they say those terrible things as if they knew what they were talking about. The Company wars with the Russians. Don't they know that? Don't they know that we are at war with the Russians and have been for what? Forty years?"

"No, Chandler, they don't know it."

"How do they think? Can you tell me that? I've always wondered just how they think."

"To them it's peacetime, I suppose. Peaceful coexistence. Détente. They have many words to kid themselves with."

"Then, indeed, there are fools," Chandler Smith said, and for a moment he was lost in thought. When he looked at her his eyes were hard and grim. "I've got something important to do," he said. "Very important. I'll need your help. You can say no if you want, Auntie M. After, I'll be gone and won't trouble you anymore."

"What is it, Chan?"

"Somebody's got to be sanitized."

"Somebody big or somebody small?"

"Big. Very big . . . I've decided to do it with a sniper shot, long range, probably in daylight. I'll need an Enfield Enforcer Model L42A1 sniper's rifle and an Aimpoint electronic sight. Can you secure one?"

"No problem."

"Two or three rounds will be enough ammunition. Venom rounds. Exploding. Venom rounds are despicable, but in this case I cannot afford to take a chance."

"Listen, Chan. I'll do any damn thing you want. You name it, it's yours. But I got to know what the fuck is going down. Ain't I got my neck out a fucking mile and a half? Come on, who's the target?"

He rubbed his face with his hands and shook his head. "It's better that you don't know, Auntie M, believe me."

She leaned back in her chair. "You weren't in with that fucking Adolf White, were you? I know you, Chan, and I know you weren't. You wouldn't wipe your ass with a fucker like that."

"Christ, no. Spies are all scum and degenerates," he said, "but there are alliances even spies would refuse." He said it with half a smile. "Just the Enfield and I'll be on my way." He reached into his pocket and took out two thousand dollars and put it on the table in front of her. "I wish it could be more."

She reached for the money and put it in her pocket. "When will you need it?"

"Maybe tomorrow. No later than the day after. Send it by Greyhound to downtown Washington for Mr. Omega."

"All right, Chan . . . . Why don't you get some more sleep?"

He shook his head, then drained the rest of the beer. "I want to get this thing done and get out of the country. When it's over, I'm just going to evaporate."

"I'll get you papers if you want. Hell, I've got connections all over the world."

286

"So do I."

"Will you take the VW? You can take it if you want until you can steal something better. It's untraceable to me. I use it for occasional private jobs. Take the fucker."

He took her hand. "I'll never be able to repay you."

"Why did you sanitize Jamison? Can't you tell me that? Did the Company want him out of the way for some reason? Why the hell would they want Haas instead?"

"It would take a great deal of explaining, M, and even then you might not believe it or understand it .t. . . Did you ever hear of *Jellyfish?*"

"No."

"It's bottled information, still. I can't talk about it."

"Did the Company have you knock over Jamison?"

"No."

"Wouldn't put it past some of those creeps."

He smiled. I've got to go. . . . It had to be done, Auntie M. That's all I can say."

He went into the bedroom and was there for almost an hour. When he came out he had been transformed. His cheeks were puffy, his nose flatter, and his skin appeared swarthy, like an Italian's or a Greek's. He walked slouched over and dragged his left foot so that he looked old and arthritic.

He came into the kitchen and looked at her through a crooked eye, then smiled, pleased.

"Oooo, Chandler! What a truly great fucking gag this one is! Truly a fucking wonderment! A wonderment!" She made a circle around him, admiring him. "Truly you are a master," she said. "Truly, truly, truly . . . Your own god — if you have one — wouldn't know you." She laughed. "You can't teach tradecraft like this—this is instinct. . . . Stay the night, Chan. Rest some more."

"Can't."

She held him by the shoulders. "Sorry you want to keep me out of this. There's still a lot of life left in this old carcass, believe you me."

"My escape route is for one only."

She nodded. "I understand. Look, I've made some coffee. Have a cup before you go, it'll warm you up. You can spare a few minutes for an old lady."

"It'll have to be quick."

He sat down at the table and she poured him a steaming cup of ink-black coffee and a cup for herself. She stirred cream and sugar into hers slowly, watching him take a hurried sip.

"Yes, sir, Chan, you truly are a fucking wonderment," she said. "You were born to the sport like a bloodhound is born to the hunt."

He took a second sip and looked at her. A strange smile was on her lips and her features had turned to marble.

"Something wrong, Auntie M?"

"No. Everything is going fucking beautiful."

He took another sip, and then he noticed it: there was a hint of bitterness in the coffee, something metallic. A drug? He went for the automatic stuck in his belt, but she caught him and held his wrist; she was strong and the drug was weakening him.

"Oh, Jesus," he said. "Stupid is what I am!"

"Don't fight it, Chan. "You can't fight it."

He tried to push her away again, but his limbs seemed to be made of paste; he swung at her and missed and the floor rolled under him like the waves on a stormy sea. She released him and he tried to find his automatic, but his hand wouldn't respond to the instructions his brain was sending it.

He cried out; the sound echoed in the vast emptiness that surrounded him. He stumbled; the kitchen spun and whirled and darkness filtered through the walls and poured from the ceiling like a giant cold fist closing over his consciousness.

FORTY-NINE

The floor was cold against his face and his legs ached; he felt warm and tingly, pleasantly so. His thoughts tumbled in his head. Now he was small again, in the country near a lake; it was summer, warm; his old bespectacled grandfather had him by the hand and was taking him to fish in a small boat. There are birds above them, free and gliding, and instantaneously he is with them, above his grandfather, above himself, above time and the world, free, happy, eternal. . . .

Someone nudged him in the ribs sharply. He turned his head and looked up through a blur and saw figures moving. Three of them — no, four. He counted them slowly and calculated: four to one. His wrists were handcuffed behind his back. The steel was hard and cold; a bitter taste of acid lingered in his mouth.

"Lift him up, put him in the chair," someone said. A man.

Chandler was transported into an arm chair. Hands held him. Through the blur he could see two men strapping him down. His jaw was loose and he had to struggle to keep from drooling. The taste of the acid was strong in his mouth.

A woman's voice said: "Give him another upper, the fucker won't tell us nothin' if we don't get his fuckin' brain unscrambled."

"Auntie M, that you?" The words came out sloppy. His tongue was thick. Spittle ran down his chin.

Someone gave him an injection. The drug made everything spin and his legs became heavier. Now they slapped his face; it stung and rang inside his head. They stopped after a moment, then things started to clear. He was still in the little house, in the kitchen. Auntie M was by the door, a stern, uncompromising look on her face. Her .45 protruded from her belt.

There were three men. Two were young, clean-cut, technician types. They would administer his treatment, Chandler Smith knew. One was white and one black; both were businesslike, indifferent. Chandler Smith recognized the third man. He was sitting down in a chair smoking a cigar, looking at Chandler like the Grand Inquisitor staring at the Devil himself. Chandler Smith knew him well. This Grand Inquisitor's name was Lucius Cole.

"We got a few questions here, Chandler," Cole said. He looked like a man ready to erupt with volcanic violence. Redness was spreading from his neck up onto his face. Chandler Smith had seen this look on men's faces before.

"You murdered the President of the United States," Cole said. "You are one of us. One of *us* has murdered the President who it is our sworn duty to protect and serve!" His voice was cold and hard. He inhaled deeply. 'Now you are going to outline for me the whole course of events which led up to your doing it, and you are going to include every damn detail, hear?" He pushed the record button on a large tape recorder.

"How are you, Lucius?" Chandler Smith said weakly.

"You know who these two boys are? They are technical services advisors we flew in special tonight on the Singapore trunk. You know what that means. They've been teaching some staff how to wring information from a stone, if you know my meaning — and don't try popping open your cyanide tooth, we already fixed that for you while you were out."

"Been good, Lucius? You look very fine. I was always proud I knew you when I heard that you were finally getting promoted. It meant so much to you, didn't it?"

"You know what we can do to you, don't you, Chan? You know we're going to make you give the whole thing to us the easy way or the hard way. We're not the kind of people that like doing things the hard way."

"I know, Lucius. You and me, we are the kind of men who do things because of what? Necessity? That is a nice convenient word. We always do what is necessary. If it is torture, then we do it. Murder, that is an easy thing. We commit brutality but we are not brutes. We do what is necessary."

"Don't preach to me! You killed the President of the United States!" he shouted, banging his fist on the kitchen table. "How in God's name could that be *necessary?*"

Chandler Smith didn't answer; his gaze had drifted to Auntie M, still standing by the door. He didn't say anything to her. She said, "You're not one of us anymore, buddy-boy. I have nobody that's outside, you know that."

"Stupidity," he said. "My stupidity made it easy for you."

Cole stood up. "It is time to get to the meat."

"I cannot stand pain, Lucius," Chandler Smith said.

Cole said, "Get the leads on him."

The two young technicians nodded and set to work.

"I cannot stand pain, Lucius."

"They're just hooking up a little monitor there, the truth thing, you know. I want the whole story."

"You will not tell them how easy it was for you to get me. Please," Chandler Smith said to Auntie M. "You will not tell them I trusted someone. There are things that I did they will talk about in the nursery for a long time. It was I who engineered the theft of the minutes for the Sixty-second Soviet Presidium. That I would like to be remembered for. But not for the easy way I was taken. Like a fool."

"All right, Chan. That much I'll do."

The technicians had the leads connected, and they switched on two little boxes with glowing dials. "We've got to have a couple of true ones and a couple of lies to get a base line."

"Answer 'yes' to the following questions," Cole said. "Am I wearing a necktie?"

"I will not cooperate with you, Lucius."

Cole sighed with exasperation. "In the end we get everything anyway. We will get what we want one way of the other."

"He's stubborn," Auntie M said. "He'll need persuading."

"What do you say?" the white technician asked Cole.

"What have you in mind?"

"Break a finger, maybe."

"Break a finger? Jesus—all right. Do what you have to do."

The technician had a small case from which he removed a pair of pliers. He held them in front of Chandler Smith's eyes. "Hard way or easy, Mr. Smith?"

"Ask your questions," Chandler said heavily.

Lucius Cole smiled. "Answer yes to all the test questions. Let's ask — Am I wearing a necktie?" He was.

"Yes."

"Is this a wristwatch?" It was.

"Yes."

"Is my skin green?" It wasn't.

"Yes."

"Is this a foot?" He indicated his hand.

". . . Yes."

Cole looked to his technicians. "You've got it?"

They indicated in the affirmative. Cole licked his lips, then rubbed his sleeve on his mouth. He paced back and forth a few times, then he turned to Chandler Smith. "I have no patience with these things, Chandler. We've known each other; we've worked with each other. Tell me straight out, have you crossed the street?"

"You really are a timid man, Lucius. I never thought you were right for this kind of work. Somewhere, deep inside you, you have a basic softness. You try to harden it with hard thoughts, but inside you are not a man for this business. After this, you will go home and it will trouble your sleep."

"Jesus, why the hell do you have to make this some sort of grand opera, Chandler? Just tell me why in hell you killed the President."

"I cannot tell you. I was not sanctioned by the Company, but it had to be done."

"Why did it have to be done? Jesus Christ. Tell me, and I swear I'll let you walk. I just *have* to know why. The

Company is paying dearly — aren't we at least entitled to know why?"

"Is knowing of such importance? It was done. Knowing changes nothing. The heat will still be on and you will not let me walk no matter. You can't have me public; that would be a bad thing for the Company."

"He's just stalling," Auntie M said. "Bring out the heavy stuff and let's get it over with."

"Patience, woman. We're getting cooperation. Why get nasty when you don't have to get nasty? We have all the time in the world. . . . Who is the Enfield for? Who are you going to kill?"

"I cannot say, Lucius."

"Why, what possible difference could it make?"

"Because he must be sanitized. There is no other way. If you knew, you would try some other way and it would not work. The country would suffer. I owe it to the country to do this thing."

Cole slid his chair closer and peered hard into Chandler's eyes. "Let's start from the very beginning, what do you say?"

"I fear what these young men can do, Lucius, but I cannot tell you. I will not tell you."

"It has to be somebody big, right? Otherwise, why would you give a damn?"

Chandler Smith wouldn't answer.

"Tell us why you sanitized Jamison. It had something to do with Ferris being blown up, right?"

Chandler Smith shook his head.

Lucius Cole looked at Auntie M. "It's like he said, we always do what's necessary. I guess we have to proceed with the necessary."

The technicians tied Chandler Smith down with nylon straps and grounded his ankle with a thick steel cable to a pipe. He did not resist. He did not speak. His body went limp; he sweated. The technicians moved with a formality now, with the slow precision of a ritual. Auntie M slid back against the wall. In the distance there was a car honking its horn wildly and further in the distance there was a train whistle. The car crusher was still smashing cars. Chandler watched as the technicians dragged a black case into the kitchen. It was heavy. The two of them struggled with it. Cole went to the sink and washed his hands and face and came back wiping himself off with a towel. Auntie M was watching Chandler and her face was as cold and still and hard as the moon. No one spoke. The technicians opened Chandler's shirt and rubbed his skin with a conducting lubricant and then attached copper wires to his nipples with cold, sharp clips.

Cole said: "This isn't my style, Chandler, you know that. I've always opposed this stuff. Honest to Christ it doesn't have to be this way. But, so help me God, I'm going to sap the truth out of you an inch at a time if I have to."

"From where we started," Chandler said, "we've come a thousand miles."

Lucius Cole sat down again in the chair facing Chandler. He was still rubbing his hands with the towel. They were dry, but he kept rubbing. "Your pious act isn't making it with me, Chandler. You've killed an important person. You iced the President, for Christ's sake! You've given the Company a big kick in the balls. Maybe worse. You may have wounded her mortally. There's talk on the Hill of a permanent on-scene Congressional oversight committee. You might as well make us part of the goddamn Parks Department."

"I can tell you nothing, Lucius."

"No, Chandler. You are going to tell everything. I swear to God you are going to spill it all. It may take time, but subjects always tell us absolutely everything. Ask these boys. Go ahead, ask them — they'll tell you."

Chandler Smith glanced at the technicians and they looked at him with interest, but no pity.

Cole tossed the towel into the sink. "Who did you want the Enfield for?"

Chandler shook his head and wouldn't answer.

"You said you would need it tomorrow or the day after. What's happening tomorrow or the day after?"

"I would tell you if I could, Lucius."

"You said it wasn't sanctioned by the Company. If not the Company, then who? What's Jellyfish? You talked about the Old Guard. Are there people around who call themselves the Old Guard? You could have been duped."

"I was more than duped."

Cole glanced at Auntie M. "He's going to give it to us. . . . How were you more than duped, Chandler? By who? By this outfit that called itself the Old Guard?"

"I can't tell you anything, Lucius."

"You mentioned Montreal. I checked your records. You were never in Montreal as far as I could tell. What happened there? Was it a special assignment?"

Chandler said nothing.

"Come on, Chandler. I want to help you. I can help you too. We can get you out of the country. We don't have to sanitize you if we get it all. Honest to Christ, can't you see I'm on your side?"

Chandler shook his head with finality. "Please don't,

Lucius. Please."

"Get on with it," Auntie M said. She was shuffling her feet with impatience. The technicians plugged in the machine. It hummed.

"Wait," Chandler said. "Listen to me." His voice had a hollow ring to it; he was pleading now. "This is true. A horrible thing has happened. The U.S. has been penetrated deeply. I must stop it. I can stop it. This cancer has gone beyond our greatest fears. It has spread to the highest levels."

"You don't mean like close to Jamison?" Cole said. "One of his people?"

"May I have a drink?"

"He's stalling," Auntie M said.

"Get him a drink," Cole said to her. "Water."

Auntie M scoffed and went to the sink and came back with the water and gave Chandler a drink. He gulped it and wanted more, but Cole said it was enough. "About this penetration. Who did it? KGB?"

"Listen to me, Lucius. Do not think of penetration as you have thought of it. It is not only that a man becomes turned, that he crossed the street for money or greed — or because he is upset with the system. There are more subtle changes that can be brought in a man. The danger is greater than you can imagine, Lucius."

"I'm listening, Chandler. Give it all to me."

"I can't. Believe me, I can't. This penetration has happened at the highest levels. Ferris wanted to prove it worked — and he proved it. Ferris cared only for the Project, only the theory, don't you see?"

"This is a lot of fucking bull," Auntie M said.

"So help me God, it isn't," Chandler said.

"All right, Chandler," Lucius Cole said. "Give me the

est of it. I'll turn off this machine. I'll have these people leave us. We'll be alone. Trust me alone. I'll keep it all to myself—as much as I possibly can. We both love this damn country, don't we? At least I do. If there is penetration I'll do everything in my power to get the bastards. You know I will. You can have my oath on that."

Chandler stared at him and thought for a long moment, and then he shook his head. "I can't, Lucius. I can't take the chance."

"Please, Chandler. *Please,*" Lucius Cole said. "You're going to give it to us anyway. Please don't make us do this thing."

Chandler bowed his head and said nothing. Cole stood up and looked to the technicians and gave them a nod. They opened their case. Cole was pale. He drifted back toward the door as the attendants started the machine that was in the case. It hummed again. There were many dials on the machine and red lights. Chandler stared at Cole, who was standing by the back door.

"I'll be right outside if you need me," Cole said to the assistants. When the door opened a whiff of cool breeze poured in. The night outside was very dark.

Chandler breathed deeply. He had heard it was best to hold your breath and empty your mind; that it was the fear of the thing that broke men, and not the thing itself.

One technician signaled to the other and a switch was thrown.

It hit Chandler Smith like a wave of pain a thousand feet high; it rocked him down to the core of his being and the force of it lifted him out of the chair. For a moment he was dizzy and the room seemed to rock. He could smell his own flesh burning and his vision narrowed to a small circle. He nearly let go of his consciousness in the vastness of his screaming.

Then they hit him again and the pain reached deeper in him and took hold; a torrent of agony flooded up and swarmed over him as if every nerve in his body had been fired by a poker. He shook until his consciousness dropped away into blessed nothingness.

The nothingness did not last.

They were slapping him and he felt the sweat of his body running over his skin. He opened his eyes and could see Auntie M standing over him.

"He's a tough motherfucker," she said to the technicians.

"Did he say anything?" Cole said. Chandler had not seen him come in; he had just appeared, hovering like a carrion crow.

"So far, recalcitrant," one of the technicians said.

Cole stood closer. "It's just a sample, Chandler," he whispered. "Have you any idea how much agony these men can deliver? What is Jellyfish? Who was in this with you?"

"Kill me, please," Chandler said. "Kill me now and don't let them go on with this."

Cole stared at him. "All right, Chandler. The hard way." He nodded to the technicians. "Up it a tad," he said.

They made an adjustment on the machine and the machine clicked and hummed. Auntie M stood by the door, watching the technicians with intense interest. Cole did not watch. He turned toward the sink, took out a cigar, and unwrapped it. He was sweating.

Chandler looked toward the ceiling; it seemed to recede up and away from him. The pain swirled under him. He told himself he could stand against it. The skin was being burned off him and he told himself he could take it all because he knew the limit. He could ride it to the limit. They hit him again and again with the pain, and each time he grew more resistant to it; his will was like concrete. He held the chair with his hands and bit down hard on his lower lip until blood ran down his chin and onto his chest. A great anger arose in him and from his center a blaze of hatred spread through him, infusing him with strength. He was determined he would not scream again; he would stand against it, outlast it; he would mount and ride the pain all the way to the suburbs of hell—and then they hit him again with it, and it cut into him and burst him from the inside. The pain fused with sound and light and the voice of his strength was meshed with other voices. In the confusion he was no longer certain which was the voice of truth, and he no longer knew who he was or what he was. . . . And then he screamed: "Ahhhhaaaa!" Like a dam bursting, the screaming shrank the world and the pain. It all fell away from him. Once again the grayness seeped into his brain and the cool blackness of unbeing swallowed him up and he welcomed it like an angel, cradled himself in it and let himself slip away.

This time they gave him an injection and the needle was still in his arm as he came out of the darkness.

"He's a cool motherfucker," Auntie M said.

"This stinks," Cole said. He paced back and forth, not looking at Chandler. His eyes were moist. He was sickened by it and it showed. He sucked on his cigar.

"It was better in the old days when all we had was a little piano wire and a pair of fucking electrician's pliers," Auntie M said. "It was over quick."

"This cigar tastes like shit," Cole said. He crushed it out on the floor.

The technicians slapped Chandler and reset the wires on his body, then made adjustments on the machine.

"What if maybe they won't break him?" Cole said. He went to the sink, rinsed his hands, and dried them on a towel. "In a way I hope they don't. He's a damn man of iron. I hope they don't break him."

"Men of iron? No such thing," Auntie M said. "They have nerves in them, they fucking break like china hit with a twenty-pound sledge. It's a law of physics."

"Don't be so sure," Cole said.

The white technician said, "Permission to elevate the treatment level, sir." He had been listening to Chandler's heartbeat with a stethoscope.

Cole looked at Chandler, who had let his bladder go, soaking his pants with urine. He was pale and bluish and his swollen tongue protruded from between his teeth. "Do whatever you have to do," Cole said.

Chandler began to speak. His eyes fluttered and his voice was hoarse and nearly inaudible.

"What's that?" Auntie M said.

A technician put his head close to Chandler's mouth. "He wants water."

"Give us a little something," Auntie M said, "and we'll give you water."

"Who's the sniper rifle for? Ask him that," Cole said.

Chandler lifted his head. He trembled; beads of sweat covered his face. "Water . . . please . . ."

Auntie M had the water in a glass and was holding it in front of his face. "Give us something first, Chan."

Cole came to him and shook his shoulders. "Who was the Enfield for?"

Chandler cleared his throat. He panted for air. They were all waiting.

"Water, please."

She held it in front of him. He coughed and vomited on the floor, and gasped for air. Then slowly raising his head he looked at them. His eyes were red and swollen and his skin was pale and his lips trembled.

"I'll tell you," he said. "Only you, Lucius. I'll give it all to you. Names, dates, places, facts. You've won. Please, no more . . . no more."

"That-a-boy, that-a-boy," Cole said. "Now then. How about a name. Start with a name. Who was the target? Who did you want the sniper rifle for?"

"Haas," Chandler said, barely audibly.

"Atta-boy," Auntie M said. "Help us out, we'll help you. Who was that again?"

"Haas. President Haas." His voice was weak, hoarse. "Undo what I've done. Got to undo it."

"Give him a drink," Cole said.

Auntie M gave him a sip of water. He tilted his head forward for more, but she refused.

"Why?" Auntie M said. "Why you going to fuck with Haas?"

"Drink," Chandler said. "Got to drink . . ."

"Give him a little more," Cole said.

Auntie M poured it into his mouth, then pulled the glass back. "Come on, Chan. Out with it."

"I will tell Lucius. Everything. All of it. Montreal, Jellyfish, all of it. The Company and the Old Guard. I will tell you all of it and then I will be done with it. You can have it for what you will do with it. I am finished. It must be undone. Must be undone. I will tell you, Lucius. I will tell it all to you. All of it. Please, no more of the machine. No more."

He was crying now, sobbing, and his head was down. He was trembling and his head wavered on his shoulders as if it were loose.

"It'll be all right," Auntie M said, patting him on the shoulder. "We'll take care of you."

Cole turned to the white technician. "Will we be needing any of this stuff anymore?" meaning the equipment.

"Once they break they don't stiffen up again."

"Get it out of here. Clean him up."

The technicians took the wires and handcuffs off Chandler and helped him to his feet. His knees bent under him; he still sobbed and shook.

"I'll tell you all, Lucius," he said weakly.

FIFTY

The technicians took him to the bathroom and he leaned over the sink. They poured water over him. The black supported Chandler's weight and the white poured water on him.

Chandler felt his muscles gradually come under his control, the strength come back into his legs. He looked into the mirror and saw himself and he hated himself because he had let himself be conquered.

Auntie M opened the door. "Hurry it up," she said. She went back to the kitchen.

His mind was becoming clear. He breathed slowly and deeply. They put his face under the faucet. His shirt was open; his chest was a mass of burned skin and congealed blood.

"You almost made it to level four," the white technician said. "Almost a record."

"Yeah," the black technician said, "level four is halfway to Mars."

They rubbed him down with a coarse towel. For a moment his mind disconnected itself and seemed to drift over them; he was back in Hungary and on the lake with his grandfather and his grandfather was reeling in a big fish.

"Least he didn't shit his pants. We give more points if you shit," the black one said. The white one laughed easily. Chandler looked at the man's teeth; they were white, pearlescent, even, perfect. Live little gems inside his mouth. Chandler turned and saw himself in the mirror again. The reflection wasn't him. Pieces of makeup and wax were globbed on his cheeks. He looked old. A hundred years old.

The white technician shook him on the shoulder. "You're doing great, friend, just great. . . . Okay now, you've got a tale to tell." He took Chandler by the arm to lead him back into the kitchen. Chandler looked at him and started to go peaceably, but he suddenly collapsed as if his strength had failed him. The technician reached for him, but he spun around and smashed his head into the mirror over the sink, shattering it into a dozen large slivers. He dropped to his knees. A gush of blood poured out over his face.

"Tsk, tsk," the white technician said. "Damaged goods."

"We'll have to give a fifteen percent discount," the black technician said.

Auntie M was in the doorway, holding her .45 in front of her.

"Slipped," the black technician said. "Accidents do happen."

"Seven fucking years bad luck," she said. "Put some water on him." She went back to the kitchen.

The technicians pulled him to his feet and stuck his head in the sink and turned on the faucet. Chandler rested on the sink with his hand on a sliver of glass. The black technician washed Chandler's head while the white one stood by the door, looking on with his arms folded. Neither, apparently, was armed.

"Seven years bad luck, that's funny," the black technician said, chortling.

Chandler shifted his weight. His hand slid down to his side, the hand with the sliver of glass in it, held like a knife.

The black technician cut off the water and reached for a towel, turning his back to Chandler for a moment. It was then that Chandler struck.

He straightened up and grabbed the man's shoulder, pinning him around, bringing the glass sliver upward in a slashing motion across his throat. The blood spurted out like a fountain onto his shirt. The technician looked surprised; his mouth opened and a gurgle of blood poured out. Then his eyes rolled back into his head and he fell back and sank to the floor.

Chandler turned to the white technician, who was heading out the door. He grabbed him by the collar and dragged him back into the bathroom, hitting him in the face until he stopped moving. A large sliver of glass lay next to him on the floor. Chandler picked it up in his bloody hand and wrapped it in a towel. He turned off the light and crouched low. He could hear Auntie M coming.

The white technician moaned.

"What's going on in there?" Auntie M said. She was just in the hall outside. She had turned off the hall light. She would not be at a disadvantage.

Chandler didn't answer. He didn't move.

"Hey, what the fuck's going on in there?"

Chandler reached up and turned on the water. He put his arm to his mouth to muffle his voice. "Okay in here."

He rapped on the wall. "Be out in a minute."

She started to open the door. "What happened to the light?"

"Watch out!" the technician hollered.

Chandler Smith jerked the door inward and suddenly sprang at her, shoving the glass at her chest. It struck home as her .45 went off. He had her, breaking the glass off and slashing at her throat, the blood spurting out over them; they rolled on the floor. She was trying to bring her weapon in position to fire again, but he had her by the wrist. They were face to face now and he pushed a wedge of glass deep into her neck. She wiggled in his grasp and tried to push him away, but he held her tight, pushing the glass deeper.

"Ah, fuck . . ." she gasped, and the last of her life hissed out of her lungs.

From above and behind him: "Hold it, Chandler." It was Cole. He was standing ten feet away, in the doorway of the kitchen, with his gun drawn.

Chandler froze. He had his hand on the hot barrel of Auntie M's .45. His leg was on fire where the bullet she fired had grazed him.

"Just don't move, Chandler."

The technician staggered out of the bathroom and stood over Chandler, breathing hard and weaving.

"Get out to the car," Cole said to the technician. "Call the reinforcement code number. Tell them what's gone down and get some help over here."

The technician grunted and staggered down the hall. Chandler still had not moved. He was gathering his strength. Cole started down the hall, cautiously. "Just stay exactly where you are, Chandler." His voice was tight with fear. "Is she dead?"

Chandler didn't answer. He glanced toward the living room, where it was dark. The darkness extended up the hall to within five feet of him.

"That's it, Chandler, just stay exactly as you are."

Chandler slowly moved his head around. He was measuring his space, his chances. His movement would have to be quick if it was going to work, quick and startling. First he moaned weakly, to distract Cole, then he suddenly screamed and twisted and fell back into the darkness, pulling Auntie M's body with him as a shield. Cole fired four times. The house shook with sounds of the shots.

Cole stood there for a moment, holding his gun in front of him with the light behind him. He waited — waited and listened, and for a long moment there was nothing.

"Chandler? Chandler, are you there?" he said. "Answer me." He knew he was exposed and vulnerable. He knew that if his shots had missed, there was no escape. He held the gun in front of him with both hands, pointing it into the darkness.

"Chandler, please — are you there? Isn't it like you said? We do what is necessary? Chandler? Let's talk. Speak to me. Are you there, Chandler? Are you there?"

He backed away an inch, then two. He backed away, on his unsteady legs. But then:

"I am here, Lucius . . . ."

FIFTY-ONE

It was windy and clear in the early morning. Knebel arrived by taxi at the White House and was met at the door by a nondescript Secret Service man in a gray suit and taken by elevator to the third floor of the south wing.

Knebel asked the Secret Service man what had happened. Had they caught Smith? The Secret Service man grunted and shrugged his shoulders and said something was going on, but he hadn't been told and it wasn't his place to ask. In the hall on the third floor there were two more Secret Service men and they, too, were wearing gray suits and neutral expressions, standing silent and bored. Knebel was led down a hallway lined with portraits of Presidents and lesser dignitaries to a room at the end. It was a conference room with a long, gleaming table surrounded by leather-covered chairs and there were more portraits on the walls of severe-looking men and elegantly-dressed matrons. A meeting was just about to begin. The President was there, looking sullen, and Hans Ober and two of his men were seated near him. Then Knebel saw Sanchez-Flint, the cool and aloof FBI Director, and Bennett Fowler, the bespectacled, balding head of the CIA. Neither seemed pleased to be there.

Wilson Wright made a few introductions, thanked everyone in muted tones for coming on such short notice, and then asked Hans Ober to bring everyone up to date on the latest developments.

Hans Ober folded his hands on the table in front of him and surveyed his audience with steady eyes before he spoke. His dark eyes were reddened and he appeared desperately fatigued, but his voice was strong and unwavering:

"There has been a major development in the assassination investigation, gentlemen. Early this morning I was summoned to the scene of a fire-gutted house in West Baltimore, okay? We found three bodies in the ashes: Lucius Cole, Deputy Director of the CIA, a technician for the CIA's Technical Services Division, and a female operative named May Westcot. A second technician is missing.

"At four-thirty this morning, Peter Wrentzel, one of Lucius Cole's administrative assistants, received a call from one of the technical-service technicians—the one now missing—that things had gone wrong and there had been killings. He said they had questioned Chandler Smith and he had revealed that he had been planning a further assassination—this time, President Haas. He wanted to undo what he had done, he said. Somehow Smith managed to get loose and he killed a lot of people. How Mr. Cole managed to capture Smith we have no idea, okay? Apparently through May Westcot."

"And then he tortured him," the President said sourly. "Isn't that right?"

"Apparently so," Ober said.

The President turned to Bennett Fowler, the CIA Chief. "I take it this isn't standard operating procedure, is it, Mr. Fowler? How is it one of your people has murdered Jamison and another of your people is torturing the suspect?" he said sarcastically.

"I have already tendered my resignation," Bennett Fowler said. "I take full responsibility, even though none of this was done with either my permission or knowledge."

"I still want answers," the President said, "and so will the Justice Department, I assure you. There's going to be no soft-pedaling this."

Fowler stiffened and stared at the President. "I'll take official responsibility, but I take no blame and suffer no guilt, personally. Lucius Cole was acting completely on his own and I'll swear to that—under penalty of perjury if you like."

Haas said, "It's easy for you to swear off and turn away; Smith isn't gunning for you, he's gunning for me." When Fowler said nothing, Haas glared at him for a moment and then turned to Hans Ober. "All those thousands of men and millions of dollars and we can't catch this one man? Do you have any idea how this looks to the world? We look like buffoons, that's how we look!"

"Okay." Hans Ober shifted. "I'm not making excuses, but he is trained, ruthless, and exceedingly cunning. Okay, sir, remember, he *was* caught. Central Intelligence had him—for how long, we have no way of knowing. They may have been hiding him for some time."

"The important thing," Wilson Wright said, "is where we go from here. The fox is still on the loose, so to speak. Let's throw this open to the floor. Where do we go from here, gentlemen?"

Knebel raised his hand and was recognized.

"The first thing," he said, "we've got to let the press in on this. They hunger for a cover-up like jackals. We've got to give them something."

"A carefully worded statement is being prepared at this moment," Wilson Wright responded. "We do expect a loud public outcry and we're bracing for it."

"In the meantime," Hans Ober said, "we're doing everything that can be done to capture Smith. This manhunt is the most intense in history. There are thirteen thousand, eight hundred men looking for Chandler Smith at any given moment on any day. That's just Federal. There are thousands more state and local agencies involved—and private citizens. Okay, we will find him. I give you my personal guarantee, gentlemen. We *will* get him, okay?"

Sanchez-Flint, the FBI Director, said he would give his personal guarantee as well.

The President smiled wanly. "So far that's about all we do have, isn't it, gentlemen? Personal guarantees."

"Actually, Mr. President, we have a great deal," Sanchez-Flint said with measured coolness. "We have the complete thing on the weapons. The second suspect, Hakim, is dead, and we have some very good leads on her ties to Adolph White and the radical left."

"Very good," the President said. "But what about Smith?"

Sanchez-Flint smiled confidently. "We do have a strategy in formation there as well," he said. He turned to Hans Ober. "Would you please outline for us what our intentions are at this time, Hans?"

"Yes, sir." He looked at his notes. "For the first time," he said, "we feel we can control the situation—we're in the driver's seat. Smith is wounded. We know that definitely because we found his blood on the sidewalk outside the house, and from the amount of blood we know he's hurting bad. We have every doctor, hospital, nursing home, and clinic within five hundred miles under surveillance at this very moment. There is no possible way he can get qualified medical help without us knowing about it, okay?" He scanned everyone in the room, then continued. "That's phase one. . . . The inauguration of C. Miller Petri as Vice President is set for Tuesday as the Lincoln Memorial. Now we know Smith was going after a sniper's rifle. He's got to try then and we'll be ready. That's phase two. One way or the other, we get him."

He was finished talking. He leaned back in his chair and reached for his coffee cup.

Sanchez-Flint said that the calculated risk was minimal. "The President will not be in any inordinately high-risk situations. The exposure is minuscule."

"How minuscule?" Knebel asked.

"I'm sure you know there is no way to measure risk with any precision."

"I'll take the risk," the President stated. "Why does he want to kill me? Anyone have any idea?"

"It's some kind of psychological pathology." Sanchez-Flint said.

"I believe it is too," Wilson Wright said.

The President sighed. "You know what we've got so far? A lot of high-sounding rhetoric. Hear this. I want this man caught. I know there is a risk involved here for me personally, but I want this man caught *now*. One lone madman cannot be allowed to paralyze a nation or its leadership. When one goes into public office, one goes into it knowing up front there are dangers to be faced. I have promised this nation dynamic and vital leadership and it is entitled to nothing less."

"Mr. President?" Knebel said. "May I say something?"

"Certainly."

"The plan does have some boldness to it, but as in all defensive operations, you must anticipate all possible contingencies and then wait to react to the suspect when he acts first. Such plans are often wrought with uncertainties. All contingencies *can't* be anticipated, for one thing."

"What do you mean, 'all contingencies can't be anticipated'?"

"We are making unfounded assumptions. First, we assume he is alone. He may not be alone. We assume he's wounded severely, but he may not be. And we don't know his motives or intentions or capacity. We don't know his resources."

The President nodded vaguely. "What else can I do, Mr. Knebel? I can't sit here in the White House and hide, can I? As long as the FBI and security people approve the plan, I'll go along. Any assistance you might give them would be appreciated."

"Might I ask you something, Mr. President?"

"What, Mr. Knebel?"

"Have you ever heard of the Old Guard?"

"No, what is it?"

"I'm not sure. . . . Have you ever heard of a CIA agent named Bernard Ferris?"

He thought a moment, then shook his head. "Ferris? No. Why do you ask?"

"Looking for motives. Thought perhaps this might be

personal."

"It isn't."

Wilson Wright adjourned the meeting.

As the others were filing out of the room, Knebe asked Ober to wait a moment.

"Why wasn't I called when this first broke?"

"We didn't know what we had or how we were going to handle it. Wilson Wright wanted me to do a prelimi-nary investigation."

"So he could figure the political side of things?"

"Yes."

Knebel smiled. "He's got you playing games, Hans Better watch it."

Hans Ober said, "You know how it is, you got to play or they kick you out of their sandbox."

FIFTY-TWO

Knebel drove Ober's car to West Baltimore. Chad Priest went along. Chad Priest was subdued and quiet. They got caught in the commuter traffic on the bridge and had to wait twenty minutes for a stall to be removed.

The bodies had been taken away by the time they arrived, and the gutted house told Knebel nothing. It had burned hot in the center and had fallen in on itself. Some of it was still smoldering and wisps of smoke rose into the cold gray sky.

"What do you think, Chad?" Knebel asked.

"I don't know. Smith must have had help. They tortured him and he must have been weak. There were four of them. I think he had to have had help."

"Lucius Cole told me Smith could kill a man six hundred ways."

Knebel talked to a fire investigator for the Baltimore Fire Department and then he and Chad Priest drove back to Washington.

"He started it with gasoline," Knebel said. "The Volkswagen bus has no gas in it, the fire captain said. He must have drained the tank."

"Taking vengeance on the corpses, you think?"

"Could be . . . You know what else I'm thinking? If he took the time to drain the gas tank, how badly wounded could he be?"

"I see your point."

When they arrived back at the Annex, the security desk at the front door told them to report to Hans Ober's office. They went up to the third floor in an elevator. Hans Ober was busy at the moment lecturing some subordinates. When he was finished he asked Knebel to come in alone. Ober was angry.

"He's got guns, Knebel. He hit a sporting goods store this morning. We had the goddamned place staked out, and he knocked it off anyway. What the hell are we dealing with here? We got two men in a car across the street and he walks right past them because he looks like a farmer. We all take disguises as a joke because they make fun of them in the movies and on TV, but by God it isn't a joke! It's a weapon, a terrible, potent weapon in the hands of a master, Knebel. I've seen it. This guy could make himself up like your mother and you'd take him out to dinner on his birthday."

"How about his wounds? How bad is he hurting?"

"That's another thing. The son-of-a-bitch got a veterinarian in Castle Island, Maryland, out of bed right after dawn. The vet stopped the bleeding for him and sewed him up. A veterinarian, Jesus Christ! This guy is making us look like a bunch of asses!"

"The TV people are going to have a lot of fun at six tonight," Knebel said.

"You bet they will. Coast to coast they'll roast us like Thanksgiving turkeys. Today I break my oath. I swore I wasn't going to down a bourbon until this guy was in

318

irons, but I'm breaking that oath today. . . . You still think we ought to scrap the idea of grabbing him when he goes after Haas?"

"It's a perilous course."

"Would you take it — the risk, I mean?"

"Yes."

Hans Ober smiled. His hard, cop features turned almost boyish. "Thanks for that, Knebel. Thanks much. Now, sit down — I'm afraid I have some bad news." His features hardened. He looked grave and folded his hands on his desk in front of him.

"What is it, Hans?"

"Wilson Wright called me this morning after the meeting. He wanted to know if I thought Lowenstein was completely trustworthy. Wright's a real sandlot politician, okay? He's buddy-buddy with Sanchez-Flint. Got the picture? Sanchez-Flint wants this whole show to be totally Bureau. Now that Stewart Ott's been rotated out, I think maybe he could get the President excited about making some changes — you get the picture?"

"What did you tell him about Lowenstein?"

"What could I tell him? I told him Lowenstein was one of the greatest detective brains that ever lived, but he was a little on the unpredictable side."

"Go on."

"Okay, the President is highly agitated by this whole business, as you might well imagine. So, for whatever reason, Wilson Wright and the President have decided that maybe it isn't such a hot idea to have a convicted felon quite so closely associated with the investigation."

"You mean they're thinking of giving him the ax."

He nodded. "The decision has already been made. Believe me, I made a case for keeping him, but Wilson

Wright said the President's mind was made up."

"You think I ought to fight them on this?"

"Bad time for dissension."

"Wonder what's behind it?"

Ober shrugged. "Who the hell knows? Maybe it's because of the autopsy business, who knows? Politics is like the tide, it comes in and goes out. You've got to go with the tide or drown in it."

FIFTY-THREE

Knebel's plane landed at Montreal's Dorval Airport at three-thirty in the afternoon. After clearing customs, Knebel was met by Walter Byron, who looked tired, but content.

"Where's Lowenstein?" Knebel asked.

"Back at our apartment, why?"

"When I called, I said I wanted *him* to meet me."

"He had to get somebody he wanted you to talk to. You know how he is, Mr. Knebel. He doesn't pay too much attention to what anybody tells him."

Knebel was angry. He shoved his hands deep into his pockets and followed Byron down the ramp. "I have a return ticket on a plane out of here in an hour," Knebel said.

"I'll try to have you back in time, sir."

Byron drove the rented Ford Fairmount. They headed north on Boulevard Maison Neuve.

"Is it something important?" Byron asked Knebel. "I mean, why you wanted Mr. Lowenstein to meet you."

"It's personal business between Mr. Lowenstein and me."

Byron was silent for a moment. "He's an amazing

man, you know. Truly amazing."

"In more ways than one."

"He's cut through this thing faster than a hot knife through soft butter. He doesn't build a case out of tiny scraps and then fit them together like a jigsaw puzzle. He grabs off chunks of it at a time. I guess he needs somebody like me around to pick up the crumbs and analyze them, but he gets most of it in a hurry."

"I never said he wasn't good. Nobody ever said he wasn't good."

"He's just not an organization man," Byron grinned.

Knebel lit his pipe. "What's he got for me? Who's this person he wants me to talk to?"

"The man who knows all about the Montreal Project. Maybe even why there was no anabase trioxin in the President's liver."

"That doesn't overly excite me at this point."

"Maybe it will when you hear it all."

Byron pulled up in front of a gray-colored apartment house. The building was shabby and the parking lot was broken up. It was on Rue St. Jacques near Old Montreal.

"We didn't know how long we'd be," Byron said. "We got this place on a weekly rent. Lowenstein says he can't feel at home in a Hilton."

Knebel followed him upstairs. Some kids were playing on the stairs, shooting each other with squirt guns.

The apartment was large, with high ceilings and old, over-stuffed furniture. The drapes were in a floral pattern. It was chilly inside and smelled faintly of natural gas.

Lowenstein came out of the bedroom. He had a coffee cup in his hand. "Have a nice flight, Knebel?"

"I wanted you to meet me at the airport. I said specifically I was flying in to confer with you in person."

"I was busy, catch?"

"What have you got?" He looked at his watch.

"I've got a Mr. Ralph Donaldson. He's been telling us some very interesting stories. Would you like to hear some of them?"

Knebel stepped into the bedroom. Donaldson was perhaps thirty, thin, with a gray pallor on his cheeks. He looked up at Knebel and there was fear in his eyes.

"You're Donaldson?" Knebel asked.

The man nodded.

Knebel looked at Lowenstein. "Who is he?"

"He worked at the Old Guard's research place. He was their pharmacologist."

"Is that right?" Knebel asked Donaldson.

He nodded and said, "Did you bring the money?"

"The money?"

"I had to promise him ten thousand to get his story," Lowenstein said. "Got any discretionary funds on you?"

"Nobody gave you any such authority," Knebel said.

"So I'm a lying cur. Sorry Donaldson, no pot at the end of the rainbow, catch?"

Donaldson came to his feet, rage flooding onto his gray face. "You swore there'd be no problem! You said I'd have my money today!"

Lowenstein shrugged. "Life is sometimes a pisser, Donaldson. Sit down. *Sit down,* I said."

Donaldson sat back down, sullen.

"What's he selling?" Knebel asked.

"He did give us some of it," Byron said. "He worked for the project the whole ten months. He's identified Smith and Ferris — who was known then as Sabel."

"Is that right, Mr. Donaldson?" Knebel said.

"I want my money. Without the money, I'm saying nothing. If they find out about me talking to you guys, I'm going to be shredded like a cabbage in a coleslaw factory."

"What's he talking about?" Knebel asked.

Byron said, "When the project was burned out he was ordered to disappear someplace. But he had this fat girl friend here he was having a good time with, so he stayed on. That's how Mr. Lowenstein tracked him down, through her. Ellen Kidd, her name is."

"All right, Mr. Donaldson," Knebel said. "You give us something good, I'll see to it you get not only money but an untraceable new identity."

"What about Ellen?"

"Ellen, too," Knebel said. "Tell me all about what went on here."

Donaldson's eyes drifted between Lowenstein and Knebel and there was fear in them. He was calculating his chances either way.

"Logically you have no other choice for your future or Ellen's," Byron said. "You might as well swim in the current, because you sure as hell can't go back upstream."

Donaldson nodded at the impeccable logic of that. "Christ, my cover's blown anyway. What the hell." His eyes drifted downward and his voice sank into a lower register. "All right," he said. "It was like he says. I'm a pharmacologist — almost a pharmacologist. I got into a little trouble when I was going to school. I cribbed a little, as they say, and didn't quite finish up. I was a junior, actually. Couldn't keep my hands off broads. Never had time to study." He sighed at the memory, then looked to Knebel, assuring him. "I'm pretty good at math and chemistry when I want to be, but broads just drive me crazy. I can't stop thinking about them. So anyway, when I got kicked out of Michigan State — which was a pretty damn harsh penalty for the tiny little cribbing I was into — I had to make a living somehow. A man's got to make his bread, as they say. So I met up with these guys from Toronto who said they were into synfuels out of river mud. What they were really into was cocaine, I found out pronto. They wanted me to test the stuff they were bringing in from South America and passing south into Detroit. I went along for the ride. It was easy work and the money was good. Shit, it don't hurt nobody but those who want to ride the mustang. The one night I was working in my lab down in my basement and the cops smash in. Just like that. The next thing I know, I'm in the boiler. Was I sweating it. Canada don't mess around with dope, you know. It's a heavy trip, maybe ten years, maybe more. I'd go crazy, no broads for ten years. So my solicitor comes to me and says he's got a deal. The Americans are doing this secret project and they can use my skills. If I go along with it, I'm off the hook. Hey, What the hell choice is that? I go along with it."

"What was the deal?" Knebel asked.

"I'm supposed to work for this psychological institute that's testing a mind-altering drug. A variant of LSD. They call it Lysergic Acid-N. I don't know what the hell it is. I ask them, but they tell me the less I know the better.

"Tell me about Ferris," Knebel said.

"He means Sabel," Byron said.

"You're sure you can get me this new identity?"

"Anything you want, any place on the planet,"

Knebel said.

"Sabel — Ferris — is a strange man. Very, very strange. He's got the strangest look about him. He's one determined son-of-a-bitch. He wants this project to succeed bad. I could see right off the bat why they needed me. This LSD-N is unstable as hell. You got to melt it down from a powder and the crystals form almost immediately. You got to use an alkaline reducer — not too much — or you blow the top of the subject's head right off. Then you got to have it ready to inject within, say, twenty minutes, or you've lost it. It separates on you. You've got to get it perfect — temperature, consistency, everything."

"What were its effects?"

"It made the subjects sort of indecisive. Wishy-washy. Vaguely fearful. It was hell on executives. They lost their magnetic north. We had it right down to a science, perfectly predictable. Sabel was getting very excited about it; then he found some new twist. It's a hallucinogen, you know — could make you imagine all kinds of stuff. Not wild visionary stuff, like regular LSD, but funny stuff, like suddenly you were in love with Sophia Loren."

"What did they intend to do with it? This wasn't done for purely scientific reasons."

"I have no idea, honest to God. They talked a lot about *the bond*. They wanted to make the bond. What the hell that meant, I have no idea. Far as I know they didn't get it. The only guy besides Sabel who knew what it was, was the assistant director, a guy named Archer Ogden. He was a real scientist type. His head was stuck in a test tube. After a while, though, he started getting antsy."

"Where do I find him?"

"He must be in a zoo or someplace. He should have been locked up. Brilliant, but goofy, you know."

"In what way?"

"Compared to him, Hamlet was cheerful."

"Two subjects committed suicide, you know about them?"

"Sure, that was early on, before they got it right."

"Anabase trioxins were in their liver tissue."

"Sure. Probably a lot."

"How long does it stay there after treatment is terminated?"

He pursed his lips. "Not sure. A week, maybe two. The psychological effects last a hell of a lot longer. Years maybe."

"Jamison hadn't had an injection for five months," Knebel said to Byron.

Donaldson's eyes went wide. "They fired up Jamison? Holy shit! Who'd want to do that? The Russians?"

"We don't know. . . . What happened with the project?" Knebel asked. "Why was it shut down?"

"LSD-N was unstable and tricky like I said, so it wasn't any good for field work. Besides, Jamison came to the Presidency and he wasn't as gung ho for this as Ronald Reagan — if Reagan even knew about it."

"Jamison scrapped the project?"

"Somebody did, unless Robert Roberts — I mean Chandler Smith — closed it on his own initiative. What the hell do I know?"

"What *did* Smith have to do with all this?"

"Not a hell of a lot with the tests themselves. He was just around. I don't think he really approved of the project. It was his job to see that we weren't infiltrated. You know, to see there was no hanky-panky. Security was his bag. Then one day he says their contract was cancelled—he gives everybody travel money and that kind of stuff. Sabel is madder than hell. He thinks he's just on the fringe of some great breakthrough and he wants Smith to go to bat for him, but Smith won't hear of it. The next thing you know, the place burns down. That's it, that's all I can tell you. Fifty-six thousand dollars they gave me and a New Zealand passport, and they tell me maybe I ought to find a better climate. I have been deep under, holding my breath ever since."

Knebel thanked Donaldson and went out into the living room with Byron.

"Get a complete statement from him. We want names, dates, times. Get some money out of Hans for them; then get him into the informant program for an identity change. His girlfriend, too. Then get an APB out on Archer Ogden."

"Sure."

"Ask Lowenstein to come out here, I want to talk with him privately."

"Okay."

A moment later Lowenstein came into the room. He was smiling and he looked at Knebel and his smile dissolved.

"You look like you've got some had news, Knebel."

"Why don't you have a seat?"

"Maybe I should have a drink." He took a pint from his coat and drank some from the bottle. "What the hell is it, did we blow our expense account or something? These aren't exactly deluxe accommodations."

"I want you to know I had nothing to do with this."

"With what?"

"Can't have you working on the case anymore."

"What?"

"Wilson Wright and the President are nervous and want you taken off the case."

"This is mighty strange."

"I wanted you to know it wasn't my decision ."

Lowenstein took a few more gulps of liquor. "Once you're down they won't let you up, catch? They just keep kicking the hell out of you." He stared vacantly at Knebel.

"I've still got friends in Pennsylvania, Lowenstein. I made a few calls before I left. The Governor is going to sign a special waiver to allow you to work for the State Police out of Harrisburg. They're going to loan you out to local jurisdictions to give assists on the tough ones."

"Throw the old dog a bone, that it?"

"It'll put you back in the trenches, isn't that what you wanted?"

"I'll think about it." Lowenstein put on his coat. "I was on a streak with this one. I'm telling you, give me a week more and I'll have this guy Smith sitting in your lap."

"Sorry, there's nothing I can do."

"I'll say good-bye to Byron. Keep him on, Knebel. For a college man he's not too bad. He's trainable anyway."

"Sure," Knebel said.

FIFTY-FOUR

The shadows of sunset were long on the pavement of the parking lot and the gray clouds of evening were cast in orange against the rippled sky. It was cool and quiet; the traffic on Highgate Boulevard was light. Chandler Smith watched the sunset from the roof of the gray abandoned building and it faded quickly. He had been resting, tending the injury to his leg. The limb throbbed with pain where the veterinarian had sutured it; blood seeped from the wound and a deep redness was spreading down his leg which was stiff and numb. He had soaked a dressing in antiseptic and had bathed the wound and bound it. It was a bad wound. The veterinarian had said it was bad; he should have gone to a hospital because the bone was chipped and there were pieces of the bullet still inside him.

He had a six-pack of beer to drink and he drank four bottles, sitting propped against the wall of the airshaft. The building had once been a farm implement manufacturing company, and it was brick, old, crumbling. The building beyond the creek was a warehouse without windows; on the other side was Highgate Boulevard. There was a sign that said the owner "will build to suit enant." It was quiet here and he felt safe for the moment.

From his place on the roof he could see across the river to the Capitol, and with his field glasses he could see the Capitol dome, lit now in the growing darkness. To the south he could see the Lincoln Monument; it, too, was lighted and grand.

As the darkness spread over the city he felt safer and was warm under a large tarpaulin he had found in the abandoned factory. He got under it and rested his head on his duffel bag. The beer was warming him from within and his leg was throbbing less. Only a tingling bothered him. He slept for a half hour, slept soundlessly and dreamlessly, and he awoke suddenly to the sound of screeching tires someplace below.

It was cool after dark and the wind had come up. He ate some cheese and French bread and had some more beer under the tarpaulin. After he had finished eating he packed everything in the duffel bag. He got to his feet and his leg was very stiff. With the movement, pain returned. He paced around between the airshaft and the wall, where he could not be seen from the street, until he could move his leg freely and then he stretched the muscles. Leaving the tarpaulin, he picked up his duffel bag and went down the fire escape at the back of the building by the marsh, down one flight to where he had forced the boards over the window open earlier. He went inside. It was cold and sound echoed off the empty walls.

This was a loft area, where there were offices and one of them had no windows. He went in the office without windows, closed the door, and lit his flashlight. There was an old table, some papers on the floor. Getting out his makeup equipment, he started changing himself. It

didn't take him long. He had a tight-fitting hairpiec
and dark skin cream and shaded glasses. There wa
great pain shooting up the right side of his leg and h
winced into the mirror he was using.

When his disguise was completed he went outside
leaving all of his things except his weapon and a fev
tools. He dragged his foot, which went well with th
character he was playing. He crossed the street with th
light and stood at the bus stop. Some young peopl
passed and paid no attention to him and he did not loo
at them. Cars went by, many of them. No one notice
the old Black man standing at the bus stop.

When the bus came a Black man was driving it. Th
driver said, "Evenin' " and Chandler Smith nodded. H
dropped fifty cents into the box and moved to the back
taking a seat by the rear door. There were a couple o
passengers and when they looked his way, his eyes foun
theirs and they turned away. He kept watch at the win
dow. At the intersection of Willow he pulled the cor
and got off at the next stop. He didn't hurry; a lame ma
never hurries.

The traffic on the Boulevard was light. There was
clock in the window of a Chevrolet dealership. It was te
minutes to eight. He crossed with the light and turne
south on the boulevard, walking in the bright light of th
lamps which arched out over the street. He walked pa
the Higate Baking Company. He stopped for a momer
to look at the bakery and the trucks lined up behind th
chain-linked fence behind the building.

He continued at his slow pace to the end of the bloc
and turned on Grant Avenue. The traffic was heavie
here; it was a main arterial between the expressway an
the suburb of Yorktown. The cars whizzed past. H

walked to the alley which ran behind the bakery and started up it.

A young man was walking his dog down the alley. He said good evening to the lame old Black man and Chandler Smith waved his hand and watched him with suspicion. Apparently, he was just walking his dog and nothing else.

At the back gate of the bakery Chandler picked the padlock. It was an old lock and the tumblers were loose and it was easy for him. Most of the trucks were all lined up in rows. There was one parked by the fence, off by itself, waiting to be pulled up into the washrack. He squeezed between two rows of parked trucks and made his way down to the washrack. It was very dark here and the cover was good.

There was a sound behind him, a scratching, and he glanced backward and there was a German shepherd racing at him, teeth bared, hurtling through the air.

Chandler Smith reacted quickly by coming to his knees and bracing for the attack; he brought his forearm forward and shoved it into the animal's open jaw.

The force of the attack knocked him sprawling backward as he groped for his automatic with his right hand. The dog had not made a sound, but had released the arm and was trying for the throat. And then there was another dog on him; it had come from the opposite way and was bigger and stronger than the first.

Chandler Smith kicked the second dog squarely in the head and bounced him to the side. He had his automatic in his hand now and he pressed it under the first dog's chin and fired, fired the silenced weapon twice, and felt the animal stiffen and flap wildly to the ground. And then the second dog struck again, but Chandler Smith was ready and fired into his chest, knocking the dog backward in his tracks.

Chandler Smith got to his feet and looked around. It was quiet except for the traffic on the boulevard. The big dog was still breathing and squirming in pain on the ground. Chandler Smith shot him again and he stopped moving.

Chandler Smith was trembling and his arm was bleeding; the wound in his leg was open and blood was running down his leg. He went down to the truck by the washrack. It wasn't locked. He climbed in. The pains in his arm and leg were very sharp. He tore off part of his shirt and bound the wounds on his arm. There was no key for the truck, so he had to break the lock on the ignition with the channel pliers he had brought with him. There was no problem starting the truck.

He could hear the watchman calling for the dogs. Chandler drove the truck quickly out the gate and down the alley to the street.

Back at the abandoned Farm Implement Company Building, it took him two and a half hours, working methodically, to clean the paint with steel wool and mask off the glass with newspapers and tape. He worked slowly because of the pain. When he was finished he loaded an airless paint sprayer with blue paint and went to work making the gray van blue. The painting took him a little over an hour and when he finished it was nearly one in the morning. He rested and napped and when he woke he painted the sides with the official seal of the City of Washington, D.C. and put an inventory number on the back door. He changed the license plates, using some he had fabricated out of cardboard and masked with dirty oil.

When he was finished he cleaned himself up and changed his disguise, carefully cleaning off the dark face cream. Then he shaved. He penciled in some longer lines around his eyes, making himself appear vaguely oriental, and he darkened his skin with almond coloring.

He had coveralls, a red jacket, a bright orange vest, and an orange cap. When he had finished he examined himself in the mirror closely and was satisfied.

The paint job on the truck was still tacky, but okay. He had some sand and dirt, and he threw it on the truck and affixed some yellow lights to the top. Then he was ready.

It was after three o'clock in the morning when Chandler Smith pulled up in front of the barber shop at 216 S. Portland Street in Westborough, Virginia. He got out of the van. The street was deserted. It was a small town and quiet. He walked down the alley next to the barber shop to a small shack behind it. He had his automatic in his hand now. He approached the shack slowly. His mouth was dry and his leg tingled and had swollen and was very stiff. He stepped up on the porch, paused for a moment, then threw his shoulder into the door, smashing it open, and shined the flashlight straight ahead. There was a little man in a bed and he had sat up and was reaching for a gun.

"Freeze!" Chandler ordered.

The little man put up his hands. He was a bony little man and his face was twisted; his chin was covered with a rash and he hadn't shaved in a few days. Squinting into the flashlight, he said: "Cops? You the Feds?"

Chandler closed the door behind him and turned on the light. The rooms were small, shabby, cluttered.

"What the fuck," the little man said. "Who are you?"

"Look closer, Reggie."

He shaded his eyes from the light. "What the fuck. That you, Chandler? Holy fuck. Man are they looking for you. Are they *ever* looking for you!"

"They aren't finding me either."

"Did you really ice the Prez? . . . Christ man, you got big, big balls."

"I need some C-5 plastique, Reggie. About twenty kilos ought to do it."

Reggie Dawes got out of the bed and put on some slippers, keeping his hands in plain sight. He had long fingers and long fingernails, which he flicked against his thumbs.

"Twenty kilos? You must want to go for a moon ride. That what you want? You want to go for a mooooooon ride?"

"I'll also need some detonators and a remote switch."

"Maybe Reggie ain't got all that shit," Reggie Dawes said. "That's a lot of stock for a little man like Reggie."

"You've got it."

Reggie Dawes flicked his nails again, then scratched at a pimple on his cheek. "Maybe I do, maybe I don't."

Chandler pulled the hammer back on his automatic. "I want it now."

"Reggie ain't doing work for the Company anymore, you know. They put all us independents out of business."

"You aren't out of business. There's always a market in death, and you enjoy it too much to retire."

"Maybe Reggie does like it." He smiled. When he smiled he showed a lot of gum; his teeth were large and gleaming white and they looked strange in the mouth of the homely little man. "Tell you what, tell you what. You come back in two hours, Reggie maybe will have your stock."

Chandler pointed the automatic at the little man's head. "I can blow you up and look for it myself."

"Better put that down, Chandler. Reggie's a businessman." His voice was steamy with fear. "Reggie detests violence. Put it down, Chandler, I'll check my stock and see if we can fill your order, no sweat." He shuffled into the next room. "What is it, man? Ain't Reggie always played it fair with you? Hey, man, Reggie plays it straight with everyone. You buying this or thieving it?"

"You never played straight with anyone in your life," Chandler said.

The place was cluttered with electronic gear and tools and it smelled of lubricants and solder. There were TV and radio parts everywhere.

"This is going to run about two grand, Chandler. You got two grand?"

"I haven't had time to get to the bank, Reggie. This'll have to be on the cuff."

"Sure, Chandler. What the fuck are friends for?" He went into the bathroom. It was the only clean room in the house. He switched on the light and turned to Chandler. He had stopped squinting and stiffened straight up.

"There's a couple hundred grand reward on you, Chandler. Maybe more. I haven't been following it all that close."

"That's right, there is."

"You can't risk Reggie keeping his mouth shut about this. You've gotta kill Reggie. Even if I give you the stuff you haven't got any fucking choice."

"If you don't give it to me, you're dead right now." He aimed his weapon again at the man's head.

"Chandler, my friend, think about this for a fucking minute. Tie Reggie up. Tie Reggie up and take him along with you." He was sculpturing every syllable. "Afterward — after you blow up whatever or whoever you've gotta blow up, you can let Reggie go, see. Man, give old Reggie a break!"

Chandler paused for a moment, then put the weapon back into his belt.

"All right, Reggie. If you screw it up, I'll see you suffer the pains of hell first before I dismember you."

"Trust Reggie, Chandler. Trust Reggie." He rubbed his hands together and his eyes rolled joyously and he smiled too. "I got this shit hidden so good the fucking Almighty couldn't find it."

He reached into the shower and pulled on the shower head. There was a noise in the wall and a panel slid open in the shower.

"More than three hundred pounds in there and a hundred detonators. Twenty kilos coming up." He reached in, removed the packets, and handed them to Chandler, who once more had his automatic out.

"We had a fucking deal, Chandler."

"Sorry, Reggie. I can't take the risk."

"Honest to God, Reggie wouldn't say a fucking word."

"You finked on Caine and Marmado once."

"That was to a Congressional committee! That was the fucking Church Committee! They were going to put me away for — what the fuck — contempt of Congress! Ferguson told me it was okay to spill it! Check with Fergie, he'll tell you, man."

"I gambled with Auntie M and it was stupid," he said,

and cocked his weapon. The little man backed against the wall and covered his head with his hands and his knees buckled beneath him.

"Jesus Christ Almighty, Chandler, don't do this thing to Reggie. Please, Chandler, oh please!"

Chandler was steady. "On your feet, Reggie. Like a man, on your feet."

"Fuck man, no, please! Reggie was always your friend. Reggie never finked on you! Ferguson cleared it!"

Chandler stepped up and leaned down, pointing the automatic at the man's heart; Reggie Dawes stiffened and jerked his head back and looked Chandler straight in the eyes, a narrow, hating look that seemed to stare beyond into a eternity of fear.

Chandler covered the man's eyes with his other hand. And then he fired.

FIFTY-FIVE

At seven-thirty in the morning Knebel took a drive with Hans Ober. The commuter traffic was heavy; the day was slightly overcast, pleasantly cool. They were in a Ford; Chad Priest was driving and Hans Ober and Knebel sat in the back seat. Hans Ober had brought maps, charts, and diagrams with him.

"C. Miller Petri is from Illinois," Hans Ober said, "so naturally he wants his inauguration at the Lincoln Monument, okay?"

They drove by the Lincoln Memorial and around the park. Knebel showed where the President's car would be coming from and where it was possible to stage an assault. On the speaker's platform, he would be practically enclosed by bulletproof glass.

"The Presidential limousine is impregnable, practically."

"No car is impregnable," Knebel said.

"Okay, didn't I say *practically?*"

"What if he stole the gun to throw you off? What if he was really planning on a bomb?"

"We've had bomb experts working all night combing every inch of ground the President will be covering.

340

Dogs will be sniffing out the crowds."

Knebel looked at the maps, charts, and diagrams for some time and then shook his head. "I still don't like it. He can come at you so many unexpected ways."

"At eight o'clock we start handing out new identity papers to every cop and press person who'll be allowed within three hundred yards of the President, okay? We've got an inner ring of two thousand security people. Nobody else gets close. But he's got to be someplace just outside that ring, okay? By ten o'clock, say."

"I suppose . . ."

"It's a virtual certainty. Okay. We have twelve thousand men that are going to close in behind him. He'll be caught someplace in the middle. It's *got* to happen." They again drove past the Lincoln Memorial; Ober pointed to the top of it. "Powerful telescopes up there. We're checking every car. We've got dogs sniffing out explosives, okay? They can tell if a man's armed with a handgun from twenty feet. . . . Well? What's your thinking now?"

"I'm thinking somehow he's going to pull it off. I hope to God you get him, but I think somehow he'll pull it off."

"No way in hell."

The crowds gathered steadily and uniformed police appeared. Knebel was given his special identity card with his photo. Ober went back to the Annex and Knebel checked out the command post where the Secret Service and the FBI were coordinating security. They had put one security man with every two persons from the press. They weren't taking any chances, they said.

At nine-thirty Knebel walked down the nine-and-a-half blocks to Memorial Park. He crossed to the review stand area and surveyed the parking lot where the motorcade would park. It was a large black-topped area, roped off with gold braid. The crowd was pressing closer and the police were holding them back. Two television crews were setting up between the parking area and the reviewing stand. It was two minutes to ten.

On his way back to the command post, Knebel was checked for proper identification by four different sets of police and two Secret Service men. The Chief Justice of the Supreme Court had already arrived for the swearing-in. At the command post, Knebel found Hans Ober pacing impatiently.

"What's going on?" Knebel asked.

Ober shrugged. "Don't know. Our people keep reporting the President hasn't come downstairs yet. C. Miller Petri and his wife went up there an hour ago and nobody's come down."

Knebel waited and smoked his pipe on the steps of the command center. At last the word came that the motorcade had started up Pennsylvania Avenue. Knebel started back toward the reviewing stand area. Ober caught up with him before he had gone half a block.

"Hold on there, Knebel."

Knebel turned to him. "Smith made his try?"

Ober shook his head. There was disgust on his hard face and an enigmatic smile on his lips. "Haas has thrown a wrench into the works."

"How's that?"

"He's just issued a press release," Ober said heavily. "Until the fugitive Chandler Smith is apprehended, he's decided the prudent thing to do is to remain within the security area of the White House itself. They'll have the swearing-in there this afternoon."

Knebel knocked the ashes out of his pipe and crushed the ember out with his foot. He smiled. "You know how they hunt tigers in Bangladesh, Hans?"

"No idea."

"They tie a small goat to a stake and wait for the tiger to come for lunch. It seems our goat has decided he doesn't want to be a goat."

"There was no way in hell the tiger would have even gotten close, okay? Now what the hell are we going to do?"

"Find another way to hunt our tiger, I suppose."

"The only way I know is to put up a dragnet even a mouse couldn't squeak through."

FIFTY-SIX

Janet Knebel was asleep and dreaming when the phone rang.

"Hello?" The dial on the clock said it was two A.M.

"They've halted the dragnet." It was Knebel. "They've brought in twenty-seven men who could have been Smith. None were. We've searched twenty-two thousand vehicles and seven thousand buildings and have nothing. Not one good solid clue. Smith's gone like a puff of smoke. . . . What time is it? What day is it?"

"You didn't call me to ask what day it is."

"Could you see me now?"

"Certainly, Richard. I'll put the coffee on."

When he arrived he was in a sullen and dark mood. He stood in her kitchen, sipping coffee, tugging nervously on his beard.

"We were laying for Smith the other morning; I suppose you know that," he said.

"I figured you were," she said.

"Haas pulled the plug on the scheme at the last moment."

"Figured that too."

"We might have had him. When the crowd cleared

out they found a stolen truck that had been painted to look like a City Water Department vehicle."

"You think Smith was going to use that somehow?"

"They found his fingerprints inside."

"What was he going to do with a truck?"

Knebel shrugged. "Ober and I tried to figure it out and couldn't. They found a dead arms dealer in Westborough, Virginia yesterday. Reggie Dawes, his name was. He was killed with the same caliber automatic as the one Chandler Smith stole in Castle Island, Maryland. If Smith did kill him — and there's every reason to believe he did — then he is now equipped with a large amount of explosives and detonators."

"They have to get him sooner or later, don't you think?"

"Even when we get him we might not have anything. He might not be taken alive. If he is taken alive, he might not tell us anything. I'm convinced this Old Guard business is somehow related to Jamison's death, but I don't know how."

"Besides Biskey, our people can find nothing on the Old Guard. There are rumors, whispers, legends, but that's about it. No one seems to take them at all seriously."

"The Bureau hasn't been much help either. . . . Mind if I smoke?"

"Turn on the exhaust fan over the stove."

He switched it on; it hummed. He packed his pipe and lit it.

"The Old Guard is as ethereal as steam, but they're real. I'm sure Harrison Cheney is one of them. He resigned under very peculiar circumstances. I know he backed the Old Guard idea when it was originally proposed. I've got him under surveillance, but so far, he's gone nowhere, spoken to no one, and done anything suspicious in the least. He lives like a hermit up in Williamsburg, as peaceful as a pet rock."

"Maybe the Old Guard is just a myth."

"Not a chance. Listen, Janet, you know how I've always worked. I've built a case like I was making a ship in a bottle, a tiny piece at a time. Meticulous, never swooping in for the arrest until I knew I was going to make it stick. When my case was done, it was as carefully detailed as a Van Dyck portrait."

"I remember."

"This case can't be built like that. Too many hidden things. Too many secrets, too many pieces. It's too big, too diverse. I've gotten my hands on a couple of the keys, but haven't opened any of the locks."

"What do you want me to do?"

He sat down. "How about sticking your neck way out? Way, way out."

"How?"

"What do you suppose would happen if there was a front-page story in the *Chronicle* tomorrow with your byline. Suppose you quoted a highly placed source in the investigation task force saying we were closing in on an as yet unnamed secret clique of intelligence operators who included Chandler Smith. What if it said Clement Jamison was assassinated because he was about to conclude a pact with the Soviets which would have ended the cold war. What if you claimed the clique has been influencing foreign affairs through bribery, blackmail, and coercion for two decades. What if you said some high government officials have already been questioned and are to be questioned further? Among them, you night say, is Harrison Cheney."

"You really want to name names?"

"Damn right I do. His, anyway . . . How about it, Janet?"

"Do you have any substantial evidence linking Harrison Cheney to this alleged conspiracy?"

"Circumstantial."

"Intuitive mostly?"

"Yes."

She thought it over a moment. "If I can get my publisher to go along, I'll do it for you, Richard. But it'll make me feel a little unclean."

"Will your publisher go along?"

"He was a supporter of Jamison's. Knew him, liked him. If he thinks this may help to corral his killers, he'll go along."

He averted his gaze. "If I'm wrong, Cheney will probably sue your socks off."

"We've been sued before." She smiled. "I'll name you as my source and he can sue our socks off together."

"Afterward, I want you to have police protection, Janet."

"Nonsense. They'll know I'm just your mouthpiece. You'll need the protection."

He gave her some handwritten notes. "This will give you the idea. Write it up any way you like."

"I can phone it in, won't take ten minutes. Then we can have a drink. Think I've got a couple of bottles of pretty good champagne."

"Got to get back to the Annex. If something breaks, I want to be there."

"They could phone you here. Come on, spend the night, relax. You're going to be hit with a fire storm tomorrow."

"Really can't, Janet."

"Too married, eh?"

"Guess so."

"You're very old-fashioned, know that?"

"Yeah."

Knebel went back to his room at the Holiday Inn, showered, put on a robe, and sat on the bed drinking a brandy from a water glass. He thought of calling Laurie, but he didn't want to wake her. He put out the light. The luminous dial on the clock said it was three thirty-five. It wouldn't be long now. He laid his head on the pillow. He was asleep in less than a minute.

The phone rang at seven-twenty.

"Knebel, you've got to be crazy!" It was Ober.

"Guess you saw the paper."

"Wilson Wright just phoned me. He couldn't believe it. Brother, is he hot! Harrison Cheney is a very important man in this town. You've just about called him a Presidential assassin!"

"Sometimes you've got to stir the coals to get some sparks, friend."

"You've got yourself more than a few sparks, okay? You've got yourself a blaze!"

Knebel was in his office at the Annex by eight-thirty. Reporters, dozens of them, wanted to talk to him throughout the morning, but Knebel refused. He told his secretary to neither confirm nor deny that he was the 'informed source' of the article. At lunchtime Ober came by his office.

"I've been over to the Main Campus all morning, Knebel. Sanchez-Flint has been chewing on my tail bone, okay? Figured I must have had preknowledge, if

348

not complicity, in this scheme of yours. Wilson Wright was there, he's rabid. There was talk about dumping you out the window, but saner heads prevailed. Chad and I convinced them the timing would be wrong. Better to wait, let things cool down, then dump you out the window."

"Thank you for that."

"You're hanging by a thread. Nobody but nobody really believes in this Old Guard business but you. You took one hell of a risk, okay?"

"It's a high-stakes game."

"You'll let me know if something crops up?"

"Thought you weren't a believer."

"I never rule out anything till the jailers turn the keys."

Knebel didn't know what to expect, exactly. He thought someone would contact him with a message, a threat, an invitation to lunch. The paper was out on Tuesday morning and by Thursday he had heard nothing. At two-thirty in the afternoon Ober phoned him.

"Thought you ought to know, Harrison Cheney held a news conference for the print media this morning. He was his old charming and gracious self. He said the story was hokum. The Bureau has pretty much said the same thing. Looks like you got a little egg on your face again, Richard. Wilson Wright thinks maybe you ought to talk to the press, deny the whole thing and get your ex-wife to say it was all a mistake."

"I'm not sure yet it was a mistake. Fishing takes patience."

Ober sighed. "Let me know when you're ready to listen to good sense."

Late in the afternoon Stewart Ott came to see him.

He sat in the chair across from Knebel with his arms folded, his eyes pointed at him like cold, cocked muskets. He was wearing a polka-dotted bow tie, which he tightened as he started talking.

"I'm not here as a friend, Richard, I've been sent."

"Somebody calling for my resignation?"

"Something like that. I think personally you ought to be committed. What the hell's the deal?"

"Harrison Cheney is Old Guard."

"Can you prove it?"

"No."

"Can you prove there is an Old Guard?"

"No."

"Then you should be committed. What the hell were you trying to do with a fool stunt like this?"

"I figured somebody might panic if they thought we were on to something. Somebody might break ranks, want to make a deal to save himself. I thought maybe they might try to find out what I know. I threw the dice, friend, and I got craps—so far. It happens."

"So the gambit netted nothing."

"So far, like I said."

"All right then, here's the deal. Senator Southerland will take you on as a consultant to his committee so long as you give your word there'll be no more shenanigans like this. First, have Janet run a retraction. You've got to bare your soul. Plead temporary insanity."

"What happens if I don't?"

"You know what happens, Richard. You either play with the team by the rules or you go to the showers— forever. You'll be back at your think tank thinking at the Second Coming."

"How long have I got before the ax falls?"

"Noon tomorrow. Wilson Wright is inflamed and he's got the President inflamed. They're ready to kick you out, damn the consequences. Noon tomorrow I'll check back."

After he had gone, Knebel called Laurie in California.

"I've been reading about your troubles, darling," she said. "It must be terrible."

"They want me to resign. They've offered to let me ride in the back of the bus on Southerland's committee."

"You thinking of coming home?"

"I'll let you know tomorrow. I was so sure something would come of this."

"Maybe it will yet."

He spent the rest of the day going over reports, had an early supper, and was back in his office at seven. He worked steadily until eleven-thirty, then had a cup of coffee and sat back and smoked his pipe. He reflected on his choices and options. He was tired and his thinking was dull. At the moment he was favoring sitting tight. They might not go through with firing him, fearing adverse publicity. If they were ready to take the adverse publicity and did fire him, it would make headlines. When he had the public's attention, he would name the Old Guard as being behind the assassination. It was a long shot, but it might get him some believers. Maybe some hotshot reporters would start looking into the right rat hole and catch themselves an Old Guard member. All he needed, Knebel figured, was one willing to talk and the roof would fall in on all of them.

At eleven-forty Janet called.

"Have they been pressing you to resign, Richard?" she asked.

"Yes."

"They've been pressing me to retract, but I'm not going to," she said. "I don't think you'll have to resign either."

"You've been contacted by one of them!"

"He says he's not one of them, but he knows all about them."

"Who is he?"

"Are you sitting down?"

"Yeah."

"I spoke to Chandler Smith himself not five minutes ago."

FIFTY-SEVEN

"Are you positive it was Chandler Smith?"

"Absolutely. I asked him about Ferris. He knew all about Montreal. This was no crank, Richard, it *was* Chandler Smith."

"What did he want?"

"He wants to talk to you," she said. "Now—tonight. In person."

"Where?"

"Listen, Richard. He told me that I'm to take you there, that I'm not to give you the location. He said *no* police, and *no* guns. He just wants to talk. Fair enough?"

"Yes. What else did he say?"

"I'm to pick you up and take you to him. He assured me he wouldn't hurt either one of us as long as no police came and we weren't armed."

"All right, Janet."

"You agree to all conditions? No police, no guns?"

"Yes. Yes, I agree."

"I'll pick you up in fifteen minutes."

She drove a Datsun 280 ZX. Knebel had trouble squeezing his large frame into the passenger's seat. She started driving west, out of the city. He looked around to see whether they were being followed. He detected no tail.

"There could be a Pulitzer in this," she said.

"It's a damn fool thing to risk your life for."

"Not to me it isn't. You aren't armed, are you, Richard?"

"No."

They went through Forestville and Upper Marlborough and then turned north on U.S. 301 and stopped in Conaways, where she made a phone call in a small diner. She got a recorded message directing her where to go.

They continued north to Benfield and then turned west and south toward Arnold before crossing back across the Severn River into Annapolis. They followed some city streets and down by the docks they found a train track which they followed to some warehouses. They finally came to a stop at an abandoned boat yard. There were some small sheds and a pier with some old boats tied to it. It was dark and still and quiet. She flashed the headlights of her car twice. The end of the pier was dark.

"I'm afraid of dying," she said.

"Most people are."

"Are you frightened right now, Richard?"

"Yes."

"Were you frightened when you went into White's place?"

"Yes."

"You didn't look frightened. I watched you on television. Look at me; I'm shaking like a leaf."

He put his arm around her.

After a moment he said, "You don't think we've been

354

tood up, do you?"

"He'll come." She rubbed her hands together to warm them. "What kind of a man is he? What kind of a man makes a spy?"

"Idealism, I suppose. With him it was idealism."

"What happened to him? What does it do to a man to cheat and lie and subvert? They're criminals, really. Sanctioned criminals. Even soldiers have some rights in the enemy country, but the spy, he is an outlaw always. Even in a war. For the idealist, it must be terrible to always be an outlaw."

"I suppose it would be," he said.

There was a ship coming up the channel, its engines throbbing, and they both watched it pass.

"Remember the time we took a week off at Fourth Lake?" she said.

"I remember."

"That was a very good time."

"It was."

"It was probably the best time I have had—as an adult."

"For me too, Janet."

"What happened to us?"

He shrugged. "We were two careers separated by a common marriage."

"I guess we were."

"Maybe in another time, another place, we'd have been Romeo and Juliet," he said.

She laughed. "Wouldn't that have been something?"

A light flashed at the end of the pier. "Did you see that?" she said.

"I saw it."

She flashed her headlights twice and the light at the

355

end of the pier flashed twice in return.

"Well, Richard, this is it."

"You wait here," he said. "I want to check it out."

"Not on your life!"

They got out of the car. It was cool down by the water, cool and still, and out a way a tanker was moving upstream. "Watch your step," Knebel said. There were loose boards on the pier and some of them were rotted. "Keep close to the pilings," he said, "the footing is more sure."

There was an old ferrous-cement hulled scow tied alongside the pier. It had a high crane on board, and beyond it lay a half-sunken tugboat.

"What is this place?" Janet asked.

"I guess most of these boats have been abandoned. Maybe the pier's been abandoned too. There's a lot of redevelopment going on."

A foghorn sounded somewhere across the channel.

"I want you to go back, Janet. Let me make the first contact. If everything's okay, I'll signal."

"No thanks, Galahad."

They started again down the pier. As they approached the tugboat, Knebel called out Chandler Smith's name, and then he called it again. They walked closer and he shone the flashlight ahead of them.

He stumbled. "Damn."

Suddenly she clutched his arm. "There. Over there behind that post."

Knebel looked into the darkness. There was a man standing at the end of the pier. Knebel shone his flashlight, but could see no one.

"Who's there?" Knebel said. "Smith, is that you? We're not armed."

A flashlight flickered. Knebel flashed his in return, then waited. Nothing. It was dark and quiet. A foghorn sounded. Small waves lapped at the pilings. There was a strong, pungent odor of stagnant water. And then, the sound of a helicopter.

"What's that?" Janet asked.

Knebel swung around. Two helicopters with powerful searchlights were swooping in on them.

"You lied, Richard!"

She suddenly dashed toward the end of the pier, waving her arms, calling out to Chandler Smith, but her voice was lost in the roar of the helicopter engines. Knebel chased after her, keeping an eye on the helicopters above. A passenger in one of them leaned out with a rifle in his hand and Knebel saw the flash of muzzle fire and heard the bullet zing in the air near him and hit the water to his right. He dropped and took cover behind a piling as the second helicopter circled around toward him. The figure at the end of the pier had leaped into the half-sunken tug moored there just as he was caught in the searchlight of the first helicopter. Janet was now near the tug, caught in the searchlight, shielding her eyes. Knebel called to her and again started running toward her, when suddenly there was an explosion.

It erupted out of the moored tugboat, bright and orange and white, engulfing Janet, and the concussion that followed lifted Knebel into the air and swept him from the pier, flinging him out into the black water. . . .

BOOK FIVE

FIFTY-EIGHT

There was a loud buzzing in his ears and there was the pain. Pain everywhere. And he was stiff as marble. He opened his eyes to the brightness and a blur. Dark figures moved around him. Nurses? Doctors? They were mumbling amongst themselves, but it was incoherent. Someone was moving his leg. A spike of pain shot up to his brain like a lightning bolt and he groaned.

"I think he's coming out of it," a woman said.

A man's face appeared in front of him. "Mr. Knebel? Are you with us?"

Knebel tried to speak, but his speech was hopelessly slurred. The man touched his shoulders. "There, there, just rest now."

The man's face was gone and now Knebel could feel himself slipping again into the blackness. Again he tried to speak, but the exertion seemed to pull him under and it was pleasant.

When he awoke he was in another room. It was daylight, but the shades were drawn and it was dim. The ringing in his ears had dulled.

"Hey, buddy, can you spare a dime?"

He turned his head. It was Laurie. Her face was

slightly blurred, but then she came into focus. She kissed him.

"What about Janet?"

"She's gone, Richard. She was killed outright."

Knebel shut his eyes tight for a moment, then opened them again. "She went to her death thinking I betrayed her. I didn't." After a moment he added, "She was a brave, brave woman."

"Yes, she was. . . . How do you feel, Richard?"

"Numb. I feel numb and tired." He tried to sit up, but a volley of pain rolled over him and he sank back down again.

"What's the damage?" he asked. "What do the doctors say?"

"The worst thing is a mild concussion. You have a lot of cuts and some very bad burns. Your whole left side looks like a Tarvia driveway. Two doctors were picking wood slivers and debris out of your skin for over four hours."

"How did you get here so quickly, Laurie?"

"It's been a day and a half," she said. "You've really been out of it."

"Call the FBI, Laurie. Ask for Hans Ober. Tell him I want to see him."

"The doctors want you to rest. Couldn't it wait?"

"I'll be all right. Call him, please."

She kissed him. "You can talk to him only for a few minutes. Promise me."

"Promise."

When Hans Ober came two hours later, Knebel was sitting up in bed drinking coffee and smoking his pipe. His beard had been shaven off along with the hair on the left side of his head and his face was blackened and wollen.

"Don't look in the mirror, Richard," Ober said. "The shock might knock you over."

"The choppers, whose were they?"

"Don't know. When we pulled up, they split."

"You must have had Janet under surveillance, right?"

"Sure, and you too. But we were holding way back, okay? We had homing devices in her car and on her person. We told our guys to hang back and they did. We came in when we heard the explosion. We found you in the mud headfirst up to your tush."

"The choppers opened fire on me."

"They did?"

"I want those choppers found."

"I've got men looking now, Richard. So far, no luck. Whoever they were, they didn't file a flight plan. I doubt we'll trace them."

"What about Smith?"

"He's dead."

"You're sure?"

"Yeah, we're sure. The bomb—or whatever it was—had a total destruct zone of twenty yards and a kill zone of forty or more. You were right on the perimeter. Smith jumped into the old tugboat just before the blast. He was at the vortex and was pretty well disintegrated, okay? We found a piece of finger."

"You got a good clean print?"

"Yes, it's at the lab now. They're checking it against Smith's records."

"He couldn't have survived?"

"Impossible. We saw him clear in the searchlights getting into the boat. Two seconds later it blew."

"What was he doing out there?"

"Okay. It looks like Smith had been hiding out in tha‌t tug for some time. Couple of days anyway. Ducca‌ Boatworks has been belly-up for maybe ten years. No‌ body goes around there. The mud has filled in the chan‌nel so you couldn't get one of those old tubs out unles‌s you were going to dredge for maybe a couple of hundre‌d yards. That tug was just sitting in the mud and Chan‌dler Smith moved in, we guess. We found some clothes‌ that sort of thing. One of the weapons he lifted from th‌e sporting goods store in Castle Island, a Remington .22‌ rifle and scope. The explosive device was placed just in‌side the cabin about four feet off the deck. The aft thir‌d of the tug is totally gone, but we found plenty of stuff u‌p toward the bow, including a sort of notebook, handwrit‌ten. It contained all the usual stuff these character‌s write—you know, ridding the world of tyrants and s‌o on, okay?"

"I want to examine it."

"As soon as McHenry's people are finished with it."

"Today, Hans. Get it here today."

"All right."

Knebel coughed and his face was tight with pain. H‌e shook it off after a moment and said, "Any further devel‌opments, I want to know about them right away. Any‌thing at all."

"Sure thing, Richard."

In the late afternoon the manuscript came. It was in a‌ large brown padded envelope, and with it were some‌ field reports Chandler Smith had filed to use for com‌parison. Laurie had been with him most of the day while‌ he had been sleeping. She woke him to tell him the man‌uscript had arrived because she knew he wanted to see it‌ badly.

He studied it for over an hour. When he was finished he handed it to Laurie and then rang for the nurse and ordered some coffee. The nurse wanted him to take a pill to relieve his pain, but he refused because it would dull his senses and he had much to think about, he said. While he was drinking his coffee, Ober phoned.

"The piece of finger we found was definitely Smith's, okay, Richard? Definitely his. No doubt at all."

"Did they find a body?"

"No. A lot of unidentifiable fragments. We can file the Chandler Smith part of the case away. The President has already made the announcement."

After he hung up, Knebel said, "They're satisfied Smith is dead."

"Then it's over, isn't it?" she said. "He's been holding the nation hostage, and now it's over."

"I want to see the pier and that boat for myself," Knebel said. "Could you drive me tomorrow?"

"The doctors want you here, Richard. They want to observe you until at least Friday."

"I'll be ready about eight," he said.

"If that's what you want."

FIFTY-NINE

In the morning it was raining. It had been raining since midnight and there was a lot of mud in the pot-holes on the road down to the old pier and there were large puddles of water in the parking area for the Duccat Boatworks.

Laurie drove slowly. There were many tire tracks on the ground, but nearly everyone had gone. Only McHenry and a few of his lab men were there. Knebel asked a uniformed policeman to ask McHenry to come to the car, because it was difficult for him to walk in the mud. He sat in the car with Laurie and gazed out on the railroad tracks and rusted barges around the pier. The half-sunken tugboat was at the end of what remained of the pier, its bow sticking out of the gray water. Most of the pier was gone; the planks at the severed end were jagged and blackened and twisted from the blast. Four divers were searching the shoals near the pier. As they waited, Knebel said nothing. He smoked his pipe and sat stiff and hurting. The skin on his face and arms burned and itched, but he still would not take narcotics.

McHenry finally came off the tugboat and up the hill to speak to Knebel. He was tired and his smooth feature showed strain. When he got into the back seat of the car, he introduced himself to Laurie and told Knebel he was glad to see him again.

"I think we ought to be through here in a day, day and a half," McHenry said. "I was sorry to hear about Janet's death. Tragic. I used to read her column faithfully and I missed it when she became an editor. She was a clear voice and had a lot to say, I thought."

"Tell me what you've found," Knebel said.

"You know about the section of finger. We found some scattered fragments of bone and internal organs as well . . . a little hair."

"Any gross structures, facial bones, anything like that?"

"No, sir. But the M.E. is satisfied it was Smith. He's issuing a death certificate."

Knebel rolled down a window and took a few deep breaths of air, then said, "These fragments you've found, are they consistent with the type of destruction?"

"Definitely. In fact, we're lucky to get much of anything. Take a look at that boat—most of it is just gone. We've collected a few hundred pieces, but most of it was pulverized."

"I want to see what you do have."

They got out of the car and Knebel followed McHenry down to the pier. He walked with a cane and went slowly in the mud. Laurie had his arm. He looked at the tug and examined the pieces they had collected from the bay. They had found a piece of Janet's coat and Knebel held it for a long time, staring at it. He asked whether they had found any of her body and they said they hadn't, except for blood and hair on one of the pilings.

Knebel heard someone coming up behind him; he

turned around. It was Lowenstein, looking unshaven and unkempt in an old, battered trenchcoat and rain hat.

"Hello, Knebel."

"Mr. Lowenstein."

"You need a new barber, Knebel, you're a disgrace to your calling."

Lowenstein walked past him out to the end of the pier and glanced into the wreck of the tug. Then he returned to where Knebel was standing.

"Big bomb, wasn't it?" he said. "Plastic?"

"Yes," Knebel said.

"Ten, fifteen kilos?"

"More like twenty, twenty-five. High-powered stuff."

Lowenstein nodded thoughtfully.

"What are you doing here?" Knebel asked.

"Just a tourist." He turned to Laurie and touched the brim of his hat.

"Thought you were back in Pennsylvania," Knebel said.

"My parole officer knows where I am. Relax. Like I said, I'm just a tourist." He turned to go.

"Wait a minute," Knebel said. "What do you think?"

"About what?"

"About all this?"

"Looks like Smith took the express bus into the next life."

"Why?"

"Maybe he was tired of living."

"Really think so?"

"No."

"What do you think?"

"I'm not on the case, remember? I'm Joe Private Citizen, I don't have to say what I think."

"You wouldn't happen to be doing some investigating on your own, would you, Mr. Private Citizen?"

"If I was it wouldn't be any of your or anyone else's damn business now, would it?" He tipped his hat to Laurie again and walked off.

Knebel watched him go. After a moment Knebel turned to McHenry. "What else have you got?"

"This way, sir."

The rest of the artifacts were kept in a small shed near the parking area. The divers had just recovered one of Janet's shoes and there were small pieces of the boat covered with mud laid out on the floor in rows. There was a chart on the wall showing where the pieces were found. Knebel looked at the chart for a long time. Laurie said he really shouldn't tire himself. "Let's go," she said. "I've rented a suite downtown."

"Not yet," he said. He started examining individual pieces of debris. Some were as big as a breadboard, some as small as a quarter. All were jagged and scorched.

"What is it you're looking for, Richard?" Laurie asked.

"I'm looking for what detectives are always looking for. Clues. Puzzle pieces. A murder was committed here and the victim was somebody I cared about."

"You're blaming yourself and that isn't like you, Richard. You have no reason to blame yourself."

He turned away from her and walked to the far end of the shack and took another piece of the mud-encrusted boat into his hands.

She followed him, stood next to him. He kept working with his back to her.

"Don't shut me out of this," she said.

He gave her no answer. He picked up another piece of the boat and then another. After a while she went out the door, up the hill to the car, and sat inside it listening to the radio. Later she went to a fried chicken takeout restaurant and bought him some supper and brought it to him. They went home late that day and came back early the next; she stayed with him, waiting. The following day he rented a camper and parked it at the scene. She brought him some clothes and food enough to stock the camper well.

"I can't stay here with you, Richard. It's like a graveyard," she said. "You'll call me if you need anything, won't you?"

"Yes," he said, not looking up from his work.

She kissed him on the cheek and went up the hill to the car. She drove down the long muddy drive slowly and turned down the street. It was raining hard.

SIXTY

Three weeks later it was again raining. In between there had been days of mild weather and some sunshine, but mostly it had been overcast and storming. The front had moved in late Monday and by Wednesday morning the area down by the dock was a mud bowl. Wide boards had been put down to form walkways, but they were slippery and walking on them was treacherous.

Ober, sitting in his car, surveyed the scene from the parking lot above. Knebel had called him that morning and asked him to come out and talk to him. He had agreed to come out of a sense of duty and respect, but he wasn't looking forward to seeing Richard. When Knebel had told him on the phone he had significant findings to share with him, Ober had tried to sound, if not enthusiastic, at least receptive. He suspected Knebel's grief had supplanted his reason. Ober dreaded the interview.

He got out of the car, opened his umbrella, and treaded his way down the makeshift stairs and across the walkways, inching his way like a tightrope walker. Knebel had spied him coming and was waiting for him in the doorway of the shack. A strong wind gusted intermittently. The mud smelled strongly of decay. Knebel appeared weary and pale; his clothes were wrinkled and muddy and his beard was a thick, black stubble.

"How are you, Richard?"

Knebel nodded and retreated into the shed. "Come in, Hans." His voice was hoarse.

Ober took down his umbrella. "Are you finished here, Richard?"

"Just about."

Ober followed Knebel into the shed. The rain beat hard on the tin roof and there were streams of water on the walls. On the muddy floor were sections of the tugboat hull; technicians were cleaning them. Walter Byron was there, too, working with small pieces on a bench. Knebel showed Ober into a small back room which had been made into a makeshift office. It was drier here and Knebel took off his slicker and put it on some boxes. Ober kept his raincoat on and stood by the window, nudging some small pieces of metal with his toe.

"McHenry filed what he said was his final report on this site," Ober said.

"McHenry is a good man with a limited imagination."

"He's proven to be thorough and capable in the past, okay?"

Knebel coughed and looked in a desk drawer for some Kleenex, and found some. He blew his nose. Then he said: "Chandler Smith is not dead, Hans. Rather — if he is, he did not die here."

Hans Ober looked at him with doubtful eyes. "Either you've slipped a notch in your cogs or I'm as simple as Simon and the pieman."

Knebel lit his pipe and sat down on a metal folding

chair. The window rattled with the wind and the blast shook the small building. When the wind died down, he said:

"Follow this closely. The explosion occurred at low tide. Low tide was at eleven fifty-seven and the explosion was almost exactly at midnight. All right. All Smith had to do was cut a hole out of the side of the vessel so when he jumped into the cabin, he could jump right out again into the shallow water, blowing the boat up behind him. The bomb was at table height, so the concussion was sideways and upward—not downward. After he got out, all he had to do was swim—or walk in the shallows—about forty yards and he could have been inside the canal area just to the north of the pier. It would be easy, even if the police had blocked off the road, to make it up to where the canal empties. There's a culvert pipe about ten yards up the canal which leads right into the deserted warehouse above the pier. There were bars inside the culvert to prevent people from doing this. The bars have been cut. Kids, I think, have been playing in there for years. Maybe they cut them. Maybe Smith did. It doesn't matter. That's how he got out of the boat."

"You find any fresh physical evidence of this? Footprints maybe?"

"Too much rain since."

"Did he leave anything behind? Traces of fabrics?"

"Not that we could trace to him. It's how he did it, though."

Ober shook his head slowly. "I don't know, Richard. I've been a cop thirty-three years. Solved tough ones and easy ones. Some got away, I admit. But I know when it's right. This one is right. Everything we've got points to one conclusion—Chandler Smith being pushed to the limit and cracking up. Blowing himself to bits in an attempt to get his number-one pursuer is completely consistent with that. You can't buck it with a few sawed bars and a lot of supposition. Give me some hard facts."

"I'll give you some hard facts. Chandler Smith used disguises. That's documented. He was a master of disguises, there is no doubt about it."

"Granted."

"He must have had the tools necessary to construct those disguises, right? Wigs and makeup — and eyebrow pencils? Am I right about that?"

"Okay."

"If the boat was his hideout, where are his tools? We've looked everywhere and can't find any. Not a trace, not a cinder, not an ash. We find this notebook where he raves like a crazy man, but we find none of his makeup stuff. Isn't that strange?"

"This is pretty thin, Richard."

"There's more to think about. The guns he stole in Castle Island, Maryland. There were three of them. We have one, which was left in the tug. Another was found in the phony water company truck. Where's the third?"

"Probably blown to hell."

Knebel shook his head. "He's still got it."

"He's dead, Richard."

"No. He's out there, waiting."

Ober lit a cigarette and paced around the small room, then he stopped and faced Knebel. "Please hear me out, Richard. I'm going to appeal to you on an entirely different level, okay? Cop to cop. Word has it maybe you need a vacation. Okay, you're a national hero. Maybe that engenders jealousies, okay? But officially Chandler

Smith is dead and the Administration wants him to stay dead. Wilson Wright told me this morning—the President wants things cool. Wilson Wright dumped Lowenstein and probably helped Stewart Ott out the door. Let's not give him excuses for shipping us off to the South Bronx, okay? He wants us to finish up our reports and be done with it. Unless you can give me something damn solid I've got to go along with that, not because it's the official view, but because reason, logic, the rules of evidence, and every damn instinct I've got tells me to. Chandler Smith was blown into a thousand pieces."

"I examined that piece of finger, Hans. It was severed cleanly. It wasn't blown off—it was cut off."

"I saw it too. It could have been hit by flying glass, flying anything. I saw a man's head come off in an explosion, okay? Back in the sixties. A two-by-four took it off like a scalpel."

"Damn it! Think, man!" Knebel was red-faced. "Think about Chandler Smith. He's a man of such skill and determination he can survive torture and still kill three people. He can elude the largest manhunt in the history of the world and march inexorably toward his target. What kind of a man can do something like that? Is not such a man capable of staging his own death? Why would he call me out there? It wasn't so he could commit suicide and take me with him. There's nothing in his history or background indicating any suicidal tendency. No, sir! He wanted me as a witness to his alleged demise. Who would dispute me and Janet? He wanted the heat off, so he feigned his own death!"

Ober shook his head slowly. "I'm sorry. I can't buy it."

Knebel looked out the window and rubbed his hands across his face, then turned to Ober. "Are you shutting down the investigation?"

"We're throttling it back. We'll still have a couple hundred men dotting the I's and crossing the T's. And we'll have a pretty good-size staff coordinating with Southerland's committee. Tie up the loose ends. There's still a lot of legwork to do. It'll be going on for years."

"What about those choppers?"

"Nothing, absolutely nothing."

"They were Old Guard. They had a chance to get me, Janet, and Smith. They were going to get three flies, one swat."

"They could have been hired by Smith."

"A good journeyman like Smith wouldn't rely on helpers. He wanted to talk, but when the choppers swooped in, he switched to his backup plan. The Old Guard could easily have a man planted in your organization. All they had to do was lay back and wait."

"We've had sixty good agents working on the Old Guard for a month and come up with nothing, Richard. It's a dead end."

"No, it isn't, Hans."

"Okay, maybe not. But we tried. That's all a good cop can do."

"Would you say I'm a good cop, Hans?"

"What the hell kind of a question is that?"

"You know what I've found about good cops? They have a kind of radar. A good cop gets little blips on the radar screen of his mind. The little blips bother him. Sometimes they keep him awake at night. Sometimes they just won't go away no matter how much he tries to ignore them."

"What are you getting at?"

"Remember when I asked Haas if he had ever heard

of Ferris?"

"Yeah, I remember."

"He said he hadn't. But he was on the intelligence subcommittee when Ferris testified in favor of the Old Guard. Seven days of testimony."

"Maybe he forgot."

"Maybe. But it's interesting to note that seven votes on that committee went against the Old Guard. One in favor. Guess which one?"

"Haas? Doesn't mean a thing."

"Maybe not, but what exactly did Chandler Smith mean when he told his torturers he was determined to 'undo' what he had done? He meant he had put John Haas on the throne, right?"

"I suppose. What are you suggesting?"

"I'm just talking about blips on the radar screen. . . . Before he was killed, Jamison told LaVale the country almost had a jellyfish as a President. I thought he meant Haas. He didn't. He meant himself. Project Jellyfish. Montreal."

"Not the drug business again. We went through the autopsy, remember?"

"He had been off the drug too long for it to show up. Jamison was drugged, Hans, I know goddamn well he was."

"But you can't prove it."

"Not yet, but I will. Ask yourself this: Why did Haas want Lowenstein off the case?"

"Pretty obvious, really. PR. That, and the fact he pressured Wilson Wright about the autopsy business."

"Not a chance. Lowenstein was onto something with the drug business. Somebody was getting scared. What kind of man is Haas? What do we really know about him? I've been taking a close look at his record. You know, he's been a lot more hawkish than his patsy-assed liberal image would have you believe."

"Okay, but so what?"

"I'm still talking about blips, remember. What I'm asking is, so what about a whole bunch of nagging little damn incidentals that don't add up? Like LaVale running Haas's campaign. LaVale was doing some pretty good hunt-and-peck for me when Haas suddenly whisked him away. LaVale had his number, but I wouldn't listen."

"Maybe LaVale's a good campaign man. . . .Whatever the hell you're getting at, say it straight out."

"Maybe I'm not getting at anything. I'm talking about blips on a radar screen. Here's another one: I can show you the draft of the speech Jamison was going to use when he nominated Senator Southerland to take Haas's place on the ticket."

Ober crushed out his cigarette on the floor. "That's enough, Richard. I don't think I want to hear any more of this."

"Think of the resentment, Hans. Put yourself in Haas's place. You're being dumped after all those sacrifices! The Old Guard knows you're sympathetic to their views on the Hemisphere Brigade thing. A nice folksy type like Harrison Cheney comes to you. You go to lunch, maybe. He talks about all the terrors that are going on in Latin America. He says the last chance is the Hemisphere Brigade. It's the last chance to get Castro before the whole hemisphere is washed in red. They talk about LSD-N. Maybe it's a way to save the hemisphere and ultimately the country. Haas knows about LSD-N rom working on the intelligence committee. So simple. They pay Belzar to administer it. There are three hundred forty thousand dollars unaccounted for in Belzar's state. He did it all right. I'm completely certain of that. Then something happened. I'm not sure what. Apparntly Belzar got a conscience. He became despondent. Finally, he killed himself. When Jamison got himself a ew doctor, Samuelson, he started to figure it out, I hink. Jamison began to get healed. They killed Jamison at the country club so they could get Samuelson oo."

"It does have a crazy kind of logic to it."

"Damn right it does. . . . So now they have Haas as resident. They can go right ahead with their plan, easy s pie. If somebody starts nosing around, whisk them way, like Lowenstein and LaVale."

"But Haas hasn't gone ahead with the Hemisphere rigade business."

"A week before the convention next month, he's flying Argentina. They'll make the deal then, I think."

Ober took a few steps, turned, and took a few steps ack, shaking his head. "Okay," he said slowly, "tell me his. Why would Chandler Smith try to kill Haas if mith is Old Guard too?"

"I'm not sure, but I'm guessing it's because they tried kill him. Remember, he refused to use his relationhip with Mme. Rousseau to gather intelligence. To the eople who make up the Old Guard, that is probably an nforgivable sin. For revenge, Chandler Smith is going undo what he did for them."

Ober sat back down. "Anything else on your radar creen?"

"A hundred small things."

"If you ever took this cock-and-bull to the press, the country would go right down the crapper."

"Nothing gets said until I've got my case."

"It could take a hundred years."

"I need your help."

"Listen, Knebel. I'll tell you up front — this is all fairyland stuff. I think you'll come to the same conclusion by-and-by. There is no Old Guard, Chandler Smith was blown into fish food, and Haas is as clean as my grandmother. . . . But you're a big roller, and when your radar blips, I won't walk away from it. I'll get you all the help I can. Only let's keep this theory between us, okay? The President is the biggest fish in the pond, a jumbo shark. Let's not stir the waters too much, okay?" Ober stood up and picked up his umbrella. "You watch yourself, okay?"

"Thanks, friend."

"And see a psychiatrist."

SIXTY-ONE

Knebel rented a large furnished apartment in a working-class neighborhood in Southwest Washington, a mile and a half from the Annex. The breakfast room had two large windows which afforded good morning light. Laurie made the room into her studio. Knebel used the living room for a study and one of the two large bedrooms to store the thousands of pages of computer print-outs and reports he had sent to him. He spent his days and nights poring over papers, sometimes falling asleep at his desk or in a chair. He ate little, keeping going on coffee and cognac. Ms. Pressman came every morning and evening, and Mrs. Mancuso often brought records and files. He usually sent her away with requests for more files and records. He didn't leave the apartment and refused to talk to reporters. He listened to the news on the radio hourly, waiting for Chandler Smith to surface. It had been seven weeks. The nation's attention was being focused on the upcoming political conventions and a border war in Pakistan, hostilities in southern Lebanon, disarmament talks.

It was Sunday, late in the evening. Laurie came into the living room. Knebel was standing with a glass of cognac in one hand and a report in the other.

She had a painting with her and wanted to know what he thought of it.

He held it up to the light. It was a still life depicting two dying red flowers in a bowl sitting on a windowsill. Outside the window it was dark, with the reflected image of something brilliant and perhaps terrible. It may have been a sunrise, a sunset, or a nuclear blast.

"It's powerful," he said. "Provocative. Very good."

"It's not me."

"It is different from what you usually do."

"I can't work here, Richard. It's not good here. It's no good for you, either."

"What do you mean?"

"You've got to take some time off. Get some rest."

"Can't. Impossible."

"Not even for a few days?"

"No."

She looked down at her hands and flexed her fingers. She had long, delicate, artistic fingers. "I'm trying to understand, Richard. There must be a whirlwind of emotion in you. It's like a sickness."

"We score a few points, I'll get better quick. You could help me, Laurie, if you wanted."

"How?"

He shrugged. "One thing you could do is help me with the coincidental material. Help me read through it, look for anything suspicious. Anything."

"I wouldn't know what was suspicious if it kissed me on the lips."

"It was just a thought."

She put her arms around him, "Let's go back to Seaside — at least for a little while."

"No."

"I'm frightened, Richard. These men you're after, they're powerful, powerful men. And even if Smith is alive, he's not going to let himself be caught."

"You don't think Smith is alive, do you?"

"I don't care whether he is or he isn't. I just want to go home."

"I'm not leaving, Laurie. Not until my work is finished."

She left the room. They spoke little to each other the rest of the day. She went to bed early. When she got up at five-thirty in the morning, she found him asleep at his desk, his pipe smoldering in an ashtray. She made breakfast for herself and sat for a while at the window, looking at the street. She had a second cup of coffee, then went to the phone and made a reservation for a noon flight to Los Angeles. After she packed her things, she called a cab and then woke her husband.

He looked up at her. "Must have dozed off." He looked around, surprised it was morning.

"I'm going back to Seaside," she said. "Good-bye, Richard."

He stretched and rubbed his eyes, then looked at her for a long moment. "Perhaps it's best. I'll be home as soon as I possibly can."

"I don't think you will, Richard. I don't think you'll ever come home."

As she was going out the door he said, "Won't we be having champagne before you go?"

"Not this time."

Knebel went back into his study and began to work. His secretary came early with a box of records and a pile of correspondence. He dictated some memos; then they had a cup of coffee together and she left a little after noon. At twelve-thirty he heard a key in the lock of the front door and went to investigate. He found Laurie coming in the door with her suitcases.

"Your flight canceled?"

"My horoscope says today is a bad day to fink out on a loved one."

He helped her carry her suitcases into the bedroom. He kissed her warmly. "Glad you're back."

"How glad?"

They made love on the bed, long and leisurely, and then they slept. When Knebel woke, Laurie had made him a thick ham-and-cheese sandwich. She served it to him with an Amstel Light. He ate hungrily and drank the beer quickly.

"Let's get to work," he said.

He showed her what to look for and she started reading the long computer print-outs, holding a felt-tip pen in her hand. He started on the correspondence his secretary had brought. The first thing he opened was a special delivery letter marked personal and urgent. There was no return address. It was unsigned and read:

ARCHER OGDEN, FERRIS'S ASSISTANT IN MONTREAL, IS POSING AS DENNIS SOMMERS, A PATIENT AT THE UPSTATE MEDICAL CENTER PSYCHIATRIC CLINIC IN SYRACUSE, NEW YORK.

SIXTY-TWO

Wilson Wright was in bed by midnight. It had been a busy day, getting the President ready for his trip to Buenos Aires. A busy and satisfying one. The President, Wilson Wright thought, was ready, finally, in all ways. Everything would go right when he met with the generals; there need be no reason to worry on that score. No reason at all. The President would sign the historic treaty uniting all the anti-communist nations of the hemisphere into a solid, indestructible block. The tide, which for so long was running more and more red, would finally be turned. Wilson Wright took great satisfaction in the thought.

He turned off the light and closed his eyes. He could hear some laughter coming from the TV set his wife was watching downstairs. The sound blended with the soft soul music coming from the maid's room down the hall. There was something else, too. He listened hard and noticed a strange hissing sound, like a tire deflating. He tried to identify it, but couldn't. It seemed to be coming from outside, steady and slow. Strange. He decided to ignore it.

He couldn't get to sleep. His heart seemed to be beating hard and fast. After a few minutes his temples were throbbing and he thought a headache might be coming on. He got up and turned on the light, put on his robe, and went to the bathroom. He took a Tylenol and, a little unsteady on his feet, got back into bed, leaving the light on. In the drawer of his bedside table he had a few Western adventure paperbacks. He took one out. Louis L'Amour's *The Lonely Men*. He had read it before, perhaps a dozen times. He started reading it again. He found L'Amour's work a pleasant diversion. It could quickly transport him back to the nineteenth-century American West, where you could tell who your enemies were by the color of the hats they wore.

But this time he found he couldn't concentrate. The words seemed to blur on the page. What was that hissing? It was definitely louder. For a moment he thought it might be in his mind. His heart seemed to be beating harder. Could something really be wrong? The Tylenol hadn't done its usual magic; the pounding at his temples was getting stronger. He reached for his watch and began taking his pulse. Twenty-eight beats in ten seconds. That would be 168 a minute. High, but not dangerously so.

Must be he was too uptight. Stress, he thought. He turned the light off and started breathing deeply, telling himself to relax. There was a pressure now in his chest. He sat up. His arms ached, as if he were being squeezed in a vise. Touching his fingertips to his forehead, he found he was sweating. He got to his feet, but was unsteady, weak. He made it to the door, opened it, and called out for help. The pains were very sharp now, shooting up his arms and across his chest. He couldn't get his breath. He held on to the doorframe. The maid was coming. "Call an ambulance. . . . Please. Hurry."

SIXTY-THREE

"Sommers is not your man, Mr. Knebel," the doctor said.

"He can't be this Archer Ogden person."

Doctor Plank was in his early thirties, serious and solicitous, with deep-set blue eyes and a small mouth and curly hair. His facial muscles twitched. He and Knebel were in his small office at the Upstate Medical Center in Syracuse, New York.

"What makes you so certain?" Knebel said, standing and leaning over his desk.

The doctor cleared his throat and leaned back in his chair. "I'm certain because he's in one of my groups and has talked at length about his wife, his children, his career, and so on. Sommers is a stockbroker, not a—what did you say?"

"Biochemist."

"It's not possible, no."

"The physical description of Ogden fits this man perfectly."

"I'm telling you, Mr. Knebel, it isn't possible."

"Does Sommers get any visitors?"

"No, no he doesn't. He has not invited them. But he

does receive correspondence."

"Personal or business?"

"Both."

"Do you monitor this correspondence, Doctor?"

"No, of course not. We never violate our patients' confidentiality."

"Why is he here? What's his diagnosis?"

"Depression. Severe."

"May I see his records?"

"Afraid not, Mr. Knebel. Not without a court order, and probably not even then." The whole left side of the doctor's face twitched as he said it. His eyes drifted away from Knebel, his cold stare. "I feel it would be too disruptive to the patient and possible deleterious to his progress."

Knebel leaned further over the desk, resting on his clenched fist. "If I don't see that man in five minutes I will have you arrested and held as an accessory after the fact in the assassination of Clement Jamison, Dr. Plank. How do you think that'll help your career?"

The doctor jerked his head around and glared at Knebel. Knebel took the doctor's telephone receiver off the hook and dropped it into the doctor's lap.

"Maybe you ought to consult your superiors or your lawyer. I'll wait in the hall. You've got five minutes to decide if you want a future."

In the hallway Knebel lit his pipe and paced around. A minute later the doctor came out of his office. "This way, please," he said coldly.

Knebel followed him down the hallway. Patients in street clothes or bathrobes loitered about, as peaceful in their barbiturate stupors as sleeping puppies. The doctor asked a couple of attendants where his patient was, checked the recreation room and then a solarium. The patient was there, sitting on a chaise longue, reading a book. He had a medium build and salt-and-pepper hair; his skin was pock-marked and ruddy. He looked up when Knebel and the doctor approached and dropped his book on the floor.

"You're Richard Knebel, aren't you?" he said, his eyes registering both fear and dismay.

"I am Knebel."

The doctor said, "This man has some insane idea you're a biochemist named Ogden, Mr. Sommers. He wouldn't listen. He insisted on seeing you. Don't trouble yourself, he'll go in a moment."

"Don't deny it, Ogden," Knebel said. "It would only make it worse."

"What name did you say?" He looked at the doctor.

"Ogden."

"No, I'm Sommers. Sommers is the name; stocks and bonds is the game. Been with Merrill-Lynch for fifteen years. Over fifteen years. Wonderful years, all of them."

"You see, Mr. Knebel," the doctor said, "this man is obviously not your Archer Ogden."

"If I found you, the Old Guard can find you," Knebel said.

"Old Guard?"

"Yes, the Old Guard. You've been a loose end they left untied and that was dandy so long as no one was on to them. But now we are on to them and sooner or later they'll get around to taking care of all their loose ends. They'd probably sleep a lot better if you were at the bottom of a deep, deep lake someplace."

"But I am Sommers," he pleaded. "I am. I'm a stock-broker from Rochester, New York. Never heard of any

Ogdens."

"Okay, Sommers. But when I file my report, you'll be Ogden. The report will get circulated, and maybe it'll find its way to the Old Guard. It probably will."

"I have no reason to care about any of this."

"That might be true. But if you are Ogden, hear this: I'll get you to a safe house, get you a new ID, even a new face. If you cooperate, maybe we'll smash the Old Guard and you won't have to go on with this sham anymore. You can check out of this mausoleum and get on with living with real people. . . . What'll it be, Ogden? A new identity, or are you going to sit here and wait for the Old Guard to send an errand boy here and have you crossed off their loose-end list?"

He shook his head and his eyes met Knebel's. He sighed. "You'll never smash the Old Guard."

The doctor looked at Knebel and both sides of his face twitched simultaneously. "I didn't know. Honest. He talked so, at length, about selling securities, about everything. His childhood, his mother who beat him . . . everything."

"I'd better talk to Mr. Ogden alone."

"Fine, yes." He backed away from them, scowling at his patient. He closed the door as he went out.

Once he was gone, Ogden said, "How in God's name did you find me?"

"Doesn't matter," Knebel said, pulling up a chair. "Tell me everything you know about the Montreal Project."

Ogden brushed his hands through his hair. "You probably think me a monster, don't you, Mr. Knebel? Some kind of Frankenstein."

"Are you some kind of Frankenstein, Mr. Ogden?"

"I don't know. I didn't start out to be. We did experiments on unsuspecting human guinea pigs. Maybe I am some kind of monster. It's hard for a man to face up to that."

"Why don't you start at the beginning?"

He nodded vaguely. "I was a research biochemist — but you no doubt already know that. I'm sure you know quite a lot about me. Did you know I was married once? Helene, her name was. She died about fifteen years ago. We didn't have any children. All we had was each other. Bone cancer. It was horrible. It took her slow. Real slow. She shriveled up. The agony was terrible. They gave her chemotherapy and x-ray therapy, but all it did for her was prolong the agony. When she died I collapsed. Spiritually, I mean. It was as if I was emptied inside. For almost a year I was like a bombed-out building. Finally I started getting myself together. I needed solace. I looked for it where people have looked for it for a million years: in religion. Mystical religion. I was seeking something valid for myself and for modern man, some escape from the modern aesthetic malaise, from this void of disbelief. I was seeking some shortcut to the mystical experience of the ancients through the only medium I knew. Drugs. Men like Huxley had gone before me, and Timothy Leary. Others. I wanted to reach out and touch God. I took a sabbatical from Colorado State and set up a lab at home. I was my own subject at first."

"How did you get connected to Ferris?"

"I published a modest paper in a small academic journal nobody ever heard of. Apparently he had. I think the intelligence community monitors scientific journals all the time, looking for anything to help them in their work. Ferris was very excited about my discovery and offered me a great deal of money to continue my researches. Like a fool, I went for it. I wish to hell I'd never heard of Ferris."

"What exactly was your discovery?"

"It's difficult to explain, but I'll try. . . . At some level there is, in the human psyche, an indestructible self, surrounded by a shell of sham and pretense we call personality. I showed how it was possible to break down the shell and leave the indestructible self naked. Through the hallucinogenic properties of LSD-N, the outer core dissolves and the inner self emerges. What I was hoping for was that the restructured individual could be free of all phoniness—all fears and misgivings, all self-destructiveness. He would be the totally authentic human being. That was my original conception. You see, I wanted not only to touch God, I wanted to *be* God."

"Is that what Ferris wanted too?"

"Ferris was a far more practical man. He was a scientist himself, you know. He looked over my data. Oh, he had quite another conception. He convinced Admiral Leher, who was the CIA Director at the time, to fund a project. Ferris called it Jellyfish. His eventual target was a KGB master spy named Volkov, the man in charge of Soviet subversion in Latin America. The Argentinian invasion of the Falklands was supposedly his brainchild. Volkov mainlined cocaine. Ferris figured to get to his source and jellyfish him—make him indecisive and cowardly. That's what he thought LSD-N was good for. I went along with it because I wanted the money for my researches. What a goddamn fool I was. I convinced myself I was being patriotic."

"What do you know about the Old Guard?"

"Not much. Chandler Smith used to positively rail against them. My impression was they were quite powerful men, some in the military, some in the intelligence community, some in the government, but what exactly they were doing I don't know."

"Do you know any of them?"

"No. All I know is they were instrumental in the continuance of the program in Montreal after the CIA ordered a shutdown. Chandler Smith was very perturbed about it. He had grave doubts about the moral justifications for the Montreal business. Finally the fire closed it down. . . . Did the Old Guard have anything to do with the murder of Clement Jamison?"

"I think so," Knebel said.

"You'll never nail them. They're much too clever."

"Why do you say that?"

"Who do you imagine the Old Guard to be?" He smiled enigmatically. "You think they're sinister old men who sit at electronic consoles petting cats and plotting Armageddon? You figure they surround themselves with huge, bald men wearing earrings in one ear like movie villains? You think they wear mustaches and skulk around in alleys after dark? I read your ex-wife's article in the *Chronicle*. Blackmail, bribery, coercion, she said. This is not what the Old Guard is about."

"What are they about then?"

"They're men who believe might makes right. They're men who believe in a perverted kind of patriotism. They believe anything is justified so long as it's in the national interest. You didn't think such men just disappeared because a couple of Nixon's boys got their wrists slapped for their misdemeanors! These men are above that kind of thing. These men have roots deep in the political and economic hierarchy of this country. Lately they've been upset by defeat after defeat in the secret war against the communists. They're men who saw the CIA rocked by scandal. They're men who saw the CIA get a bad rap about Vietnam and Cambodia. They're men who see ten or fifteen KGB agents operating in the U.S. for every U.S. counterinsurgency agent. They're worried men. They're men who are impatient with a liberal Congress. They're vigilantes, Mr. Knebel. Chandler Smith told me how they work. It's an 'Old Boy' network. Say sometimes an official agency gets into a little trouble. Sometimes they can't quite prove a case to satisfy a jury. Sometimes a double agent shouldn't be exposed, but should be gotten rid of. Sometimes the regular boys are constrained by cumbersome legalities and Congressional snoopers. So one Old Guard brother calls another. Harry? Got a little mess here. Need a U.N. diplomat to get hit by a car, need a troublesome politician in Italy to disappear, need a secret experiment carried out. No trouble, anything you want, brother, you just name it."

"How many are there?"

"They don't publish a membership list. A few dozen, perhaps. A hundred. Not all that many. But they've got an army of ex-CIA and military people at their disposal. Security people, mercenaries. The mercenaries even have their own slick magazine, for Christsake. We've created a monster with all this spy business and it's going to eat us up. They pervert the press, they pressure politicians, they manipulate foreign governments."

There was a thin line of sweat on Ogden's brow and he shivered every few moments, after which he wiped his arms with his hands, as if he were shooing away inisible bugs.

"I want some names, Ogden. Who are these people?"

"Honest to God I don't know. I don't think Chandler mith knew either."

"The end result of the Montreal Project was bonding, ght?"

"Bonding? Oh, yes." Ogden's lips quivered. The eads of sweat on his forehead grew larger. He wiped nem with his sleeve, shivered, and once more attacked ne invisible bugs on his arm.

"What is bonding, Ogden?"

His eyes drifted upward. "How much I wanted to for- et I had ever heard of it, how much I wanted to undo vhat I had done. It was accidental, you know. We didn't ave any idea there was such a thing when we started. and then all of a sudden it was there. A totally unex- ected development of my research. We'd opened Pan- ora's box, Mr. Knebel, and loosed a vast evil on the vorld. We had discovered the bond. The N-Bond, 'erris called it. LSD-N was the drug, the N-Bond was he product. Perfect bonding. Perfect and complete. Chandler Smith had a growing terror and so did I. Per- ect bonding." His eyes widened. "Chandler and I saw it or the Devil's work that it was. You could just bond any- ne at all. Anyone. Anyone on earth. Armies. You ould bond whole armies if you wanted to. What if .SD-N got into the wrong hands? Don't you see, Mr. Knebel?"

"Maybe it did get into the wrong hands."

Ogden's eyes narrowed with fear. "They did use it on amison, didn't they?" He said it softly. "When they ex- umed his body to examine his liver, I knew."

"I think they did use it on him."

"My God, my God!" Suddenly he grabbed Knebel'
arm. "You'll never let them find me. Swear to me you'
never let them find me!"

"They'll never find you, Ogden. Never. Now tell m
just one thing . . . what is the N-Bond? What does
mean to bond someone?"

Ogden slumped back into his chair and shivered. H
looked off someplace toward the ceiling, shaking hi
head and wiping his arms furiously. "You'll never be abl
to hide me well enough. If they want me, they'll find m
They'll find me some day."

"The N-Bond, Ogden. Tell me."

He looked at Knebel and smiled enigmatically. "Yo
use it to make men slaves, Mr. Knebel. Complet
slaves. Lifetime slaves. Anybody you want. That
right. Anybody from a shoeshine boy to the President o
the United States."

SIXTY-FOUR

The phone at his bedside rang and Walter Byron opened his eyes and looked at the clock: it was six-fifteen. The girl beside him stirred. The phone rang again. The girl was a Pan Am stewardess with creamy brown skin and jet black eyes; she smelled sweet and warm and she looked at him and smiled sleepily.

"Tell them nobody home," she said.

He kissed her and reached for the phone, rubbing his head to wake himself. "Nobody home," he said into the receiver.

"Walter Byron?"

"Yes, speaking."

"Richard Knebel."

Byron sat up. "Mr. Knebel, how are you?"

"Are you on leave, Walter?"

"No, I'm working with Hans Ober. They've got me doing field report audits over at the Main Campus. Assassination backlog . . . How have you been? What have you been doing?"

"Talking to Archer Ogden."

"You found him!"

"I was sent an anonymous tip on where to find him.

The whole thing is beginning to look clear to me. . . . Did you see on the news Wilson Wright is dead?"

"Yes. Quite a shocker, wasn't it?"

"The autopsy is scheduled for this afternoon. Can you meet me afterward?"

"No problem, Mr. Knebel. Where?"

"Do you know the Sandie's Restaurant on the Leesburg Pike near Falls Church?"

"Yes."

"I'll meet you there about six or six-thirty. If I'm late, please wait."

"Sure thing, Mr. Knebel."

Walter Byron arrived at the restaurant at five-thirty and waited for almost an hour, drinking coffee and reading the *Washington Chronicle*. It was hot and humid outside, but inside the restaurant it was air conditioned and cool.

When Knebel arrived he looked introspective and thin. They left immediately, taking Byron's car. Knebel handed Byron a slip of paper with an address on it. "Wilson Wright's home," he said.

"Can you tell me what this is all about, Mr. Knebel?"

"It's possible Wilson Wright was murdered."

"Murdered? Who would murder him?"

"I don't know for sure, but I have my suspicions."

"Chandler Smith?"

"Yes."

"Why?"

"I'm not sure."

"How?"

"That's what we're going to try to find out first."

The maid answered the door. She was young and black, wearing a black-and-white uniform and a black apron. At the sight of Byron she sparkled with delight. He showed his FBI identification.

"A policeman?" The sparkle faded.

"We'd like to see Mrs. Wright," Byron said. "We know it's a bad time, but it's important."

The maid showed them into the foyer and asked them to wait. She returned a moment later with Mrs. Wright, who was dressed in black with a string of small white pearls around her neck.

"Gentlemen with the police, ma'am," the maid said.

"I'm Mrs. Wright; how may I help you?" Her eyes were clear, but she had the pale complexion and the dull expression of grieving.

Byron held out his identification; she nodded. "It's about your husband, ma'am," he said.

Knebel said: "I'm sorry we don't have time to handle this with more delicacy, Mrs. Wright, but where can we talk?"

"You're Richard Knebel, aren't you?"

"Yes. We have reason to believe your husband didn't die of natural causes, Mrs. Wright."

She seemed jolted; she paled. "Are you saying he might have been killed?"

"Perhaps you ought to sit down, Mrs. Wright," Byron said.

She nodded and showed them into the spacious, elegant living room. She sat on the couch; the two men remained standing.

"I don't understand," she said. "The doctors said it was his heart."

Knebel said, "It's possible to induce a coronary occlusion, Mrs. Wright, using certain toxins. . . . What time did your husband get home last night?"

"About eleven-thirty. Carson had just come on TV— he was doing his monologue."

"Did he have Secret Service protection?"

"No—he didn't want it. He said it didn't stop them from shooting Mr. Jamison. He didn't like being conspicuous either."

"Where had he been?"

"At the White House."

"How was your husband feeling when he came home?" Knebel said.

"Fine. He was in very high spirits."

"What did he do when he got home?"

"We talked."

"Where?"

"We have a sort of family room by the kitchen. He came in through the garage. We talked for a few minutes. He had milk and cookies."

"Then what did he do?"

"He went into his study and checked with his answering service to see if he had any messages. A couple of minutes later he came out here and said he was going to bed."

"Did you and your husband share the same bed?"

"Why do you ask?"

"I'm sorry, Mrs. Wright, but it may be important. Please answer the question."

Her eyes drifted downward. "No," she said. "No, we didn't. He went to bed and after a while the maid came down and said he'd taken ill. We called an ambulance right away, but it was too late. He expired on the way to the hospital."

"Had he had any previous history of heart trouble?"

"No. None that I knew of. They can't always detect it

coming on, that's what they told me. My husband almost always missed his annual checkup, I'm afraid. He did exhibit a lot of — what do they call it? — Type A behavior. He was always at full throttle."

Knebel nodded. "May we see his bedroom?"

"Certainly."

She took him upstairs and down the hall to the bedroom. Knebel looked over the room quickly and then turned to the window. He examined it carefully, then joined Mrs. Wright and Byron by the door.

"Thank you, Mrs. Wilson," Knebel said. "Sorry to have bothered you."

"Is that all?"

"Yes."

She went back down to the front door with them. At the door Knebel said, "My condolences, Mrs. Wright. I respected your husband despite some differences we had. He was very capable and did his best for his country."

"Thank you for that, Mr. Knebel. . . . I'm afraid you've confused me a great deal. Was my husband's death from natural causes or wasn't it?"

"There's no way to know for sure. The medical people say it was a heart attack, we'll have to go along with their findings."

She seemed relieved. She smiled at him tentatively.

"I'd like to know about the services," Knebel said.

"The funeral is Wednesday," she said.

"The President, I believe, is scheduled to be in Buenos Aires. Will he be canceling his trip?"

"No. There'll be a special Mass for close friends and relatives, it's being scheduled so the President can attend. Ten tonight."

"Where's the Mass to be held?" Knebel asked.

"At our parish church. Saint Cecelia's."

As Knebel and Byron drove down the street, Byron said. "What do you think, Mr. Knebel?"

"There was a small hole in the window frame big enough for a small tube. A little sodium cyanide gas and that's all there is to it. Simple and neat as inflating a tire."

"There's no doubt in your mind then. Wilson Wright was murdered."

"He was murdered."

The sun was going down and darkness was descending quickly. The last of the commuter traffic had ended. They were on Cypress Boulevard. It ran along a steep ridge; on the right there was a view of the Potomac and the bridges. The lights of Washington and McLean were flickering in the dusk.

"You said this morning on the phone that you'd spoken to Archer Ogden," Byron said.

"He's been posing as a mental patient in an upstate New York hospital."

"He explained this bonding business?"

"Yes. According to Ogden, bonding is a dependency relationship. It's a natural process which occurs in children. It also occurs between neurotic patients and psychotherapists, prostitutes and pimps, athletes and coaches, and so on. The dependent person surrenders his judgment to his controlling influence. Ogden claimed that LSD-N enhanced the effect a thousand fold. Ten thousand fold. The victim becomes so dependent on his control he hardly has an independent thought. They successfully bonded thirty-one people in Montreal that Ogden knew about, but they hadn't quite perfected the process when they were shut down. The Old Guard wanted the Hemisphere Brigade thing badly. They had the N-Bond in their bag of tricks and they hauled it out and put it to use when it looked like Jamison was backing away from the scheme. The way I figure it, Belzar was their weak link. He was shaky probably from the start. His conscience got to him, despondency set in, he jumped. Jamison had at that time maybe twenty-five treatments in him and was well on his way, but the process at that point was still reversible. The bonding effect quickly dissipated and he had a falling-out with his control — Harrison Cheney — almost immediately. Cheney actually resigned eleven days after Belzar's suicide. Dr. Samuelson, Jamison's new doctor, probably suspected something. That's why I think they chose the Fire Creek Country Club. They could get Samuelson too. Knocking off Jamison was easier than rebonding him. Besides, they had another bonded servant to take his place."

"Haas."

"Exactly. I had it wrong all along. I'd figured Haas was one of them. He's not. He's one of their victims. He was bonded to Wilson Wright."

Knebel had his pipe out and was cleaning it with his pocket knife.

"How much of this could you make stick with a Grand Jury, Mr. Knebel?"

"Not a goddamn lick of it."

They stopped for a signal light. Byron drummed his fingers on the steering wheel. "I still don't see how Chandler Smith got involved with the killing of Jamison."

"Simple. Here's the way I figure it and I'm probably pretty close: Chandler Smith was already on to the dirty business when he worked for the Montreal Project. He had grave misgivings about the Old Guard. He was instrumental in closing down the project. All Ferris had to do was convince him Jamison had been drugged by, say, the KGB, and Chandler Smith would have knocked Jamison off as a patriotic duty. Afterward they planned to get rid of Smith. It would be easy to make it appear that a disgruntled and disgraced CIA agent had gone off his trolley and knocked off the President. But they missed when they tried to kill Smith. He must have been stunned by the attempt on his life. It got him to thinking. He started checking on what really happened. That's what he was doing in Connecticut — where he killed those two cops — he was there to do some checking on Haas, who has a summer home in Hamptontown. And so does Wilson Wright. The computers doing cross-indexing of nonsignificant material coughed up that little fact for me."

"How was Haas drugged?"

"Haas has allergies and there's a world-famous allergy clinic at Hamptontown. They had a break-in the night before Smith shot those two cops. Nothing was stolen, so they didn't report it."

Byron shook his head. "The implications of this bonding business are enormous. Two or three dozen powerful people doing your bidding and you could run this country."

"Why would you stop with just this country?"

SIXTY-FIVE

It was dark and quiet; warm. St. Cecelia's Church was large and gothic and vine-colored. Byron pulled into a parking place. Knebel lit his pipe and looked at the church. The Secret Service was already there, going over the grounds. There were lights on inside; an organist was practicing.

"One thing bothers me, Mr. Knebel," Byron said. "Why doesn't Chandler Smith go to, say, the *New York Times* with his story?"

"Because it would undermine the legitimate efforts of the intelligence services, I guess. Remember, he's in complete agreement with the Old Guard in terms of goals. He disagrees only with the method. He's having his own private civil war."

"I see."

Knebel fell silent, lost in thought.

"Why are we here, Mr. Knebel?" Byron asked after a moment.

"I keep asking myself *why now?* Why did he hit Wilson Wright at this particular time?"

"To break the bond?"

"Then why didn't he hit Harrison Cheney instead of

Jamison?"

"I don't know."

"Haas is supposed to be leaving for Buenos Aires tomorrow for the Latin Summit. I doubt he'll call it off. Not if his control has programmed him to go. But Wright's death must be terrible for him. He would be desperate to come to some kind of memorial service, I'd think. Haas is Catholic too, remember. A devout Catholic. I wonder if Smith would have counted on something like that."

Byron looked at him. "You don't think Smith killed Wilson Wright just to set up Haas? That's bizarre."

Knebel put away his pipe. "Let's have a look around."

They got out of the car and crossed the lawn and went up the front steps of the church. A White House Secret Service man was there and recognized Knebel.

"Services aren't until ten," the Secret Service man said.

"I know," Knebel said. "Mind if I have a look around?"

"Go ahead. . . . This gentleman with you, sir?" Byron showed him his FBI identity card.

"Fine, thank you."

Knebel and Byron stepped inside the church. Half-a-dozen janitors were polishing the floors and two Secret Service men with dogs were working the altar area, searching for bombs. Two other Secret Service men were installing infrared surveillance cameras and, near the door, metal detectors.

"Too bad about Mr. Wright, wasn't it?" the Secret Service man said with genuine sympathy. "He was a nice man."

"How many are coming tonight?" Knebel asked.

"Thirty to thirty-five."

"You're doing advanced screening of the guests?"

"Been too sudden for that."

"Any press coming?"

"No. Only close friends and relatives and the Presidential entourage. Full complement of us, two ushers."

"How about the clergy?"

"The priest. One altar boy."

"Choir?"

"No choir. There'll be a choir tomorrow at the regular funeral."

"How's Mr. Haas taking it?"

"Between you and I, Mr. Knebel, word has it he hasn't been bearing up too awfully well. I understand he nearly broke down completely when he heard the news and hasn't been at all himself. They were close, you know."

"I know," Knebel said.

Knebel and Byron looked around the church for a few minutes and found nothing out of the ordinary. Then they went outside to inspect the grounds.

SIXTY-SIX

Chandler Smith, standing on the doorstep wearing wire-rimmed glasses and a neat, trimmed mustache, showed the old woman a green plastic identification card which identified him as Henry Ransom Wise of the United States Secret Service.

"What is it you want?" the housekeeper asked.

"Is Father Callahan in?"

"He's been with your people all evening long and he's fit to be tied."

"A few questions, ma'am, won't take but a minute."

She sighed with exasperation. "I'll tell Father you're here."

Chandler stepped into the vestibule and took off his hat. He closed the door behind him. There was a long stairway directly opposite the vestibule. The housekeeper stood at the bottom and called, "Father, a gentlemen to see you . . ." But there was no answer. She swore under her breath and moved awkwardly upstairs on a game leg, clutching the railing as she went.

Chandler went into the living room and silently pulled the shade down and closed the curtain. He listened for a moment to the housekeeper talking to the priest upstairs, but he couldn't make out what they were saying. He threw his hat on the couch and removed his wig, mustache, and glasses and set them down on a table. He then took out a small revolver from a shoulder holster and affixed a silencer to the barrel. He turned off one of the lights, then stood in the shadows and waited. While he waited, he refitted the prosthesis he used to replace his missing finger. A few moments later he heard voices again and someone on the stairs. He cocked the revolver.

The priest came into the living room and clicked on a light. "Why is it always so dark in here?" he asked with vexation; then he turned to him and said, "Yes, what is it? Secret Service again? Haven't we got it all straight yet what I'm to do and not do in my own church?" The priest's voice was harsh, his tone, cranky. He looked at Chandler with a cold stare. The priest had thick gray hair and thick jowls, heavy eyebrows, and a ruddy complexion. He stepped forward into the living room. "Well, what is it, man?"

It was then he saw the gun and he stopped, putting his hands up like a baseball umpire signaling for a time-out. "Wait a minute here. . . ."

"Do not move," Chandler said. His voice was calm, even. "Put your hands down and come and stand here." He pointed to a place on the living-room floor. The priest complied. Quickly. The priest was shaking his head and his ruddy face was suddenly white with fear.

"Call your housekeeper down here," Chandler said, almost whispering.

"What are you going to do, mister?"

"I'm going to kill you and the old woman if you don't do exactly as I say."

"I understand."

"Call her down here, *now*."

The priest called loudly: "Mary!"

She answered a moment later; he asked her to come down immediately.

"Be right there, Father."

"The priest had his eyes closed and his lips were moving in silent prayer. When the housekeeper approached he opened his eyes and said, "Please don't be alarmed Mary. He isn't going to hurt us."

"Sit on the couch, both of you," Chandler said.

The housekeeper was looking befuddled. She glanced first at the priest and then at Chandler. "Father," she said, "what is it that's going on here?"

"He won't harm us," the priest said, reassuring her. He took her arm and led her to the couch.

"I need your keys, Father."

He nodded and handed them to Chandler. "The one for the car is the gold one," he said.

"It isn't the car I want."

"What do you want?"

"How many Secret Service men are on duty over there at the church?"

"I have no way of knowing. Many, many, for sure."

"Did they set up a metal detector? Like at the airport?"

". . . I don't know."

"I don't know either," the housekeeper said.

"What time is the President to arrive?" Chandler asked.

"I don't know," the priest said.

"Will he be taking communion?"

"I don't know. Why do you want to know?"

Chandler pointed the gun at the housekeeper's knees. "Do you think, Father, you might be a little more helpful if I put a bullet or two into Mary?"

The housekeeper's eyes went wide. She turned to the priest in terror: "Don't let him, Father!"

"Please, no!" the priest said. "No—no! What can I tell you? Things to help you hurt the President? I can't tell you anything. I'm a man of God. I can't tell you anything, whatever you do to us."

Chandler looked at his eyes. They were pleading eyes, tearing. After a moment Chandler took a small leather case out of a pocket and handed it to the priest, who opened it. There were two small hypodermic syringes inside.

"Sodium Pentothal," Chandler said. "You'll both be out for two hours, maybe a little more."

When the two were safely asleep on the couch, Chandler went outside and picked up a large suitcase he had left alongside the front steps. He carried it inside and upstairs to the bedroom and opened it. Inside he had a black suit with a Roman collar, black socks, black shoes, a gray wig, and a makeup kit. He quickly dressed and went into the bathroom. There he put on a wig and face putty, making up the jowls that gave his face the right shape.

He had been studying the priest for two weeks. He knew his slightly stooped walk, his gravelly voice, his brusque, abrasive manner. He had practiced the imitation for a hundred hours. It would be perfect. It would have to be—there would be people there who knew the priest well and they would not be fooled by a shoddy performance.

Last came the skin. He put on a powder which

burned and irritated his skin and made it reddish; then he deepened the color with toner. The last thing he did was tape a small container of white powder to his right wrist.

He went downstairs and looked himself over carefully in the hall mirror. He practiced his speech. It was difficult and he had spent many hours on it. He kept it low, solemn. Wilson Wright had been a parishioner and a friend of the priest. The priest would naturally be shocked at the death; shocked, yet hopeful — because of the promise of the life to come, which was the priest's stock and trade.

Now Chandler slouched over and practiced his walk, looking at himself in the mirror. He was ready. He stood by the door and thought for a moment. He could not take the chance they would have metal detectors at the church. He dropped his gun into the umbrella stand by the door and went purposefully out the front door, down the stairs, and across the lawn, heading to the church.

SIXTY-SEVEN

Knebel and Byron had inspected the grounds thoroughly. It was a massive church and the lawn spread out from it eighty or ninety yards to the south and fifty to the north, where it ended at the driveway to the rectory. There were many shrubs and hedges, and the land fell away to the rear of the church where there was a rose garden and more hedges and a parking lot. A broad flagstone walkway led around both sides of the church to the rear parking lot. Beyond the parking lot there was a woods and, someone said, a religious retreat with enormous grounds beyond that. Knebel took a look up and down the block while Byron looked over the cars in the parking lot. They met again at Byron's car in front of the church. The temperature was falling. An intermittent cool breeze had started from the south. People attending the service had started to arrive. It was ten minutes to ten.

"A lot of security to penetrate here," Byron said. "It's all being treated routinely, though. They certainly don't expect anything."

"No, I don't think they do."

"I've been thinking, Mr. Knebel. It wouldn't make

sense for Smith to try anything in the church — how would he get out?"

Knebel was watching the priest cross the lawn and meet two Secret Service agents, then go inside with them.

"I don't know how he'd plan to get out, Walter. Maybe he's planning on a kamikaze hit."

"You really think so?"

"No."

Knebel knocked some ashes out of his pipe, then reloaded it from his leather pouch.

"The Secret Service is going to be very damn careful about who they let into the church," Byron said. "Everyone is to be screened through a metal detector. Everyone has to show identification — even though most of them will be with groups who all know each other."

"Say you did have some way to get out, how would you crack the security to get in if you were Smith?"

"Don't know. Bomb maybe? Guided missile? It wouldn't be easy."

"Bombs are messy. Smith so far has been more fastidious."

"Sniper rifle?"

"Maybe, but the only good cover seems to be the woods in back. Besides, you don't know the entrance the President is going to use. There's the front, both sides, two little ones in the rear. Smith went to a lot of trouble to set this up. He'd figure out something more certain."

"How do you think he'd do it, Mr. Knebel?"

"Don't know."

Knebel lit his pipe and leaned back against the car. "What I'm worried about is what we do if we don't get Chandler Smith. Or if we do get him and he won't talk

414

Or he isn't taken alive. I've been thinking about the Old Guard. How the hell are we ever going to nail them?"

"I don't think I understand what you mean, Mr. Knebel."

"Do we go after them with subpoenas and Grand Juries? Congressional hearings? Undercover infiltration and surveillance?"

"I suppose so."

"We've been using those weapons on the Mafia for fifty years and haven't given them more than a mild headache."

"What are you getting at, Mr. Knebel?"

"I don't know if I'm getting at anything."

There was a sudden gust of cold wind. The two men shivered.

"That's a grave digger's wind," Byron said. "A cool southerly in the summer is a grave digger's wind. That's what my Jamaican grandmother always said. Death rides high and proud on a grave digger's wind."

Knebel heard the motorcycles just then. He turned to see the President's small motorcade approach from the south and turn into the circular drive which led to the side door of the church.

SIXTY-EIGHT

The Secret Service men had handled him with deference to his priestly calling, apologizing profusely for making him walk through the metal detector. He grumbled as Father Callahan would grumble. The President would arrive in a few moments, they told him, and he could begin the service any time he wished afterward.

"All right, all right," he said. "It's late enough as it is. Tell them there'll be no sermonizing or eulogizing. The sacrifice of the Mass to help the man's soul is why we're here. The funeral tomorrow will be time enough to say all the good words."

They nodded and said they would pass on the word to the President and Mrs. Wright.

Chandler crossed in front of the altar, genuflecting at the tabernacle, and entered the sacristy on the south side of the altar. The altar boy was there, waiting. He was a teenager, tall, lean, with a shock of blond hair splashed over his forehead and large blue eyes.

"Evening, Father."

"Hello, son."

The boy helped Chandler off with his coat, hung it up, then helped him put on his priestly vestments. First the long white alb, tied with a cincture, then the stole, then the chasuble. The boy kept looking at him as if he thought something was wrong, but he said nothing.

"What's bothering you, son?" Chandler said gruffly.

"Nothing, Father."

"Come on, what is it?"

"You just don't seem yourself, Father."

"Getting old, maybe."

"Yes, Father." The altar boy grinned. It seemed to put the question to rest.

Chandler went to the locked cabinet to get the chalice. He took the keys out of his pocket clumsily, quickly realizing the sensible thing would have been to have gotten out the chalice before putting on the vestments. There were many keys on the ring and many of them seemed to fit, but none of them would turn the lock. The altar boy came to his aid:

"Anything wrong, Father?"

"No, no, I'll get it." He was again fumbling with the keys. Suddenly he noticed his finger prosthesis had slipped sideward and the boy was looking at it and recoiling. He looked at Chandler's hands, then at his face, and his eyes were alive with wonder.

Chandler took two steps forward and hit him in the jaw, staggering him. Chandler hit him again and he went down on the tile floor. Chandler quickly pulled a knife and knelt down next to him. It was sensible to kill him. It was necessary to kill him. There was not enough time to handle it differently. Wasn't it enough that he had spared the priest? He raised the knife, but couldn't strike. Not a boy.

He went quickly to the door and looked out into the church. People were still being seated. The lector was talking to the Secret Service man. Chandler closed the door and went to the curtain, cut some cord loose, tied the boy and gagged him with some altar cloths, then locked him in the closet. He broke open the cabinet and removed the chalice; it was full of communion wafers. He checked at the door again. Everyone was seated. The President, his head lowered, was seated down front. The altar candles had been lit and there was soft organ music playing. The votive candles at the sides of the church flickered. The rear of the church was darkened; still, he could see the Secret Service men in the shadows. He counted six, but there were probably more; outside, he knew, there were motorcycle police.

He waved his hand and got the lector's attention.

"Yes, Father."

"We'll begin," Chandler said.

"Fine."

"The boy's ill. I've told him to rest. I don't want him disturbed, I think he's sleeping."

"All right, Father."

"The boy should not have come if he was ill."

"Of course he shouldn't have, Father."

"Let us begin the Mass or we shall be here until midnight."

The lector nodded and mounted the lectern. The lector was a middle-aged man, sour-faced, with a melodious, baritone voice. Chandler stepped out into the sanctuary. The people rose. Chandler placed the pall-covered chalice on the altar, genuflected, straightened up, and made the sign of the cross. This was done with dignity, slowly, as Father Callahan always did it. Chandler made the sign of the cross again and said:

"In the name of the Father, and of the Son, and of the

Holy Spirit." His voice echoed off the walls of the church.

The lector answered, "Amen." Some of the people answered with him, but they were barely audible. There were few of them and they were not Catholic and didn't know what to say. Chandler continued:

"The grace of our Lord Jesus Christ and love of God and the fellowship of the Holy Spirit be with you."

"And also with you. . . ."

SIXTY-NINE

Knebel and Byron had made another trip around the grounds and had walked up and down the block. Knebel peeked into the church and then they walked back toward the street.

"I expected something to happen by now," Knebel said. "They're reading the Epistle, it's almost half over, I think."

"Maybe he isn't setting up the President."

"Maybe."

"But you don't think so, do you, Mr. Knebel?"

"No."

They stopped walking and stood in front of the church by the street. It was still and quiet. The Presidential limousine was parked nearby along with a dozen motorcycles. Uniformed police and Secret Service men stood by the front doors and were posted at intervals around the lawn and down the sidewalks that ran down the sides of the church. They all seemed relaxed, easy.

"Hello, Knebel. How you doing Walter?" someone said. Knebel and Byron turned around — it was Lowenstein.

"Arthur!" Byron said. "What the hell are you doing

here? How are you?"

"Got something to show you guys. . . . Like to take a little walk?"

"Sure," Knebel said.

SEVENTY

Chandler held the host over the chalice, his eyes and voice raised dramatically:

"Father, may this Holy Spirit sanctify these offerings. Let them become the Body and Blood of Jesus Christ our Lord as we celebrate the great mystery which He left us as an everlasting covenant. He always loved those who were His own in the world. When the time came for Him to be glorified by You, His heavenly Father, He showed the depth of His love. While they were at supper, He took bread, said the blessing, broke the bread, and gave it to His disciples, saying: Take this, all of you and eat it: this is My Body which will be given up for you. . . ."

Chandler paused, looked around, then reverently showed the host to the people, genuflected, and went on:

"In the same way, He took the cup, filled with wine. He gave You thanks, and giving the cup to his disciples said: this is the cup of My Blood, the Blood of the new and everlasting covenant. It will be shed for you and for all men so that sins may be forgiven. . . ."

It was then that he heard what sounded like thumping

coming from the sacristy. At first he didn't know what to make of it, but there was only one thing it could be. The boy in the closet. He looked around. No one else seemed to hear it, but he would have to hurry before they did.

SEVENTY-ONE

There was a large dent on the left front fender of the Chevy van. Its bumpers were rusted, and on the side it said "Margolis Carpets, *the best for less,*" in faded letters.

"Is this what you want to show us?" Knebel asked.

"In the back," Lowenstein said.

The back doors had been pried open and the lock was broken.

"Lucky you found this vehicle open, Mr. Lowenstein," Knebel said, "Otherwise we might suspect you of vehicular breaking and entering, a misdemeanor."

"Yeah, I'm lucky all right."

In the back of the van there were two rolled carpets and some large boxes, a footlocker, and some sacks. Lowenstein pulled back the corner of one of the carpets and switched on a flashlight. Rolled inside the carpet was the body of a man. He was black, massively built. There was a bullet hole in the back of his head. The blood was thick and dried in his matted hair.

"Turn his head — I want to see his face," Knebel said.

Lowenstein and Byron rolled the body over.

"His name's Benny," Knebel said. "I don't know his

last name." He looked at Lowenstein. "Is there another body in there?" He indicated the other carpet.

"An old duffer . . . You know this Benny?"

"He was a bodyguard."

Lowenstein and Byron unrolled the other carpet and Lowenstein shined the light. Knebel took a look. "Benny's boss, Harrison Cheney."

"Looks like somebody worked him over pretty well," Byron said. "Burn marks too. And wire. Jesus."

"Done by a master," Lowenstein said. "Knew right where to put the pressure. This guy went through hell before he was snuffed."

Knebel said, "What do you bet Chandler Smith knows all Harrison Cheney knew about the Old Guard. Let's see what else we've got here."

They started going through the boxes and sacks and the glove compartment. There were tools, clothing, a rifle, two .38 revolvers, two cameras with telephoto lenses, binoculars, ammunition, three small tape recorders, and bugging equipment.

"Everything but a keg of beer and a pretty gal," Lowenstein said. "Hey, what's this?"

It was a small suitcase, locked tight. Byron had a jackknife and opened it quickly. Inside was an elaborate theatrical makeup kit.

Knebel picked up one of the .38s and checked to see if it was loaded. It was. He put it in his belt.

"He's got to be inside that church made up as one of them."

"Yeah," Lowenstein said. "But *which* one?"

"The one that tries to kill the President," Byron said, heading out the door.

"May this mingling of the Body and Blood of Lord Jesus Christ bring eternal life to us who receive it."

The lector responded:

"Lamb of God, You take away the sins of the world, have mercy on us. Lamb of God, You take away the sins of the world, have mercy on us. Lamb of God, You take away the sins of the world, grant us peace."

In a hurried, hushed voice, Chandler continued:

"Lord Jesus Christ, Son of the living God, by the will of the Father and the work of the Holy Spirit, Your death brought life to the world. By your Holy Body and Blood free me from all my sins and from every evil. Keep me faithful to Your teaching and never let me be parted from You."

He raised the host to the people and said:

"This is the Lamb of God who takes away the sins of the world. Happy are those who are called to His supper."

The lector responded:

"Lord I am not worthy to receive You, but only say the word and I shall be healed."

Chandler came down to the front of the sanctuary. The lector opened a gate in the altar railing and some of the people lined up to take communion. Out of the corner of his eye Chandler could see the lector heading for the sacristy. Chandler cleared his throat loudly and gestured with a jerk of his head for the lector to come to him.

"The boy must be needing something," the lector whispered.

"Leave him alone, he's fitful in his sleep. After Mass we'll get him home."

"But Father . . ."

"After Mass!" Chandler whispered sharply.

"If you say so, Father," the lector said lamely.

Chandler let out a deep breath and turned to the communion line. Haas was fourth in line, looking pale and shaking, his hands held prayerfully in front of him, his head lowered. Chandler could feel the hard knot of anticipation rising in his throat. It would be over in a minute. If only the fool lector would stay put.

The first to take communion was Mrs. Wright, her eyes staring fixedly in front of her. Chandler handed her a communion wafer:

"The Body of Christ," Chandler said hurriedly.

"Amen."

Chandler was suddenly aware of the side doors at the rear of the church being opened and closed. Three men slipped in. He couldn't make them out in the shadows, but he knew they were coming quickly down the side aisles and he knew there was danger.

A man was standing in front of him, Wilson Wright's uncle, a former New York Governor.

"The Body of Christ," Chandler said hurriedly.

"Amen."

Chandler could see the three men moving in the shadows, one on his left, two on his right. They seemed to be looking people over. So they weren't on to him quite yet. There would be enough time. Just a few minutes more. The Secret Service was not on the alert. There were two Secret Service men by the doors to either side of him and half a dozen more sitting in pews behind the small congregation.

The next person receiving communion was the President's mother.

"The Body of Christ," Chandler said.

She took the wafer on her tongue. "Amen," she said.

The President was next. Chandler turned his wrist and deftly flicked open the small vial he had taped there and dropped some powder onto his hand and spread it on the communion wafer. The President looked at Chandler, and with dull, bewildered eyes and a trembling hand, reached for the wafer, but his attention was drawn to the sacristy, where the altar boy had just pushed the door open and was saying something excitedly to the lector.

"Body of Christ," Chandler said, pushing the communion wafer at the President. But the President didn't take it. His eyes were alert now, watching the lector, who was frantically signaling the lanky Secret Service agent posted near the altar railing.

"The Body of Christ," Chandler said again. "Please, it is nothing."

The President nodded vaguely.

"This is the Body of Christ," Chandler said firmly.

The President took the communion wafer and started to put it in his mouth.

Then from the side of the church: "Halt!"

It was Byron, his .38 leveled at Chandler from forty feet away. Chandler gave him a stern look, as a priest would in reprimand for interrupting service. The President, thinking the gun was aimed at him, cried out and fell forward in panic against the altar railing. He dropped the communion wafer. Chandler's hand flashed inside his vestments for his throwing dagger. The communion chalice hit the floor. The President was no more than two feet from him. Chandler lunged toward Haas as Byron fired, the bullet hitting Chandler in the left

428

shoulder, staggering him; Byron fired again, hitting Chandler in the ribs, knocking him backward off his feet.

A woman screamed; a Secret Service man yelled, "Mayday! Mayday!"

Simultaneously, the two Secret Service men standing nearest to Byron had reacted swiftly, reflexively, to what they regarded as a clear and present danger to the President. Seeing the priest hit, they assumed that Byron had been aiming for the President and missed. In an instant they drew their weapons and fired on Byron, hitting four times in the back and once in the neck. Byron spun around and tried to put up his hands, and they fired again, hitting him in the chest and face. He fell backward onto the stone floor.

Three other Secret Service men from the back of the congregation rushed to the President while one of the two Secret Service men stationed by the side door went to the aid of the wounded priest, who was struggling to get to his feet. The Secret Service man saw the dagger too late. Chandler plunged it into his throat with one hand as he wrestled his gun away from him with the other.

By then a half dozen Secret Service men had the President on his feet and were shielding him, trying to get him moving toward the rear of the church. The center aisle was blocked by panicked members of the congregation trying to make it to the exits. Chandler got to his feet with the gun in his hand and that's when he saw Knebel standing to his right, pointing a gun at him.

"Give it up!" Knebel shouted, but Chandler seemed not to hear; he looked at Knebel and shook his head. Knebel was in a crouch, both hands on his gun, sighting down the barrel at Chandler's chest, but his finger froze on the trigger. Ignoring Knebel, Chandler stumbled a few steps forward to the center of the church and lifted his gun in the general direction of the President.

"No!" Knebel shouted.

The President, surrounded by five Secret Service agents, was being ushered up the center aisle, behind a phalanx of Secret Service men who were clearing the way ahead of them. Chandler fired two quick shots from thirty feet away, hitting the Secret Service man directly behind the President in the back of the head. The second shot hit the agent to his right just below the ear as he turned to see where the shots were coming from. As the two agents fell, the President was a target for a split second and Chandler fired twice more, but couldn't get off a third as fifteen Secret Service men from around the church opened fire on him, dozens of shots blending together into a roar. Chandler's body jerked wildly as the bullets slammed into him; he looked like a marionette being shaken by its strings. And then, as if the strings were cut, he dropped to the floor. The roar stopped. It was quiet.

Knebel rushed to Chandler and stood over him. Chandler's priestly white and purple vestments were drenched with blood and more blood was splattered on his face and hands and there was a piece of flesh torn from the side of his neck. He looked toward Knebel with vacant eyes and managed a small nod as if something secret and important was shared between them. Then his eyes closed softly.

A Secret Service man knelt down and took Chandler's pulse and said he was dead. The Secret Service man with the dagger in his throat was dead and the two others who had been shot were dead too. Everyone was quiet except the altar boy, who was crying. His cries echoed off the cold stone walls of the church as they led him out the door. The President had been hit, someone said. He had been rushed outside and no one knew how badly he was hurt, but there was blood on the floor and a lot of it. Knebel wanted to check Chandler Smith's pockets, but a Secret Service man said the FBI would have to do that. They were on the way.

Lowenstein took Knebel by the arm and they went over to where Byron was lying on the floor. Someone had put a coat over his face. There was a large pool of blood under him.

"You did good, Walter," Lowenstein said, his voice cracking. "As good as any college man could."

"As good as *any* man could," Knebel said.

Knebel and Lowenstein went outside and walked to the front of the church where the Secret Service men had taken the President. They were trying to revive him by pushing on his chest and breathing into his mouth, but it was doing no good. Knebel pushed his way into the small crowd that had gathered and saw the two exit holes the bullets had made on the front of the President's shirt. At least one of them and probably both had hit the heart.

Knebel and Lowenstein walked down the block. Knebel lit his pipe. His lighter, he was surprised to see, was steady in his hand. Lowenstein took a half pint of sour-mash bourbon out of his pocket and took a long drink from it.

"You had a good bead on Smith there," Lowenstein said.

"I guess I did."

"If you keep letting Presidential assassins go, before you know it you'll be committing real bad misdemeanors, Knebel, catch?"

"The gun jammed."

"Ah. They have a way of doing that."

He offered Knebel a drink from his half pint. Knebel took the bottle, wiped it off and took a couple of swallows, and handed it back. Neither of them said anything for a few minutes. An ambulance had arrived and the paramedics were working on the President. More police were arriving, an army of them. The sirens were deafening.

"You suppose Chandler Smith might have passed the information on the Old Guard he extracted from Harrison Cheney to anyone?" Knebel asked.

"Might have."

"Who?"

"The only person in the world he trusted, I think, was Madame Rousseau."

Knebel nodded and relit his pipe. "We'll start with her," he said.